You're a
Colonel?"

"I came all this way just to record your name in my logbook when I shoot you down," Colonel Yuri Yakanov transmitted to Captain Gaines from his Soviet-made Mi-8 helicopter.

Captain Rat Gaines lined up his Huey Cobra on the enemy chopper. "I hope you brought your fucking lunch, Ivan, because shooting me down is going to take all day."

"The last time I shot down an American pilot he did not have time to make jokes."

"Well, Ivan, I'm not just any American pilot. I'm the best snake driver there is."

The Russian chopper bore straight in at the American Cobra. Yakanov fired. Big glowing orange balls of 23mm tracer rounds flashed past Gaines canopy.

Gaines bore in closer, triggering his own cannon in short bursts.

The enemy pilot had one last trick.

He hauled back on his cyclic, kicked down on the left pedal, and feathered the rotor blades to minimum pitch all at the same time. The heavy Russian machine put her nose up and skidded sideways, losing speed as fast as if he had opened a dive brake.

The maneuver caught Rat completely by surprise. His speeding Cobra flew right past the HIP.

The Russian pulled his pitch back and dropped the nose of his ship. Now the Cobra was right in his gun sight!

Other books in the **CHOPPER 1** series:

CHOPPER 1

#11 SKY STRIKE

Jack Hawkins

IVY BOOKS • NEW YORK

To Harry, Jack, and Dennis.
Thanks for all your help.
And, as always, to Claudia.

Ivy Books
Published by Ballantine Books

Produced by Butterfield Press, Inc.
133 Fifth Avenue
New York, New York 10003

Library of Congress Catalog Card Number: 88-91135

ISBN: 0-8041-0315-1

Manufactured in the United States of America

First Edition: November 1988

AUTHOR'S NOTE

The Vietnam War has been called the first helicopter war and for good reason. Without the use of rotary-winged aircraft, the war could not have been pursued in the manner that it was. Let it never be forgotten that the United States Army was not defeated on the battlefield in Vietnam. It won every battle that it fought and it won through the extensive use of helicopters, both gunships and troop-carrying slicks.

The lessons learned in Vietnam regarding the use of armed choppers has dramatically changed the face of modern warfare. Every modern army in the world now uses armed helicopters and uses them in the way that was pioneered by the U.S. Army's First Air Cavalry Division in Vietnam.

Among the nations that closely watched the development of our helicopter tactics in Vietnam was the Soviet Union. The Russians were early developers of rotary-winged aircraft and made use of armed autogiros in World War II for recon and artillery spotting. In the postwar era, however, while further tentative experiments with armed helicopters were made, nothing much came of it. It took the American experience in Vietnam to provide the example for the Russian air force to follow.

When the Russians saw how effective armed choppers

were, they realized that once again, they had to play catch-up with American military technology and they had to do it fast.

They sent helicopters to North Vietnam during the war for field armament testing under combat conditions. One of the Russian choppers used for this purpose was the Mil Mi-8T, codenamed HIP. Similar in concept to, but much larger than the Bell UH-1 Huey, the HIP could carry two squads of infantry as well as various external weapons loads.

Had the North Vietnamese Army made more extensive use of these machines, they could have presented a serious problem to the American forces. As it was, they were rarely seen, and most Americans were completely unaware of their deployment. Usually enemy choppers were only talked about in bars and clubs by men who had seen them on clandestine operations—men such as the Green Berets or the Roadrunner teams.

This is the story of one of those teams and two of the Russian HIP helicopters.

CHAPTER 1

Near the Cambodian border

Nguyen Cao Duc, ex-lieutenant colonel of the People's Air Force of Vietnam, eased forward on the control stick of his Russian-built Mi-8 helicopter gunship and cut the power to its two 1,500-horsepower turbines. He had approached his target at normal cruising altitude so he would not be heard on the ground. Now, he wanted to lose airspeed and altitude to get a better shot for the folding-fin, 57mm high-explosive rockets.

His hand shot forward to flick on the arming switches for the two air-to-ground rocket pods that hung from pylons extending from the sides of his machine, and for the two deadly accurate 23mm cannon mounted in the chopper's nose. He scanned the target area through the gunsight as he made his turn. Once leveled out, he started his firing run on the American infantry company clustered in the clearing below.

He felt contemptuous as he swept down onto his target. They were such fools to stand in the open like grazing cattle. This time he would not hit just one or two of them. He wanted to kill dozens of the "long-nosed" bastards. He was jubilant.

When the unsuspecting Americans grunts were centered

in the lighted pip of Duc's gunsight, his gloved finger tightened around the gun switch on the control stick. The HIP's airframe shuddered from the muzzle blast of the two cannons. Clusters of the small rockets lanced out in front of him, trailing streams of white smoke.

Captain Mike Torrence, commanding officer of Charlie Company, 1st Battalion, 7th Cavalry, glanced up briefly from studying his map when someone yelled.

"Hey look! There's a chopper coming in from Cambodia."

"What is it?" someone else asked. "A Jolly Green?"

Charlie Company had been inserted down the valley earlier that morning. They were taking a break in the open before they moved back to the jungle to conduct a routine sweep of a one-time enemy stronghold west of Pleiku. This densely wooded, mountainous region was a real motherfucker to hump, and Torrence wanted to give his people a rest before they tackled it. A recon team from the Blues had been put into a blocking position further down the wood line. The two units were to join up later in the afternoon for their extraction.

Torrence wasn't even remotely concerned about the approaching helicopter. American infantrymen in Vietnam never had to worry about overhead aircraft. Anything in the sky of South Vietnam was American. The North Vietnamese air force had never ventured down from the north.

Without giving a thought to the approaching chopper, Torrence mopped the sweat from his forehead and went back to reading his map.

A slender, nineteen-year-old infantryman in the 2d Platoon, who had spent hours as a kid building model airplanes, was leaning back against his loaded ruck watching the chopper as it approached in the clear blue sky. A frown slowly built on his young face.

"That's not a Jolly Green," he said to no one in particu-

2

lar. "The nose is wrong, and I've never seen one painted that way."

He sat up and looked a little more closely at it. He saw rocketpods hanging on its sides. Jolly Greens were not armed.

"Hey! That's a Russian chopper!" he screamed, just as the first cannon shells tore into Charlie Company.

Behind his helmet face shield, Colonel Duc smiled. The cannon shells and rockets exploded among the clustered men, flinging their bodies into the air like rag dolls. The projectiles tore the grunts to bloody shreds.

He was still smiling when he kicked down on the rudder pedals and slammed the cyclic over to the side to snap the tail around for another run. The Americans were so stunned by his attack that they hadn't even tried to defend themselves. He leveled out again and bore down on them, his cannons and rocketpods spitting fire. One of the rockets exploded between a man's feet, throwing him into the air. Another soldier was hammered to a red pulp by the cannon shells. Duc laughed at the carnage below him.

He pulled out of his firing run and banked sharply away to the left. Keeping low to the ground to evade any possible ground fire, he twisted the throttle all the way against the stop and streaked for the Cambodian border a few miles away.

Suddenly he caught a glimpse of three men breaking out of the tree line in front of him. Dropping the nose slightly, he gave them a short burst from the 23mm cannons as he flew past them at over a hundred fifty miles an hour. He went by so fast that he didn't see if he scored any hits, but he didn't mind. He had already made a great killing today.

Duc was very pleased with his day's work. Normally the North Vietnamese pilot didn't risk coming into South Vietnamese airspace. There was too great a chance of American radar picking him up and sending fighters after him. Usually, he spent his time taking out lone recon teams who were working deep inside Cambodian or Laotian territory. This time, though, he had not been able to resist the chance to shoot up an entire American infantry company caught in the open.

3

The Russian Mi-8 gunship he flew was his unit's only operational attack helicopter, and he had put it at risk to make this attack. It had been well worth it.

Lieutenant Colonel Nguyen Cao Duc, former North Vietnamese pilot, was now the chief and only gunship pilot of the Cambodian Khmer Rouge Air Force. He was temporarily at peace with himself.

Sergeant Treat Brody, Spec-4 Chance Broken Arrow, and PFC Jungle Jim Gardner were only a little more than a click away from Charlie Company when Duc swept down out of the sky. They were on a recon working with the C Company grunts, and their mission was to keep track of any NVA who tried to slip out of the bag when Charlie Company swept the woods.

"Treat!" Broken Arrow hissed.

"Yeah, I got it."

Both of the men heard the gunships cannon and rockets as Duc strafed the company.

"We got any air support working out here today?"

"We're not supposed to. The ell tee said that it's all on call today."

"What's going on? I didn't hear anyone call for air support on the radio."

"I don't know. We'd better have a look-see."

"JJ!" Brody whispered loudly.

The third grunt, a big, burly man, peered out of his hiding place in the foliage and nodded. Brody made a move-out signal and nodded again.

The three men raced through the jungle. Broken Arrow, a modern-day comanche warrior, always took the point position. He prided himself on his Plains Indian tradition and took the war seriously. To him, crawling around out in the jungle was like playing cowboys and Indians. But the way he played it, the North Vietnamese were the cowboys.

Broken Arrow carried a sawed-off, Remington twelve-gauge pump shotgun instead of an issue M-16 rifle. He wore

4

a black and green striped tiger suit camouflage uniform. A razor-sharp K-Bar knife strapped to his right boot top completed his armament.

The Indian's buddies all called him "Two-Step." He earned that nickname when he was bitten by a krait snake. Of the thirty-three species of snakes found in Vietnam, thirty-one of them were poisonous. The most deadly is the krait. Usually after being bitten by the small, light green snake, a man took only two steps before falling over dead from the venom.

Somehow, the Indian survived his bite. While he was recuperating in the hospital, their platoon sergeant, Leo Zack, hung the nickname on him and it stuck.

Everyone called him Two-Step now, but a better name would have been the Tiger. He moved through the jungle with the same grace and swiftness of the big cats. And when he struck, he was just as deadly. He handloaded the ammunition for his sawed-off, replacing the lead balls in the shotgun shells with steel ball bearings. Working the pump so fast that the shotgun sounded like it was firing on full automatic, Two-Step could clear a path in front of him half the size of a football field.

Treat Brody followed Two-Step through the thick, lush rain forest. Brody was a sun-bronzed Californian with a wild shock of blond hair and a bushy moustache. He looked like he should have been riding a surfboard in the Pacific instead of stalking the jungles of Vietnam. And in fact, before he came to Southeast Asia, he had stalked the beaches of Malibu. That had been almost two long years ago. Since then he had found a new sport as a door gunner and grunt with the Blues, the Aero Rifle Platoon of the 1st Battalion of the 7th Cav.

On the shoulder of his faded jungle fatigue jacket, he wore the big "Horse Blanket" patch of the First Air Cavalry Division, the Pony Soldiers. Brody now lived to fly and fight with the Air Cav. It was his entire life.

Jim Gardner was following in the drag position. Gardner was known in the Blues as Jungle Jim because of his size. He had developed his muscular build logging the fir forests

5

of Washington State's coastal mountain range before he joined the army. Though he had only been in-country for three months, he was almost as much at home as the veteran grunts. He carried an M-79 grenade launcher as well as an M-16 slung over his back. In his big hands, the thumper looked more like a child's plastic toy. But the big man had proven that he could put its deadly little grenades wherever he wanted with pinpoint accuracy.

These three men were a deadly team.

The three grunts broke into the clearing just in time to see a big chopper sweeping down on them.

"Hit it!" Brody screamed as the HIP started firing.

Cannon shells exploded all around, showering dirt on them. With an ear-splitting roar, the big machine flashed overhead. Brody looked up to see gray camouflage stripes painted on it and a bright red tail boom. Two gun barrels stuck out of its nose and rocketpods hung on the sides. With a scream of turbines, it was gone.

"What the fuck was that!" Gardner yelled, picking himself up off the ground.

Brody watched the chopper disappear in the distance, a puzzled expression on his face.

"Fucked if I know, JJ."

The three grunts looked down the clearing and saw a scene of utter devastation. Charlie Company had been hit bad. They took off running to see if there was anything they could do to help.

The kid who had recognized the chopper as a Russian design was moaning softly as the Charlie Company medic, "Bac Si" Thompson, finished tying a tourniquet around the stump that once was his left leg. A 23mm round had taken it clean off below the knee.

"It was a HIP," the wounded soldier sobbed. He was referring to the NATO designation for the Russian-built Mi-8 helicopter. "I know it was a HIP."

He repeated it over and over again until the third vial of morphine finally took hold and he drifted into a drug-induced sleep. Bac Si adjusted the IV bag of blood expander that was

6

plugged into his patient and put the severed leg on the blood-soaked poncho with the rest of the young soldier.

"Man, I've had about enough of this already," he muttered as he went to care for his next patient. "Fucking gunships just ain't cuttin' it."

Captain Torrence was still on the horn reporting the incident when the first Dustoff medevac chopper from Ah Khe touched down in the open field. It would transport his seven wounded and four dead to the hospital. The blast from the Huey's rotors blew fine red dust into his eyes.

"Negative, negative," he shouted angrily into the handset of his Prick 25 radio. "I have positive ID that it was not a U.S. aircraft. It was Russian, I say again Romeo, Uniform, Sierra, Sierra, India, Alpha, November. Russian. Do you roger, over?"

"Roger that, Boulder Six. Out."

"Those stupid, fucking bastards!" he muttered.

He gave the handset back to the RTO and wiped his face again, looking around at his men. They were lucky the enemy pilot hadn't gotten even more of them the way they had all been clusterfucked in the open.

Torrence turned to his runner. "Get the Platoon Sixes over here ASAP."

"Yes, sir."

When the two lieutenants from First and Second Platoon and the E-7 who ran Third arrived, Torrence turned to one of the men, a tall officer with a sweat-stained brush hat pulled down over his eyes.

"Blake, I want you to take the rest of the company into the woods and conduct that sweep. The C-and-C bird is coming to take me back to Battalion. I've got to talk to those assholes about what happened here. They think we got hit by a fucking Huey."

Second Lieutenant Blake didn't even blink. He was an old field hand and had learned a long time ago to expect the unexpected. "I can handle it, *dai uy*," he answered. "No sweat."

Torrence looked his favorite platoon leader squarely in the

eyes and smiled grimly. He could depend on Blake, better known to the men of the Company as Roger Roger.

"Don't fuck up, man," he warned. "I've lost enough people out here today already."

"Roger, roger, sir." Blake nodded affirmatively.

CHAPTER 2

Camp Radcliff, An Khe

PFC Ralph Burns, known to his buddies as Farmer because he came from a potato farm outside Pocatello, Idaho, was taking his usual afternoon nap. The two things that Farmer never missed out on was food, even army chow, and the chance to get a little bag time, even if it was only fifteen minutes or so. He was just about to start disrobing dark-eyed beauty in his dream when someone kicked the end of his bunk.

"Hey!"

Farmer reluctantly opened his eyes to see a skinny, dark-haired soldier with a duffel bag thrown over his shoulder standing at the foot of his bed.

The man kicked his bed again and Farmer opened his eyes a little wider.

"I know you," Burns said. "I met you out in the woods last month. You're that redleg FO with the funny name."

"Yeah, Bernie Rabdo. But they all call me 'the Bunny Rabbit.' "

"Nice to see you again, Bunny. What're you doing here?"

"This is the Blues, right?"

"You got that right," Farmer said proudly. "The ass-

9

kicking Aero Rifle Platoon, Echo Company, First of the Seventh Cav.''

"Well," Bunny grounded his duffel bag on the empty bunk next to Farmer's. "It looks like I'm going to be your new artillery FO.''

"Hey, that's great!" Farmer swung his feet over the side of the bunk. "I'm Ralph Burns, but everybody calls me Farmer. You can have that bed there, it's empty and I'll see if I can find you a foot locker." He glanced at his watch. "It's a little early for dinner, but I can probably steal you a cup of coffee from the orderly room.''

Bunny laughed. "No, I'm fine. Thanks anyway.''

"Well, if there's anything else I can do for you, just let me know. I was beginning to think that we weren't going to get any more replacements.''

Bunny looked up from unpacking his duffel bag. "I'm not really a regular replacement.''

"What do you mean?''

"I had to find a home real fast and I found out that you guys needed an FO.''

"Yeah," Farmer thought back. "We ain't had an FO since I got here and that's been almost three months now. Why'd you have to leave where you were?''

"The Ninth Cav." Rabdo leaned back on the bunk and looked Farmer straight in the eye. "Somebody gave me a ration of shit about being a Jew boy and I punched his fucking lights out.''

"Who did that?''

"My platoon sergeant.''

"No shit! Why'd he do that?''

"I don't know, I guess that he just doesn't like Jews.''

Farmer thought about that for a while. "Well, that doesn't make much sense to me. I've never met many Jews except for a couple of guys back in basic, and they were okay. But I don't see that being a Jew's any reason to give a guy a hard time.''

Bunny laughed. "You're okay, man. Now how about giving me the hot poop on this company and the Blues.''

10

Farmer was happy to tell Bunny everything he knew. It made him feel like a real veteran.

"Well, you met some of the guys that day out in the woods. That was my squad, Second Squad, and Sergeant Treat Brody is squad leader."

"Is Brody that lifer E-Six you had with you?"

"Oh, God, no. That was Sergeant Wilcox. He got killed four or five days later. Brody's a young guy like us. Then, there's the ell tee, Lieutenant Vance. I haven't seen too much of him, but he seems to be okay for an officer. Our platoon sergeant's Leo Zack, a great big black dude who's really okay. He's the best sergeant I've ever met. Nobody ever sees Top Richardson, the first sergeant, unless you go into the orderly room, and he don't bother nobody."

"What about your CO? What's he like?"

"Captain Gaines? He's great. He flies that Cobra with the shark's mouth painted on the front, and he saved our lives when we went into Cambodia after Sergeant Zack. He's from Atlanta so he talks a little funny, but he's a great guy."

"What happened on that Cambodian thing? I heard something about you guys going AWOL, but I never did hear the full story."

Farmer got comfortable and launched into the long tale of Brody's raid into Cambodia to free Zack from the North Vietnamese and Major Tran.

"What kind of man is this Mike Torrence?" the G-2 intelligence officer of the First Air Cav Division asked as he looked up from the report on his desk. "Is he reliable?"

"He's very good in the field," Lieutenant Colonel Maxwell T. Jordan replied. Battalion commander of the 1st Battalion, 7th Cavalry, he was standing across the room, looking at the big situation map on the wall. "He's been running that company for quite a while now and he's proven to be very reliable on everything I've seen."

"You believe his story then?"

"Yes, I do. I think that Charlie Company got hit by an enemy aircraft."

"The kid who ID'ed that thing, does he remember any markings on it? Insignia or anything?"

"I talked to him at the hospital as soon as the Dustoff brought him in. All he remembers is that it was painted dark green with gray stripes and that it had a bright red tail boom."

The G-2 leaned forward in his chair. He was silent for a moment. "You don't have need-to-know status," he said finally. "But I'm going to tell you something about your Russian gunship."

Jordan looked startled. "Are you telling me that was an NVA chopper?"

"Yes it was. It is an experimental Mi-Eight HIP gunship stolen from the North Vietnamese Air Force a couple of months ago. It seems that an NVAF pilot—we think it was a light colonel named Duc—simply took off on a mission one morning and never returned. The NVA listed him missing in action, but a few weeks later we started hearing about this chopper from some of the Special Forces Roadrunner teams across the fence. They started reporting strafing attacks by a lone helicopter gunship operating in Cambodia. We think that this guy Duc has teamed up with the Khmer Rouge for some reason and is conducting a one-man air war against us."

"Why?"

"To be honest with you, we haven't the slightest." The G-2 looked frustrated. "But this is the first time that he's strayed over the border. He's cut down a couple stragglers from clandestine missions and that sort of thing, but mostly he hits ground targets, shoots them up and disappears. Frankly, I don't know what else to tell you about this guy. Just warn your people not to be too trusting of lone choppers in the future. And, Mack," the G-2 added grimly. "This thing goes down as a friendly fire incident."

"You're shitting me!" Colonel Jordan exploded. "I can't tell my people that. Dammit, those guys aren't that fucking dumb. That Russian chopper story is all over my battalion already."

"Friendly aircraft, Mack. That's the way it is. I've told you too goddamned much already."

Late that afternoon, Brody, Two-Step, and Jungle Jim walked into the big platoon tent together. Farmer jumped up off his bunk and greeted them. "Hey, guys, look who's joined us. Bunny Rabbit, the FO. He's been assigned to work with us."

Brody walked up to the slim, dark-haired young soldier and stuck his hand out. "Welcome aboard, Bunny. We've been needing an FO for a long time now."

"Yeah, that's what Farmer was saying."

"Good, I see he found you a bunk. After chow tonight, we'll make a run down into Sin City and I'll show you where we hang out. I could definitely use a couple cold ones myself right now."

Farmer noticed the look of exhaustion on the faces of the three men. "You guys don't look too good. What happened out there today?"

Gardner dropped his ruck in his bunk. "We got hit by a gunship. Charlie Company got all sorts of fucked up."

"Jesus, what happened? Couldn't they see you guys were GIs, not a bunch of gooks?"

"It wasn't one of ours."

Now Farmer and Bunny were all ears.

"I didn't know the gooks had choppers." The new FO was surprised.

"Well they sure as hell have that one, and it tore those guys a new asshole," Brody continued the story.

"Did you get a good look at it?"

"Not really." Gardener said. "We hit the dirt when it started firing at us, and it went past so fast that I didn't see a thing. We did see what it did to C Company, though. They had to dust off almost a dozen guys."

"Jesus."

Brody started stripping off his dirty, sweat-stained jungle fatigues. "Bunny, I'm going to grab a shower before chow.

Then I'll meet you back here at eighteen hundred, and we'll hit the strip for a couple of beers.''

Big Mama, the Vietnamese woman who ran the Pink Butterfly Bar, was in trouble again. Major Nguyen Van Tran, the North Vietnamese officer she spied for, was furious with her. He was angry because the Air Cav had destroyed an operation of his last month and he wanted vengeance. Specifically, he wanted his vengeance on that new Cobra gunship pilot. It was easier for him to vent his frustration on Big Mama than it was to take it out on the Air Cav. He had ordered the bar and brothel owner to get as much information as possible about the pilot and his machine quickly.

And that was Big Mama's problem. Beyond the fact that the machine was flown by Captain Rat Gaines of Python Flight, and that the Cobra itself was one of only two such helicopters in the Air Cav, she had learned very little. She knew Gaines commanded Echo Company of the 7th Cav and flew with Python Flight, but that was of little use to the North Vietnamese Major. What was worse. Big Mama didn't know how she was going to get what Tran really wanted.

Her information came from what her customers told her girls. Unlike many of the young Air Cav officers, Gaines didn't visit her establishment. As far as she knew, he didn't visit any of the whorehouses in the strip area outside the main gates of Camp Radcliff that the GIs called Sin City.

Big Mama's place was the perfect establishment for her kind of intelligence work. The bar was always well stocked with cold, black-market Budweiser, real American Coke and hot girls. Her place was very popular with GIs of all ranks. In fact, the men of the Echo Company Blues used her bar almost exclusively.

The madam was confident that her girls could get Captain Gaines to talk if she could just get him to visit. She knew that Gaines couldn't help but be aware of the services her place offered. The Pink Butterfly was known as far away as Hue.

14

She had learned a few things about Gaines from his men. His troops seemed to like him, he was not married, he didn't have a "Round Eyed" girl friend that any of the men knew about, and his vices seemed to be limited to smoking cigars and drinking Bourbon.

She also knew that he did not visit any of the other whorehouses. That's what bothered the old madam. In her experience, a man that did not do what men normally did had a sexual problem. Therefore, she concluded that Gaines must have a problem. Just exactly what kind of problem, she had been unable to discover.

The Pink Butterfly could accomodate almost any sexual taste, from ducks to little boys or virgin nuns. Nothing was a problem. But before she could offer Gaines something, she had to know what kind of bait to use.

From her twenty-five years of working in a whorehouse or running one, Big Mama knew the sexual mind of western men quite well. She had met very few of them who could resist the delicate, petite bodies of Asian girls or their well-developed sexual skills.

"Maybe he just doesn't like girls," she sighed. "Maybe he is one of those who have no interest in the charms of the flowers of the Orient. Maybe he is a secret boy lover. What am I to do? What am I to do?"

Big Mama sweated in spite of the blast of cool air from the big American PX floor fan in her room. She rolled her naked bulk onto her stomach. A small Vietnamese girl sitting on the bed next to her started massaging her lower back.

The madam liked the new girl. She was going to work out quite well. Not only was she a rare beauty in a land known for its beautiful women, but she was completely in awe of Big Mama, just the way Big Mama liked her girls to be. Most importantly, she was taking to her training very well. The older woman sighed again as the girl's small fingers danced over tense muscles buried under layers of fat.

Suddenly Big Mama had a great idea. She rolled onto her back.

"Come!" she told the girl. "Help your honored mother relax."

As Big Mama relaxed to the young girl's eager fingers, she thought of a new idea.

Maybe the elusive long-nose pilot was just shy. Maybe he feared getting a disease. But perhaps he could be lured there by a virgin. It was worth a try.

CHAPTER 3

Camp Radcliff, An Khe

First Lieutenant Michael Alexander, the Echo Company executive officer, stared vacantly at the pile of paper work on the desk in front of him. He was not quite sure where to start this morning.

Over the last three weeks, no matter how hard he had worked, the pile got bigger, not smaller. He was beginning to think that being a company XO was the most thankless job in the army. Now that Alexander was on board, Captain Gaines, the Echo Company commander, spent all his time down at Python Operations while the XO was stuck in the orderly room doing paper work.

He signed another supply requisition and put it in the outbox. Alexander was a mechanized-infantry trained officer fresh out of Germany, and he desperately wanted to learn about airmobile warfare. When he took the XO's job, Gaines promised that he would get the opportunity. So far, all he had seen was paper work. He hadn't gotten within ten feet of a helicopter.

Alexander was going over a vehicle deadline report when

Spec 4 Jenkins, the company clerk, knocked on the opened door.

"Come in!"

"Need your signature on these, sir." Jenkins handed him another stack of papers.

Alexander added them to his pile.

"Ah, Lieutenant." The clerk retrieved them from the top of the stack. "If you don't mind, sir, I need these ASAP to meet a battalion suspense date."

That was a valid reason to take a look at them, so Alexander put down the vehicle report and took the papers from the clerk again. Jenkins had arranged them so that all the signature blocks were exposed at the bottom of each page. All he had to do was to sign them.

"If you'll just sign here, sir, I'll run them over to the S-One."

Something about Jenkins's manner was making Alexander suspicious. "I'm familiar with army paper work, Specialist," he said. He started reading through each document before signing it 'For the Commander.'

Jenkins stood nervously in front of the desk while the XO read and signed the papers. So far Alexander hadn't seen anything out of order. The first few pages were routine reports, ammo inventories, supply requests, and the like. Then, on the next-to-the-last page, the XO found what he was looking for. It was a request for the award of the CIB, the Combat Infantryman's Badge, to a dozen men of Echo Company.

In a war that had over ten men sitting on their asses in secure bases for every man who was out in the woods with his finger on a trigger, the CIB was sacred. It, alone, was proof that a man was a warrior, a real soldier, and not just another REMF, a rear-echelon motherfucker.

In Vietnam, more than any other war in history, there were two distinct classes of soldiers—those who put their lives on the line and got shot at, and the REMFs who didn't. Those who actually fought the enemy wore the wreathed rifle of the Combat Infantryman's Badge.

A grunt might not wear his division's shoulder patch, his

18

name tape, or even his rank stripes, but if he had earned a CIB, he wore it proudly. One of the reasons Alexander was chafing behind his desk was that he wanted to earn his own CIB, and to do that he had to get out into the woods.

Although he had only been in the unit for a couple of weeks, a few of the men's names stuck in his mind. He spotted one man on the list, a Spec 5 cook in the mess section, that he knew for sure didn't merit the coveted award.

Still not one-hundred-percent sure, Alexander asked the clerk for a copy of the company roster.

Jenkins turned white under his Nam tan.

The XO pushed his chair away from his desk and stood up. "Specialist," he barked. "consider yourself under charges."

"Yes, sir," the unhappy Jenkins answered.

"And send the first sergeant in here with that roster."

Considering Jenkins's crime, there were several things Rat Gaines could have done. He could have had him court-martialed on formal charges and sent to Fort Leavenworth, Kansas for a five-year stint in the army's disciplinary barracks. But since the court would probably only give Jenkins a six-month tour in-country at the LBJ stockade, he decided to handle the matter in-house.

Gaines knew that most of the men in the company had stopped trying him out, testing him to see if he really had the balls for command. Now that he spent most of his time down at Python operations, they were testing his new XO instead.

It was the way it always worked. Every time a new officer came into a unit, he had to show the men that he had what it took to wear his bars. Gaines decided to turn the matter completely over to Alexander.

"Mike," he told his XO over the phone, "since you caught this, I want you to take care of it. I'll okay anything you decide to do to him."

First, Alexander had the clerk type up a complete set of

19

general court-martial papers with his name on the top, his crime, and the extract from the UCMJ, the court-martial manual, specifying the punishment required were he found guilty. Second, the XO had him go through all the award orders he had cut and make a list of the men he sold the awards to. Then Jenkins cut new orders rescinding the phony awards.

This was going to cause the clerk some problems in the barracks because the men had paid good money for the awards. Many of them were still in the company, and they were not going to be too happy.

"That's just tough shit," Alexander growled when he saw how long the list was. "Let them take it out of Jenkins's hide."

Finally the executive officer gave the clerk the chance to choose his own punishment. "You're an Eleven Bravo, right?"

Standing at attention in front of his desk, the stunned Jenkins nodded affirmatively. His basic MOS, his military occupational specialty, was Eleven Bravo, an infantryman.

"Well, I'll tell you what I've decided to do about this. You can either be court-martialed and run the risk of doing five years in the stockade," Alexander smiled and waved the court-martial papers under the man's nose.

"Or if you'd rather, you can trade your typewriter in for an M-sixty, hump the brush with the Aero Rifle Platoon for the rest of your tour, and earn your own CIB. Take your pick."

To help the clerk along with his decision, Alexander added, "If you decide to go to the Blues, on the day you DEROS I'll hand you these papers, and we'll be even. But until then, if you piss me off even just a little bit, I'll have the old man sign these and send your sorry ass straight to jail."

Needless to say, Jenkins chose to take his chances in the jungle with a machine gun rather than with the MP guards in a military prison.

"Report to Sergeant Zack and tell him that you're his new First Squad machine gunner."

"Yes, sir!" The newly assigned Hog Humper Jenkins saluted and did a quick about-face.

20

Captain Rat Gaines and his co-pilot and gunner, Warrant Officer Joe Schmuchatelli—better known around the flight line as Alphabet—were only a few klicks out of the Special Forces camp at Dong Pek when the warning light on the oil-pressure gauge started blinking bright red.

Rat banked his Huey Cobra gunship, *Sudden Discomfort*, around and headed back to the camp.

"Bold Lightning, this is Python Lead," he radioed ahead. "Request permission to put down on your pad and check my bird. Over."

"Python Lead, this is Bold Lightning, permission granted. You don't happen to have any cold beer or hot broads on board? Over."

"This is Lead, sorry 'bout that, boys. Just rockets and a couple of miniguns. Over."

"Oh well, it never hurts to ask. Lightning, out."

Rat flared out to a landing on the tiny dirt pad and cut his turbine. He was just stepping out of his cockpit when he heard a voice behind him, one he knew well.

"It's about time you showed up here, Gaines, you still owe me twenty bucks."

Rat spun around. It was Green Beret Captain Larry "Lightning" Ringer, a man to whom he owed a lot more than just twenty bucks.

"Larry!" Gaines pounded his friend on the back, almost knocking the smaller man flat. "What in the hell are you doing way the hell out here in the sticks? You're supposed to be down in Nha Trang working with Project Delta."

"I had to come up here and look after you, asshole," Ringer answered, disengaging himself from Rat's enthusiastic greeting and straightening the beret on his head. "I heard that you were up here with the Air Cav and since I know that you can't find your own ass with both hands and radar, I thought that I'd do you a favor and keep track of you."

"Why didn't you call me and let me know that you were here?"

"I've been busy, man. There's a war on, you know."

"You asshole."

Gaines couldn't believe Ringer was here. The last time he had seen the short, wiry Special Forces officer had been over a year earlier. He and Ringer went back a long way. They had started out together in infantry officer's basic back at Fort Benning. Since then, their paths had crossed more than once. Ringer was a legend in Special Forces. He had won every medal that his country could award him except for the Medal of Honor and there were many men who believed that he deserved one of those as well. Rat was really happy to see him again.

"You still don't know enough to come in out of the sun, do you?" Ringer laughed. "Come on down to the Team House and have a cool one. There's someone here that I want you to meet."

"You go ahead, Captain," Alphabet called out, his head stuck in the open engine compartment of the Cobra. "I'll poke around inside this thing and see if I can find what's wrong."

Gaines followed Lightning Larry into the underground command bunker of Mike Force Company A-248. A hand-lettered sign over the door read; WELCOME TO CAMP BUM-FUCK. HOME OF THE MUSHROOM DETACHMENT.

"Mushroom Detachment?" Gaines queried.

"Yeah. They keep us in the dark and feed us bullshit."

Rat chuckled. At least Larry hadn't lost his famous sense of humor.

"Actually," Ringer said after they caught up on the latest news, "my Cambode CIDG and I are supporting the MAC-SOG Roadrunner operations. You know, the Project Delta cross-border watch teams. We're a reaction force, a hatchet force, they call it. If one of the RTs gets their asses in a crack, we go in there and get 'em out."

Rat grinned. "You've been going into Cambodia? Bad boys. Haven't you heard that's a no-no? USARV keeps telling the press that we aren't doing that."

"Right," Larry answered grimly. He raised his beer can

22

in mock salute. "Just like Hanoi Hanna keeps saying that the NVA aren't over there, either. Shit, if they would just quit screwing around in Saigon and zero those bases, we could get this thing all wrapped up and go home."

Ringer ran his hand over his short, cropped hair. "Rat, I swear that I've seen stateside-type bases on there less than ten miles from the border. White painted buildings, supply dumps, flagpoles, the whole nine yards. It's unfuckingbelievable what they've got in there, and we can't touch them because we might piss off Sihanouk. I'll tell you, man, sometimes this whole war is enough to make you want to puke in your boots."

The Special Forces officer took a long pull on his beer. "Well, anyway, enough of that. I want you to meet one of the best Roadrunners of them all. He's spending a few days with me to relax. Hey, Panama Jack!" he called out. "Come in here a minute."

The man who answered Ringer's call was a short, stocky kid wearing Bata boots and a tiger suit totally devoid of insignia. His hair was cropped short, Airborne style, and he was so young that were it not for the steel in his faded blue eyes, he could have been a high-school football hero.

Instead of football, though, this smiling young man played a far more dangerous game. He was a Roadrunner, a member of one of the clandestine, cross-border recon teams that kept a watch on the Ho Chi Minh Trail and NVA infiltration into Vietnam. At twenty years of age, he was the youngest Green Beret in-country.

"Rat, meet Sergeant Panama Jack Wilburn of RT Sleeper. PJ, this is the guy I told you about, Rat Gaines."

The young sergeant shook Rat's extended hand. "I've heard a lot about you, sir. But knowing Captain Ringer, I'm sure that most of it's pure bullshit."

Ringer laughed. "Another beer?" he asked Gaines.

"No, thanks, I'm driving. But I'll take a cup of coffee if you have one."

"Sure. How do you take it."

"Barefoot."

"Captain Gaines," Wilburn broke in. "You mind if I take a look at your Cobra? I haven't had a chance to see one up close."

"Sure. Tell that gunner of mine out there to give you the fifty-cent tour."

"Thanks."

Ringer came back with the coffee, and the two men continued to talk about old times and mutual friends who were no longer with them.

Gaines finished his coffee and stood up. "Larry, I've got to go see if Alphabet has found what's wrong with that bird. If he can't fix it, I've got to call for a shithook to pick her up and take her home. I don't want to leave her here overnight."

Outside on the helipad, Alphabet was closing the access doors to the turbine bay while Wilburn sat in the front cockpit checking over the gun controls.

"I found it, Captain," Alphabet called out when the pilot walked up. "The wires to the oil-pressure sending unit were loose. I put 'em back on and we're ready to go anytime you are."

Gaines turned to his friend. "Look, Larry, if you can get away, give me a call. I'll come and get you and show you the bright lights of An Khe. Make sure you wear your shoes though, we're a pretty civilized bunch in the Air Cav."

Ringer laughed. "And if you get too bored down there shining your boots, come on up here for a week and I'll show you what the war's all about."

CHAPTER 4

Sin City, An Khe

Rat Gaines felt a little uneasy when he walked into the Pink Butterfly Bar with his driver, SP/4 Bronski, but he was greeted with cheers. He looked around and saw that most of the Aero Rifle Platoon and many of the men from Python Flight were already there, and the party was in full swing.

The company commander usually didn't go bar-hopping with his troops, but since this was a promotion party for one of his helicopter mechanics, he felt he at least had to make an appearance.

The men made a place for him at one of the small tables. As soon as he sat down, the most beautiful Vietnamese girl he had ever seen brought him an ice-cold beer, a real Budweiser, not a *ba-muoi-ba*. He was staring so hard at her that he almost didn't hear Bronski make introductions.

"Captain," the driver said, with a big grin half hidden under his bushy black moustache. "I'd like you to meet TNT."

The girl smiled a demure, but vividly sensual smile that made Gaines shiver.

"She's called TNT because she's dynamite."

25

The men in the bar cheered enthusiastically. Gaines could only agree and did so without taking his eyes off her. He had seen many beautiful girls in Vietnam, but this one was more than beautiful. Her eyes were dark and her skin was golden like honey. She wore a bright silk *ao-dai* and he could clearly see her slim but full body outlined perfectly under the thin cloth. He took a long drink of his beer.

TNT smiled again and walked away with a slight provocative twitch of her hips. Rat's eyes followed her all the way to the bar. He sighed.

Big Mama watched the American's reaction to the girl's performance from under another one of her big army PX electric fans. She realized that she had been completely wrong about the captain. He did like girls.

The madam had totally misjudged the reason why Gaines had not visited her establishment before. It wasn't that he was afraid of Oriental girls. Evidently, he rather liked them. Obviously he had been so busy running his company that he had very little time to think about sex.

When Gaines did have time for it, he made a point of not frequenting the same cathouse that his men used. That policy helped him keep his command presence and prevented any problems arising from accidentally screwing one of his troopers' girl friends. Lately, however, he had started feeling the need to take a short flight down to Saigon for a night. It was either that, or collect on his rain check with Lisa Maddox.

A month earlier he had been in bed with her and just about to get down to the main event when he had been called away to make an emergency extraction. It was very tempting to take the blond nurse up on her offer of a rematch, but he knew that it might cause more problems than he had time for.

The blond, green-eyed nurse had been away from An Khe for the last few weeks, so he hadn't seen her. She was working at a forward hospital, and he was too busy to fly down to see her. Now that he hadn't seen her for a while and had time to think about it, he realized how dangerous she could be to him.

Rat Gaines was a confirmed bachelor. He took his career very seriously and didn't want anything to interfere with it. This didn't mean that he didn't like the ladies—just that he didn't need to get seriously involved with anyone. And he was afraid that if he finally did take Lisa to bed, it would ruin his resolve to remain a free man. He wasn't sure that he could keep a relationship with her on the fun-and-games level. Something told him that things would get very serious with her, very fast.

Bronski noticed that his CO's beer was empty and yelled for another one. TNT brought it to him.

"What your name, *Dai Uy*?" she almost purred as she set his beer on the table.

"Rat Gaines."

"That nice name. I like it."

She cocked her head to one side and looked at him through half-lowered lashes. "You buy me drink, *Dai Uy*?"

"Sure, I'll buy you a beer."

"TNT no drink beer," the girl pouted, rubbing her sleek belly. "Beer make me *ti-ti* drunk and bookoo fat. Why you no buy me Saigon Tea?"

Rat knew all about Saigon Tea. All the bar girls in Vietnam drank Saigon Tea, usually weak tea or watered-down Coke. The GI had to pay outrageously inflated prices for it, and the girl got a percentage of the take. If the girls drank beer or a cocktail instead, they didn't get a cut of the price like they did with tea. It was a racket, but it was the only game in town, and everyone who wanted a piece of the action had to play.

Rat, however, liked bucking the system. "Saigon Tea number ten." He had a big grin on his face. "I'll buy you a Coke instead."

The girl smiled. "Okay, *Dai Uy*, you buy me Coke." She rattled off a rapid-fire order to the bartender in Vietnamese.

Rat was stunned. He had never seen a bar girl cave in that quickly. She smiled at him and abruptly sat down in his lap. Bronski and a couple of the men laughed.

Gaines had a reputation to uphold so he settled back and

let her get comfortable while the men cheered. He had to admit that, reputation or not, she was a very tempting little lapful. She snuggled against him, purring like a cat, and he slipped his arm around her waist. He could smell her subtle sandalwood perfume, and her firm little breasts were pressed against him. Through the thin silk of her blouse he could feel her nipples become erect.

He smiled at her and patted her on the ass. "You're a very nice girl," he said. "Bookoo *dep*."

From the other side of the room, Big Mama saw the time to strike. "Oh, *Dai Uy*," she called out. "You like girl friend, no? TNT make number-one girl for you. I give you special price."

Rat grinned and shook his head. "No, thanks, Big Mama. I have number-one girl friend back in the States."

Everybody roared at his answer. They all had girl friends back in the States, but that didn't keep them from having one in The Nam as well. TNT snuggled even closer to him, grinding her soft buttocks against his crotch. He felt himself start to get hard.

"You no like me, *Dai Uy*?" she pouted. "I like you bookoo. You number-one *Dai Uy*."

Rat laughed. "You got that right, girl. I'm a number-one *Dai Uy* and you're a number-one girl. But I've got to go back to work."

He deposited the girl on her feet and stood up, taking his can of black-market Bud with him. "Big Mama," he nodded slightly to the old madam. "Boys, thanks for inviting me to your party, but I've got to run. You boys don't get in too much trouble now."

The men cheered in reply. He turned to his driver, "Bronski, I'll take the Jeep, and you can get a ride back with one of the other guys."

"Yes, sir." The driver was relieved not to have to take his CO back to camp. He had five hundred P burning a hole in his pocket and he intended to get his ashes hauled before the afternoon was over.

"Christ!" Gaines muttered as he drove back to operations. "That little bitch just about had me coming in my pants. I've got to get my ass down to Saigon real fast."

Te Lan smiled to herself as Gaines walked out into the street. Now she knew his sexual preference. The girl that the long-noses called TNT had already told her how fast he had come erect and how big he had been. Captain Gaines liked girls, that was for sure.

Oh to be young again, the old madam thought.

Big Mama had learned something else about Gaines. She had seen the way he handled himself with the girl. The man was strong, he had pride, and, unlike most of the Americans she met in her business who acted like pigs at a trough, he was disciplined. The Yankees she had catered to for the last two years were like schoolboys. Gaines reminded her of the German sergeants of the French Foreign Legion, whom she had serviced when she was a young girl.

Those were men, she remembered happily.

The American had the determination that the Germans had shown, the same sense of duty. It was not going to be easy to lure him into an ambush, but she had a better idea how to do it.

"What a waste," she sighed. Big Mama really liked hand-some western men.

Gaines couldn't take the time off to get laid in Saigon, so he tried to put it out of his mind. The next night the battalion was having a steak-fry at the officers' club, and he decided to get half drunk instead.

The night of the party, Gaines looked around at the men and women clustered around a Jeep trailer full of iced-down beer. The young officers, nurses, and Red Cross girls were socializing as if they were at any lawn party back in the States. The main difference was that almost everyone was dressed in o.d. green. Except for the doughnut dollies, even the women wore jungle fatigues.

The exception to the dress code was, of course, Captain Mike Torrence, the CO of Charlie Company. Mike was known for his flashy wardrobe, and tonight he sported one of his usual off-duty outfits—shower sandals, red-and-white checkered bermuda shorts, and a loud Hawaiian shirt.

"Hey Torrence," Gaines called out. The slightly drunk Charlie Company commander looked up.

"How far did you have to chase that guy to get his shirt?"

Torrence shot him the finger and Gaines laughed.

He wandered over to the grill, a cut-down fifty-five gallon oil drum. Thick steaks sizzled on glowing charcoal, sending their savory smell into the warm evening air. The steaks were almost ready, and he was hungry. He looked down at the empty beer can in his hand. It was time to get another one.

Walking over to the beer trailer, he spotted a blond nurse with her back to him. Thinking that it was Lisa Maddox, he stopped in midstride and started over to her. Just then, she turned her head. It was someone else. "Careful, Rat old boy," he said to himself. "You're losing it."

He dug through all the Hamm's and Miller beer in the cold water in the trailer and found another can of Bud hidden under the ice. He opened it with the church key tied to the trailer hitch. He caught himself wondering when Lisa was coming back. He knew that he could call the 45th Surge and find out easily enough, but he didn't want to be too obvious about his interest. At least not to other people.

He took a quick drink and got into line for a steak. "A rare one," he told the fat mess sergeant behind the grill.

"Here you go, Captain, one still kicking." The cook grinned as he forked a thick slab of barely seared meat onto Rat's plate.

Not everyone in Binh Dinh Province was partying that evening. Some forty klicks outside Camp Radcliff near a small village along the Song Ba River, a man in oak-leaf-pattern camouflage fatigues and face paint slowly took up the slack on the trigger of his XM-21 sniper's rifle.

The XM-21 was a modified version of the M-14 rifle. With its match-grade barrel and hand-loaded ammunition, it could reach fifteen hundred meters and hit a six-inch target every time. Centered in the ghostly green glow of the sniper's Starlite scope was the figure of a man standing on the river bank.

A man he had been ordered to kill.

The sniper made a slight sight adjustment, let out the breath he had been holding, and the silenced rifle spat.

Some five hundred meters away, the man fell like a puppet with its strings cut, a 7.62mm bullet deep in his brain. The sniper liked head shots, and he knew without having to examine the body exactly where he had hit the target.

At the edge of the river, another man spun around at the sound of the round impacting in the head of the man beside him. The second man, a North Vietnamese courier on a mission to deliver messages to the local Viet Cong cell at An Khe, looked out into the darkness surrounding the small village, frantically seeking the cause of the other man's death. He saw nothing in the black velvety night.

Panicked, he tried to run back to the safety of the darkened village. Before he took two steps, another silenced bullet cut his leg out from under him, and he went down.

The military intelligence agent at the sniper's side briefly laid his hand on the man's shoulder in approval, but the shooter shrugged it off. He did not like to be touched. By anyone.

Around Camp Radcliff, the MI agent was known as the Spook. His job was to operate against the VC infrastructure in Binh Dinh Province. That meant he tracked down and killed or captured VC tax collectors, gunrunners, messengers, and agents. He employed manpower from many sources to perform his missions. Tonight it was a sniper from the 75th Rangers at Camp Radcliff and a small force of Vietnamese rangers to surround and isolate the village.

The Spook's ARVNs quickly moved down to the river, captured the wounded courier, and faded back into the night. No one in the sleeping village had heard the silenced rifle.

In the morning, the villagers would wake and find the body of their headman by the river, and they would know the price for aiding the Viet Cong—silent death!

CHAPTER 5

Camp Radcliff, An Khe

Rat Gaines poured himself another cup of coffee from the ever-brewing pot in the radio room and took it back to his small office in the operations shack. Sitting down at his desk, he stared vacantly at the pile of paper work flowing out of the in-boxes.

"I've got to find myself a mission," he muttered. "If I don't get a vacation from this, I'm going to go bat shit."

Even though Lieutenant Alexander was handling all the Echo Company paper work at the orderly room, there was still aviation-related work that Gaines had to do himself. There was nothing of great significance in the pile this morning. Requests for the usual routine bullshit, aircraft maintenance reports and an evaluation of the new Cobra chin turret that had been fitted to his bird.

He was halfway through the pile when he heard a knock on his door. Looking up, he saw the Spook standing there, a big grin on his face.

"Mind if I come in?" As usual, the military intelligence agent was sporting one of his more snappy outfits. A Hawaiian shirt, khaki British military shorts, polished jungle boots and a .357 magnum in a shoulder holster. The operative's cover was an assignment with the Rural Development Agency, teaching the local farmers how to grow rice. He was so obviously an agent that Gaines wanted to laugh every time he saw him. His dress was just the thing for an agricultural advisor.

Gaines was glad of the interruption. "Not at all. What's up?"

"You're going to love this." The Spook reached into a manila envelope and pulled out a folder with a coversheet stamped Secret on the front. It was the report of the interrogation of the wounded NVA courier he had captured the night before.

Gaines was silent while he read the report. "You're shitting me!" he exploded. "Big Mama at the Pink Butterfly is a VC agent?"

"Check the last paragraph."

Gaines read on and slowly looked up at the MI man. "It looks like somebody doesn't like me." His voice was cold as steel.

"Somebody likes you enough that they're willing to pay twenty thousand piasters for your sweet ass. Dead or alive." The Spook laughed.

"This shit isn't funny!" Gaines snapped back.

The report stated that the courier had been taking instructions to Big Mama to post a reward for the capture of Captain Rat Gaines. If he could not be captured, he was to be killed.

"What in the hell is this all about?" Gaines asked.

"We're not really sure. All we know is that the orders came straight down from the headquarters of the Two hundred first NVA Division."

"Well, I'm going to find out what the fuck's going on around here." Gaines stood up and started buckling on his pistol holster.

"Wait just a fucking minute." The Spook jumped up. "You can't do that!"

"The fuck I can't," Gaines stated flatly. "Anyone who

thinks that they're going to get my head had better bring their fucking lunch 'cause it's going to be an all-day job.''

"Hey, man, calm down, calm down." The Spook grabbed his arm. "We're going to take care of her, but listen up just a minute. I've got a plan."

"This had fucking better be good, my man."

"It is, Rat," the Spook grinned. "Believe me, you're really going to love this one."

Two days later, when Bronski went to the laundry next door to the Pink Butterfly Bar to pick up Gaines's clean uniforms, he came back with a note from Big Mama.

Dai Uy Gaines, the note read. So sorry that you did not stay for party last week. You work bookoo too much. TNT cry because she think you no like her. If you no like TNT, maybe you like Baby San instead. She see *Dai Uy* at party and fall bookoo in love. She cherry girl, but she want to be girl friend for you too. Maybe you come visit me soon and I give for you a very special show with TNT and Baby San.

With Great Respect,

Than Te Lan (Big Mama)

Gaines grinned as he folded the note and put it in his pocket. The MI agent's plan seemed to be working. He picked up the phone and put a call through to the Spook's office.

Early the next evening Gaines dressed very carefully for the Special Show that Big Mama was giving in his honor. For once, he was not wearing a flight suit. Instead he put on a set of loose-fitting jungle fatigues. Tucked under his belt at the small of his back was his Browning Hi-Power 9mm pistol. He put another thirteen-round magazine for the gun in his left rear pants pocket. In one of the side pockets of his fatigue pants, he carried a roll of two-inch-wide adhesive tape and a folding, lock-blade knife.

It had been a hectic day getting everything ready for the main event that evening. The Spook had provided the necessary manpower from his various assets, both MI and ARVN. All Rat Gaines needed to provide was his own self.

"Rat, are you sure that you really want to go through with this?" The Spook sounded concerned when they met in Gaines's office in the Python operations shack. "We can always bust them earlier, you know. If you're not real careful, buddy, you're more than likely going to get your ass shot off instead of getting your dick wet."

Rat looked up from checking the ammunition in his pistol magazines. "You need to catch them in the act, right?"

"Yeah."

"Then it looks like I've got to go through with it." He smiled grimly. "What a way to die. I can see it now, the headlines in the Atlanta newspapers 'LOCAL BOY KILLED DE-FLOWERING VIRGIN FOR HIS COUNTRY.' "

The Spook laughed.

"Just as long as your boys aren't fucking the dog," Gaines continued, "we should be able to pull this thing off just the way we planned. The only thing I'm worried about is that if Big Mama has more than just a couple of the local cowboys waiting for me, I may have my hands full. Are you sure that your man is going to be in there to back me up?"

"That's the plan. She thinks that he's the NVA courier, the contact. He's using the real courier's name and the correct identification codes. Since no one in the local VC cell has ever met this courier before, it should work."

"It's the 'should' part that I don't like. But what the fuck," Rat sighed. "All they can do is kill me. If anything does go wrong, Spook, have that bitch killed for me, will you?"

"Don't worry, Rat. I'll do it myself."

"I'll sleep a lot better knowing that."

Gaines could feel his erection grow as he stared at the two naked girls making love to each other on the bed in front of him. He was no stranger to Asian whorehouses and had seen porno flicks at the club on film nights. But he had never seen anything like what was going on less than three feet away.

TNT and the girl they called Baby San were writhing in ecstasy, coupled in the most pornographic tableau he had ever seen. His eyes were filled with glimpses of golden skin, jet-black hair, firm breasts, sleek thighs, and almost hairless pussies as the girls brought each other to orgasm. Unconsciously, he wiped the sweat from his forehead.

From the corner of the room, Than Te Lan glanced at the American officer. She could tell that he was as ready as he was ever going to be. It was time to let him at the girls before he had an accident in his pants.

Big Mama wished that she could take the place of one of the girls and take this handsome long-nose to bed herself, but she had had her turn at that many years earlier. Now it was time for her Little Flower, time for her to discover the joys that could be found between the legs of a Western man.

It was too bad that he had to be taken away, but Major Tran wanted to interrogate him as soon as possible. Big Mama was to collect her reward of twenty thousand piasters, almost two thousand American dollars, for her troubles, so she wasn't too upset about it. The reward would almost bring her secret retirement fund to the point where she could leave the dangerous life she had been leading for the last two years, and live comfortably far from the major's intrigues.

Than Te Lan was not a Communist at all. In fact, if the Viet Cong ever did come to power, she intended to leave the country the minute they took over for Bangkok or Singapore. Politics aside, she was a business woman and she made her living selling goods to the highest bidder. In this case, it was the North Vietnamese.

Unknown to Major Tran, Big Mama also sold information to the Khmer Rouge across the border in Cambodia, the ARVNs, and anyone else who paid for it. She had started her career selling bedroom information to the French back in the old days of the battles against the Viet Minh. But when the Americans came to Vietnam, they had foolishly turned down the offer of her intelligence services. They told her that they didn't deal with whores. In order to stay in business, she had been forced to sell to the Communists.

Big Mama raised her bulk from the lounge chair.

"Girls," she clapped her pudgy hands. "It is time for the *Dai Uy* to choose."

The two girls disengaged themselves, put down the various implements they had been using on each other, and walked over to the American.

Turning to Gaines, the madam bowed slightly. "Which one do you want, *Dai Uy,* TNT or Baby San?" The woman giggled behind her hand. "Or maybe both?"

Gaines tried to answer but his throat was dry. The two naked girls were all over him, rubbing their lush bodies against him, caressing him, teasing him. He tried to back away, not because he didn't want their attentions, but because he was afraid that their searching hands would find the Browning pistol tucked into the back of his belt.

Fortunately for the operation, the two girls concentrated on the front of his pants, their soft little hands making him even harder.

"I know, *Dai Uy*!" The woman clapped her hands again. "You take both girls. You bookoo man. You need two girl friend."

"Go now," she said.

Gaines headed for the back rooms accompanied by the two naked, giggling girls.

When the American went into the bedroom, Big Mama quickly headed for the laundry room in the back of the bar where three Vietnamese man waited for her. One of them was the phony courier. The other two were from the Binh Dinh Province VC cell. The madam greeted them.

"We will wait until the American is asleep before we act," she said. "There must be no struggle, no fighting. I don't want the other customers to hear anything. When he does not return to the camp, the MPs will come and question everyone about him."

"Then you should send a girl in for us while we wait," the phony NVA courier said. "Why should the Yankee dog have all the fun tonight?"

"Do you have money?" Big Mama asked bluntly, always the madam.

"Money!" the man spat, keeping in character. "It is for the struggle that she will give her services, not for money. She should be proud to service a fighter for the people's struggle."

Big Mama sighed. *Communists,* she thought. They always wanted something for nothing, particularly sex. She was a business woman. She fed the girls, she clothed them, and she cared for them like they were her own daughters. But the Reds always said that it was for the struggle and she was left to pay the bills. Resigned, she went to fetch whatever girl wasn't busy at the moment.

While Big Mama went to get a whore, Gaines was busy trying to get out of his uniform without the two girls seeing the Hi-Power. Finally, when he had stashed the pistol with his cloths under the head of the big bed, he joined them.

Back in the laundry room, the phony NVA was busily pumping away between the open thighs of the girl Big Mama had brought for them. The girl calmly chewed gum while he labored, and the two Viet Cong watched and waited their turn. Suddenly one of the VC pulled a Tokarov pistol from his belt and violently struck the North Vietnamese behind the ear.

The madam gasped. Before she could say anything, the Viet Cong pulled the limp body of the courier off the girl and rolled him over.

Then she saw what the VC had seen. On the man's chest, right over his heart, the words *Sat Cong,* "kill Communists," was tattooed. It was the slogan of the hard-core ARVN Rangers.

The man was a plant. In his exertions with the whore, his shirt had come loose, exposing the tattoo. The counteroperation was blown.

They had to kill the American officer. Immediately.

CHAPTER 6

Sin City, An Khe

Behind the Pink Butterfly Bar, the Spook and his team waited.
The bar was at the end of a built-up area along the road to
the base camp, and they were in blocking positions all around
it to prevent anyone from reinforcing the enemy inside. Two
snipers from the Ranger Company, Chief and Gambini, were
covering the rear of the building which faced open ground.
The Spook's ARVN Rangers were covering the front and
sides. Their plan was to wait until they heard shots inside the
bar or saw the VC take Gaines's body away—whichever came
first.

Everything was in place. It all depended on Gaines and
the Spook's ARVN inside the bar.

In the back room, Big Mama argued with the two VC who
wanted to shoot Gaines, noise or no noise.

"You cannot do that!" the madam said shrilly. "Someone
will hear the shots and call the MPs. The *cahn-sat* will close
my business and send me to the monkeyhouse. And if that
happens, the People's Committee will get no more information from my girls."

"You useless old whore," one of the VC spat. "You brought this upon yourself. The Yankee must die right now."

"How was I to know that this one was a puppet of the long-noses?" she pleaded, kicking the unconscious ARVN. "How was I supposed to know? He came with the right papers and he knew the code words."

"They must have captured the real courier and tortured the codes out of him. The bastards!" The VC hit the comatose Ranger on the back of his head again. This time, his skull broke with a sickening crunch.

"We must kill the Yankee to avenge our comrade!"

"Yes, he will die," Big Mama agreed. "But we must stay with the plan. Major Tran will kill him after he has learned what he wants to know. Let me send my daughter to get another man to help us capture him. If we have to, yes, we will kill him. But Major Tran wants him alive so we must try to capture him first. The girls will keep him busy for quite some time yet."

The VC grudgingly agreed with Big Mama's plan. He wanted more manpower, however, if he was going to try to take the big American alive. Big Mama went out and found her oldest daughter, Lan. She quickly told her what was needed, and the girl hurried out to get more VC to help them.

Gambini was watching the back of the building and caught the girl in his nightscope as she slipped out the back door into the alley.

"One coming out," he whispered to the MI man crouched down beside him. "Wait! I think it's a girl."

"Where's she going?"

"Up the alley."

"Drop her!" the Spook commanded.

"But it's a girl, sir!"

"Goddamnit, sniper, drop her ass. Now!"

Gambini shivered. He had never killed a girl before. He focused the Starlite scope, took up the trigger slack, and the silenced rifle spat. Once.

A hundred meters away, the girl fell without a sound. Gambini always went for a head shot. A 7.62mm round in

41

the head insured that the target wouldn't make a sound when hit, not even a gasp or a cry.

Inside the Pink Butterfly, Big Mama waited with the VC for help to arrive. The leader hit the dead ARVN again, just to make sure he was dead. The other VC took out a joint and lit up to calm his nerves. Big Mama sat, fanned her fat face, and prayed that there would be no trouble and that Gaines would not be killed in her bar.

"*Aiee,*" she moaned softly under her breath. "I am so close now. I will have enough money to leave here when this is done. Please, Lord Buddha, do not let anything go wrong."

The minutes passed slowly. Outside, the Spook and his men held their positions and waited patiently. Gambini kept checking the girl's body with his scope. In the green glow of the Starlite scope, her small body lay still.

Killing was Gambini's profession, and, like all snipers, he was good at it and took pride in his work. The problem tonight was that he had never killed a girl before. He briefly thought of his sisters back in Chicago and shuddered. "Holy Mother Mary," he whispered, crossing himself. "Forgive me, please forgive me."

In the bedroom, Gaines fought to catch his breath. He smiled and looked over at Baby San laying next to him with a grin on her face. Now that she had been initiated into the world of commercial sex, Asian style, she could go out and make her fortune renting her cute little ass to anyone with the ready cash.

"You like me, *Dai Uy*?" the girl purred softly, her dark, half-closed eyes making her look even more like a cat.

"Yeah, I like you," he answered, running his hand over her. "You're a number-one girl."

He forced his mind back to the matter at hand. It had certainly been fun—one of the high points of his Vietnam experience—but someone was going to come and try to kill or kidnap him very soon. He really wanted to be ready for it.

TNT started caressing him, trying to get him back in shape

for the second round of the evening's entertainment. It just wasn't working.

"No." He pushed the young whore's hands away. "You wait *ti-ti*. I smoke cigarette now." He reached under the bed as if to get his smokes. "You go get me a beer, okay?"

The girl left the room, and Gaines sprang into action. Sitting up with a roll of adhesive tape in his hands, he rolled over onto Baby San and clamped a hand over her mouth. The girl was shocked, her eyes darted from side to side as if she were looking for help. She tried to wiggle out from under him, but she couldn't move.

With his other hand, Gaines took the free end of the roll of tape, put it between his teeth, pulled off a strip, and slapped it over her mouth. He flipped the girl onto her stomach and taped her wrists together behind her back. Finally he taped her ankles, put another strip or tape across her mouth and pulled the sheet up to cover her.

Leaving her on the bed, he dressed as quickly as he could, pants and boots first. Flicking the safety off on the Hi-Power, he kept it in one hand as he wrapped the boot laces around the tops of his boots and tied them. Slipping his arms into his fatigue jacket, he moved silently up against the thin wall on the hinge side of the door.

Crouching there, he listened for footsteps in the corridor. Nothing. All he could hear was the muffled voices and sounds of other customers screwing in the adjoining rooms.

In the back room, the VC leader was getting anxious. "Where is your daughter, old woman? She should be back by now. Why hasn't she returned?"

The madam was getting worried, too. Lan should have returned since the Viet Cong safe house was only a few hundred meters down the alley. She worried frantically about what could have gone wrong.

"I can't wait any longer," the VC leader said. "Come, we will kill the Yankee now."

"Just a moment longer, please," Big Mama begged, her pudgy hands clasped in front of her face in a gesture of prayer.

"No! We do it now!"

Gaines hugged the wall when he heard heavy footsteps coming down the corridor toward him. He could tell that there was more than one person coming, but not how many.

Suddenly, the pilot wasn't quite as confident as he had been before. He felt like a rat in a trap. This wasn't a firefight in the jungle where he could maneuver and see the enemy. Here he could only sit tight and shoot it out.

He glanced over to the bed. Baby San was still covered by the sheet, but now he saw that it didn't really look like there was a man in bed with her. He hadn't even thought of that, and he didn't have time to put pillows under the sheet with her. In the dim light of the room, however, it still might work. He sure hoped it would.

The door opened slowly, and Gaines tensed himself to spring when the man came through. Without even stepping into the room, the VC stuck the barrel of his pistol through the partially opened door and started firing into the bed.

"Oh, no!" Big Mama screamed.

Outside, the Spook heard the shots. "Get it!" he yelled. He started sprinting for the bar.

With the first report of the VC's Chinese-made Tokarov pistol, Gaines's combat reactions took over. He put three shots through the back of the partially opened door, spun around, and emptied the rest of the Browning's thirteen-round magazine through the thin wall, aiming for the ones he had heard in the hallway.

Before the shots had stopped ringing through the corridor, in the other back rooms GIs started shouting, and their girls screamed.

"VC! Stay down!" Gaines yelled as loudly as he could. "Stay down!"

He dropped the empty magazine out of the butt of the pistol, slapped in a new one, and released the slide. Crouching low against the wall, he listened. All he heard was commotion throughout the whorehouse.

He crawled across the floor to the door. The body of the first VC blocked it open. Gaines quickly checked him. He was dead, two shots in the chest. Using the dead man's body for cover, he opened the door a little farther and cautiously peered around it.

In the poorly illuminated hallway two more bodies lay, Big Mama's and the other VC's. He moved out a little farther and looked up and down the hall. All he saw were frightened faces, both GI and Vietnamese, looking out of partially opened doors.

Gaines got to his feet and went over to Big Mama. Two growing pools of blood spread on the floor beneath her, but she was still breathing. He looked at the other VC. He was dead with a hit in the neck as well as a couple in his body.

Someone crashed down the hall. Gaines dropped to one knee and was bringing the Browning up when he saw that it was the Spook, his Swedish K submachine gun in his hands, and his ARVN running behind him. Rath lowered the pistol.

The MI agent glanced down at the two bodies and then over to Gaines. "You okay?" he panted.

"Yeah. I'm okay, but you'd better get a medic in here ASAP if you want to question her." Gaines pointed his pistol at the madam lying on the floor. "I think I got her pretty good."

"*Bac si!*" the Spook yelled for his ARVN medic. "*Lai dai!*"

"By the way," Gaines asked. "Just where the fuck was that man you had inside? The one that was supposed to keep this shit from happening."

The MI man looked up from the bodies on the floor. "He's dead."

Gaines turned and went back into the room to check on Baby San. As he had feared, the girl was also dead. He didn't even need to check her pulse to see that. The blood soaking the sheet looked black in the dim light. The VC had fired three times before Gaines's bullets cut him down. At such close range, there was no way that he could have missed.

What a fucking waste, Gaines thought, walking over to the bed. The young girl's dull, dark eyes had a very puzzled look in them. Gaines wondered if she had known what was really supposed to happen. There was no way that he would ever

45

know. In his own mind, he decided she was guilty of nothing more than wanting to have a good time.

Leaning over her body, he gently peeled the tape away from her mouth and closed her eyes.

By now the whole bar was swarming with people. The Spook's men were looking for more VC, the MPs were interrogating everyone in the building, the GIs were pulling their pants on and trying to leave, and the whores were running around screaming and crying hysterically.

Only then did the postcombat reaction finally hit Gaines. Instantly, the adrenaline of battle fled his body. He suddenly felt weak all over and completely exhausted. He headed out front to the bar.

The two snipers, Chief and Gambini, were already in the bar helping themselves to a bottle of Big Mama's Jack Daniels.

"You okay, Captain?" Chief asked, pushing the bottle his way.

Gaines took a deep breath. "Yeah." He took a long drink straight from the bottle. "I'm fine. How 'bout you guys?"

Chief looked up at him. "Gambini killed Big Mama's daughter." The Indian sniper's voice was cold. "The Spook made him do it."

"What happened?"

Gambini looked up at him, and Gaines could see that he was in shock. His face was pale, he was shaking all over, and tears were forming in the corners of his eyes.

"I didn't know who it was," he said in a shaking voice. "He told me to shoot, and I shot. I knew that it was a girl, but I didn't know that it was her. Lan and I used to get together when I could get time off."

Now the tears really came. He put his head in his hands and wept. Gambini was a blooded sniper with over fifteen kills in his log book. But he was also barely twenty years old, and he had just killed his girl friend.

Gaines handed him the bottle. "I don't know what to tell you. You saved my life. She was going to get reinforcements.

I don't think that I could've handled any more of them by myself."

Gaines laid his hand on the man's shoulder. "I owe you one, and if there's anything I can do for you, just let me know."

"Thanks, sir," Chief said. "He'll be okay tomorrow, I'll take him back to the barracks now."

Chief helped Gambini to his feet, and the two snipers left. Gaines grabbed another black-market bottle from behind the bar and had a second drink. He put the rest of the bottle in his side pocket and went looking for the Spook.

CHAPTER 7

Camp Radcliff, An Khe

The next morning, the story of the raid on the Pink Butterfly Bar raced through the big Air Cav base camp. Almost everyone was shocked to learn that Big Mama was an enemy agent. Jolly, fat old Big Mama? The madam who not only ran the best bar and whorehouse north of Saigon, but who was always willing to listen to a GI's troubles and even let a few broke grunts run a tab. Big Mama a VC spy? It was hard to believe.

In daylight, even Gambini was having a hard time believing that it had all happened. The night before when his buddy Chief had taken him back to the barracks, he had drunk the rest of the Jack Daniels to get to sleep. Even that hadn't helped. He lay awake on his bunk until dawn, running the scene over and over through his mind, the moment when he pulled the trigger on the girl.

A couple of times he had almost gotten up to sneak back to Sin City to see if Lan was there and the shooting a bad dream. But try as he could, he knew that it wasn't. Morning had finally come and there was something he had to do.

He was still wearing his dirty camies and face paint but

he really didn't care. Getting up from his bunk, he slipped into his jungle boots, buttoned his fatigue jacket, and walked across the street to the Ranger Company orderly room.

"Top, I want to see the CO."

The first sergeant was aware of what had happened down on the strip the night before and he tried to put the sniper off. He had a pretty good idea what Gambini wanted to see the captain about.

"I don't know, Gambini, he's real busy this morning. But, I'll tell him that you want to see him."

The young sniper leaned over the first sergeant's desk. "Top, you tell the captain that I want to see him now." His voice was low. "You tell him that I'm turning in my gun."

This was serious. All of the army's snipers in Vietnam were volunteers, and the rules were that anytime one wanted to quit, he could, no questions asked by anyone.

There were sound reasons for that policy, and it was strictly enforced. Not only was sniping a dangerous business, it was not to everyone's taste, not even to all combat infantrymen. It was one thing to kill a gook in a firefight—most of the time no one was ever sure if anyone had actually been hit or not. But not every man could look another man in the face through a sniper's scope while he put a bullet in his head. It made the war just a little too personal for most men.

If Gambini wanted to quit, the CO had to reassign him. That's all there was to it.

The first sergeant got up from his desk. "Wait here, Gambini. I'll see if he's in."

Gambini wasn't the only one who was having trouble dealing with the aftermath of the Whorehouse Raid, as it was called around the base camp. The other sniper in the Spook's team, Chief, was very glad he had been stationed to keep watch in the other direction and not the one ordered to kill Big Mama's daughter.

Killing men was one thing. He had never had a problem

with that. But killing a woman was something that he didn't want to do. If a woman warrior was armed and attacking him, that was another matter. He would kill her without a moment's hesitation. But killing an unarmed girl was entirely different, something that he didn't want to even think about.

For some reason that he couldn't quite explain, Chief felt protective about Gambini because he killed Lan. Even though both men were in the same platoon, Chief had never been tight with the other sniper. They had gone on several missions together, but they had not become friends.

Snipers tended to be loners—Chief, especially so. But the primary reason the snipers had not become friends was their backgrounds. Gambini was a big-city boy, an excitable Italian from Detroit who had gone into the army to keep from going to jail. Chief was quiet and reserved. He had been born into the warrior tradition.

Chief's given name was John Miluk Metcack and he had been born on the Siletz Indian Reservation in western Oregon. He was the grandson of a California Tutuni Indian warrior who had been rounded up by the army in the early 1900s and sent to a reservation in Oregon to keep him out of trouble. Metcack's father was a logger, as were many men of his tribe, and the young boy had been left in his grandfather's care when his father was away for months at a time at logging camps.

Under the old warrior's tutelage, young Metcack had first learned how to hunt illegal deer for the family's table. He had spent many cold, wet hours hiding in the mountains of the Oregon coastal range, waiting for a target to appear. The old man only gave him one round of ammunition at a time for the family's old lever-action Winchester deer rifle. If he missed his shot, his family went hungry.The young Indian quickly learned to shoot accurately. He had no other choice.

When he grew to manhood at fifteen, the old man initiated him into the warrior tradition and taught him how to hunt men as well as deer.

At the first opportunity, Metcack joined the army and volunteered for duty in Vietnam. He saw himself as a modern

Indian warrior practicing his trade, proud of his heritage and of his ability to kill his nation's enemies.

The white men in the Ranger Company called him Chief, but he didn't resent the nickname. He was proud because he was very good at what he did. When it came to the silent, long-range kill, he *was* the Chief.

Chief was troubled. He felt there must be something he could do, one warrior to another, to help Gambini get over the aftermath of the killing. One of the biggest differences that he had seen between white men and Indians was that white men didn't have a constructive way to deal with the emotions that arose from the killing of other men.

The Indians, however, knew that while all life was sacred, there were times that a man must kill his enemies without remorse. He decided that he would seek out the other sniper and would try to pass on to him some of the ancient warrior's wisdom that he had learned from his grandfather.

He was deep in thought as he walked down the dusty company street, thinking of the things his grandfather had told him about the difficulties that a man faced when walking the path of the warrior.

"Hey, Chief!" One of the other Rangers called from the door of his hooch. "How's it going, man?"

"Nun ya." The Indian called back, giving his customary answer.

"Hey, man, I don't speak Indian, what's that mean?"

"It means *nun ya.*"

Chief walked on, a secret smile on his face.

Rat Gaines was also in a foul mood. The Spook had called him earlier to report that Big Mama had survived her wounds and ratted on the entire An Khe Viet Cong network. Dozens of Viet Cong agents were being rounded up and thrown in jail at that very moment. That was good news, of course, but it brought the company commander little joy. He kept seeing Baby San's dull, dead eyes.

Gaines was a realist. He had been in The Nam long enough

to know that people were getting killed every day—lots of people. And many of them weren't carrying guns for either side. They just got caught up in the crossfire; the shorts and overs and human error of the war.

The Communists were fighting a total war and they were more than willing to involve what the Western world called noncombatants in their fight. Most Americans simply did not want to believe that women and children could also be the enemy. He remembered a bombing in a restaurant in Nha Trang that killed a pilot friend of his. The bomb had been emplaced by a ten-year-old shoe-shine boy.

Gaines thought about it bitterly as he did his morning's paper work. Regardless of what happened, the war always went on, and there was always more work to do. He picked up his phone and rang through to Lieutenant Muller, the harrassed battalion adjutant.

"Muller, this is Gaines. Where's my goddamned supply sergeant? . . . No, Lieutenant, that's not going to cut it, I want my supply sergeant, and I want him on board now! . . . I don't want to hear that, Muller. That's the division's problem, not mine. . . . I'm going to be your problem, Lieutenant, if you don't come up with a man for me ASAP."

He slammed the phone down. As usual, Muller had blamed division-wide shortages in supply personnel. Rat knew that it was a real problem, but he didn't care. It was nice to have someone like an adjutant to yell at when he felt the way he did today.

Treat Brody woke up suddenly in a cold sweat. He looked around the big GP tent in confusion, disoriented for a moment. He was alone. He glanced at his watch. Everyone else was at breakfast.

He had been dreaming again, bad dreams. It had been several nights now since he had slept peacefully, and it was beginning to tell on him. His repeated nightmares were full of vague, shadowy shapes which menaced him. The shapes floated above him wherever he went, and he couldn't escape them. And try as he did, he couldn't clearly see what they were. When he turned to look, they vanished. Then, the minute he turned around and tried to run away, they followed him.

He sat up, swung his legs over the edge of his bunk, and tried to light a smoke. His hands shook so badly that he could hardly get the cigarette out of the pack. He finally got it lit and dragged the smoke deep into his lungs.

"Fuck," he muttered to himself. "I've got to get my shit together."

He finally stood, walked to the end of the tent, and looked out onto the airfield that the GIs had nicknamed the Golf Course. As always, dozens of helicopters were flying in and out of the world's largest helicopter landing field. The drone of rotor blades cutting through the air was a constant background noise at Camp Radcliff.

Brody flicked the cigarette butt out the open tent flap and turned back to get his soap and towel. Though the sun would not have heated the water in the shower tank yet, he wanted to wash the slick, sticky sweat away. Maybe the cold shower would clear his head.

He didn't know what was wrong with him lately. He couldn't think of anything that could be causing him to have the dreams. He used to have nightmares about the jungle when he first came to Nam, dreams that the vegetation was trying to reach up and drag him out of his door gunner's pocket in the back of his chopper when he flew low over the trees. But he had gotten over them long ago, when he finally convinced his subconscious mind that the only thing to fear in the jungle was other men, and not the jungle itself.

He rubbed a hand through his wild shock of blond hair. It was grimy with sweat and the all-pervading red dust of An Khe. He slipped into his shower sandals, wrapped his issue o.d. towel around his waist, and headed out.

The cold shower felt good, and the veteran door gunner let the water run as long as he dared. He would have given anything to be able to stay under it for an hour or so. But he had to leave some water in the tank for the next guy. He

53

toweled his hair dry, quickly shaved, and brushed his teeth. He noticed that his bushy mustache badly needed a trim. He didn't want Zack on his case about it again.

Halfway down the duckwalk coming back from the shower tent, he ran into Corky heading the other way.

"Buenos dias," the Chicano machine gunner called out cheerfully.

"Fuck you."

"Hey! Lighten up, amigo. That's no way to be on a beautiful morning in sunny Southeast Asia."

"I've got your Southeast Asia hanging." Brody grabbed at his crotch.

Corky laughed and walked on by.

Back in the Blues' tent, Brody dressed in a clean set of jungle fatigues and started getting his gear squared away. They didn't have a mission laid on today, but he wanted to get his stuff ready in case something came up at the last moment.

As he worked, he realized how much he missed his old buddy, Elliot Fletcher, the Snakeman. Snake had DEROSed a couple of weeks back, and things just hadn't been the same around the Blues without him. Brody missed the Texan's constant bitching about anything and everything and his schemes to get out of work. With Fletcher gone, Brody didn't have anyone to get pissed off at when he felt like biting ass.

He repacked his ruck, put the refilled canteens back in their carriers, and shoved it under his bunk. He started to reach for his rifle, but stopped. It was clean enough, and he didn't feel like fucking with it.

He got up and headed out the door, wondering what to do with himself. Most of all, he wished that someone would give them a mission.

CHAPTER 8

Kangor Wat, Cambodia

The sun was setting outside the small Cambodian village of Kangor, some sixty klicks from the Vietnamese border and ten from Laos. In the jungle, the dark trees all but hid from sight the ancient stone temple of Kangor Wat. The massive stone structure was all that stood intact of a large religious complex built by the kings of the ancient Khmer empire.

Over the centuries, wars and marauding bandits had destroyed the many smaller buildings that had once surrounded the large one reducing them to piles of jumbled, blackened stones. The relentless tropical rains erased the vivid carvings that had once adorned the stones, so they looked like nature had scattered them there, not the hand of man. In time, war, the rain, and the jungle would destroy the huge temple as well. For now it still defied the elements.

The whine of a helicopter turbine cut through the other sounds of the jungle. A dark green-and-gray camouflaged helicopter made a low pass over the temple. The monkeys who made their homes in the ruined temple didn't even look up at the sound. They were used to the comings and goings of the Russian built Mi-8 HIP and paid it no heed. Grooming and mating activities were far more important to them.

North Vietnamese Air Force Lieutenant Colonel Nguyen Cao Duc unlocked the pilot's door of his chopper and swung it open. The hot, fetid air hit him in the face, and he gasped. City born, Duc hated the heavy, thick atmosphere of the jungle, rich with the stenches of life and death. He longed for the cool, clean breezes that blew off the South China Sea.

Duc unbuckled his harness and stepped to the ground. As he walked over to the huge stone temple with his helmet in hand, Khmer ground crewmen hurriedly pulled the camouflage netting back into position, hiding the narrow airstrip hacked into the jungle.

Only a very low-flying aircraft could ever spot his secret base. And to do that, it would first have to fly through the ring of antiaircraft guns that surrounded it. Duc felt secure.

Even if the base were found, he knew that the Americans would never bomb it. They could not dare risk damaging the ancient temple of Kangor Wat, second only to Angkor Wat as a sacred shrine of the Khmer people. One bomb on the temple grounds, even a little one, would send Prince Sihanouk running to Moscow for aid. The Americans would never risk that.

Cambodia's one-sided neutrality was far too important to the 'peace-at-any-price' faction in the United States. Duc laughed. He could not understand how any people could be so blind. Chairman Mao was right. The Westerners, particularly the Americans, were decadent and doomed to fall. What other reason could there be for the stupid, incompetent way they conducted their war in the south? Any nation as powerful as they liked to think that they were, would have destroyed North Vietnam years ago, grinding it into the dust. Instead, they played at war, wasting the blood of their young men in a stupid game, fighting by the rules.

Duc snorted. Rules! Rules were written by winners, not by losers. And to win, one had to be bold.

Duc lived to kill Westerners, particularly Americans. In fact, to his way of thinking, his adult life had begun the night

56

he killed his first American in a parking lot at the University of Washington in Seattle.

Nguyen Cao Duc was born the pampered only son of a Hanoi University professor and his very young wife. Raised in an academic environment, Duc had been destined for the career of an educated man, a Mandarin in the ancient tradition. He was well on his way when fate suddenly intervened and gave him a glimpse of the future.

He was fourteen years old when he saw his first airplane up close. He was on a bus traveling to the mountain summer home of a school classmate when it stopped in front of the French airfield at Phuc Yen, north of Hanoi. Right next to the road, a French air force F8F Bearcat was parked on the tarmac.

Young Duc had never seen an airplane at close range and he was very interested in it. He got off the bus, walked over and stared at it through the fence. The more he looked at the silver fighter, the more his young heart leaped. Something about the beauty of the American-built fighter spoke to him. The power of the four 20mm cannon in its short wings and the huge, 2,000-horsepower radial engine were images that burned into his brain.

When the bus continued on its way to the mountains, Duc was not on it. He walked back and forth on his side of the fence for over an hour as if in a trance, soaking up every detail of the war bird. Finally he caught another bus back to Hanoi. Before he returned to his house, however, he went to the temple and burned joss sticks at the altar. As he prayed, he vowed that one day he would become a fighter pilot.

That night, when he announced his intentions to his father, the elder Duc forbade him to even think of a career in the military. He was the son of a Mandarin family, the educated class of Vietnam. He patiently explained that the military was for the sons of the middle classes and the peasantry, not the gentry. Over the next few years, however, the younger

Duc persisted in his dream. Finally, as he always did, his father gave in.

But the father made his son compromise. The old professor sent the eighteen-year-old boy to the United States to study aeronautical engineering. If his son was to be a pilot, he would be an educated one, not just another man who flew a machine. Nguyen Cao Duc would also know why and how the machines flew.

Duc excelled at his studies at the University of Washington. As the son of a Mandarin, it was expected, and it came easily enough. Unfortunately, the slender young Vietnamese failed completely in the social arena.

As an Asian, he was not accustomed to the freewheeling social life of young Americans. And at five feet four inches and one hundred twenty pounds, Duc looked like a child and was treated as such by his far bigger American classmates. Far worse than that, however, was the humiliation he suffered three times a week when he went to his mandatory physical-education class. Most small-statured Vietnamese men have small penises, but Duc's was small even by Asian standards.

In Vietnam, being from a privileged class, Duc had never been exposed to taunts about the size of his genitalia. In fact, he had never seen his high-school classmates nude, and didn't know that he was so small in comparison. The maids of his father's house had never said anything to him about it, and they had shared his bed since he was fourteen.

The first time he saw young American men in the locker room of the university, he had been shocked. He had not known that a man could be so huge. He was intimidated by them and tried to hide his inadequate member as best he could. At the same time, those big emblems of masculinity fascinated him, and he covertly looked whenever he could.

One day, he made the mistake of paying too much attention. Someone caught him staring. Grabbing the slightly built young Duc by the shoulders, the American forced him to his knees.

"You want to look at it you little queer, get a good look!"

Duc's nose was just inches from the big American's crotch.

The strong body smell of meat-eating people made him sick to his stomach. Duc gagged and swallowed hard to keep from vomiting. Tears came to his eyes.

"You like that thing, you little queer?" the man taunted him. "That's a real man's tool. I'd shove it down your throat, but you'd like that wouldn't you?"

Loud laughter rang in his ears and filled his heart with shame.

Duc was jerked roughly to his feet. "Are you sure you're not in the wrong locker room, little girl? Let's have a pecker check here." The American was enjoying himself. Too late, Duc's hands went to cover his small organ.

"You call that thing a dick? I've seen bigger wangs on cockroaches!"

Once again, Duc's ears rang with harsh laughter.

"Hey, guys, it's Needle Dick the Bug Fucker! In person!" the man roared, howling at his own crude humor. "Needle Dick the Bug Fucker."

From that day on, Nguyen Cao Duc was known on campus as Needle Dick the Bug Fucker.

Duc never went back to his physical-education class and managed to get a medical excuse for the remainder of the term. That way, he was still able to graduate without the credit. He avoided the men who had witnessed his shame, but word of his humiliation got out in the engineering school. No one said anything to his face, but everytime he saw an American classmate with a smile on his face, Duc felt that he was being taunted.

Duc did so well in his engineering classes that he was invited to the school academic awards dinner that June. He was so elated about his academic accomplishments that he foolishly lowered his guard and let himself be talked into going to the engineering-school party that followed later that evening.

The party was great and, for once, Duc didn't feel inadequate. He had done well in all his classes and he mingled freely with his classmates, talking about the kind of things that were important to college students. Just as he was about

59

to leave, the big American who had humiliated him in the locker room came in the front door.

With the man was a beautiful American girl, one of those whose golden skin and hair had so haunted Duc's erotic dreams. He had not dated any American girls on campus, but his dreams had been full of them, and this was a girl he had dreamed about.

Duc panicked. He tried to turn away and hide, but it was too late. The big man had spotted him.

"Hey!" the man bellowed drunkenly. "Look! It's Needle Dick the Bug Fucker! How ya doing, Needle Dick ole buddy?"

To his horror, Duc felt the man's hands on his arms again. He struggled and tried to run, but could not break free of his grasp.

The man turned to his date. "Sweets, I'd like you to meet Needle Dick the Bug Fucker, the man with the shortest crank in history."

The room burst out in laughter, and Duc wanted to crawl away and die. Worse, the blond girl looked down at him and giggled.

"You're kidding!" she smiled at her date. "He looks like such a nice boy. He doesn't really fuck bugs, does he?" She giggled again, and Duc realized that they were both drunk.

"Sure he does," the big man said. "See."

To his even greater horror, Duc felt his pants pulled down, his tiny penis exposed for everyone to see.

With a cry of rage, Duc pulled himself loose and fled the party, pulling his pants up as he ran. Behind him, he heard howls of laughter.

Hours later, he still heard them as he wandered in an aimless daze around the campus. He would have revenge, he repeated to himself over and over again, he would have revenge on all those smelly, big Americans and their huge, animal-like organs.

Around midnight, Duc's wanderings took him to a parking lot behind a girls' dorm. He came out of his daze when he heard gasping noises coming from a big sedan parked in the far corner of the lot. He knew those noises well, the sounds of lovemaking, and they drew him to the car.

The light from a streetlamp faintly illuminated the car's interior, and Duc saw a half-naked man kneeling in the backseat. The man turned his head slightly, and Duc recognized his tormentor. He panicked and turned to run again, but he saw that a pair of female legs were wrapped around the man's hips, and the man humped his torso up and down.

Instinctively, Duc knew who was receiving him, the blond girl who had witnessed his humiliation at the party, the golden-skinned girl who had laughed at him.

Rage filled the young man's heart. It was bad enough that the girl had seen his humiliation, but watching her have sex tormented him. Her cries of pleasure fueled that outrage. Duc felt his own small member stiffen. He tried to fight it back, but it had a mind of its own. Shaking and shuddering, he tried to turn away, but he could not.

Rage filled Duc's mind, blanking out all else, and he moved toward the car. The two lovers had finished, and the man had fallen back against the front seat. When Duc opened the door, the smell of alcohol mixed with the reek of sex hit his nose. The were both dead drunk and had passed out.

Powered by his rage, Duc's mind instantly devised his revenge, and he fell upon the girl who still lay in the backseat. She looked up through a fog of alcohol, but she was too drunk to resist. Duc wrapped his hands around her slim throat.

The Vietnamese was small but he was strong, and the girl was totally defenseless. His hands crushed her windpipe. Her green eyes blinked at him pleadingly, she waved her hands aimlessly in the air, and her small feet drummed a tattoo against the seat.

Duc continued squeezing her soft throat long after she had stopped breathing. He squeezed until his arms ached. When he finally let her go, gasping for breath, he stared at the slim body beneath him. The girl's green eyes were open wide and stared at him. Her swollen tongue stuck out between her soft, red lips, and her throat was bruised where his hands had squeezed the life from her.

Duc shuddered at the sight. But almost of their own accord, his eyes traveled to her crotch and fixed on her patch of blond pubic hair. To his horror, his member became stiff again.

In a frenzy Duc fell on her body, ripping at her blouse, tearing it from her body. At the sight of her full breasts, his rage exploded anew. Grabbing hands full of her long, golden hair, he slammed her head against the side of the car again and again.

The Vietnamese would have torn the dead girl's head from her body had not her boyfriend groaned in his drunken stupor. Duc panicked and fled, running as fast as he could.

The next morning, Duc left the campus for his summer vacation back home. At the Seattle airport, a newspaper headline caught his eye. CO-ED BRUTALLY SLAIN it read. Below the headline the story reported that her date had been arrested for the crime.

Duc smiled all the way on the long flight back to Vietnam.

The next year, young Nguyen Cao Duc continued his studies in France, where he joined Ho Chi Minh's Vietnamese Communist Party.

CHAPTER 9

The Cambodian border

Since that night in Seattle so long ago, Duc had killed several more Americans, but it was not enough to quench the burning hatred he felt in his heart for all things American.

Duc's love of aircraft and his belief in the Communist doctrine of Ho Chi Minh earned him a spot as a student in the Russian Air Academy at Morineo. Once again he excelled in his studies both on the ground and in the air. Upon graduation, he was commissioned an officer in the Peoples' Air Force of North Vietnam and assigned to fly one of the MiG jet fighters the Soviet Union had supplied his nation.

From the cockpit of his swept-wing MiG-17 high over North Vietnam, Duc met and killed several American pilots in aerial combat. Duc made his aerial kills the same way that he had killed the co-ed in Seattle. He specialized in seeking out crippled aircraft and finishing them off in a frenzy.

When he was scrambled to meet an American bombing raid, he always headed for the coastline. Loitering at high altitude, he waited for a helpless Phantom or Skyhawk trying to reach the open sea. Screaming down in a dive, he would fly up behind the American aircraft and start shooting holes in it.

Even though a long burst from the MiG's two 23mm and single 37mm cannons was usually more than enough to down his prey, he was never in a hurry to finish them of. He would play with the American pilot, flying close enough to see his terror-stricken face. If the pilot ejected from his crippled plane, Duc followed shooting holes into his parachute. Finally, he would close in and blow him apart with the cannon.

Duc's aerial success brought him to the attention of North Vietnamese leaders, and he was invited to join the air-force operational staff in Hanoi. There he was assigned to work on plans for the surprise attack on the south that was to take place during Tet of the coming year. Midway through the long planning process, Duc had been outraged to learn that no role in the offensive was being given to the People's Air Force of Vietnam.

The North Vietnamese air force was small and primarily defensive. They had a small squadron of Russian IL-28 twin-jet attack bombers, and the MiG-15 and 17 fighters were equipped to carry bombs and rockets in the ground-attack role.

Duc had been well schooled at the Russian air force academy, and he knew the tactical value of a well-coordinated air and ground attack. He was convinced that the planned ground offensive was doomed to failure without proper air cover and support. Without aerial protection, the Americans and their giant air fleet would grind the North Vietnamese infantry into dog meat.

He had strongly argued his point at the planning sessions. To some degree, they had agreed with him, but the final decision had been not to launch air attacks against the hated Americans.

The Hanoi leadership was afraid of two things. If their air force suffered big losses from the superior American power, there would be no one left to protect the capital city from American bombers. Also, North Vietnamese air attacks in the south might cause the Americans to step up their bombing raids of the north in retaliation. Thus far, the limited bombing was bearable and could be endured. But if the restrictions were removed, and the Americans conducted a real air war against the North, like the one waged against the Germans and the Japanese in World War II, Hanoi would be destroyed.

Also, Duc had been told that even if the ground forces were defeated, by some perverse logic the offensive would still be a victory for Ho Chi Minh. The American president had told his people that the war was almost over, and they believed him. If their television programs were to show the Communist forces fighting in the cities of the south, the American public might panic. The peace party in Congress and in the streets of America would be so frightened that perhaps they could force an end to the war.

Duc had been outraged. He lived for the people's struggle and he was ready to die for it, but only for total victory. To win the war without killing every last long-nose bastard in Southeast Asia was unthinkable. He was disgusted, and saw the decision of the Hanoi leadership as pure cowardice.

Since that night in Seattle, Duc had never lost control of his burning hatred. But when his own leaders denied him a long-awaited chance to kill them, something inside him snapped.

He resigned from the planning staff and asked to be reassigned to flight duties. His request was granted. With his engineering background, Duc found a place as a test pilot in the armed-helicopter test program.

Russian air-force advisors had flown four of their Mi-8 helicopters into North Vietnam and were conducting experiments on their usefulness as gunships. The Russians were very impressed by the American success with armed helicopters in the south, and saw great potential for helicopters on the battlefields of the future.

The Mi-8 helicopter, NATO codenamed HIP, was a big machine, over twice the size of a Bell Huey and considerably faster. Powered by twin 1500-horsepower turbines spinning a big, five-bladed rotor, it could carry a squad of infantry as well as a heavy-weapons load at over 150 miles an hour. The machine that he was assigned to fly had been equipped with a pair of 23mm cannon firing forward, and four, thirty-two round, 57mm air-to-ground rocketpods hung from pylons on each side. Though it was not as maneuverable as a Cobra, it carried a greater weight of ordnance at a slightly higher speed.

Duc loved his new ship and he started making unauthorized ventures, seeking targets along the border. The first time he saw the explosive 57mm rockets tearing into an American recon team on the north side of the DMZ, he was ecstatic. This was the way he wanted to kill Yankees, close enough that he could see their blood.

One day, while returning to his base, he had an idea. If Hanoi wouldn't let him take the air war to the Yankees, he would do it himself. A single gunship operating in the vicinity of the American army would do more damage than the entire MiG fighter force up north. He started reading maps and making plans.

Colonel Duc's border excursions had not gone unnoticed by the Soviet air contingent. Russian Colonel Yuri Yakanov, the commander of the air advisors, was well aware of them. He was also aware of Hanoi's reluctance to allow their aircraft to engage targets in the south. The Russian air force wanted front-line combat testing of their helicopters, not just target shooting. When Colonel Yakanov learned that Duc was checking out maps of the Cambodian border region, he quickly figured out what the North Vietnamese pilot was planning and made plans of his own.

When Duc's preparations were completed, he simply loaded up his experimental HIP gunship with all the ammunition it would carry, took off one morning, and flew south to join the Cambodian Khmer Rouge. Unknown to him, a small, but powerful transponder in his helicopter told the Russian colonel exactly where he had gone.

At first the Cambodian Communists didn't quite know what to think of the renegade North Vietnamese officer. The Cambodian and Vietnamese people had been mortal enemies for centuries, and even the Communist factions of the two countries didn't always see eye to eye. At first they thought

66

he was a spy, but after a lengthy interrogation they sent him to Pol Pot, the leader of their party.

In Pol Pot, Duc finally found a kindred soul, another French-educated Asian whose hatred of the West was just as twisted and pathological as his own. Pol welcomed Duc and his Russian gunship, the first aircraft in the Khmer Rouge arsenal.

At Duc's suggestion, Kangor Wat was chosen as the perfect site for a hidden airfield. From there he could range out and attack the entire central portion of the Vietnamese border region. The airfield was built quickly. Fuel supplies, ammunition, and spare parts were stolen from Prince Sihanouk's Cambodian air-force stores and transported to the temple. Two American-trained Cambodian aircraft mechanics were recruited and sent to the jungle to maintain the ship. Within a few weeks, the HIP went into action along the border.

Since then, by his calculations, he had killed at least fifty Americans with his strafing attacks and the ambushes of the occasional Air America aircraft he happened upon.

Today he had ambushed another recon team inside Cambodia. This time he caught them just as the pickup helicopter was touching down for their extraction. He destroyed it as well, adding at least another ten men to his tally. The North Vietnamese pilot was well pleased with his day's work and he decided to celebrate. He had his eyes on a village girl who had been brought into the camp last week. She looked young enough to properly appreciate him. He would see that night.

Though Colonel Duc would celebrate his victory, one American had escaped his ambush of the Special Forces Roadrunner Team; twenty-year-old Green Beret Sergeant Panama Jack Wilburn.

Everyone else, however, was dead. Even the four helicopter crewmen on the extraction chopper had died when one of the HIP's 57mm high-explosive rockets slammed into it. Wilburn had a 23mm shell splinter deep in the muscles of his right thigh, but he was otherwise unhurt.

When the scream of the chopper's turbines finally faded in the distance, Wilburn picked himself up from the edge of the jungle clearing where he had taken cover and looked around.

The extraction chopper was a blasted, flaming wreckage. It had taken the rocket just as it touched down. Through the black, oily smoke of the burning JP-4, Wilburn could see the blackened, burning figures of the pilot and co-pilot still strapped in their seats. The doorgun ammunition was cooking off in the flames, adding to the danger. There was nothing that he could do for either man.

A ruined body in a Nomex flight suit lay close to the wreckage, the legs still on fire. It was one of the door gunners. The other gunner was on the other side of the bird and in no better shape.

His own team members were dead, too. They had been caught too close to the chopper and sprayed with rocket and cannon fire. He survived only because he had been covering the extraction from the edge of the clearing.

He quickly checked each of his teammate's bodies in the vain hope that one of them might still be alive. Only then did the young sergeant stop and tie a bandage on his own wound. He could feel the sharp, jagged piece of steel deep inside his leg, but he didn't have time to probe for it. He had to get moving.

He went back to the bodies and collected their dog tags and documents. At the same time, he rummaged through the wreckage of their rucks and pockets to collect water, food, and extra ammunition.

RT Sleeper had been at the end of their mission, so there was little water or rations left. He found some cold rice balls in the packs of the Nungs on his team and enough water to fill his two-quart canteen. They had not had a contact, so he still had his basic ammo load for his weapon. However, he took no chances and grabbed all the extra ammo he could carry.

The last working radio was on Wilburn's back. Taking out his compass and map, the Special Forces man quickly plotted a course back to South Vietnam some thirty klicks away, and started moving out as fast as his wounded leg could carry him. He didn't want to be in the area when the North Vietnamese ground forces came in to check out the attack. There was no way for Wilburn to know that the NVA were not chasing him—indeed, that they had no idea his team had been hit, or that the red-tailed chopper spitting cannon shells and rockets had been working on its own.

The terrain wasn't that thick, but with his wound it was tough going. The young sergeant felt the sharp piece of metal inside his leg tearing and cutting the muscles with every step he took. It hurt badly, but he shut his mind off and gutted it out.

By nightfall, he had made some ten klicks before he stopped.

After a long drink and a quick meal of cold rice and a nut bar from his Lurp rations, Wilburn took the radio off his back and got out the reel of copper wire from the pouch on the side of the PC-77. Tying a short piece of stick to one end he threw it as far as he could into the tree above him. He then cut the wire from the reel and hooked the other end to the external antenna connection on the radio.

The Prick 77 could only reach five miles with the eight-foot whip antenna, but with the wire antenna, it could reach over twenty miles on a good night.

"Broken Rainbow, Broken Rainbow, This is Dizzy Sleeper. I say again Dizzy Sleeper, over."

Wilburn listened intently. There was nothing but static hissing on the handset. He transmitted again.

"Broken Rainbow, Broken Rainbow. This is Sleeper, this is Sleeper, over."

Again nothing.

Wilburn changed the frequency on the radio. "Black Slider, Black Slider, This is Dizzy Sleeper. Over."

The voice of the retransmission station on top of the mountain outside of Kontum answered faintly.

"Dizzy Sleeper, this is Black Slider. I hear you weak, but steady, over."

"Slider, this is Sleeper. Can you retrans to Broken Rainbow on this push for me. This is a blue-star call, over."

"Roger, can do. Wait one."

"Dizzy Sleeper," a deeper voice cut in a few minutes later. "This is Broken Rainbow on your push. Over."

"This is Sleeper. Go to secure. Over." Wilburn turned a knob on his radio and waited.

"This is Rainbow on secure. Go ahead."

Speaking in the clear, Wilburn told Rainbow, the Special Forces CCN operations center, what had transpired with the gunship attack and his present situation.

"Roger, Sleeper, I copy. Stand by for extraction information."

Using a grease pencil, Wilburn wrote the eight numbers given by the radio operator on the acetate covering on his map.

"Rainbow, this is Sleeper, roger, copy. See you tomorrow. Sleeper out."

At first light in the morning, another slick would come to the coordinates he had been given to pull him out. For the first time since the enemy gunship had suddenly swept down on them, Jack Wilburn began to think that he might survive.

He turned the radio off. It was on its last battery, and he had to save its remaining power. He would need it in the morning to vector the chopper in.

He checked the compress bandage on his leg and was relieved to see that the wound wasn't bleeding much. He checked the magazine in his M-16 and the grenades on his belt. Then he leaned back against the trunk of the tree and tried to stay awake till dawn.

CHAPTER 10

USARV Headquarters, Saigon

In most wars, many critical decisions are not made by the military commanders on the battlefield. Instead, they are made by politicians safely sitting behind their desks in the halls of government.

In Vietnam, however, more so than any other war in history, what occurred in combat was almost always decided primarily by political whim, not by military necessity nor even common sense. Rarely was any decision made on the basis of what was most effective in military terms. The American political response to the situation in Cambodia was a very good case in point.

Since the formation of the modern state of Cambodia with the breakup of French Indochina in 1954, the country had been ruled by Prince Norodom Sihanouk. Sihanouk was a fairly typical Asian leader of the old school. He was fat, treacherous, despotic, inept, and not too bright. He was also completely out of touch with the mood of the people he governed.

In the struggles between the Asian Communist nations and the Free World, Sihanouk loudly proclaimed Cambodia's neutrality. But he also favored the Communist Chinese and the North Vietnamese every chance he got.

Sihanouk knowingly and willingly allowed the North Vietnamese Army to build giant base camps and supply dumps in his country, and then he screamed bloody murder in the United Nation's General Assembly when the United States tried to expose him. Although it had been proven to be a fact time and time again, Prince Sihanouk hotly denied that the NVA were using his country as a sanctuary and threatened to move Cambodia into the Communist Bloc if American forces crossed the border.

For some perverse reason, the peace-at-any-price crowd in the American media and Congress loved fat Prince Sihanouk and swallowed his line completely. They worked overtime to see that the American military was effectively prevented from doing anything about the North Vietnamese Army in Cambodia. This allowed both the NVA and the mainforce VC units to use Cambodian camps as staging areas for attacks on South Vietnam with complete impunity.

Not all Cambodians agreed with Sihanouk's left-wing politics, however. There were two major political parties working against him, the Blues and the Reds. The Reds were, of course, the radical leftist Khmer Rouge Communist Party. Their maniac leader, Pol Pot, was allied with the Red Chinese, and he wanted the North Vietnamese out of Cambodia so his party could take over the entire country.

The Cambodian Blues was a Western-leaning party run by an army officer named Lon Nol. He wanted the North Vietnamese out of Cambodia as well, along with all Communists, including the Khmer Rouge. To accomplish this mission, Lon Nol's people fed a considerable amount of intelligence information about NVA activities in Cambodia to American headquarters in Saigon.

When continued reports filtered into Saigon of a large buildup of enemy troops, ammunition, and supplies in the Cambodian sanctuaries along the Vietnamese border, the United States Army Vietnam Headquarters was alarmed. General William Westmoreland wanted more information and ordered that an operation be mounted. He wanted the Fifth Special Forces Group to send their long-range recon teams into Cambodia to get a firsthand assessment of the situation on the ground.

For once, military common sense seemed to be in command instead of the vascillating politically inspired bullshit that held sway most of the time in Saigon. However, to keep the Jane Fondas in Congress and the American press from wetting their pants, this would be a clandestine operation conducted by the Green Beret Roadrunner teams. They were to cross the Vietnamese border, sweep through the NVA base camps in these areas, and report everything they found.

In the planning process for this extended recon operation, someone in the USARV G-2, the Intelligence Staff Section, found the First Air Cavalry Division's report of the Russian gunship operating in their AO. This report was tied into other Special Forces sightings, studied carefully, and assessed. The conclusion was that the gunship posed a possible threat to the planned operation.

The G-2 was assigned the task of finding out more about the enemy aircraft. Even using ARVN sources, some of which ran all the way up into high-ranking Communist officials in Hanoi, they were unable to come up with any information at all about the location of the gunship's base.

Since even one enemy gunship could cause great damage to the recon teams, it became imperative that the HIP's base be found and that it be taken out before the operation kicked off.

It was 0400 hours at Kadena Air Base, Okinawa, home of the Ninth Strategic Reconnaissance Wing of the United States Air Force.

A 103-foot-long, entirely black aircraft, which looked more like a spaceship from a science-fiction movie than an airplane, was towed from its hangar. Two men wearing astronaut-type spacesuits climbed into the cockpit of the Lockheed SR-71 Blackbird and started their preflight checks.

The checklist readoff took over an hour, but with bright flames finally shooting out of her afterburners, the big black spy plane was airborne as dawn broke over the island.

At 25,000 feet over the Pacific Ocean, the SR-71 made contact with a Boeing KC-135Q aerial tanker aircraft to refuel. The Blackbird's two huge J-58 engines were thirsty. She needed a long drink of JP-7 jet fuel before starting her high-speed recon run.

Once refueled, the pilot of the SR-71 lit up her 'burners again. Quickly she broke Mach unity and streaked up to cruising altitude at 85,000 feet—sixteen miles high. Once up there, she settled down to a cruising speed of Mach 3.5, three and a half times the speed of sound or two thousand miles per hour, faster than a 7.62mm round. She turned north, heading for the land mass of Southeast Asia. The heat of her speed made the titanium skin on the aircraft's nose and the leading edge of her delta wings glow a dull orange-red at twelve hundred degrees Fahrenheit. She started her recon run along the Cambodian-Laotian-Vietnamese border region.

In the backseat of the Blackbird, the RSO, the recon systems operator, turned on his cameras and sensors. They would cover a path sixty miles wide along the aircraft's route. The sensors that he controlled could detect a burning cigarette at night, and the cameras could read a newspaper's headlines from that height.

Sixteen miles below the speeding SR-71, Colonel Nguyen Cao Duc sat in the cockpit of his Russian gunship, running his preflight checks before taking off on a mission. The camouflage netting had been pulled back from his hidden jungle airstrip, and he was naked to the sky as the Blackbird flashed overhead.

Duc was totally unaware of the skyplane as it passed. It could not be seen with the human eye and Duc's radar was not powerful enough to detect anything that high. Even had the renegade North Vietnamese pilot known of the Blackbird, there was absolutely nothing that he could do about it.

Several minutes later, the SR-71 throttled back and made a slow turn in the sky over Red China to head southeast again. It was a leisurely turn that took hundreds of miles to complete, but the pilot wasn't at all concerned about being in Red Chinese airspace. There wasn't a fighter plane in the world that could reach him where he was, flying on the edge of the stratosphere. Not even the most advanced Russian antiaircraft missiles could reach that high. The sky was his own to do with as he pleased.

Once he was turned around, the pilot aimed his skyplane on a path that would take him over the Red Chinese border with North Vietnam, then down to Hanoi and Haiphong. He figured that as long as he was in the neighborhood, he might as well use up the rest of the camera's film on the French and Russian cargo ships offloading in Haiphong harbor.

A little over an hour later, the SR-71 settled back down to earth at Kadena Air Force Base. Another Blackbird mission was completed.

Four hours after that, at USARV Headquarters in downtown Saigon, the Blackbird's photos and sensor readouts had been studied, and Duc's base was located.

"Hot damn!" the USARV G-2 exclaimed when the photo interpreter pointed out an airstrip hacked out of the jungle in front of an old temple. The enlarged photograph clearly showed the big Russian helicopter sitting at the end of the narrow runway. Even the helmeted pilot in the chopper's cockpit and the 57mm rocketpods hanging on its sides were clearly visible.

"I'll be a son of a bitch! Will you look at that! There it is at Kangor Wat. Those bastards have cut a runway right next to that goddamned temple, and we can't touch him there."

The G-2 stabbed his finger at the aerial view of the ancient Khmer temple. "One bomb on that pile of rocks, and Prince Sihanouk will have the whole fucking United Nations down on our backs. Shit! I know Westy wants this operation to work, but the press will shit a brick if we try to bomb that temple."

He turned to the G-3, the operations officer, who was in his office going over the photos with him.

"We're going to have to take this guy out from the ground. Who do we have that we can get on short notice to do it?"

"I'll call down to Fifth Group and see if I can borrow a Mike Force Hatchet Team from them. Also, since this is in their AO, I'll see what the Air Cav can put together."

"Better put a move on it. This is top priority!"

CHAPTER 11

Camp Radcliff, An Khe

A very sleepy Rat Gaines walked into the big air-conditioned briefing room at the Third Brigade headquarters building. He had had another one of his sleepless nights. He was going to have to do something about that, something to help him relax. Maybe more flying time or a run down to Saigon would do the trick.

He took a seat and looked around the crowded room. Something big was going on, but for the life of him he couldn't figure out what it was. He was the only company commander in the room, so it had to be something specifically to do with Echo Company. Only his battalion commander and S-3 were there. The brigade's other infantry battalions weren't even represented.

Colonel Jordan's early-morning call hadn't given him a clue about the mission. Gaines was beginning to think Jordan didn't know anything about it, either. The strange thing was that most of the officers standing around in the room were wearing the USARV shoulder patch. And with the exception of the brigade commander, his colonel, and the battalion S-

77

3, he didn't see anyone else wearing the big Horse Blanket patch of the First Air Cav Division.

Gaines wondered what all of the Saigon warriors were doing so far from home. He took a seat in one of the folding metal chairs. They were supposed to be back in their comfortable, air-conditioned offices in Saigon, patting secretaries on the ass and writing each other up for another pretty medal. They were not supposed to be up in grunt country, where they might scuff their nice spitshines.

At that moment, a Special Forces officer wearing a pressed tiger suit came in the door. Gaines looked up in surprise to see his old buddy, Lightning Larry Ringer from the Mike Force camp at Dong Pek.

Larry sauntered up and plopped down in the empty chair next to Gaines. "What's happening?"

"Damned if I know. What're you doing here?"

"Beats the shit outta me." Ringer looked around the room and shook his head. "CCN called up and told me to get my young ass over here ASAP."

A full colonel wearing spitshined boots, staff brass, and a USARV patch on starched jungle fatigues stood up and called the meeting to order.

"Take your seats, please," he said. "Gentlemen, you are probably wondering why you have been called together today."

The men in the room all laughed at the age-old military joke.

"USARV needs someone to go into Cambodia and do a little job for us."

The laughter stopped instantly. This was the greatest wish of any soldier in Vietnam, a chance to take the war to the enemy instead of waiting until the North Vietnamese brought it to him. Now that the colonel had everyone's undivided attention, he continued.

"This briefing is classified top secret, gentlemen, and it's on a strict need-to-know basis. At zero six hundred hours, twenty nine April, long-range recon teams will start crossing the Cambode border all along the Two Corps's AO." He pointed to a large map on the wall.

"Their mission is to check out numerous reports of enemy movement and buildup in this region." Again he pointed to the map. "But that is only part of why you men are here."

Now everyone was confused.

"Up here," the map pointer moved right, to an area where a small finger of Cambodia extended up into Laos. "There's a target that has to be taken out by that date to insure the success of this mission. Due to the fact that this target is located in an ancient Khmer temple complex, it cannot be attacked from the air. It must be taken out with ground troops."

An aide placed an enlarged aerial photograph over the map. One of the shots taken by the SR-71.

"Here you can see the temple complex. And here is the target." The pointer tapped against the top view of a large helicopter. "A Russian Mi-8 HIP gunship."

A buzz filled the room. Almost everyone had heard about the gunship attack on Charlie Company of the 7th earlier that month, even though it had been officially denied.

The colonel faced the room again. "We do not know why this machine has been based there, but we do know that we cannot take any chances with it. Over the last few months this aircraft has operated against MACSOG recon teams, and it even strafed a U.S. infantry company in South Vietnamese territory not too far from here. Therefore, this thing has to be taken out, and that's where you people come into the picture."

"Captain Gaines? Captain Ringer?" the colonel addressed the two men.

"Yes, sir," Gaines and Ringer both answered as they stood up.

"Gaines, your Aero Rifle Platoon is to accompany a Hatchet Team from Ringer's Mike Force on a raid of this airstrip. Their mission is to destroy that helicopter. All air assets required to transport the assault element will be provided by your Python Flight and will be under your command. Your ground element will be guided into their attack position by men from a Special Forces Roadrunner Team."

"Yes, sir."

"Ringer, you will provide an element from your Hatchet Team to accompany Gaines's people on this operation. You will coordinate with him for lift requirements."

"Can do, sir."

The colonel handed the two officers thick packets with a red stripe and the words Top Secret stamped across the front. "Here are your mission orders. Read them over now."

As the two company commanders read their operation orders, the colonel briefed Colonel Jordan and his S-3 on their parts in the coming operation—logistics and support functions.

The colonel turned back to the two young officers. "Do either of you gentlemen have any questions at this point?"

Neither did.

"Good. Now I will turn this over to Major Worthington, who will go over the operation in detail."

The major, also wearing a USARV patch and spitshined jump boots, stood up and faced the room. "Okay, here's what's going to happen."

When the briefing was over, Gaines hurried back to his orderly room to start preparing for the raid. He had just a little over twenty-four hours to get everybody ready, and there was a lot of work to be done. Suddenly his lack of sleep was totally forgotten.

The attack force wasn't going to be very large. Gaines was to contribute seven men from the Blues, including an officer. A sniper from the division Ranger company would also be attached to them for the operation. Larry Ringer was to provide another twelve men from his Mike Force unit. In addition, the reconstituted Recon Team Sleeper, consisting of four men including Sergeant Jack Wilburn—sole survivor of the old Sleeper Roadrunner Team—would guide the two groups into the attack position.

They had a total of twenty-four men to do the job, three slicks' worth when they reached extraction at the end of the mission.

If they all make it that far. Gaines went over the company roster trying to get an idea of whom Vance should take with him. He yelled through the open door of his office.

"Top! Can you come in here a moment?"

"Yes, sir."

"Can you send someone to round up Lieutenant Vance and Sergeant Zack ASAP?"

"Right away."

The assault group was to lift off from the small airstrip behind Ringer's camp in two flights. Because the North Vietnamese were known to have radar in use along the Cambodian border, they could not fly directly to their target. An airmobile assault on the airbase would tip off the North Vietnamese alerting them to the USARV base-camp recon mission that was to follow.

Therefore, the group would be split into two parties. One group under Vance's command would fly to the border north of Pleiku, get off the choppers, and continue on foot. Ringer and his Mike Force people would do the same, but starting some twenty klicks farther north of the Blues.

Having the two groups move into the target area on different axes was good insurance. If one group was discovered and hit on the way in, the other one could still continue the mission. If both groups got through, they were to meet at an assembly area some four klicks away from the temple of Kangor Wat. Once there, Captain Ringer would take command of the entire unit, and they would attack the base together on the third night.

It was going to be a hairy operation. Rat wished that he could go in with the ground element, but he couldn't. He was a company commander now, and it was his job to stay back and see to the aerial operations. He gave a quick thought to letting Lieutenant Alexander take the mission, but the XO didn't have any field experience. Gains had no other choice but to let Jake Vance have the honors on this one. He just hoped the Lieutenant was up to it. He had to admit that Vance had done a creditable job in Tray Ben village a month ago, but he still didn't have complete confidence in him.

There was a knock on his door. He looked up to see Vance, with Sergeant Zack at his side.

"Come on in, gentlemen, grab a seat."

Gaines spread the operations overlay out on the floor in front of them. "Okay, here's what's happening. Jake, you and part of the Blues are going to Cambodia tomorrow. And this time, it's legit."

"How many men, sir?"

"You'll be going in with one squad. But one thing first. Sergeant Zack won't be going with you. He has to stay back here to run the platoon in your absence. So, who do you want?

Vance glanced over to Sergeant Zack. "I'll take Second Squad. Brody's people."

"Good, that's who I was thinking myself. Okay here's the plan."

When Gaines's briefing was over, Jake Vance told Sergeant Zack to get Brody's people ready. He walked back to his hooch to get started on his own weapons and equipment.

Normally this was something that the young officer always enjoyed doing. Some officers had their RTOs keep track of their gear, but not Vance. No one had ever cleaned his weapon or packed his ruck. He always did it himself.

The routine was part of his mental preparation for combat and helped him get over his premission jitters. He had learned that the more apprehensive he was, the more time he took getting ready.

As he got started, Vance realized that he was unconsciously expecting a very rough time. He found himself disassembling his M-16 magazines and checking the spring tension of every one. Then he carefully wiped the dirt and sand off of every round of ammunition before reloading them.

He was also careful to count out the cartridges, loading only seventeen rounds into each one.

The so-called twenty-round magazine for the M-16 rifle was a bad piece of work. Nineteen or twenty rounds in it almost always made it jam on the second shot. Veteran grunts loaded their magazines with only seventeen rounds. Some went in the woods with eighteen, but Vance didn't want to risk it. He had never had a seventeen-round load malfunction on him yet and he didn't want to press his luck.

The army was not unaware of this magazine problem, however, and a new thirty-round magazine was currently being tested by some elite units in-country. The reports said that it worked well, but none of them had been issued to the grunts in the divisions yet.

As each magazine was reloaded, Vance tapped the back of it against the top of his footlocker to seat the rounds against the wall of the magazine. Only then did he put them into his magazine pouches and bandoliers.

Next, the lieutenant stripped his Colt .45-caliber pistol, thoroughly cleaned it, and checked all of its magazines, as well. When he was finished with that, he sharpened the blade of his survival knife.

Finally, he went over his four hand grenades, checking their pins and fuses to make sure that they were tightly screwed into the body. Then he taped the spoons down with black electrician's tape. That way, if the pin snagged on something and pulled off, the spoon wouldn't fly off. It was unhealthy to have a grenade spoon fly off before you wanted it to.

When his weapons were ready, he turned to the rest of his personal gear.

First he chose the C-ration meals he would take. Often he went short on rations in the field to avoid having to hump the extra weight, but this time he took enough to keep him going for two days over the scheduled mission time as well as coffee for several days more. He also packed several small rolls of C-ration toilet paper in a plastic bag with two pairs of extra socks. He hated to run out of ass-wipe and dry socks.

All of this went into his ruck with his poncho liner, two sticks of C-4 plastic explosive, a Prick-25 battery, and two extra bandoliers of M-16 magazines. His compass, penlight, grease pencils, C-4 stove, malaria pills, and salt tablets were already in pouches on his field belt, but he checked them over as well.

Finally he put fresh water in both of his two-quart canteens. Now he was ready.

Vance laid his gear aside and, getting out his writing pad, started a letter to his father, Lieutenant General Joseph R. Vance III. Trying to find something to tell the general about, he couldn't help but think about the coming mission again.

He knew that the CO was right in ordering Sergeant Zack to remain behind to take care of the rest of the Blues, but he was going to miss his platoon sergeant. He had come to depend on Leo Zack's extensive combat experience to keep him out of trouble in the field. There was no telling what could go wrong on a mission like this. And once across the border, they would not be able to call for someone to come running to their rescue if the shit really hit the fan.

Vance knew that if something did go badly wrong, it was going to be up to him to make the right decisions. He just hoped that the Special Forces Roadrunners that were guiding them in knew what they were doing.

CHAPTER 12

Camp Radcliff, An Khe

In the Blues' tent, Brody and his people were also getting their gear together for the raid.

Over in the corner by the door, Two-Step was putting together a new batch of tailor-made ammunition for his Remington pump gun. The army-issue 12-gauge shotgun round held only nine .36-caliber lead balls. That was fine for civilian use, but it wasn't good enough for the Indian grunt. Not in Nam.

Broken Arrow opened a dozen of the shotgun shells at a time and took out both the lead balls and the gunpowder. First he measured out a new powder load, ten percent greater than the standard, and poured it back into the empty hulls, creating his own Magnum loads.

Then he counted out twelve .25-caliber stainless-steel ball bearings for each shell. That gave them 25 percent greater killing power. Since the ball bearings were lighter than lead balls, they traveled farther and hit harder. Also, unlike the lead balls, which deformed when they hit something, the steel balls kept their shape. They plowed right on through and kept going.

Once he had killed two NVA with a single blast of the pump gun. The steel balls had torn through the first man's chest and had gone on to kill the man standing behind him. Two-Step had been real proud of that.

The Indian's relatives back home had just sent him a new twenty-five-pound keg of ball bearings, so he had plenty of makings on hand. Usually he only carried a hundred rounds in the field, but today he was making up an additional hundred—more than enough in case things got rough.

On the bunk next to him, Treat Brody was cleaning his weapons. Like his platoon leader, Lieutenant Vance, he, too, was careful to count the 5.56mm ammunition he was loading into his M-16 magazines.

When he had loaded up enough magazines to fill five bandoliers, he took out his secret weapon, the special magazine that would be in his M-16 when he unassed the chopper at the Cambodian border. It was a modified Russian AK-47 assault-rifle magazine.

The AK mag had been extensively reworked so that it would fit into the M-16 rifle. First, its throat was ground down so that it fit into the narrower magazine well of the sixteen. Then the original AK magazine catch had been ground off and a square hole cut into the sight side so it would clip into the magazine catch of the American rifle.

This modification worked because the 7.62mm AK-47 and the 5.56mm M-16 cartridges were almost the same length, the AK being just a little longer and much fatter. When filled with AK rounds, the Russian magazine held thirty rounds, but a man was able to load thirty-eight of the skinnier M-16 rounds into it. That was over twice the capacity of U.S. army-issue magazines.

It took a lot of work to modify the AK magazine, well over an hour in a machine shop, but it worked, and it worked well. It gave Brody a little added firepower on initial contact when he needed it most. And on this mission, he wanted to carry as much firepower as he could.

The veteran grunt didn't like the feeling of the latest mission at all, and he wasn't quite sure what was making him

Gardner turned away and slowly walked back to his bunk. It had been two weeks now since he had gotten a letter from his wife, Sandra. When he first arrived in-country, she had written him several times a week. Then she had cut back to once a week, and now she rarely ever wrote at all. He tried to tell himself that there had to be a reason for it, something harmless, but he knew better. He could read between the lines as well as the next man. Something was seriously wrong back home in Gray's Harbor, Washington, and he was afraid that he knew exactly what it was.

He sat down on his bunk and continued cleaning his rifle. Jim Gardner and Sandra Dunning has been high-school sweethearts, married right after they graduated. At the time, it seemed like the right thing to do, but now he wasn't so sure. At first things had gone well, but then the sawmill in the small logging and fishing community shut down right after their baby boy was born.

Not only had the army seemed like a real good idea at the time, but even with the war going on it was his only real option. For one thing, when his two-year hitch was over, he would have the GI bill to go to school with. He figured that he could get a degree and find a decent job. Right now, though, he wasn't too sure how good an idea it was after all. For the first time, he really envied the single guys in the company.

Being in the army was no place for a married man. He fully understood what his old drill sergeant meant, that if the army wanted him to have a wife, he would have been issued one. It was hard enough trying to stay alive without having to worry about a wife and a kid at home.

His first few weeks in Nam, things had gone okay back home. Before too long, however, he could tell that Sandra was having a hard time trying to work and take care of their son at the same time. He knew that if he was back there, he could help her over the rough spots and everything would be okay. But he wasn't going to be home for another nine months. He was beginning to wonder what he would find waiting for him when he finally did get home.

From her letters, he could also tell that Sandra was lonely, and it was beginning to look like she had found a local solution to the problem. That was something that he didn't even want to think about. He decided to write her another letter, hoping against hope that there was something he could do to straighten things out.

"Hey, guys!" Brody called out. "I got a letter from the Snakeman!"

"Read it!" someone called back.

" 'Hey, dudes,' " Brody began reading. " 'Fort Hood, Texas sucks dirty donkey dicks. There are more no-time-in-Nam lifers, profiles, skates, and REMFs here than you can shake a dick at.' "

That got a howl from all the men.

" 'All of us Nam returnees get all the shit details on post. I've been cutting grass and painting rocks nonstop ever since I got here. They even have us taking PT tests. Man, I ain't done no push-ups since Basic, but I'm sure as hell doing them now. All the lifer NCOs here have some kind of medical profile that keeps them from going to Nam and they love to get on our case. I even had one asshole tell me to take the ribbons off my khakis until he could check my two-oh-one file to make sure that I'd been awarded the medals.' "

"That sucks!" Corky cut in.

"FTA," someone else commented. Fuck the army.

" 'Anyway,' " Brody continued reading, " 'I'm on CQ again for the second weekend in a row, but I'm short. I've got less than three months to go and I can do that standing on my head. You take care now and tell all the guys that I said hello. Your old buddy, the Snakeman.' "

"It don't sound like our man Snake is having a good time there at all," Two-Step said.

"No, it doesn't," Brody agreed. "I sure hope that he keeps his fucking mouth shut. It sounds like he could get his young ass thrown in the stockade real fast around that place."

"I wonder why the Snake didn't say anything about his leave at home?" Corky asked.

"I don't know, Corky." Brody folded the letter and put it

in his footlocker. "Maybe that didn't work out too well, either."

Brody knew all about his going back to the Land of the Big PX and finding that, in his absence, it had turned into something that he didn't recognize at all. He had gone back once to escort a friend's body home, and it had not been a good experience. Even stopping off in L.A. to see his family had been a total disaster.

It had seemed to him that everything in the United States had changed, but he knew that the world hadn't changed at all. He was the one who had done all the changing. The only place on earth that he truly felt comfortable now was in the Nam.

On his trip back he had left three days early to return to the war. He didn't even want to think about what he was going to do if and when the war ended. As much as he hated to admit it, now that he had made his sergeant stripes back, he was turning into a real lifer. As the troops always said, NCO meant, "no chance outside."

He put Fletcher's letter out of his mind and went back to getting his gear ready for the mission. That was something that he understood completely. He knew that if he took care of his war gear, it would take care of him when he needed it.

A stocky, black master sergeant with a shaved head walked in the end of the tent and looked around.

"Hi, Sarge," Farmer spoke up.

"You boys got everything you need for tomorrow?"

Leo Zack was obviously concerned. The platoon sergeant wished that he was going out with them. He knew that the company commander was right in having him stay back to run the rest of the platoon, but he couldn't help but be a little apprehensive about the mission. Lieutenant Vance wasn't the best field officer that the veteran NCO had ever seen. In fact, Zack felt Vance would have trouble finding his ass with both hands and a radar set if someone wasn't right there to tell him exactly where it was located.

"Yeah, Leo, we're pretty well squared away," Brody replied as he stood up.

"Treat," Zack nodded his head toward the door. "Come outside with me a minute."

"Sure, Sarge."

"Look, Brody," the black sergeant said once they got out of earshot of the men in the tent. "I want you people to take it real careful out there tomorrow, okay. Once you get to the assembly area, Captain Ringer will take command of the operation. But until then, don't let the lieutenant get you guys in trouble."

Brody laughed. "Yeah, I know what you're saying. Without the old Black Buddha to hold his hand, the ell tee is going to be completely lost."

Zack agreed, but he didn't say so openly. "At least he'll have those two Special Forces sergeants to ground-guide him, and maybe they can keep him from stepping on his pecker."

"If he has one to step on."

"Anyway, Treat, don't take no chances over there, none at all. It just ain't worth it, man. Not in a situation like that where you don't have no backup or support."

Brody was touched by his sergeant's obviously genuine concern. He had come a long way from the days when Zack was always ragging his ass about something.

"Don't worry, Leo, I'll try hard not to."

CHAPTER 13

Camp Radcliff, An Khe

The next afternoon, right before dusk, Vance and the Blues stood at the edge of the alert pad waiting for Gaines's slicks to return. Rat had already flown Ringer's Mike Force element to their L2 earlier that afternoon and he was on his way back to pick them up now. Ringer had a longer distance to travel so he had been inserted first. Also, it added to the deception plan for the two assault groups to be inserted in separate flights as well as at separate locations.

As he looked around at the men, Vance felt a little more confident than he had before. This was not going to be an easy mission, but he couldn't think of a better bunch of grunts to do it with. He wished Captain Gaines had let him bring Leo Zack along, but he knew Brody and his people were the best grunts in the platoon.

Vance's own men had been joined by the sniper from the Hotel Company of the 75th Rangers and two Green Berets from RT Sleeper who would act as their pathfinders on the way to the target.

The Ranger sniper had that cold-eyed, casual look that said he could handle himself under any circumstances, and the Special Forces men had previously operated in the part of Cambodia they were going to. One of them was Jack Wilburn, the sole survivor of the old RT Sleeper that had been shot up by the very same Russian gunship that they were going after. Though his leg wound had not yet fully healed, Wilburn had a personal account to settle with that chopper, and he had insisted on being included on the mission.

As the grunts waited for their lift ships, Vance checked out each man. The inspection wasn't because he didn't trust them to be ready. They were all veteran boonie rats and knew better than to go into the woods half-prepared. He just wanted something to do to keep his own mind occupied while he waited.

The men from the Blues, with the exception of Broken Arrow, wore their jungle fatigues with brush hats, and their faces and hands camouflaged with green and black grease paint. Two-Step wore his usual tiger suit and had a camouflage neck scarf tied around his head. Vance had long since stopped trying to get the Indian grunt to wear a standard uniform. Or to get a regulation haircut, for that matter.

Everyone's ruck was loaded down with a double basic load of ammunition and grenades as well as extra water and rations. They would be humping almost eighty pounds a man, not counting their individual weapons, but they couldn't go with any less. If they were spotted before they reached their objective, they would need every last round they were carrying.

Gardner and Rabdo were further burdened down with the two Prick-77 radios and batteries. They had borrowed a pair of Prick-77s because they had a secure voice capability, and on this mission they could not risk any interception of their transmissions. The extra radio was backup in case the first one went down. It was a burden, but it was also their sole link with the outside world and Ringer's Mike Force.

Cordova had the only M-60 machine gun, but both Gardner and Two-Step were carrying thumpers, M-79 grenade launchers. Gardner packed an M-16 slung over his back as well and the Indian had his sawed-off shotgun, the perfect point-man weapon. Everybody was carrying extra bandoliers of 40mm grenades for the thumpers, as well as extra link belts of M-60 machine-gun ammunition and one claymore mine apiece.

The Ranger sniper wore the oak-leaf-pattern camouflage uniform and carried his 7.62mm XM-21 sniper rifles with both day and night scopes strapped onto the sides of his ruck. He carried an Army-issue .45-caliber pistol on his belt and a Bowie knife upside down on his assault harness.

The Green Berets in their tiger suits had NVA-style rucksacks on their backs. Sergeant Wilburn carried one of the new, experimental XM-203 M-16 rifle-and-grenade-launcher combination weapons while the other man had a CAR-15. Both of them were also armed with Browning Hi-Power 9mm pistols in shoulder holsters.

Fighting knives and machetes were hanging on most of the men as well, completing the picture of walking arsenals. In the distance, the lieutenant heard the sound of rotors. The slicks were coming back.

"That's it, men! Saddle up!" he shouted.

Tails high in the air like hovering dragonflies, the two slicks touched down on the alert pad. Hunched over to clear the spinning rotor blades, the raiders sprinted through dust kicked up by the rotor blast and scrambled on board. Overhead, Rat Gaines's Cobra and the two other gunships of his Light Gun Team circled protectively.

Vance climbed on board the lead slick, Cliff Gabriel's ship, *Pegasus*. One of the door gunners handed him a flight helmet, and he quickly plugged it into the intercom before he took his seat in the open door.

"We're go," he called up to the pilot.

"Roger that, Jake," Gabe called back. "Hang on!"

The pilot pulled pitch, the tail came up, and they were away. The mission was on.

Vance and his men sat in the open doors of the chopper with their boots hanging down over the side. As the cool evening air buffeted his face and the wop-wopping of the rotor blades rang in his ears, Vance felt his pulse pound faster and faster with the adrenaline that raced through his body. There was a feeling about riding in the open door of a slick, locked and loaded for war, that was beyond description. The young officer couldn't put this heart-pounding, gut-twisting feeling into words. And after all this time in Nam, he still didn't know if it scared him more than it excited him.

From the air, the countryside below looked peaceful and calm, but there he was, flying through the sky with a chopperload of men, armed to the teeth just looking for someone to kill. Vance was very conscious of the weight of the loaded ruck on his back and the trigger of his sixteen lying under the fire finger of his right hand. It was a powerful feeling.

He looked around at the men sitting in the door beside him. They, too, were feeling the excitement. He saw it in their eyes, and their faces wore the same tight grin that was on his own face, the smile that hid the hammering of their hearts.

He caught Brody's eye and gave him a thumbs-up. Brody laughed and made the arm-pumping signal to go faster. Vance grinned.

It was a short flight to their landing zone half a mile from the Cambodian border. Rat charged ahead of the two slicks and swooped over the clearing to check it out while the other two gunships and the slicks stood off to one side.

"Python, this is Lead. The Lima Zulu is green. Execute. Out."

While Rat's Cobra did figure-eights overhead, its chin turret trained toward Cambodia, the two slicks dropped down and flared out a foot off the ground.

Vance pulled the flight helmet off and jammed his brush hat down over his ears. "Go, go, go!" he shouted as he jumped down to the ground.

The twelve men unassed the birds in less than ten seconds, running crouched over to clear the rotor blades. They went to ground in the tall grass for a moment as the slick drivers pulled pitch and rose back into the darkening sky. Vance saw Gabe raise his hand in salute as he flew off.

Now came the second part of the deception plan. The slicks would fly on along the border and make several more dummy insertions before they returned to An Khe—dropping down and landing for a few seconds, pretending to off-load people. That would confuse North Vietnamese radar operators who might be watching them. The enemy wouldn't know where they had actually dropped troops or if they had landed any at all.

As soon as the sound of the rotors faded in the distance, the men got to their feet. Sprinting for the cover of the tree line a hundred meters away, they slipped back into the sheltering darkness.

Vance and his twelve men were on their own.

Once in the tree line, they quickly formed into a patrol formation with the two RT Sleeper men taking point and slack. The sniper took the drag position. He would check out their backtrail with his Starlite scope to insure that they weren't being followed. After a final glance at the maps, they moved out.

Vance made no radio calls back to An Khe. It was vital that they preserve strict radio listening silence. Captain Gaines would report their departure when he returned to Camp Radcliff. Except for unseen emergencies, the raiders were to maintain complete radio silence until they hit their objective.

Moving at night was always difficult, even in the best of circumstances. And moving in unfamiliar territory anywhere in Southeast Asia is never the best of circumstances. Nonetheless, the men covered ground quickly. The two Green Berets were well practiced at night navigation, and before they stopped for their first break they had made some six klicks into Cambodian territory.

During the break, Vance went forward to talk to the point man. Wilburn was huddled under his poncho liner, reading his map with a red filtered penlight.

"How're we doing?" Vance whispered, crouching at his side.

"So far, so good, sir," the young Green Beret answered. "This was the easy part, though. There's not much between here and the fence.'' He referred to the Vietnamese border behind them.

"From here on, however, it's going to get a little rougher. Also, a month ago, we ran into a small camp not too far from here and we're going to have to bypass them carefully."

"I'll tell my people," Vance replied. "We'll be ready to move out again in one-five mikes."

"Roger that, sir. There's no point in getting everyone worn out too soon. Wake me then."

When they moved out again, Wilburn set a killing pace. He wanted to get past the NVA camp before first light. Though toughened by months in the field, Vance and his men tired quickly on the night march. It took a great deal of energy out of a man to go a distance in the dark, and it was very dark in their part of the world that night. There was no moon and no reflected city or base-camp lights to even partially lift the veil of darkness.

"It's blacker than the inside of a cat's ass!" Vance heard someone mutter softly and he had to agree. Though his eyes had long since adjusted to the darkness, straining to see what was around him was giving him a headache. Trying to move silently, but constantly stumbling on unseen obstacles was tiring.

Worst of all though, was trying to identify the night noises all around him. He was straining to filter out the normal sounds of the jungle so he would be alert for sounds that might mean danger. At least the monkeys were asleep, and that was helpful. More than once, jumpy grunts had fired at monkeys crashing through the trees.

Though it was tough going, they continued on throughout the night, taking only short breaks every hour.

At first light, Vance halted the raiding party, put out their security, and told his people that they could have breakfast. The sun wasn't up yet, and the morning mist hovering above the ground gave the jungle a mystical, eerie quality, muting the vivid daytime colors to shades of greenish gray.

Most of the men found places in the thick undergrowth and wrapped their camouflage poncho liners around them to ward off the chill morning air as they ate. It was a cold breakfast. They could not afford to light even a small C-4 fire to heat coffee. The smell of coffee or heated rations would carry through the chill air for a mile or so.

Most just opened a C Ration can of fruit or a B-2 unit, and washed it down with water. Farmer, however, had managed to score some of the prized Lurp rations and went about fixing one for his breakfast.

Lurps were freeze-dried, long-range-recon rations and were packed in plastic bags. To rehydrate one of them, you tore open a corner of the bag, poured in a little water, resealed the bad, and put it under your shirt. A man's body heat would soften the food and bring it to body temperature in just fifteen minutes or so.

While Farmer waited for his rice and pork Lurp to warm up, he tore into a can of peaches. He had worked up a real appetite on their night march.

Vance finished off his can of pound cake and a Lurp nut bar, and made a canteen cup of cold coffee. He had to have his morning coffee—hot or cold. He took his cup to the point position to talk to the Roadrunners.

"How are we doing, Sarge?" he asked Wilburn. He sat down beside him on the damp ground and tucked his poncho liner tighter around his body.

"Not too bad at all, sir. I figure that we're here." He pointed to a location on the map. "It looks like we made about twelve klicks last night. You know, sir, for legs, your guys are pretty good at this."

"We try," Vance answered, proud to hear praise from the Green Beret. "God knows we try."

The Special Forces sergeant laughed softly. "As soon as the mist burns off, we should get going again. I figure that it's going to be about ten hours to our night position."

Vance checked the map. "That gives us only eight klicks to our marry-up point with Ringer's Mike Force people."

"Yeah, I figure that we'll want to move a little slower on that last leg and keep an even better eye out. We'll be in Khmer Rouge territory and we'll have to be very careful."

"Sounds good to me. You want me to rotate point, Sarge, give you and your buddy a little rest?"

"A little later maybe," the Roadrunner said. "We've got it for now, sir. But you can send your shooter up behind the slackman in case we need him."

CHAPTER 14

Kangor Wat, Cambodia

Lieutenant Colonel Nguyen Cao Duc woke to the chatter of monkeys outside his quarters in the temple complex of Kangor Wat. Crumpled on the floor beside his bed lay the bloody, naked body of a young Cambodian village girl. She had been strangled, and her face was battered beyond recognition. Her small breasts, thighs, and vagina were covered with blood, abused and torn as if she had been mauled by a wild animal.

"Orderly!" Duc called out sharply. "Orderly!"

The orderly, a teenaged private of the Khmer Rouge, quickly answered the colonel's call, a timid knocking on the door.

"Enter!"

The young soldier went in the room, trembling in the presence of the officer. Back in the soldier's barracks, the men made fun of the renegade North Vietnamese colonel. They called him "Mad Dog Duc", a take off on his middle name, Cao, which also meant dog. They were very careful, however, that they used his nickname only when there was no chance that they might be overheard. The Vietnamese officer's murderous rages were well known.

Once Duc had torn open the scrotum of a man who had displeased him, and then tied him to stakes over an anthill with the wound next to the opening of the nest. It was said that the man's screams were heard all the way to the village. It was also said the Duc sat calmly in a chair next to the anthill and read *Thoughts of Chairman Mao* until the man finally died.

The young Cambodian soldier shuddered.

"Take this carrion away," Duc said, pointing to the girl's battered body. "Feed it to the pigs."

The soldier moved quickly to obey.

Filthy peasants, Duc thought, watching his orderly drag the body out by the arms. They fornicated like animals. The lying little bitch had told him that she was a virgin. She should have been since she was certainly young enough. The colonel's rage built when he remembered the slight smile when the girl had seen his erect penis the night before. A smile that meant that even although she was only thirteen, she had known a man before. His rage subsided, however, when he remembered her punishment.

He had not had to beat her too long before she admitted that she had already lain with a man. Pleading for her life, the girl offered her anus to him, saying that she was a virgin there. He finally took her that way. Even though she had been telling the truth, it had not been enough to wipe out the insult of her smile. After savagely taking her, he had beaten her to death and mutilated her body.

The next time the villagers would bring him a virgin or he would execute each and every one of them.

Duc washed in his room, dressed in a clean flying suit, and walked over to his command post deep inside the ancient temple to read the morning's reports from the Khmer Rouge Headquarters. Word had been sent down that the Yankees were mounting some kind of recon operation against the border sanctuaries. Communist agents in South Vietnam had reported that several recon units had been alerted for cross-border missions.

So far, the Khmer Rouge agents had not been able to determine where the units were being sent. But in his heart,

Duc knew that it was the secret NVA bases in Cambodia and Laos. He could think of no other target for such forces, particularly with the buildup that was taking place to prepare for the big attack next spring.

He bent over his maps and studied the reported locations of the Yankee recon teams.

Though Duc had deserted his nation's air force, he still felt very protective of his own people. He had not abandoned the land of his birth nor had he abandoned the struggle. He had only deserted their cowardly leaders. When those men were deposed and replaced with men who shared his revolutionary zeal, he would return and proudly wear his nation's uniform again. But until then, he wanted to fight the imperialists where he was, with the Khmer Rouge.

It was ironic that it was the Cambodians. For centuries the traditional enemies of the Vietnamese people, they now showed the true spirit of the revolution, and led the fight against the Yankee imperialists. Ho Chi Minh had started the struggle in Southeast Asia, but he was old, and the men who spoke for him lacked courage. Only the Cambodian Pol Pot continued in the true tradition of the People's Struggle.

Nonetheless, when the Yankees crossed the borders, he would take to the air to protect his countrymen from them. He would show the North Vietnamese leadership what they had refused to believe before, that even a lone aircraft used properly in a tactical-support role would make a great difference in the outcome of a battle. The blasted bodies and burned-out helicopters of Yankee recon teams would prove that he had been right all along.

Duc turned to his operations officer. "Send the supply sergeant in to see me. And tell him to bring the latest ammunition supply report with him."

"Right away, Comrade Colonel."

Duc went back to studying his maps. A few minutes later, the supply sergeant appeared. "You wanted to see me, Comrade Colonel." He stood at a rigid position of attention.

"Yes. Where are the ammunition reports?"

"Right here, Comrade."

Duc quickly went over the papers. "You only show sixty rounds of rocket ammunition on hand?"

"Yes, sir, that is all we have. Our people in Phnom Penh have had a difficult time obtaining more."

Duc glared at the man. "They will have to do better. I must have rockets if I am to kill more Yankees. Send a message immediately. They are to get the rockets to me at any cost."

"Yes, sir." The supply sergeant saluted and did a smart about-face.

The major problem that Duc faced with his remote operation in the jungle was obtaining ammunition and fuel supplies for his machine. And fuel was far easier to obtain than ammunition. Some of his JP-4 jet fuel came directly from American air-force stocks, one barrel at a time. Most of it was supplied by European petroleum companies that did business in Vietnam and Cambodia. In return the Viet Cong did not attack their storage facilities. They considered it another form of taxation.

The ammunition for his gunship was another matter, however. All of it had to be stolen from Prince Sihanouk's Royal Cambodian Air Force. The 23mm cannon and 57mm air-to-ground rockets that armed the gunship were also standard armament of the Russian MiG-17 fighters of the Cambodian air force. Khmer Rouge agents simply stole what they needed from Sihanouk's ammo dumps, but there were very few MiG fighters in the Cambodian inventory. The stocks of ammunition on hand for them were not large. Pol Pot was trying to secure an ammunition supply pipeline from Red China for his use. So far, it had not been established, and Duc was having to manage on what Pot's agents could steal.

If the American recon operation went the way he thought it would, Duc was going to need all the ammunition he could get his hands on. He bent over his map and continued studying the reported enemy locations.

All that morning, Vance and his nine men continued on the march to their planned lager site for the second night. They

104

were moving much faster now than they had during the previous night and were making good time.

So far, they were the only humans in their part of the world. They had not encountered anyone, either military or civilian, and the only signs of human habitation were small, isolated villages in the distance, and the occasional Cambodian farmer working in his rice fields.

The apparent peacefulness of the countryside, however, only made the lieutenant more anxious. He preferred a little more activity in his AO. Then at least he knew where everyone was. This was a little too spooky for him.

They halted in the early afternoon, during the heat of the day to rest and eat. This time, Vance let the men light small C-4 fires to warm their food. The smell would not carry far in the hot air of the daylight hours.

The platoon leader ate his own food cold, if one could call something that was blood temperature cold. He did make himself a big cup of hot coffee.

Brody was deep in thought as he held a C-ration can of beanie wienies over a small lump of burning plastic explosive. He had had another one of his nightmares again that morning when he dozed off, and this dream had been clearer, more vivid than the others.

He had dreamed that he was being chased by something in the sky. A huge, dark, formless thing with a giant, fanged mouth. He had been naked and unarmed, running across an open field trying to escape the thing chasing after him. He could see cover in the distance, but each time he ran to hide in the brush, it disappeared.

He had been having this same dream time and time again recently. Each time it wrenched him from his sleep in a cold sweat. The frustrating thing was that he didn't know what was chasing him. He couldn't identify it. Every time he turned to look at it, it vanished. All he knew was that it was trying to kill him, and there was nothing he could do to stop it.

He had had bad dreams when he first came to Nam about the jungle trying to devour him. But he had shaken them off once he realized that the jungle was his ally rather than his enemy. He had had the first bad dreams because, as a guy from the concrete jungles of Los Angeles, he had never been in the woods before, and they were alien to him.

He could understand that then, but now he didn't have the slightest idea what was causing the new nightmares. He shook himself, pulled the hot can off the fire and ate his meal.

Broken Arrow was burying his empty C-ration cans when the Ranger sniper walked up and knelt down beside him. "You're a Redskin, aren't you?"

"Yeah, Chance Broken Arrow," Two-Step replied, sticking out his hand.

"John Metcack," the sniper answered. "Siletz from Oregon."

"I'm from the Comanche people in Montana," Two-Step said proudly. "I didn't know there were any Indians out in Oregon."

Metcack laughed. "A lot of people don't, brother, but we've got three reservations, and there's over a dozen tribes scattered all over the place."

"Well, I'll be damned."

"Yeah, I saw you at the chopper pad and I knew that you had to be a brother. So I thought I'd come over and introduce myself. By the way, the white men all call me Chief."

Broken Arrow grinned. "Yeah, my buddies call me Two-Step, but that's got nothing to do with being an Indian. I got hit by a Krait and lived through it."

"Shit! I've never heard of anyone living through that."

"Yeah," Two-Step laughed. "You know what they say, there's thirty-three different kinds of snakes in Nam and thirty-one of them are poisonous."

"How'd you ever get into the Rangers?" Two-Step asked, changing the subject.

"Well, back in Basic, the drill sergeants learned that I knew how to move through the woods without tripping over my fucking feet, so they talked to me about going to Ranger school."

Chief looked around the dense, tangled jungle surrounding

them. "We sure as hell didn't have woods like this at home, but I'd sure rather be out here than down in some fucking line company. A guy can get killed crashing around out there with those clowns."

"Yeah, that's why I'm in the Blues, I didn't want to have to run around in the woods for weeks at a time in an infantry platoon. I'd rather fly." Two-Step looked at the XM-21 cradled in Chief's arms. "When did you become a sniper?"

"When I got in-country they checked my records and found that I had scored a hundred percent on the rifle range. They asked me if I wanted to get into the sniper unit they were forming. I figured it would give me a chance to work by myself so I went for it."

The sniper patted the stock of his weapon. "This is sure as hell a better piece than the one I used to kill deer back home. I'm trying to figure out a way to take one of these things with me when I rotate."

"We could sure use some snipers with us in the Blues," Two-Step commented. "That long range would come in real handy sometimes."

"How do you like that airmobile stuff?" the sniper asked. "Doesn't the pucker factor get a little high when you hit some of those hot LZs?"

"Na, it's not really that bad. Also we've got some of the best chopper pilots in the Air Cav flying for us."

"I guess that makes a difference."

"It sure as hell does."

From the head of their column, Vance called out.

"Saddle up!"

"Well, it was nice talking with you, brother," Chief said, getting to his feet. "I've got to get back up to the point. I'll catch you later."

"Sure thing."

Five minutes later, the raiding party was on the move again.

CHAPTER 15

In Cambodia

To the north of Lieutenant Vance's group, Captain Lightning Larry Ringer and his Mike Force unit were moving through the jungle as fast as they could, desperately trying to make up for lost time. For once, Ringer was not living up to his reputation. They were badly behind schedule.

Earlier that morning, Ringer had stumbled onto a North Vietnamese infantry company that had spent the night camped along their path. They barely escaped detection when they walked right up on the enemy camp in the thick of the morning-mist. By the time the Mike Force point man had spotted them, he had almost stepped in one of their campfires.

They were so close to them that Ringer had been afraid to pull back and bypass their camp. With limited visibility, he couldn't see how far they were strung out along the trail or where their positions were. There was just too great a chance of stumbling into them again or of being heard as they tried to break contact. If they were spotted and it came to a fight, Ringer's small force was hopelessly outnumbered. The only thing they could do was go to ground right where they were and try to wait them out.

For most of the morning, the Mike Force troops had laid in the wet foliage and watched the North Vietnamese leisurely cook their breakfasts, collect their gear, and slowly amble off to the north.

The NVA had given Ringer's people an unexpected rest. If staying perfectly still for several hours in the morning chill could be called rest. It had also cost them valuable time that had to be made up if they were going to get to the assembly area on time. Lightning Larry was pushing his people as fast as they could go.

The Mike Force was moving along a tree line at a dog trot. Ringer was close to the point element. The woods made a slight jog to their right front some two hundred and fifty meters ahead.

It was a nice place for an ambush. He decided to check it out. He didn't need another fuck-up at all. He motioned for one of his Cambodes to go forward and look it over when the tree line exploded with automatic-weapons fire.

The first burst of AK fire took out both the Cambode point man and the slack, both hit with full bursts from about seventy-five meters away. There was no doubt that they were dead.

"*Didi*," Ringer yelled. He dove for cover in the trees. The rest of his Strikers sprinted after him, firing as they ran. Enemy fire shredded the vegetation around their fleeing figures. Even when they got deeper into the jungle, they continued running as hard as they could, crashing through the brush trying to break contact. It was every man for himself until then.

Minutes later, Ringer found a concealed spot and halted. The panting Strikers quickly pulled into a defensive perimeter around him and tried to catch their breath.

Ringer turned to the Mike Force interpreter at his side. "Lon," he gasped, "See how many made it."

"Yes, *Dai Uy*."

As the Cambodian NCO went to check his men, Ringer whipped out his map and compass to plot a way out.

Sergeant Lon quickly came back.

"It's number ten, *Dai Uy*. Three men dead and two more hurt. One man can walk okay. The other is hurt bad, hit in back. The *Bac si* say he hit in lung, but we no leave him. We take him with us, no?"

"Yeah, we'll take him with us, Lon," Ringer said. "Tell *Trung si* Tom to come up here."

"Yes, *Dai Uy*."

"Shit!" Ringer muttered softly to himself. "What a fucking mess."

Sergeant Thompson flopped down in the brush beside him. "You get the casualty report?" he gasped, wiping the sweat from his eyes.

"Yeah, I got it."

"Other than that, though, *Dai Uy,* we're okay. We didn't lose any equipment."

Though he had lost some men, Ringer knew that it could have been one hell of a lot worse. Had the slopes waited just a few more minutes to pop their ambush they would have gotten even more of them.

Lightning Larry's luck was still holding strong.

Now all he had to do was evade the enemy following him and get to the attack position on time. He went back to his map and compass.

Ringer heard faint voices, as the enemy followed the trail broken through the brush. One command rang out loud and clear. The language was Vietnamese. Now they were really in Shit City.

Had they been hit by a roving Khmer Rouge force, they probably could have evaded them with no problem. It was not going to be so easy getting away from a North Vietnamese regular infantry unit on their home turf. They were in a real bind now.

For starters, the enemy had probably checked the bodies of the dead and discovered that they were Mike Force strikers. The North Vietnamese had a special hatred for the Special Forces Mike Force, so they wouldn't just let them go. They would be hot after them. That changed everything.

Ringer turned to his team sergeant.

110

"Tom, we're going to have to break this off and run for home. Those guys aren't just going to let us go, and they've got radios. Even if we cross into the Khmer AO, they'll just call ahead and let them know we're coming. We can't take the chance of their following us to Vance's people or alerting the Khmers that we're operating in their territory. I'm afraid that young Lieutenant Vance is going to have to pull the job off on his own. I don't think we can help him now."

"You're probably right," the NCO answered.

Ringer stood up. "Well, let's get this show on the road. I'll take point, you take drag. We'll head south and east, back for the fence. Tell Lon to put the wounded striker in the middle, but they've got to keep up with us. I'll try to get through to Vance and then see about getting us an extraction."

"Hook Talon Bravo, Hook Talon Bravo. This is Hook Talon Alpha. Over."

Vance looked up to see Bunny Rabdo, his RTO, running over to him. "Lieutenant, it's Talon Alpha on the horn!" he shouted.

Vance suddenly felt sick to his stomach. This was what he had feared. Something had gone wrong. Vance took the Prick-77 handset from the radio operator.

"Hook Talon Alpha, this is Talon Bravo, go ahead."

"This is Alpha," Ringer's voice came over the radio. "Switch to secure, over."

Vance turned the knob on the face of the radio. In the secure mode, they could talk openly and not be overheard. Ringer didn't want to take any chances with coded messages that might be misunderstood. "This is Talon Bravo on secure. Go ahead."

"This is Alpha. Look, I've got a real problem here. We've been hit by at least a company of November Victor Alpha. I have three Kilo India Alpha and two Whiskey. I am trying to break contact, but I can't shake 'em."

There was a pause in the transmission.

111

"I don't think I'm going to be able to complete the mission, Bravo. I'm going to have to call for an extract and get what's left of us out of here ASAP. Sorry 'bout that, over."

"This is Talon Bravo. Roger, I copy. Good luck, Lightning. Bravo, out."

Now the shit was really in the fan. Vance badly needed Zack's years of combat experience. But Zack was back at An Khe and the lieutenant was going to have to get out of this one on his own.

Vance called a halt and sent for Wilburn. He remembered a favorite saying of his company commander, Rat Gaines.

"Somedays you get the bear, somedays the bear gets you, and somedays it just doesn't pay to go out in the woods."

Vance didn't have to be a southerner to know that this was going to be one of those days.

His call to Vance completed, Larry Ringer went back to his immediate concern, trying to get out of his situation as fast as he could. But the pursuing North Vietnamese were not making it easy.

They were doing okay, so far, but the NVA trackers were hot on their trail. This was going to turn into a footrace all the way to the border unless he could get some help real fast.

Carrying the stretcher with the wounded Striker, there was no way that they could possibly outrun the pursuing North Vietnamese for very long. All the slopes had to do was to rotate fresh men out to their point position and they would run his people into the ground. It was an old Apache Indian trick, and it worked as well in the jungles of Southeast Asia as it did in the deserts of Arizona.

Right now, the Cambodian Strikers were passing the stretcher with the wounded man around, taking turns carrying him. But that was going to get real old before very long. Also, once the Vietnamese figured out the general direction they were headed, they could call other NVA units into blocking positions along their route to cut them off.

Were it a little later in the day, he might be able to simply keep going till nightfall and evade his pursuers in the dark. But there were too many daylight hours left. They would never be able to keep up their killing pace that long.

As much as he hated to do it, Ringer knew that he had no choice but to find a PZ somewhere along his route and call for an emergency extract. He took a sweat-stained map out from under his tiger-suit shirt as he ran.

Vance was sitting cross-legged on the ground with his map out and one of his rare cigarettes in his mouth when Wilburn walked up.

"Pull up a chair," the lieutenant told the Special Forces sergeant. "I'm afraid that we've got a real problem here. I just got a call from Captain Ringer. He ran into some NVA regulars and can't get away from them. He says that he doesn't think he'll be able to join us for the attack."

Wilburn squatted down on his heels beside the officer, his over and under, thumper sixteen cradled in his arms. "I hope to hell you're shitting me, *Trung uy*."

"I wish I was, Sergeant." Vance looked scared. "He ran into a company-sized unit and took several casualties. He is trying to evade, but he says that they're hot on his trail and he's going to have to extract. So if we decide to continue this mission, we're going to be all on our own."

Wilburn looked into the distance and rubbed his hand across the back of his neck. He wondered why things always turned to shit in Cambodia.

"I don't know if we can pull this off by ourselves, Lieutenant," he said quietly. "Captain Ringer's people had all the RPGs."

"Oh, fuck!"

Vance leaned his head back against the tree trunk and closed his eyes for a moment. All he needed was more bad news.

The American army hadn't had a decent rocket launcher in its entire arsenal since they dumped the old Korean War-vintage 3.5-inch bazooka. The 66mm LAW, light antitank

113

weapon, that was supposed to have replaced it, had turned out to be a real piece of shit. It couldn't be trusted to function properly under combat conditions, and no one liked to use it.

Therefore, Special Forces units in Vietnam often captured Russian-designed RPGs when they needed to have a dependable rocket launcher with a decent range. The RPG was heavy and a bit awkward to carry, but it always fired. It also had a bigger warhead than the LAW.

In fact, the RPG was so good that General Westmoreland had tried to get the army to put it into production in the United States. As usual the congressman, in whose state the LAW was produced, screamed his head off about American soldiers using foreign weapons. The plan was dropped. It didn't matter that the RPG was the best shoulder-fired rocket launcher in the world, bar none. It was un-American. Their assault plan had called for the RPGs to take the gunship out from five hundred meters away.

"I hadn't even thought of that," Vance said. "The only long-range weapons we have now are the two seventy-nines, and they don't fire as far as an RPG. That means we'll have to get a lot closer to that helicopter than we had planned on."

Vance looked up from his map. "I need your advice, Sergeant. The way I see it, we still have an obligation to try to get in there and take that chopper out. Can you see anyway that we can possibly do that without committing suicide?"

Wilburn sighed and studied the map for a moment. He had always wanted to be a general, and this was his big chance.

"What do you think about this, sir? Why don't we just keep going and move on to the edge of this mountain tonight." He pointed to a volcanic peak some twelve klicks north of the temple at Kangor Wat.

"We'll lay up there tomorrow, get caught up on our sleep and hit them the next night. We can get under way right at dark, attack at midnight or so, and get back to the mountain by dawn. Not only is that mountain a good staging area, it's also a good pickup point."

This was the part he hated, but it had to be said. "I've

got a nasty feeling that we're not going to be walking out of this one, sir. If we make it back, they're going to have to come in and get us out.''

Vance looked at the map, glad that Wilburn had come up with a plan that sounded like it would work. ''That sounds fine to me, Sergeant, but we're still going to have to get real close to the gunship to destroy it. Like hand-grenade range close.''

''I know, sir, but I can't think of any other way to do it. Can you?''

''No, I can't. So I guess that's it.'' Vance folded the map and put it back in his side pants pocket. ''You'd better tell the men about our change in plans.''

''Yes, sir.''

Wilburn went from one man to the next telling them of the changes. Most of them took it calmly with a minimum of grumbling. It was only midafternoon, but since they were going to have to march all night until they reached the mountain, the sergeant gave them an hour to eat and rest before they moved out.

Finding a soft spot under a tree, the platoon leader leaned back on his ruck and grabbed a few Zs himself.

CHAPTER 16

On the Cambodian Border

Panting into the radio while he ran, Ringer got through to CCN, Special Forces Command and Control North, at Kontum and scrambled a rescue mission. His old buddy Rat Gaines and Python Flight had lifted off from Camp Radcliff and were hauling ass to extract what was left of his people. All they had to do now was to stay ahead of the North Vietnamese and get to the Papa Zulu on time.

It sounded simple enough, but it was going to be real tight.

After a quick conference with his team NCO, Sergeant Thompson, Ringer ordered the sergeant and one of the Cambodian Strikers to drop back to ambush the pursuing NVA point element. Ringer hoped that the two men would cause the slopes to deploy and hold them up for fifteen minutes or so, giving the rest of them a chance to break free.

It was a good idea, but Ringer really didn't think that it was going to work, The slopes would probably just bypass Thompson and keep on their trail.

Ringer and the six men with him were running much more slowly now. Carrying the litter with the wounded man was

116

wearing them down quickly, but he wouldn't leave him behind. It was bad enough that he had been forced to leave his dead where they had fallen in the ambush, but he had never left a wounded man, American or indigenous, and he wasn't about to start now.

To the rear, he heard the sharp rattle of automatic-weapons fire and the dull crump of grenades. Thompson had sprung his ambush on the enemy point.

Ringer picked up the pace.

As he ran, he prayed that Tom would make it back. Thompson was a good man and they had worked together for a long time. It was only another ten or fifteen minutes to their pickup zone.

In the air, Rat Gaines was inbound to the Papa Zulu with a heavy-gun team at his back. The four Huey gunships and his Cobra were loaded down with everything that the armorers could hang on them. Following behind as fast as they could go were three slicks of the lift element. Each slick had a medic on board.

Gaines keyed his throat mike, "Hook Talon Alpha, Hook Talon Alpha. This is Python Lead on your push, over."

"Python, this is Talon Alpha," Ringer panted into the transmitter.

Gaines heard gunfire in the background.

"Go ahead."

"This is Python Lead. I am inbound to your Papa Zulu, Echo Tango Alpha six mikes. What's your situation now, over?"

"This is Talon Alpha. I'm at least ten mikes November Whiskey from Papa Zulu, and I'm up to my ass in alligators. Can you scratch it for me? Over."

"This is Python Lead. Roger, can do, I'll be there most *rikky-tik*. Be prepared to pop smoke, over."

"Talon, roger, out."

Gaines switched back to the Python gunship frequency. "Python, Python, this is Lead. Two and Three, turn the wick up and follow me. Four and Five, you stay with the lift ships. Over.''

A chorus of rogers followed as two of the C-model Huey guns broke away to follow their leader.

In the front seat of *Sudden Discomfort*, Alphabet tightened the fingers of his Nomex gloves. Reaching over to his control panel, he flipped on the arming switches to his 7.62mm minigun and the automatic 40mm thumper in the ship's chin turret and the 2.75-inch rockets under the stub wings. He was going hunting again.

From behind him, Ringer heard more firing, both AK and M-16. At least one of his men was still alive. He yelled at his Cambodians to run faster.

''*Di di!* Goddamnit! *Di di mau!*''

Through the breaks in the treetops, Ringer saw black specks in the sky closing fast. The gunships. He keyed the hand set to the radio.

''Python, Python, this is Talon Alpha. I have you in sight to my November Echo and I'm popping smoke. The target is right behind me, a company of November Victor Alpha. Smoke out, over.''

He pulled a smoke grenade from his assault harness, pulled the pin, and dropped it on the side of the trail as he ran. Behind him, thick, purple smoke billowed up through the tops of the trees.

''Talon Alpha, this is Python Lead, I see Goofy Grape, over.''

''This is Alpha, roger Grape. Go get 'em, Rat, they're right on my ass.''

''Roger, Talon, I copy. Move past the smoke and continue to the Papa Zulu. We'll cover for you.

''Python guns, this is Lead. Hit behind the smoke and watch out for the good guys.''

It almost looked like the lead ship, Gaines's Cobra, was going to fly into the ground. It passed not thirty feet over Ringer's head. He felt the rotor blast and the concussion of the explosions as Alphabet fired everything he had into the jungle—rockets, 40 mike mike and the minigun. It felt like

118

the world was coming to an end around him, and for all he knew, it was.

The Strikers beside him were running as fast as they could now, drawing on their last reserves of energy. Ringer put his head down and ran flat out. It was all up to the gunships now. If they could keep the gooks off their asses while they ran the last few hundred meters to the clearing, they'd make it.

He glanced around behind him and saw a tall figure in a tiger suit stagger out of the smoke from the rocket explosions. It was Thompson.

Ringer stopped in midstride and turned around. The sergeant was coming, but he was not coming fast enough. As he watched, Thompson stumbled and fell on the side of the trail.

"Lon, keep going!" Ringer yelled to the Cambode interpreter who had stopped when he did. The Special Forces officer spun around and started back to help the downed man.

Gaines had cleared his first firing run and was banking *Sudden Discomfort* around for another pass when he saw the first of the Strikers break out of the tree line into the open ground.

"Python, this is Lead. Get those slicks on the ground now!"

The slicks turned onto their final approach. With doorguns hammering at likely enemy hiding places, they flared out and settled to earth a few meters from the running Cambodes. The four Strikers carrying the litter with their wounded comrade clambered onto the first bird, and it lifted off instantly. The other two men ran back to the second slick.

One of them scrambled on board, but Lon ran to the pilot's window. "No go! No go!" he yelled. " *Dai Uy* and *trung si* come *ti ti*!"

The slick driver shook his head and yelled back. "Get on, I can't wait!"

"No! Wait, please!"

Rolling in for his next firing run, Gaines saw the interpreter waving his arms as he yelled at the slick pilot.

"Python Seven, this is Lead. What's going on down there?"

"This is Seven. The Cambodian says that his advisors are coming, but I don't see them."

"Are you taking fire?"

"That's a negative."

"Hang in there until you do."

"Roger, copy."

Gaines leveled his gunship out, and Alphabet started playing with his firing controls again. He walked the chin turret from side to side as they swooped in low over the edge of the trees, peppering the jungle with 40-mike-mike grenades. Gaines looked down through the foliage and spotted two figures in cammies. It looked like one of the men was trying to carry the other one to the PZ.

"Python, this is Lead, we've got two more men in there, and I'm not leaving without them. Let's go guns, get in their shorts. Get it, 'rat' now!"

As Gaines pulled out of his run, two more gunships came charging in side by side right behind him, their rotors almost touching. Their noses were ablaze with fire and 2.75-inch high-explosive rockets lanced out from the pods hanging on their pylons.

The forest was coming apart below them. The rockets, miniguns, and thumper rounds were a storm of steel tearing into the jungle, shredding the foliage and dropping huge trees like they were matchsticks. Fires started by the explosions added more smoke to the already darkened sky. It was getting difficult now for the pilots to see their targets, but the gunships still came on.

Python Flight was doing all that men in flying machines could possibly do to protect the two men on the ground. Now it was up to Ringer and Thompson to get to the Papa Zulu.

Back at Kangor Wat, only some forty klicks away from where Ringer and his men were running for their lives, Colonel Duc was monitoring the North Vietnamese radio transmissions as

120

they chased after Ringer. His excitement was growing by the minute.

The renegade North Vietnamese pilot got most of his kills when NVA tactical radio broadcasts informed him that an American unit was operating in the vicinity. Then he went hunting.

Usually he stayed away from engagements like the current one. He didn't want the NVA units to know that he was operating in the vicinity. But when he heard the Vietnamese radio operator say that Yankee helicopters were in action there, including one of the new, sharklike Cobra gunships, Duc couldn't resist. He'd never shot down a Cobra yet, and he wanted to add one to his growing collection of kills.

"Get my helicopter ready," he shouted to the Khmer who acted as his crew chief. "Hurry!"

As the Cambodian ran to the HIP, Duc quickly got into his flying gear.

The big gunship's turbines were spinning the big five-bladed rotor when Duc scrambled into the cockpit and buckled himself in. After a fast check of the instrument panel, he twisted the throttle all the way up against the stop. With the twin turbines screaming, the tail of the HIP came up, and he lifted off the ground in a hover. Lining the HIP up with the narrow airstrip, he hauled up on the collective and pushed forward on the cyclic. The five rotor blades bit into the air and the chopper started down the strip. Within seconds, the red-tailed Russian helicopter was airborne.

Duc stayed low to the ground with his turbines at full RPMs. He headed toward the contact site at well over a hundred fifty miles an hour. As he turned on his gunsight and flicked the switches to arm the chopper's two belly cannons, he felt the familiar tension building in his stomach.

He was anxious to kill again.

Ringer was panting so hard he could hardly breathe. The thick, blinding smoke from the explosions and the fires they had started was choking him. Coughs racked his body as he

121

staggered toward the PZ with Thompson on his back in a fireman's carry. The NCO was hit in several places, but if he could get him to a Dustoff soon enough, he would live.

The Mike Force commander was totally oblivious to the destruction all around him. The rockets slamming into the trees, the crump of the thumper rounds detonating, and the ripsaw sound of the miniguns as the four gunships worked the woods behind him. Over the burning jungle, Gaines's *Sudden Discomfort* flew figure-eights in the sky acting as the C and C bird directing the fire from the other gunships.

The Special Forces officer was also oblivious to his own wound. He had a piece of shrapnel in the shoulder, as well as the weight of the man on his back. He was oblivious to anything except the need to keep going at all costs, to put one foot in front of the other until he cleared the trees. His reserves of energy were all but gone, and he was moving solely on stubborn willpower. As long as Larry Ringer was alive, he would keep on running.

Suddenly, out of the smoke in front of him, two figures ran at him. Ringer tried desperately to bring his weapon up to fire, but his aching arms would not obey his brain's commands.

"Don't shoot!" one of the figures shouted when he saw Ringer try to raise the sixteen. "Goddamnit, don't shoot!"

It was the two door gunners from the slick that was still waiting on the ground. They had come looking for them.

One gunner took Thompson from his back. Cradling the wounded NCO in his arms like a child, he sprinted for the bird. With the man's weight suddenly gone from his back, Ringer stumbled and fell. He was finished.

Hands shot out, grabbed him by the assault harness, and jerked him back onto his feet.

"Run, goddamnit, run!" the other door gunner screamed in his ear.

With the gunner pulling him along, Ringer started running again and they broke out of the trees into the clearing. The slick was already in a hover moving closer to the wood line, the rotors at full RPM.

The gunner shoved Ringer into the cargo compartment and scrambled in behind him. The second he was inside, the pilot pulled pitch and the slick lifted into the sky.

Just then, from his position orbiting the PZ, something caught Gaines's eye. He looked up through the plexiglass canopy over his head.

There it was again! A flash of sunlight on polished metal. He looked again and saw a large, dark helicopter diving down on top of them and it was coming on fast.

The chopper looked big enough to be a Jolly Green Giant, the air-force HH-3 that was often used for search and rescue. As it drew closer, however, he saw that it was painted dark green with irregular gray stripes and marked with a bright red tail boom. Nothing that the U.S. Air Force had in the skies over Southeast Asia was camouflaged that way. Also, there weren't any Jolly Greens operating by themselves over Cambodia anyway. They always had an escort of Skyraiders on their rescue missions.

The pilot suddenly remembered the Russian gunship that had mauled Charlie Company the other day. This had to be it!

"Python, Python," Gaines's urgent voice broke in on the chopper command radio frequency. "Break and run for home fast! We've got an enemy gunship on us. Call for help, stay low, and watch out for this bastard. Get the hell out of here. Now!"

CHAPTER 17

On the Cambodian Border

Captain Roger Rat Gaines was the son of a World War II air-force bomber pilot from Atlanta. Since his boyhood, he had dreamed of flying fighters and read every story about World War II fighter pilots he could get his hands on, as well as building dozens of models of his favorite airplanes.

When he graduated from high school, he signed up for air-force ROTC in college and started pilot training. Things were going very well for the young Gaines until his sophomore year when, to his complete disbelief, he flunked his P-1 category physical examination. The flight surgeon said he had a slight heart murmur and disqualified him. Faced with a non-flying job in the air force, Gaines quickly switched over to the army ROTC infantry program. If he couldn't fly, at least he could fight on the ground.

Three years into his army career as an infantry officer in Germany, First Lieutenant Gaines read that the army was looking for chopper pilots. The war in Nam was eating them up at a rapid rate and the army was taking anyone who wanted to fly. Gaines applied for flight training, passed the physical, and went to Fort Wolters, Texas to learn how to fly. He graduated at the top of his class and requested a gunship assignment in Nam. His request was granted.

Though he had been flying gunships for months now, Gaines still longed to fight in the air, and it looked like he was finally going to get his chance. It would be a rather strange fight, but a real aerial battle nonetheless. Maybe he would go down in the history books as the first chopper pilot to ever shoot down another chopper in combat. But just as likely, it would be the other way around—he'd go down as the first dumb fuck to die trying to dogfight in a helicopter.

At their leader's call, the Python birds hit their RPM-increase switches, ran their turbines all the way up past 6,600 RPM, and split for the border. The slicks stayed close to the ground since they had a better chance of surviving that way, but the gunships climbed higher to put themselves between the enemy and the loaded-down slicks.

Gaines took a deep breath and racked *Sudden Discomfort* around to face the HIP just as the big helicopter started its firing run. A million things ran through the Cobra pilot's mind at the instant he turned. This was going to be the aerial dogfight that he had dreamed about all his life.

If he dumped his empty rocketpods under the stub wings of his Cobra and turned the wick up all the way, he could make almost a hundred and fifty miles an hour. He had the 7.62mm minigun and the 40mm grenade launcher in the chin turret to fight with. The Mi-8 HIP, on the other hand, could do almost two hundred miles an hour and was at least armed with rockets and machine cannon, probably two of the same deadly 23mm weapons that armed the Russian MiG fighters.

The odds were definitely in his favor. Those machine cannons could reach out over three times as far as his light-caliber 7.62mm minigun. On top of that, the Russian's 23mm guns fired high-explosive shells.

"Joe," Gaines called up over the intercom. "Let's see if we can keep this bastard off the slicks long enough for them to get home."

"That's a rodg."

Duc was intent on the slower slicks frantically jinking from side to side to get away. He didn't see the Cobra off to his left when he swept down onto his targets. The Hueys were centered in his gunsight, and he was just about to press the cannon trigger when a stream of bright red tracer fire cut across his nose. Instinctively, he banked his HIP sharply away to escape the enemy fire.

Quickly he scanned the sky for an enemy jet fighter, but saw nothing, but the new Cobra gunship was off to his left between him and the fleeing helicopters. Duc turned back to his target, and the lone Cobra fired at him again with a short burst from its nose-mounted machine gun. Rat Gaines wanted to fight.

Duc gave up all thoughts of attacking the fleeing American machines. They were sitting ducks, and promised no sport in shooting them down. Especially when one of the other ducks wanted to shoot back. He wanted to add a Cobra to his kill list. Now he had found one, and it wanted to make the kill even more interesting by fighting back.

He ran the HIP's twin turbines up to maximum RPM and turned into the Yankee gunship.

"Good, he took the bait and he wants to play," Gaines called up to his gunner. He was pleased. "The slicks should be able to get away clean now."

Gaines watched the HIP turn into him and waited. He knew the enemy pilot would start firing his cannons long before he got in range of the Cobra's minigun. He had to stay alive in the air until he could get close enough to use his lighter-caliber weapon.

He read once about a propeller-driven Navy AD-1 Sky-raider attack bomber that had downed a MiG-15 in the Korean War. The Skyraider had made the kill because the pilot had been able to outmanuever the jet-fighter opponent.

Rat wasn't facing a Mig-15, but he was facing the same machine cannons that armed the MiGs. With those guns, the Russian helicopter could stay out of range and blow big holes in Rat's Cobra at his leisure. A single hit almost anywhere from one of the high-explosive cannon shells would put him in a world of hurt. The secret to survival today lay in not getting hit.

Since helicopters were the most maneuverable machines ever to fly, and the AH-1 Huey Cobra was the most maneuverable of them all, maybe he could take a page from the Skyraider's book and outfly the Russian gunship. It was worth a try. At least he didn't have anything to lose.

"Hang on, Joe!" he yelled to the warrant-officer gunner in the front cockpit. "I'm going after him."

As Gaines banked *Sudden Discomfort* around, Duc seemed to retreat by turning away from him and climbing higher up into the sky. But the North Vietnamese pilot wasn't running from the Cobra. He just wanted more room for his opening moves in a deadly aerial ballet.

For the first time since he started flying his Cobra, Gaines wished that he had one of the optional 20mm Vulcan cannons bolted under the stub wings. Either that or at least another minigun in place of the automatic thumper.

The Cobra's chin turret could be fitted with a variety of weapons, but Gaines usually carried a turret that mounted a 40mm grenade launcher and one 7.62mm minigun. That combination worked best against ground targets. He kept his stub-wing hardpoints available for 2.75-inch rocketpods. But that armament mix didn't give him much to fight an aerial dogfight with. He also knew that the HIP was armored, and light-caliber minigun rounds weren't going to be very effective. To make matters worse, the thumper, with its short, thousand-meter range and slow muzzle velocity was all but useless for air-to-air combat. He figured that he had about half of his minigun ammunition left on board, but at a firing rate of four thousand rounds per minute, it wasn't going to last long.

A mile away, the enemy gunship completed his turn and started back for *Sudden Discomfort*. As the HIP lined up for a head-on shot, Gaines twisted his throttle back a little to cut his RPMs and hauled up on the collective to change the pitch of his rotor blades for maximum maneuverability. It was time to dance.

With a kick at the rudder pedals and a savage pull on the cyclic stick, the Cobra suddenly wasn't where she had been in the sky anymore. She had jumped off to the right and was hanging almost motionless in the air, her tail high.

Glowing bright orange, the HIP's 23mm cannon tracers flashed through the spot *Sudden Discomfort* had occupied just a moment before. Rat snapped the tail around as the Russian machine flew past them. Alphabet gave it a short squirt of the minigun as it passed.

"Lead him, Joe!" Rat yelled over the intercom when he saw the 7.62mm tracers fall far behind the speeding gunship. "Lead the bastard!"

In the cockpit of the Russian-built helicopter, Duc cursed. He had had the Cobra locked in the center of the lighted pip of his gun-sight when it had vanished. He racked the big machine around and drove at the American ship again. Now he had it in a side deflection shot. He made a slight gun-sight correction and squeezed the trigger to the cannons.

This time, Gaines turned into the HIP, presenting the narrow frontal area of his smaller bird to the cannon fire. Duc's rounds passed on either side of him.

"Yaaa hooo!" Gaine's piercing rebel yell rang out. He whipped the tail of the Cobra around to give his gunner a better shot. The HIP screamed past right in front of them.

This time, Alphabet triggered off a few rounds of the 40 mike mike along with a quick burst of minigun fire. He missed again. The Cobra's firing controls and gun sight were designed to shoot at ground targets, not something moving at a closing rate of almost four hundred miles an hour. It was impossible to feed in enough lead to hit something moving that fast.

Duc saw the flame blossom from the nose of the Cobra and hauled his chopper around to evade the stream of tracers. The Russian gun sight in his machine had come from a MiG-17 fighter. Against the slower, highly manueverable Cobra, it was of little use. It had been designed to shoot at heavy bombers flying in level flight, not at aircraft that could dart from side to side like a Cobra. He was going to have to do some old-fashioned bare eyeball shooting to hit the Yankee ship. He would get closer next time and wait until the last possible moment before firing.

Duc increased his turbine RPMs and turned away from the Cobra again.

"You okay?" Gaines called up to his gunner.

"Yeah," Alphabet answered back, taking a deep breath. "I can't lead that fucker, Rat, he's going too fast. I can't keep the sights on him."

"I know. You're going to have to use a little Kentucky windage on him while I try to stay out of that bastard's road. Heads up! Here he comes!"

This time the HIP didn't make a gun run on them. The enemy pilot circled around them like Indians circling a wagon train in a western movie, looking for a place to strike. Gaines turned his gunship with the Russian machine, keeping him in clear sight. Suddenly, the HIP climbed straight up, high into the sky above them.

"Watch him Rat!"

"I got him."

The enemy gunship dropped down on top of them like a diving hawk. Duc had figured out their weak spot—an attack from above.

Gaines whipped the tail of his machine around and twisted his throttle to max RPM as he pulled the nose up in a climb to meet the diving HIP. He was trapped. If he tried to run now, he was dead. With the HIP above him, any direction that he tried to turn, the Russian chopper would easily turn, bring his cannons to bear, and blow him out of the sky. All Gaines could do now was to meet the enemy face to face and shoot it out.

Duc started firing short bursts from his cannons, jinking his bird from side to side as he fired, spreading the pattern of the shells.

Gaines saw the flicker of fire from under the gunship's nose, but there was little he could do about it now. He could only try to snake his chopper around to present as difficult a target as he could. If he tried to turn or dive away, he'd be cold meat.

In the gunner's seat in the front cockpit, Joe Schmuchatelli's slim, gloved fingers were wrapped around the twin firing controls of his weapons, and he had the diving Russian machine centered in the turret gun sight. When he saw the fire winking from the cannon barrels in the nose of the HIP, he fired in return. His fingers caressed the minigun triggers, conserving ammo by rapping out short twenty- or thirty-round bursts.

The HIP flew through his 7.62mm tracers seemingly without damage just as *Sudden Discomfort* was flying through the large glowing orange balls that were 23mm high-explosive cannon shells. Alphabet kept firing the mini, his thumbs hovering over the triggers to the 40mm grenade launcher. He waited for the Russian gunship to get just a little closer.

One of the glowing orange balls flashed right at the gunner's face. he ducked instinctively. It missed and exploded somewhere behind him. Over the intercom, he heard his pilot grunt with pain as the Cobra skidded off to one side.

"Rat!" he yelled.

"Keep shooting!" Gaines answered. "I've got it. Get that bastard, that motherfucker's trying to kill us."

"You hit?"

"Keep firing!"

Now the nose of the diving HIP filled Alphabet's gun sight. It was going to fly right into them. Joe Schmuchatelli decided he wasn't going to just sit there like a good little boy without at least trying to take somebody with him.

The turret's thumper belched flame as he triggered off all of his remaining grenades in a single long burst. The 40mm rounds had no tracer element, so he couldn't see where his fire was going, but he swung the turret slightly from side to side to spread the grenades like a shotgun blast.

Rat pulled the Cobra into an almost vertical climb and the HIP passed just under their belly, the five-bladed rotor missing them by mere feet. As the HIP flashed past, Alphabet thought he saw a small explosion on the rear of the engine compartment.

The Cobra shuddered and went into a stall. Gaines rolled his bird onto her side and pushed her nose down to unload the rotor head and regain his airspeed. Alphabet looked over his shoulder. The shell that had hit them had torn up their starboard stub wing. It was half-gone, and the jagged remains of the metal skin were flapping back and forth in the slipstream.

Suddenly, a piece of aluminum ripped off and flew into the tail with a crash. Alphabet felt the ship shudder and shake. They were in trouble. Gaines fought to keep the damaged machine in the air. The piece of metal peeling away from the damaged stub wing had hit something in the tail section, probably the small elevator on the tail boom. The sleek Cobra was now stumbling all over the sky, and it was all Gaines could do to keep her under control.

"Joe! I'm getting turbine surge! We've got to get the fuck out of here. Watch that bastard!"

Colonel Duc was having his own problems. The explosion that Alphabet had seen was one of the 40mm grenades hitting the exhaust of the portside turbine, shredding the metal skin of the engine compartment.

The twisted metal sticking out into the slipstream made his machine skid in the air. Duc had trouble keeping his gunship lined up on the fleeing Cobra. He bore in on it anyway, triggering off another short burst of cannon fire only to see it go wide.

As the HIP passed to one side of the Cobra, Alphabet swung the turret over and triggered off another burst of minigun fire. *Sudden Discomfort* was hurt, but she could still bite back.

In Duc's helicopter the tailpipe temperature warning light for the portside turbine came on. The Cobra's hit had done more than just damage the airframe. Duc shut down the overheated turbine and banked to the west heading back to his base.

"Rat!" Alphabet shouted back. "He's leaving!"

"Mayday, Mayday, this is Python Lead," Gaines shouted into his transmitter. "I've got engine and airframe damage. I am heading back for the fence. Mayday, Mayday. Python Lead going down."

CHAPTER 18

Inside Cambodia

Vance and his nine men moved out at fifteen hundred hours and continued their march to the mountain. They moved quickly but cautiously, and Wilburn kept the point element well out to the front. He rotated between himself, Brody, Two-step and the Indian sniper named Chief. He was very much aware that they were deep into enemy territory and extremely vulnerable. It was imperative that the point man be fresh. A single Cambodian woodcutter catching a glimpse of them sneaking through the brush would have them all in very deep *kim chee*.

The afternoon passed uneventfully, however and not too long after the sun went down over the jungle they reached the flank of the mountain where they had decided to lay up overnight. The Special Forces sergeant had the men move halfway up the slope of the southwestern face before he let them make camp for the night. From that location they had better observation of the plains below as well as good fields of fire to cover the approaches.

"Lieutenant," Wilburn approached Vance. "I've got the security out covering the valley and I put the snipers out on the flanks. I reminded the men that it's a cold camp tonight, but I told them that they'll be able to light fires in the morning.''

"Thanks, Sergeant. I guess that's all. I can't think of anything else. Oh, yes, put me down for the early-morning guard shift."

"Will do, sir."

It looked good so far, but Lieutenant Vance was still uneasy. Unlike his exhausted men, he didn't go to sleep right away. After shedding his heavy ruck, he sat on a rock overlooking the valley and ran through his mind the assault they had to make the following night.

Without the RPG rocket launchers, they were going to have to get right onto that Russian chopper to take it out and that was worrying him. With only ten men, counting himself, he did not have enough manpower in his small command to split them up and make a proper two-element attack, one assault team and one support element. He was going to have to make the assault with all of his men in one group and there was a far greater risk if they did it that way. If they got into trouble, there wouldn't be anyone in place to give them covering fire when they made their withdrawal from the attack site.

He felt the exhaustion of the forced march. He and Wilburn could work something out in the morning. He had to get some sleep before it was his turn to pull guard. Vance rolled up in his poncho liner, found a flat spot in between the rocks, and was asleep within seconds.

On the right flank position, Chief sat motionless with his sniper rifle cradled across his folded arms. In his camouflage fatigues and face paint, he blended into the shadows and looked like he was just another rock.

Every so often the Indian sniper slowly brought the rifle up to his shoulder. Peering through the Starlite scope, he checked out the approaches to the mountain. He looked carefully, but he really didn't expect to see anything. Everything felt peaceful.

The Indian had learned to trust his instincts. More than

134

once it had warned him of some impending disaster, an ambush, a booby trap, or just a sergeant looking for a man to put on a work detail. He regarded this sixth sense as part of being a warrior and he didn't think it was anything special. He had observed the same sensitivity in white men, too, sometimes, those whom he considered to be true warriors. The starlit plain below felt peaceful, and the Indian relaxed as much as he ever allowed himself to on a mission.

Back at Camp Radcliff, things were rocking and rolling again in the 7th Cav's club. The juke box was blaring out Mick Jagger and the Stones and a couple of early starters were already dancing on the tables. It was a little early for that kind of activity, but nobody minded. They were all too busy celebrating the fact that Rat Gaines and Alphabet had survived their epic air-to-air encounter with the Russian helicopter.

After the HIP had broken off the engagement, Gaines had managed to nurse his wounded *Sudden Discomfort* back across the border into South Vietnam. He made it, but it had been a real close call. It had taken every last bit of flying skill he had just to keep her in the air. The stub wing and elevator damage and been bad enough, but the air intake on the portside had been damaged as well, and it wasn't feeding enough air to the turbine. The turbine kept surging, it wouldn't run at a steady RPM and it had threatened to quit on him any second.

As soon as he knew that they were safely back across their side of the fence, Rat quickly called in his coordinates and greased her down for a landing in the first clearing that he spotted.

When the pilot climbed out of the Cobra and took his helmet off, he saw the jagged piece of frag from the HIP's cannon shell sticking out of the fiberglass shell. No sooner were he and Alphabet on the ground when they saw the choppers of Python Flight coming in fast. Their mayday calls had been monitored back at An Khe, and the pilots had scrambled to rescue their commander.

Everything with guns and rotors that wasn't already committed somewhere else came running. Within minutes, they were circling overhead. Python Flight had to protect Rat Gaines at all costs. If he got killed, their next commanding officer might not be a drinking man—and they didn't want that.

As his gunships swooped in close to the ground, Rat waved to let them know he was okay. In the distance, he also saw a lumbering "shit-hook" coming to recover his broken bird. The big twin-rotored Chinook settled down in the clearing and three men came storming out of the rear ramp, the maintenance chief, Rat's crew chief, and one of the mechanics.

The crew chief and the mechanic headed straight for *Sudden Discomfort* while the old maintenance warrant ran up to him.

"You okay, Captain?"

"Yeah, I'm fine, Chief, I'm okay. Just get my bird out of here."

"No sweat, sir."

Under the circling protection of three gunships with itchy fingers on their firing controls, the wounded Cobra was rigged to be sling-loaded under the shit-hook. In less than ten minutes, *Sudden Discomfort* was lifted out and on her way back to Camp Radcliff.

Once his machine was clear, one of the C-model gunships dropped down and flared out for a landing. Warrant Officer Lance Warlokk leaned his head out of the side window. "Hey, Captain! Get in! The beer's getting cold."

Rat and his gunner scrambled aboard and found a seat in the rear compartment with the ammo cans. Warlokk pulled pitch and they, too, were on their way back. It had been less than fifteen minutes since he had nursed his damaged Cobra in for a safe landing.

Now that the excitement was over, and everyone was safely home, the men of Python Flight were letting it all hang out. After all, the drinks were on Rat Gaines tonight.

136

The word about Rat's battle with the Russian gunship had quickly spread throughout the Air Cav and the club was jammed with people wanting to congratulate him and his gunner. Staff REMFs in pressed uniforms and spitshined boots, doughnut dollies in their crisp, light blue uniforms, and infantry officers were rubbing shoulders with chopper mechanics with black grease under their fingernails and the other pilots of the company. It was a typical chopper-pilot party, and everybody was well on their way to getting blasted.

It had been quite awhile since there had been a big battalion blow-out in the 7th Cav and this was the best excuse they had had to get drunk in weeks. It simply wasn't every day that a pilot could lay claim to having fought the first air-to-air helicopter battle in the history of aviation.

As always, Rat had showered and changed into a clean flight suit, his party suit that had the big Python Flight insignia on the front and full-color Air Cav patch on the shoulder. He was wearing his cavalry yellow ascot and his one pair of shined jump boots. One of his thin cigars was clamped between his teeth, and a glass of bourbon and branch water was in his hand. Rat Gaines had everything he needed.

"Hey, Gaines!" Walt Greenfield, the aviation maintenance officer from the division G-4, stormed up to the pilot. "You sorry son of a bitch. You promised me that you weren't going to let my Cobra get all fucked up this time."

"I'm really sorry 'bout that, Walt." Gaines threw his arm over the maintenance officer's shoulder. "But that guy in the HIP didn't give me much choice, you know how it is. But, man, I'll tell you, you would've been real proud of your bird. Considering how he outgunned us, we really didn't do that badly."

"Don't give me any of your fucking excuses, Gaines. Didn't anyone tell you that you're not supposed to try to dogfight in one of those goddamned things, you crazy bastard? What stunt are you going to try to pull next, take on a fucking MiG maybe?"

Rat thoughtfully blew a smoke ring. "You know, Walt," he drawled in his best southern accent. "That's not a bad idea. All I'd have to do is to get your people to borrow a couple of sidewinders from the air force and mount them on the pylons. Let me see, I could probably shoot them from the backseat. Hummm . . . Let me think about it, and I'll give it a try.''

The aviation maintenance officer blanched. ''Hey, I'm just kidding. Jesus Christ! What's wrong with you?''

Rat grinned. ''Aw, come on, Walt! At least we could give it a try. Don't you want to get written up in *Air Progress?*''

''Anyway,'' Walt shook his head, ignoring this new bit of craziness. ''Your machine's not hurt that badly. We had to put on a new wing and elevator on the starboard side, but the turbine checks out okay. We'll have her back to you by mid-day tomorrow.''

''Outfuckingstanding!'' Gaines threw his arm over the maintenance officer's shoulder. ''Walt, my man, this calls for another drink.''

At the end of the bar, Alphabet accepted the congratulations of dozens of well wishers. He sipped at a gin and tonic and puffed on one of Rat's thin cigars as he watched his aircraft commander mingle with the crowd. The warrant officer was drinking alone because his date, a new Red Cross girl he had just met, hadn't shown up. It was just as well. He was not really up to any strenuous activity anyway. It had been quite a day for the gunner as well, and he was content just to sit back and watch his boss bask in glory.

It was hard to imagine two more different people than Joe Schmuchatelli and his aircraft commander. They came from totally different backgrounds and had completely different personalities, but the thin warrant officer from New Jersey practically worshipped the stocky southern pilot. The reason for this hero worship was simple, Rat Gaines was the best gunship pilot Schmuchatelli had ever met.

Alphabet had flown with quite a few pilots since he first arrived in Vietnam. Some of them had been good and some had been only so-so. But before meeting Rat Gaines, even the good ones had lacked the one quality that made Gaines stand out—his complete single-mindedness about what he was doing.

Gaines lived to fly his gunship and inflict maximum damage on the enemy. He did not allow anything to interfere with that objective, not women, booze, letters from home, or some COs ranting and raving about nickel-and-dime bullshit. Gaines only lived to fly and fight. And since Joe had started flying with him, that attitude had rubbed off.

"Can I have your attention, please!" Gaines shouted. No one paid him the slightest bit of attention. Most of them didn't even hear him over the blare of the music.

Before he could shout again, Alphabet reached around behind the cash register, got the .45-caliber automatic pistol out from under the bar and handed it to him. Gaines jacked a round into the chamber and held it straight up into the air.

"Can I have your fucking attention!"

The partygoers saw the pistol and shut up fast. Gaines had a reputation around Camp Radcliff for blowing holes in ceilings when people didn't listen to him.

Back in his college days, Rat had made his living delivering moonshine to backwoods Georgia taverns. His black-sheep uncle had been in the moonshine business and wanted someone he could trust to handle deliveries. Among the many things that the young Gaines had learned was how to quiet a brawl. Back then he used a sawed-off shotgun.

When everything calmed down, he handed the .45 back to his smiling co-pilot who stashed it back under the cash register.

"I've just been told that my Cobra, *Sudden Discomfort,* will fly again."

Cheers broke out.

"And now, I would like to propose a toast to the best Huey Cobra in the entire United States Army. *Sudden Discomfort,* long may she fly."

The crowd went wild, cheering, whistling, and stomping their feet.

"Also, I would like to drink to the best front-seat man who ever rode a Huey Cobra, our own Joe Schmuchatelli. If it wasn't for his shooting, I wouldn't be here tonight.'' The pilot turned to his gunner. "Take a bow, Alphabet.''

A grinning Alphabet raised his glass to his pilot and took a drink. The crown went crazy again, screaming, yelling, and calling the gunner's name. He felt his face getting red. He wasn't used to all the attention.

Someone pulled a chair over to the end wall and climbed up to the 7th Cav's big black scoreboard. It bore the 7th's raised sabre and Garry Owen insignia, and recorded the battalion's tally of NVA they had killed and equipment they had destroyed or captured since they had arrived in the Nam. It was quite an impressive score and it was growing bigger every day. No one could ever say that the fighting men of the First of the 7th Cavalry weren't trying to do their share to win the war.

Taking a piece of chalk, the man on the chair wrote Mi-8 Helicopter—Damaged and the date. Under the scoreboard, he hung Rat's battered flight helmet with a piece of Russian 23mm cannon shell still lodged in the side.

The party lasted long into the night.

CHAPTER 19

Inside Cambodia

"Lieutenant, Lieutenant Vance!" The low, insistent voice close to his ear brought him instantly awake.

"Yeah, what is it?" he whispered.

"Your turn on guard, sir."

"Okay."

Vance sat up and looked around. He had been dreaming about being back in the States, something about not being ready for a test in one of his classes at West Point. It took him a moment to get reoriented. He picked up his sixteen and, with his poncho liner still wrapped tightly around him, stumbled over to the guard position on the right flank.

He relieved the man on duty, took the sniper's rifle from him, and tried to get comfortable in between two boulders. As always when he first woke, he craved one of his few daily cigarettes and a cup of coffee. It would have to wait till the sun came up.

Throwing the rifle up to his shoulder, he scanned the plain below with the Starlite scope. Nothing. It was still too early for anyone to be out yet. Not even Charlie moved around at 4 o'clock in the morning. He wrapped the poncho liner tighter around his body and resigned himself to a long, cold wait until dawn.

It got very cold at night in the tropics, particularly up in the mountains. Vance wished that he had been able to bring his field jacket along. The young lieutenant always pulled his turn on guard duty when he was in the field. It was a sign of good leadership, but he really didn't like it any more than his grunts did.

He was still on guard two hours later when it started getting lighter in the valley below. The mist formed ever so slowly, obscuring the field. It would burn off in an hour or so, once the sun cleared the horizon. But at the moment it made the land look like something from a vague, shadowy dream.

Everything was so quiet that Vance let his men sleep a little longer, not calling for stand-to until nearly six-thirty.

When everyone was up, Vance went back to where he had been sleeping and started getting his gear together. Now that he saw exactly where they had spent the night, he realized that it wasn't as good a defensive position as it had looked in the dark. He decided to find a better location a little further up the hill.

He called Wilburn over. "Sarge, I don't like this camp here. Can I get you to take a look around and see if you can find us a better place. I think we should get moving before the mist burns off."

The sergeant agreed and started up the hillside. By now everyone was awake and going about their morning routines. No fires were lit yet, but the men talked quietly, smoking and eating cold rations. Hot coffee would have to wait until later, when it was light and the mist had cleared away. The smell of hot coffee carried too far in the chill of early-morning air.

Wilburn came back soon and knelt down beside the platoon leader.

"I've found us a real good place, sir, just about fifty meters or so further up. There's a little shielded pocket behind a ring of boulders that's almost as good as the Alamo."

142

Vance looked at him skeptically, "You remember what happened at the Alamo don't you?"

"Yeah," Wilburn laughed, "but this place has a rat hole out the back."

"Good. Let's go."

Silently, the ten men climbed the short distance to their new position. It was as good as Wilburn had said. They had excellent observation and fields of fire as well as an escape route out the back if they got their asses in a crack. It was also big enough for a chopper to come in and extract them.

"This is perfect!" Vance said looking around, "Tell them we'll stay here all day. And, Sarge, after you've had breakfast, I'd like to get together with you and your other Green Berets for a little skull session."

"Yes, sir."

Colonel Nguyen Cao Duc was in a nastier mood than usual that morning. He was up prowling around before daybreak.

The damage to his helicopter was worse than he had thought, and it wouldn't be completely airworthy for several more days. The hydraulics had already been repaired and the few minigun holes in the airframe were patched. But the turbine exhaust still needed to be replaced. In the condition that it was in now, the helicopter would fly, but it wouldn't reach full speed.

Khmer Rouge troops who hadn't been able to find a good excuse to get out of the temple area all made certain that they were in full uniform with clean weapons, and kept themselves busy at their duties. Even the cooks wore clean shirts as they prepared the midday meal. When Duc was in one of his moods, everyone knew enough to lay low. No one wanted to bring attention to himself and become the object of his anger.

Since the helicopter crew chief and his two mechanics were already adequately terrorized and worked as fast as they could to repair his machine, Duc decided to inspect the perimeter defenses around the temple.

By about nine o'clock, the morning mist had burned away, revealing the details of the valley below Vance's mountain campsite. On his right, to the west, he could see the green tree line of a river, the river that the map said went past the far side of the temple complex. The valley itself was mostly made up of small, terraced rice fields, many of them not being farmed. There were a few clumps of trees and another small stream moving directly across their front. In the far distance they could see the small Cambodian village of Kangor that took its name from the famous temple.

Vance, the two Green Berets, and Brody stood at the edge of the clearing overlooking the valley and oriented themselves to the terrain. Since they would be making the attack on the temple at night, they needed to be as familiar as they could with the terrain they would be moving through.

After several minutes, Vance spread his map and the aerial photographs out on a rock. "The way I see it, we have only two possible avenues of approach. We can go right through the valley," he pointed out a route on the map, "or we can go down the river."

He turned to Wilburn. "Do either one of you guys know anything about that river?"

"I've crossed it a couple of times further north, sir." The Green Beret pointed to a place on the map. "Up in that area, at least, it's not too deep and it's very slow moving. I expect that it's about the same down here."

"What do you think about moving down the river bed?" Vance asked. "Hitting them from the west and coming back through here?" His finger traced a route on the map. "At least if we do it that way, we won't alert anyone going in and won't set ourselves up for an ambush on the way back out. What'd you think?"

"I don't like getting wet any more than anyone else, sir, but it makes sense to me. The only bad thing is that on our way out, we'll be going through defenses that we haven't scouted on the way in."

"Yeah, I thought about that. But we won't run the risk of their detecting us while we're trying to scout out their perimeter, either. Without a fire-support element to back us up, I really don't want to risk it. This thing's going to be hairy enough as it is."

"You're right," Wilburn agreed. "Did anyone remember to bring the water wings?"

Vance turned to Brody. "Sarge, what do you think of this?"

"Well, sir, I don't like water any more than Sergeant Wilburn does, but I don't see that we have any other way to do it."

He looked up from the map at his platoon leader. "This thing's going to be a real motherfucker no matter which way we try to go in."

"Yeah, Sarge, I know."

Vance turned back to the map. "As you can see, the airstrip is cut into the jungle right in front of the temple. Intelligence thinks that the HIP is probably kept under some kind of cover at night, a netting or something, because the photos don't show a hangar. If that's the case, they can park it anywhere they want, so we're going to have to sweep through the area until we find it. If we can before they spot us, we'll put some timed charges on it and pull out. But if we get caught going in, we still have to find it, hit it with the seventy-nines, and fight our way back out.

"Now the only problem I see is keeping away from their troop barracks and weapons positions. Unfortunately, as you can see, with the heavy tree cover the photos don't tell us much about how they're set up. About the only thing they could ID for sure is the mess hall here." His finger pointed out a small building behind the temple.

"And the boat landing to the west. There seems to be a trail leading from the landing which probably means that they have their weapons set up covering that road. Other than that, the photo-interpretation people couldn't spot anything else. But I don't think the base is going to be unguarded."

"You can bet on that, sir," Wilburn commented. "Even

though they know that they're safe from attack, the gooks usually keep pretty good security over here.''

"That's where you and your buddy are going to come in. You'll be walking point and will guide us in.''

"That's fine with us, sir. I kind of figured it that way. I'd like to have the shooter up front with us, though. I'll need his weapon to take out any sentries I run into.''

"That makes sense. Also, I want us to stay together in one group. I don't think that this is any time to try linking up at night.''

"I agree with that, sir.''

The officer turned back to Sergeant Wilburn. "Just put out a minimum guard today and let the men get all the rest they can.''

"Yes, sir.''

"Brody, have your people break their gear down. I want them to go in as light as they can. Tell them to take only their assault harnesses, grenades, ammo, and water. I want to be able to move as fast as we can. We'll leave the rest of the stuff here and try to pick it up when we come back. Tell them to take it easy today and I'll brief them right before the sun goes down.''

As the men broke their rucks down, Vance sat on the rock looking over the valley. Although he had tried to sound confident when he was talking to the two sergeants, he really didn't feel that way at all. In fact, he was scared. He knew that if the mission did go well, it would be a feather in his cap. But he also knew that it was not a sure thing. There were a hundred and one things that could go wrong.

This was the first time the young officer ever had to operate on his own without any backup available. The Air Cav wouldn't be coming to their rescue this time. Not deep inside Cambodia.

Not for the first time on this mission, the young officer wished that Sergeant Zack was with him. He always felt more secure when the combat-hardened NCO was at his side, making helpful suggestions. Vance listened when the black platoon sergeant said he should do something a certain way.

146

Even though Wilburn was young, he seemed to know what he was doing. But he wasn't Leo Zack.

During the day, the men who weren't sleeping sat around quietly, smoking and talking.

Bunny Rabdo sat next to Farmer and looked down into the valley. "You know," he mused. "This would be a great place for a hotel. Look at that view."

"Hotel?" Farmer looked astonished.

"Sure, my family is in the hotel business. Oh, I'm not talking about a Hilton or anything like that, just a small resort hotel. It's too bad that my Uncle Sol isn't here. He'd be down in the ville right now talking the headman into signing a ninety-nine-year lease on this place."

"Hey, Bunny," Corky walked up. "If you build the hotel, can I run the concessions?"

"Sure, what'd you have in mind?"

"Oh, I was thinking about a laundry, bar, and whorehouse combination, you know. Also, maybe I'd handle parking the choppers."

Now Bunny had a blank look on his face.

"Yeah," the machine gunner continued. "Choppers. The only way you're ever going to get people up here is to fly 'em up. If someone's got enough money to take a vacation in the tropics, he sure the fuck ain't going to walk up here like a grunt."

That got a big laugh.

"I know what I'll do, Corky," Farmer said. "I'll run the training program for your bar and whorehouse. And I'll tell you what, amigo, I won't charge you much for my services at all. Just a few beers a day and all the pussy I can eat."

"That stuff's going to rot your teeth, if you're not careful," Brody laughed.

Farmer had a silly grin plastered all over his face. "That's why the U.S. Army issued me a brand new toothbrush, Sarge."

Brody walked away shaking his head.

Gardner sat off by himself instead of taking part in the grunts' gab session. He particularly didn't want to get into any discussion about women. If he started thinking about Sandra, he knew he was going to get pissed off.

Wilburn came up to where Brody was napping under a rock. "Sarge."

"Yeah." Brody opened his eyes.

"Your ell tee says that you're pretty good with booby traps."

Brody grinned. "I guess I'm not too bad."

"Can you help me rig the stuff we're leaving behind? If we can't make it back here, I don't want the slopes to get their hands on it."

"No sweat. What do you have to do it with?"

"I thought that I'd rig some pressure-release fuses on a grenade or two and maybe a trip-wired claymore."

"That'll work okay, but my guys have C-Four if you'd rather work with that. Save claymores in case we need them in the bush."

"Yeah, that sounds better. Why don't you get four sticks and we'll set it up."

The two men quickly pulled up all their spare equipment and laid the fused explosive charges under it. If the NVA found their hiding place while they were gone and tried to move any of their gear, it would blow up in their faces.

CHAPTER 20

Kangor Wat, Cambodia

Colonel Duc walked back across the airstrip to his operations room in the ruined temple. The inspection had gone quite well. Very few of his men had not had their uniforms and equipment perfectly turned out. The worst of the offenders, a man who didn't have all of his ammunition magazines with him was being taken care of now. Even inside the temple he could hear the screams.

He had just walked under the massive lintel of the main entrance to the huge stone structure when one of his radio men came running.

"Comrade Colonel," the man said anxiously. "There is a call for you on the radio. The man says that he is the Red Falcon."

Duc stopped cold. He was stunned. Red Falcon was the radio call sign for the commander of the Russian air advisory team in Hanoi and the renegade North Vietnamese colonel knew him. He was the pilot who had checked him out to fly the Mi-8 helicopter, Colonel Yuri Yakanov. He hurried for the radio room.

"Red Falcon, this is Kangor Wat," Duc said into the microphone. "Do you have a message for me? Over."

"This is Red Falcon. That is affirmative. I will be arriving at your location in fifteen minutes. Please tell your gunners not to shoot me down. Over."

Duc hesitated before answering. He was close to panicking. How had the Russian known where he was? And what did he want with him? He pushed the transmission switch on the microphone. "This is Kangor Wat. You are cleared to land, the gunners will be notified. Over."

"Thank you, Kangor Wat. Red Falcon, out."

While Duc's men pulled the camouflage netting back from the runway, he strapped on his pistol holder. Whatever Yakanov wanted, he was prepared for it.

An anxious fifteen minutes later, Duc heard the helicopter approaching low to the ground. As it drew closer, he made out the characteristic whine of another Mi-8. With a whoosh, the big dark-green-and-gray-striped helicopter flashed overhead and banked hard to make its approach.

A cloud of dust blew up from its rotors as it settled to earth in front of the temple. The pilot shut down the engines, the door opened, and a stocky man in a white flight helmet and khaki flying suit stepped out. He pulled off the helmet to reveal a shaved head and faded blue eyes. Duc hurried to greet him.

"Ah, Colonel Duc," the Russian flyer said warmly, extending his hand. "How nice to see you again."

"Colonel Yakanov," the North Vietnamese officer replied, shaking his hand. "Welcome to Kangor Wat. What brings you all the way out here to the jungle?"

The Russian looked around the temple grounds. "I have received such good reports of your experiments out here that I thought I would visit and see how you were doing for myself."

Duc was stunned. How had the Russian heard of his operations?

"Also," Yakanov gave him no time to reply, "I have brought some spare parts that I think you need, and some

150

more ammunition. You must be running low on the rockets by now.''

Duc suddenly realized that there was a Russian spy somewhere in his camp or at the Khmer Rouge headquarters. He smiled when he thought of catching that man, whoever he was.

"Won't you please come inside, Colonel. It's cooler in the temple.''

"Yes, thank you.'' The Russian pilot mopped his forehead. "I could also use a cool drink right now, if you have one.''

"But of course. I have good Russian vodka. If you will follow me please.''

Yakanov turned back to his ship. "Captain,'' he called out, "you can come out now.''

Another Russian flyer came out through the pilot's door. Obviously the Russian colonel had not been certain of his reception at Kangor Wat and he had prepared for all eventualities. That pleased Duc. It told him that the Russian took him seriously.

"This is Captain Gregor Zerinski, my co-pilot.''

Zerinski saluted Duc. "Honored to meet you, Colonel. I have heard many good things about you.''

Duc shook the slender, blond officer's hand. "Well, gentlemen, if you will come inside please.''

Lieutenant Colonel Maxwell T. Jordan, battalion commander of the First of the 7th Cav was uneasy. He had just been to the Air Cav division headquarters for a briefing on the progress of the mission against the gunship. The division operations officer had speculated that Lieutenant Vance was going in after the Russian chopper even without the additional men from Ringer's Mike Force. He had not called for an extraction, so they assumed that the mission was still go.

Jordan was uneasy about it. He wasn't too sure Vance really knew what he was doing out there.

He picked up the phone on his desk and rang through to

Echo Company. "This is Colonel Jordan, let me speak to Captain Gaines . . . He isn't? . . . Thank you, I'll try reaching him there."

He dialed down to Python Flight Operations. "This is Colonel Jordan, is Captain Gaines down there? . . . Will you have him call me when he gets back?"

The Echo Company commander reportedly was up in the air testing his Cobra gunship now that it was out of the repair shop.

Jordan lit up another cigarette. Not for the first time since he had been briefed on the chopper-hunting mission, he wished that he had had someone else to send instead of Vance. Jake Vance wasn't a bad officer, but he had not shown a great deal of original thinking or the ability to work independently of the command structure. Like most West Pointers, Vance was a little too much of a by-the-book officer. Unfortunately, the book they used at the military academy didn't cover the war in Vietnam.

Jordan prided himself on being good at independent operations. On his first tour in the Nam, he had been an advisor to an ARVN Ranger company down in the Delta. And he was proud to say that his Ranger company had been one of the best in all Four Corps. They specialized in night patrolling and ambushing, something that not every ARVN unit wanted to do. In fact, damned few South Vietnamese troops were any good at night.

Jordan had figured that if the VC could work at night, then the ARVNs could do it as well. All they really needed was some decent leadership. The mission that Vance was on now would have been just the thing for his old unit—sneak in, blow the goddamned thing up, and then sneak back out.

Back in the good old days when he had been known as "Mack the Knife" for the Randall fighting knife he always carried, he had made many night raids like that.

He sighed. One of the worst things about having been promoted to lieutenant-colonel was that he didn't get to go out in the woods anymore. Commanding a battalion was the goal of every regular army officer, but he had to admit that

152

it really wasn't that much fun. When he was honest with himself, he knew that most of the time it was a royal pain in the ass.

"Muller!" he called out for his adjutant.

"Yes, sir," the young butter bar answered from the open door. Jordan heard the sound of him pushing his chair back from his desk.

"Where's those reports of survey?"

"The S-Four still hasn't sent them back yet, sir."

"Go get them. I want to see them now."

"Yes, sir, right away."

Jordan heard Lieutenant Muller's footsteps heading down the hall at a dead run. Not for the first time, he wished that the inept Lieutenant Muller had been assigned to someone else's battalion.

The battalion commander reached into the pile in his in-box and pulled out another piece of paper. Another dumb blivit from MACV, this one was a request for information about their vector-control program. The colonel wished that the Saigon warriors would just leave him alone and let his people kill rats on their own time. Why did they have to have an officer certify the body counts on fucking rodents?

Speaking of rats, the Colonel wondered when Gaines was going to get back to him.

At that exact moment, Captain Roger Rat Gaines and his co-pilot-gunner WO1 Joe Alphabet Schmuchatelli were about fifty feet off the ground, flying balls out along the coast just south of Bong Son. Rat had his Cobra's wick turned up all the way, and they were looking for trouble at almost a hundred and fifty miles an hour.

Specifically, Gaines wanted to try out his new 20mm cannon on something nice and hard like a bunker. He thought that it was really too bad that the gooks didn't have any tanks or trucks in this part of the country. He would have loved to see what the twenty mike mikes would to do a vehicle.

Before he got his shark-mouthed Cobra back from the division maintenance shop, Rat had talked Walt into letting him mount one of the XM-31 20mm cannon pods under his port-side stub wing. After his encounter with that cannon-armed HIP, he had wanted to carry something with a little more punch than the standard 7.62mm minigun. Although, at seven hundred rounds per minute, his new cannon wouldn't fire as fast as the minigun, it reached out almost two thousand meters farther. If he ran into that Russian gunship again, he would have something to fight back with.

Right now, though, he needed to find something to practice on. He had never fired the 20mm before and wanted to know what the H.E. armor-piercing and incendiary rounds that filled the linked ammunition belts would do to a target.

As they swept on up the coastline, Alphabet kept a sharp watch out as well.

"Capt'n," the gunner called back on the intercom. "Where'd all these fishing boats come from?"

To their right front was a cluster of a dozen small fishing boats flying the South Vietnamese flag. They were being shepherded by an ARVN patrol boat about twenty feet long. It was not uncommon to see fishing boats in the coastal waters of the South China Sea, but usually one didn't see so many clustered in one place and not so far away from a village or town. These boats were out in the middle of nowhere.

"Don't know, let's go take a look."

Nudging forward on the cyclic, Gaines sent his ship into a shallow dive. He rolled back on his throttle to cut their airspeed and take a better look. The people in the boats looked up as they passed overhead. Some waved at them, trying to be friendly.

Rat flew on for half a mile before going up into a high orbit.

"Joe, you notice anything funny about those guys?"

"No. What do you mean?"

"They just don't feel right to me. I didn't see a single woman in any of those boats, and all the men are military age."

"But they were being guarded by an ARVN boat."

154

"When did the ARVNs start using twelve-point-seven mike-mike ack-ack guns on deck mounts?"

"That thing's mounting a Fifty One?" Alphabet squeaked. The Russian M-1938/46 12.7mm heavy machine gun was the most dangerous chopper-killing weapon in the entire VC arsenal.

"You got that shit right. Didn't you see that big muzzle brake on the barrel?"

"Now what are we going to do?"

"Well, first I'm going to motor on out of the area, so they'll think we've gone. Then I need to make a couple of phone calls."

"Phone calls?"

"Crazy Bull, Crazy Bull," Gaines radioed back to An Khe. "This is Python Lead, over."

"This is Crazy Bull, over."

"This is Python Lead, let me talk to the Three, over."

"Python Lead, this is Crazy Bull Three, do you have traffic for me? Over."

"Three, this is Python Lead, that's most affirm." Rat proceeded to tell Three, the battalion operations officer, about the boats they had spotted and his suspicions that they were not quite as they seemed on the surface. "Can you check with your Swab Jockey buddy down at Bong Son to verify their status? Over."

"Lead this is Three, Roger. Wait one. Out."

"Captain," Alphabet called up from the front seat. "Who's he calling?"

"I'm having him get in touch with the navy advisor to the ARVNs to find out if they have a coastal patrol boat escorting a bunch of fishermen today. If they don't, we're going back there and blow that bunch of bastards out of the water."

"Python Lead, this is Crazy Bull Three. That's a negative on friendly naval operations. But you have not been cleared to take your targets under fire. The province chief is not available at this time to okay your clearance. Be advised that the normal rules of engagement apply, I say again, the normal rules of engagement apply. Do you roger? Over."

"Bull Three, this is Lead. Roger, copy. How about scrambling one of my light-gun teams? Tell them to meet me north of Bong Son at seven-three-six five-four-nine. I'm going to shadow these people till they get here. Over."

"This is Three. Wilco, out."

Gaines flew his orbit for a few minutes. "Fuck this waiting," he growled to himself. He knew that the boats were full of NVA or VC making a supply or reinforcement run. The normal rules of engagement that the Three had reminded him about meant that he could not take the boats under fire unless they shot at him first. It was a stupid fucking way to fight a war, but even the most stupid rules could be bent.

"Joe," he called up. "I'm going to make a fast pass over that patrol boat and see if I can shake those guys up a little bit."

"Roger that. Let's go get 'em." Alphabet's gloved hands rested lightly on his firing controls as he centered the distant group of boats in his gun sight.

Gaines twisted the throttle grip all the way up against the stop as he nudged *Sudden Discomfort's* nose down into a slight dive, picking up all the speed that he could get out of her.

The gooks in the patrol boat looked up at the sound of the diving Cobra's screaming turbine. They had seen the sharks in the South China Sea, but this was the first one that they had seen in the air.

They ran for the chopper-killing heavy machine gun mounted on their forward deck.

CHAPTER 21

Over the South China Sea

As Rat bore down onto his target, the small, grey patrol boat flying the South Vietnamese flag, the black-uniformed sailors on the deck were in a blind panic. One of them stood behind the 12.7mm heavy machine gun tracking his approach while another man struggled to fit an ammunition can in place on the gun mount.

"Joe," Gaines tensely called forward. "Track him, but don't shoot until you see his muzzle flashes."

"Roger."

This was a stupid game they were playing, but they had to wait till the gooks fired first. That's what the rules of engagement said.

"And, when you open up on him, nail his ass fast. We'll take care of the fishing boats later."

"Roger."

Suddenly, Rat noticed two men in the back of the patrol boat frantically ripping a tarp off of something mounted on the rear deck. The canvas fell away to reveal the nastiest-looking twin-barrel antiaircraft gun mount that Rat had ever seen in his whole life. One of the men jumped into the seat behind the guns and started swinging the muzzles around to bear on the helicopter.

Di di time!

Kicking down on the right pedal, the pilot slammed the cyclic all the way over and frantically banked away from the antiaircraft gun. In the front cockpit, Alphabet swung the nose turret over to the side as the Cobra turned, trying to cover their retreat.

The ack-ack gun started firing. Black puffs of smoke shot from the muzzles, and glowing orange tracers rushed after them. Over the roar of the turbine, they heard the heavy chunk-chunking sound of the 14.5mm machine cannon in operation.

With his turret in full traverse, Alphabet triggered off short bursts from the minigun and thumper, but he didn't see any hits on the patrol boat. Rat headed out to sea, away from the boats. Skimming over the top of the waves, going balls-out, he snapped the tail of his machine from side to side to present a more difficult target to the enemy gunner.

He had to get away from that cannon fast.

Rat didn't mind taking a chance with the Fifty One, but he wasn't going to fuck around with that other thing, whatever it was. And from the looks of it, he really didn't want to stick around and find out what it was. Not until he had somebody to help him.

"Python, Python," he radioed. "This is Python Lead. Over."

"Python Lead, this is Python Niner Two." Gaines recognized Lance Warlokk's voice in his headset. "My Echo Tango Alpha your location is three mikes, over."

"This is Lead. Roger, copy. Turn it on, boys, we got some serious work to do."

"Lead, this is Niner Two. Roger, we're overrevving 'em right now."

"This is Lead. Roger. Be advised that the target is a twenty-foot patrol boat flying the ARVN flag and a dozen or more fishing boats. The patrol boat is armed with a Fifty One up front and a heavy machine cannon mounted in the back, so keep at least two miles away from that guy on your way in. Over."

"This is Niner Two, Roger, copy. He sounds like a mean motengater."

"This is Lead, that's most affirm. Orbit west at three thousand. I'll join up with you there, over."

"This is Niner Two. Roger, we'll be on station in zero two. Out."

Safely away from the patrol boat, Rat climbed into the sky and went into his orbit. Down below, the small flotilla was making for shore as fast as they could. In a few more minutes they would be able to beach the smaller craft. The supplies and men they were transporting would disappear into the jungle.

Rat was not about to let that happen if he could help it.

"I've got 'em, Rat," Alphabet called back, pointing off to his left.

"Roger, I see 'em." Gaines clicked in the radio. "Python, Python, this is Lead, I am on your ten o'clock and at twenty-eight hundred. Form up on me and we'll get to work. Over."

"Lead, I have you in sight now, over."

"Niner Two, this is Lead. I want you to take one of the boys and make a run on that patrol boat from the north. Come in high, shoot some rockets at him to draw his fire, and then get the fuck outta there. Don't get too close, that big gun can reach out at least two klicks. While you're doing that, I'm going to come in from the other side, down on the deck, and see if I can poke some holes in him with my new twenty-mike-mike. I want the other ship to try to keep the fishing boats away from the beach. Everybody got that? Over."

A chorus of rogers came in over the radio.

"Python, this is Lead, let's get down there and earn our flight pay."

Warlokk's Huey C gunship peeled off, followed closely by another one. Side by side, they bore down onto the patrol boat like olive-drab sea hawks. Two-point-seven-five-inch

159

folding-fin aerial rockets lanced out from the pods on their side pylons, trailing white smoke.

The first rocket rounds were short and exploded harmlessly in the ocean, but the gun crew in the rear of the patrol boat swung their twin-barreled mount around to meet the threat.

Coming in at wavetop level from the other side, Rat saw the first puffs of black smoke from the antiaircraft gun as it took the two diving Hueys under fire. The glowing tracer rounds reached up to claw the gunships out of the sky.

"Lance! Break away! Break away!"

Warlokk ignored his commander's radio call and continued his firing run. His H.E. rockets were bracketing the ship now, the explosions throwing columns of water high up into the air.

Rat's Cobra was right on the deck, the turbine screaming on overrev.

Since the 20mm cannon pod was rigidly mounted under the stub wing, it had to be fired by aiming the helicopter's nose at the target. The pilot peered through the gun sight at the rapidly approaching gray hull of the patrol boat. When he figured that he was in range, he opened up.

The heavy roar of the twenty shook the small gunship. Rat's first rounds fell short and off to the right. He nudged the cyclic back a hair and over to the left to correct his aim.

This time, the bright red tracers reached out and disappeared into the side of the boat. Small puffs of dirty gray smoke appeared on the hull when the H.E. shells exploded. The crew of the Fifty One swung their gun around to bring it to bear on him, but he ignored it. Blazing green tracers swept past his cockpit. He kept firing into the hull of the craft.

With a tremendous explosion, the patrol boat disappeared into a huge orange-and-black fireball that engulfed the entire vessel. His 20mm cannon's armor-piercing and incendiary shells had found the fuel tanks. Pieces of patrol boat, antiaircraft guns, and bodies flew into the air. Very small pieces.

Rat hauled back on the cyclic to climb away from flying

160

debris. Glancing over his shoulder as he turned, he saw that one of his Hueys was trailing smoke and flame from its turbine.

"Mayday, mayday," he heard Warlokk's calm voice on the radio. "Python Niner Two, hit and going down."

Russian air-force Colonel Yuri Yakanov leaned back in his bamboo wicker chair and lit another one of his long, filtered black Russian tobacco cigarettes. "Thank you for the refreshments, Colonel Duc. Now perhaps we should get down to business, no?"

For the last half hour, the three men had sat in Duc's day room in one of the temple's side chambers. So far nothing of importance had been discussed. The Russian colonel had rambled on endlessly about life back in Hanoi and other pleasantries while he drank Duc's good Russian vodka.

Captain Zerinski sat off to one side, nursing a drink and never taking his wolflike gray eyes off the North Vietnamese.

Duc had said almost nothing during this time, only replying when it was necessary. He felt like a mouse in a trap and could barely contain his anger. He knew that the Russians had not flown all the way down into Cambodia to pay him a social visit, they had something more important on their minds. Duc felt that the Russian colonel was toying with him, and it angered him.

He knew Yakanov. He had flown with him back at the airtest center, but he had no idea who Zerinski really was. He wore the badge of an aviator, but he had the eyes and mannerisms of a KGB agent.

The stocky Russian colonel blew out a lungful of smoke and leaned forward across the table. "Now, Colonel, I think that we should talk about a missing helicopter that is the property of the glorious Red Air Force and the heroic Soviet people."

The Vietnamese started to speak, but the Russian raised his hand. "I have not finished, Colonel." His voice was cold.

"But if that missing machine is logged out to a pilot who is making test flights for us, then it is not missing, is it?"

Colonel Yakanov sat back with a big smile on his broad Slavic face. Duc wasn't sure if he trusted a smiling Russian bear, but he had no other choice but to go along with him for now. At least until he found out what Yakanov really wanted.

"The records of my flights and the results of the weapons tests are available for your review," the North Vietnamese replied calmly.

"Excellent! I have had glowing reports of your 'tests,' but that is not the same as actually talking to you about it, one pilot to another, now is it?"

Duc had to agree.

"The first thing that we must discuss is your combat with the American Cobra helicopter. I am very interested in that enemy machine and I think that your combat experience with it can be very helpful to our gunship development program."

Now Duc was really taken aback. That aerial battle had been fought only three days ago. How had Yakanov learned of it so soon?

The Russian read the expression on his face and laughed. "Colonel Duc, do not look so surprised. Did you really think that I would let one of my helicopters get away from me completely?"

Yakanov laughed openly. "I have known exactly where you were from the moment that you first touched down here. Also, I have followed your missions every time you went up. I applaud your many successes, Colonel. We have learned quite a bit of useful information from the missions you have flown."

He took another drink and leaned forward in his chair. His voice lost all its humor. "Now, however, I think that it is time that you get a little more serious about your work."

"How can you say that?" Duc shot back, straightening up in his chair. "I am always serious about killing Yankees!"

"Please, Colonel," the Russian said, raising his hand. "Spare me. Everyone is well aware of your intense hatred for the Americans. But sometimes you let it cloud your better judgment.''

Now Duc was deeply offended. ''And how is that?''

''Your raid across the border to strafe that American infantry company is a good case in point. You should have never allowed yourself to take that risk.''

''But, I killed many Yankees and . . .''

''You only killed six men,'' the Russian officer said angrily, stabbing his finger at Duc's chest. ''Six men. Several others were wounded, but only six died.''

Duc was stunned. He was certain that he had caused more damage than that. What had gone wrong?

''And,'' the Russian continued, a grim look on his face, ''because you could not contain your hate, you brought attention to yourself. Very unwelcome attention, I might add. The Americans are working overtime trying to find your base here. And when they find it, I am afraid that your usefulness to us will be over. They intend to kill you and destroy your machine.''

Duc's thin face showed his anger. ''We will see who is killed,'' he spat. ''They dare not attack me from the air because of the danger of damaging the temple. And my base is well guarded against ground attack.''

''But,'' the Russian continued as if he hadn't heard a word that Duc had said, ''I have come up with a plan to avoid that unpleasantness.''

''And what is that?''

''First, we are going to finish the repairs on your machine in the morning. The parts that your mechanics need are in the cargo compartment of my helicopter. Then you and I are going to fly out of here to another location that has been prepared for us. After we arrive, other helicopter gunships will join us and we will start using them properly. No more of these mad-dog tactics of yours, going out all alone.''

Duc bristled at the Russian's inadvertent use of his nickname. ''I have done well, flying alone!''

Again the Russian officer ignored his outburst. ''You will start flying and working with other helicopters like the Americans do with theirs. You may hate the Yankees, Colonel, but you have to admit that they are the masters of helicopter warfare. If we are to learn how to use our helicopters efficiently, for now we have to copy what they are doing.''

Duc raged inside but he said nothing.

"Well," Yakanov said, getting to his feet. "Let us relax this evening, so that we will be refreshed for our flight in the morning."

The Russian flyer had a leer on his face. "I understand, Colonel, that you will be able to provide us with entertainment for the evening, and I am looking forward to it."

He rubbed his hands together in anticipation. "Since coming to your country, I have learned to fully appreciate some of the finer things that Asia has to offer a man."

He threw his thickly muscled arm over the small Vietnamese's shoulder. "I have always preferred my entertainment to be well experienced, if you know what I mean. But Captain Zerinski here, he prefers to be able to play the role of the instructor. Rather like you do yourself. Or so I am told."

Duc boiled inside at this reference to his tastes for virgins, but he kept his tongue. It was no time to lose his temper. He would have his revenge for these insults later.

"I am certain that something can be arranged to suit both of your tastes."

"Excellent, excellent." The Colonel beamed his approval. "I am looking forward to it."

From the other side of the room Zerinski smiled as well, but his gray wolf's eyes never changed expression.

CHAPTER 22

Over the South China Sea

"Lance! You're on fire! Get out!" Gaines called to the pilot of the stricken bird.

The flames shooting back from Niner Two's turbine had spread and were rapidly engulfing the cargo compartment, but Warlokk flew on. He dropped lower over the water until his skids were almost brushing the wavetops. Gaines saw the left-hand-side cockpit door came open as Warlook's crew jumped into the water.

It looked like both the co-pilot and the crew chief made it safely, but the gooks in the fishing boats produced AKs from the bottoms of their crafts and started shooting at them in the water.

"Get 'em, Joe!" Rat yelled up to his gunner. He slammed his gunship into a turn and bore down on the cluster of smaller boats. Alphabet opened up with the minigun and the thumper in the turret. Each time that his rounds found a target, he swung the turret into another fishing boat and continued firing. Behind him, Rat was using his new twenty-mike-mike cannon with deadly effect again.

The water churned from the explosions of the thumper

grenades and the cannon shells. The smaller boats and the men in them came apart in the heavy-fire storm. The waves were churned into a bloody foam.

Warlokk's wing man was also firing at the fishing boat as he followed the burning chopper down. Between the two blazing gunships, they managed to clear an area around the two men in the water.

When the enemy fire stopped, the third ship of the gun team swooped down and came to a hover over the waves. The two men scrambled up onto the skids and were helped into the rear compartment.

By this time, Warlokk's burning gunship had started bucking and flailing around in the sky. The fire was eating at the hydraulic systems of the flight controls. Gaines could see Lance in the cockpit fighting to keep his machine under control.

Warlokk had stayed with the ship too long. He was stuck and couldn't bail out. The chopper was so unstable that the second he took his hands off the controls, it started to tumble out of control. If he tried to jump out, it would fall out of the sky right on top of him.

All the pilot could do was ride the burning Huey down and hope that it didn't explode in mid-air. It looked like Warlokk was trying to make it to the beach, but Rat didn't think that the flaming chopper would hold together that long. If the fuel tanks didn't explode, the ammunition cans in the cargo compartment would.

"Lance," he radioed. "You've got to get out. The fire's out of control, you're not going to make it to the beach! Put her down in the water!"

Gaines saw Warlokk shoot a quick look over his shoulder at the roaring inferno behind him. That seemed to decide the issue for him. He nosed his chopper over and aimed it for the ocean.

Rat flew after him and was only a hundred meters away when Warlokk tried to flare out above the waves to kill his forward momentum. But Lance's luck had finally run out. The Huey impacted heavily into the water.

166

The chopper lurched to one side and the still-spinning rotor blades cut into the waves. With a second splash, the chopper flipped over onto its left side and started sinking fast.

Through the spray kicked up by the crash, Rat saw the pilot struggling with his shoulder harness. The impact had spread burning JP fuel on the water and it engulfed the cockpit.

Rat flared out above the rapidly sinking wreckage, and went into a hover. The blast of air from his rotors flattened the waves and blew the flames away from the cockpit. They saw Warlokk struggle out of the pilot's door and fall into the water.

"Tell him to swim away from it," Gaines yelled up to his gunner. "We'll pick him up on the skids."

Alphabet opened the side of the canopy to the front cockpit and shouted down to the pilot. "Lance! Lance! Grab onto the skids!"

Warlokk couldn't hear his shout over the roar of the rotor blast. He foundered around in the water, headed away from them and disappeared beneath the waves.

"Rat," Alphabet yelled, slipping out of his shoulder harness. "I'm going after him."

The gunner ripped his helmet off. Opening the canopy wider against the downblast of the rotors, he climbed onto the skid of the hovering Cobra and dove into the water. He came to the surface, oriented himself, and dove back down after Warlokk.

This time, he came up with the unconscious pilot in his arms. Gaines maneuvered the Cobra down even lower until the skids were touching the water. Alphabet paddled up to the hovering gunship. Holding one arm tightly around Warlokk's waist, he hooked the other one up over the Cobra's skid.

"Take it up, Rat!" he yelled up to the pilot.

Gaines feathered the pitch controls, coming up on the collective ever so slightly. The Cobra rose a few feet into the air, bringing the men up out of the water. He lifted the tail of the bird and nudged forward slightly on the cyclic. The Cobra started flying forward.

If Rat Gaines had ever needed a delicate touch on the controls of a helicopter, this was the time. Alphabet's percarious hold on the skid was the only thing keeping the two men alive. He wasn't sure that Warlokk could survive another drop into the sea.

Warlokk's wing man had seen the rescue and flew cover for the Cobra as it inched its way toward the beach a little over a mile away.

"Eight four," Gaines radioed. "This is Lead. Get your crew chief and co-pilot ready to make a water pickup if Alphabet falls off my skid. Warlokk's hurt, so you're going to have to get to him first."

"This is Eight four. Roger, copy. We're ready."

"Also, call for a priority Dustoff to meet us on the beach, over."

"Lead, this is Eight Four. Why don't I take him back myself? I can get him there faster than if we wait for the Dustoff. Over."

"This is Lead, good point. Get ready to haul him on board as soon as I drag 'em onto the beach."

"Roger, that."

The Cobra reached the surf line and Rat brought her down until Warlokk's boots were dragging in the stuff. As soon as they touched the wet sand, he came to a hover and gently lowered the ship all the way down. Alphabet turned loose of the skid and stood on the beach, holding Warlokk in his arms.

In a flash, Eight Four was on the ground. The co-pilot and crew chief dashed across the beach to take the wounded pilot from Alphabet's arms. Running back to their ship, they loaded him on board and were back up into the air in mere seconds.

A wet and weary Alphabet climbed back into his cockpit and put his helmet on. "Anytime you're ready, Rat." he called back. "Let's go home."

"Roger, pulling pitch now."

As *Sudden Discomfort* rose back up into the sky, Gaines

called forward on the intercom. "How 'bout a cold one? It's on me."

"That's the best idea I've heard in the last ten minutes or so."

"Just let me make one last pass over our fishermen and we'll head on back to the club."

"Roger."

There wasn't much to see on the water. All that was left of the VC fotilla was bits and pieces of wood and debris and a few bodies that hadn't sunken beneath the waves. Already, the sharks were moving in to feed.

Rat turned the nose of his ship for An Khe.

At 1800 hours, Lieutenant Vance assembled the men for their briefing. Everyone had stripped down to just their weapons, ammunition, and canteens and had painted their faces and hands with camouflage grease-paint sticks. They were stripped for fast-moving action, but if for some reason they couldn't get back to the gear they had stashed they were going to be in a world of hurt.

"Okay, here it is, men," Vance said. "We're going to kick off from here about nine o'clock or so. Sergeant Wilburn and Macmillan will be taking point with Specialist Metcack in slack. Broken Arrow will take the drag with Gardner. I'll be in the middle with Rabdo as my RTO."

"Once we get down off the mountain here, we'll head west until we hit the river. Then we're going to go south down the river bed to here." He pointed to a small clearing along the river west of the big temple.

"This is supposed to be the boat landing for the temple. From there we are going to go right straight through the temple complex, blow up the chopper, shoot up anybody who gets in our way, and get out of there as fast as we can. Once we're out, we'll return here, secure our equipment, and I'll see if I can get us extracted by chopper tomorrow morning.

"Now, we're all going to stay together in one group, and this is not going to be a John Wayne operation. We're going to try to do this without anyone seeing us, but if they do spot us, we'll have to hit 'em as hard as we can and get the hell out of there fast. Any questions so far?''

"I can't swim, sir," one of the men piped up. Vance turned and saw that it was Bunny Rabdo, his artillery FO.

Laughter broke out.

"No, goddamnit, I mean it!" Bunny said angrily. "I can't swim, I'm afraid of the water.

Vance looked at him. Rabdo had come to him highly recommended, so this had to be for real. Just what he needed, another complication.

"Okay, Rabdo, I'll talk to you about that later. Anyone else have any questions?"

There were several more questions, and the officer discussed each of them. Vance had finally learned to run an open outfit. He had discovered that he got the best from his people when they knew exactly what was going on. Back at West Point he had been taught to be a believer in blind military obedience. The realities of handling troops in the Nam had finally gotten through.

"Now, we're going to try to put fused explosives on that helicopter to give us a little time to get away. But if we're discovered on the way in, Gardner, you and Broken Arrow are going to have to take it out with your seventy-nines. Just about any place that you hit will put it out of action for a while, but I want it taken out for good. I want you to keep shooting as many times as you can until it catches on fire. Are there any more questions about any of this?"

"Is is too late to get a transfer, sir?" a small voice came from the back of the group. Farmer had finally realized that this was not going to be fun trip. Everyone, including the platoon leader, laughed.

"I'll tell you what, Burns, if you can get it worked out before dark, let me know, I'll go with you," he said, making one of his rare jokes.

When the briefing was over, Vance took Bunny off to the side to talk to him. The short New Yorker looked miserable.

"Lieutenant," he said, "I'm not trying to get out of anything. I really am afraid of water. You know how some people are afraid of heights? Well, I'm the same way about water. Anything more than a bathtubful gives me the shakes. I just can't go down the river, sir. Can I walk down the bank beside the other guys?''

It was obvious to Vance that the man was telling the truth. He wondered what the hell he was going to do now. He couldn't leave him behind to guard the gear because they might not be able to get back. He couldn't let him walk down the river bank like he had suggested, either. There was too great a chance of him running into someone there.

Suddenly he had an idea. ''Look, Rabdo, I can't leave you behind or let you walk down the river bank, either. It's just too dangerous. How do you feel about boats?''

''Boats, sir?''

''Yeah. Boats.''

''I haven't been in too many boats, sir. Just a rowboat in Central Park. It's scary, but it's a little better. I don't completely lose it.''

''I'll see what I can do about finding you a boat.''

''If you say so, sir.''

Vance went to find Wilburn. The Special Forces taught their people all sorts of ways to improvise things. Maybe he knew how to make a boat out of banana leaves or something like that.

Wilburn laughed when the officer brought him Bunny's problem. ''No sweat at all, sir. All you have to do is find one of your men with an air mattress in his ruck. They make real good boats for river crossings.''

Vance was angry with himself for not having thought of that solution in the first place. It was one of the field expedients that they had been taught in patrolling classes back at the Point, but it had slipped his mind.

''Good idea, Sergeant. I'm sure that somebody brought an air mattress.''

''Yes, sir, someone has to have his rubber date with him.''

When Vance went off to find one, Wilburn sat back next to his buddy, Jim Macmillan.

171

"What do you think of our young ell tee?" Macmillan asked.

"Oh, I'd say that he's about typical," Wilburn replied. "He's probably okay if there's someone around to tell him what to do. But I've got to admit that I'm not too happy about Captain Ringer not being here to take us into that temple."

"That's a big rodg. We could really use old Lightning Larry right about now."

"Well, fuck it. He ain't here, and that leg ell tee is."

"That's what I'm afraid of."

"What's the matter, Mac, you want to live forever?"

"Fuck you, Wilburn."

CHAPTER 23

Kangor Wat, Cambodia

As the sun went down over the jungle surrounding the ancient stone temple, the monkeys ceased their chatter and settled down for the night.

Inside the Cambodians' mess hall, the Khmer troops who had guard duty that night hurriedly finished their evening meals and fell in outside their barracks for the nightly inspection. The young Cambodian sub-lieutenant in charge of the small infantry detachment carefully checked each man's weapons and equipment to make sure that he was more than ready.

With Colonel Duc's Russian visitors spending the night in the compound, absolutely nothing could be allowed to go wrong. Not if the young Cambodian officer wanted to see the sun come up in the morning.

His inspection completed, the officer turned the guard over to the Khmer NCO who marched the men out to their guard posts. The lieutenant went back to his command post and started making communication checks. It was going to be a long night.

Inside the temple, Duc had produced several more bottles

of his rationed vodka as well as the women the Russian aviators had requested, and they were well on their way to having a party.

The Russians poured vodka down like water, but Duc was only drinking tea. He knew better then to get even a little drunk around them. Anger was a better intoxicant than the strongest liquor, anyway. And the North Vietnamese was very angry.

The older woman with Colonel Yakanov was enjoying the strong spirits the Russian kept forcing on her. She laughed loudly at his crude caresses. The younger girl with Captain Zerinski, however, was panicking. She had never been around a western man before and she was deathly afraid. Her dark eyes kept darting over to Duc as if he could protect her from the Russian, but in vain. She belonged to the Russian tonight, body and soul, and he would do with her as he pleased.

Watching the two blond Russian men with the Cambodian women reminded Duc of his college days back in Seattle. Particularly when he saw Zerinski openly fondling the young virgin as casually as if she was a common whore. He was not even giving her the time that a virgin needed to accustom herself to his advances. The Russians were as openly shameless about sex as American college boys had been, and Duc had to look away.

Though he tried to keep a friendly smile on his face for his guests, inside Duc seethed. He had been saving the young Cambodian beauty for himself. Since he did not have the time to make other arrangements for the men, he had had no choice but to hand her over to the cold, gray-eyed Russian officer. When Zerinski was done with the girl, Duc would send her back to her village or down to the troop barracks. After tonight's experiences, she would be of no further use to him.

As he watched the Russians, Duc realized that like the Americans, they, too, were barbaric pigs with no idea of civilized behavior. Their only saving grace was that they were Communist barbarians.

Duc could endure being around the Russians only because

174

of all that their country had given him, not only his education and his pilot's training, but the combat aircraft that made up his nation's air force. He appreciated everything but he had never felt comfortable around them. Even when he had been in pilot training at their air-force academy at Morineo, he had not liked either the people or their frozen country. In fact, the only thing that he had liked about the Soviet Union was the superb weapons they made and their vodka.

He could put up with the boorish manners of his two guests tonight, with the stench of their sweat and their light-colored animal eyes. He could do that because they had provided the helicopter that he used to strike at the Americans. Even had the Russians been worse barbarians than they actually were, he would have patiently endured them—only because they were the enemies of his enemy.

"Oh, Colonel," Yakanov called over to him. "You do not look like you are enjoying yourself tonight. You should have gotten a woman for yourself, too."

Duc looked up to see the Russian officer leaning back in his chair. His pants were undone and the Cambodian whore had her face in his lap. Her head was slowly moving up and down.

"As soon as this one is done with me," Yakanov said. "I am sure that she will be more than happy to service you as well."

Duc got to his feet. "If you two gentlemen will excuse me, I must make my evening inspection of the guard posts."

The Russian soldier laughed.

The ten-man American raiding party snaked down the side of the volcanic mountain in the darkness. When they reached the plains, they moved into patrol formation and headed west to the river. They moved silently but quickly through the thick underbrush, anxious to reach it.

At the river bank, they paused long enough to inflate the air mattress that would be Bunny's raft.

"Here you go, Admiral," Wilburn whispered. He pushed

the makeshift boat out into the water, holding onto it with one hand.

"Oh, shit." Bunny looked panicky. He took a deep breath and lay down on it while the rest of the men slipped into the river. Gardner grabbed onto the side of the mattress. "I got ya," he said softly. "Just lay back and enjoy it."

Bunny shivered and closed his eyes so he couldn't see the dark water inches from his face. He tried hard not to think about drowning.

They moved slowly through the waist-high water, the rippling of the river covering the slight sounds of their passage. Since the water retained the heat of the sun, it was not uncomfortable. In fact it was almost pleasant.

The Indian sniper was up at the point position with Sergeant Wilburn. He used the Starlite, mounted on his rifle, to scope out the banks on either side, since the local trails ran parallel to the river.

The main body trailed about a hundred meters behind the point and out of sight. Since they were in the river, they couldn't get lost, and they needed to have the extra distance to get away in case the point element got into trouble.

The moon had not come up yet, so it was pitch black. The limbs of the trees overhanging the banks prevented even the faint light of the stars from breaking up the darkness. By keeping to the middle of the stream, the grunts had little trouble staying clear of the tangled brush along the banks.

In a little over an hour, the point reached a wide spot in the river that served as the boat landing for the temple. By then, the moon had risen, casting a silvery light on the clearing. The main body halted and pulled into the brush on the bank. Chief and Wilburn went ahead to check out the landing.

When the two men got to the edge of the cleared area, they saw a small guard shack at the side of a road leading down to the river. They hid back in the brush, their camouflage uniforms making them all but invisible against the shadows. The sniper scoped out the area around the landing.

"All I see is that one guard," Chief whispered to the Green Beret. "The one over across the road."

"Can you take him out from here?"

"Is a pig's pussy pork?"

Wilburn bit back a laugh. "Now that you mention it."

The sniper threw the scoped rifle up to his shoulder. Resting the forestock against a low-hanging limb, he ranged in the Starlite and took up the trigger slack. He took a deep breath, held it, and was just starting to squeeze the trigger when he heard voices coming down the road to their left.

He instantly released the trigger and froze in place. Beside him, Wilburn crouched a little lower in the water. The silvery figures of three men walked up and stopped in front of the guard shack.

One of the men barked out a sharp command, and the guard scrambled out of the shack to stand rigidly at attention in the moonlight. One of the men spoke sharply to the guard, and the soldier answered apologetically.

Wilburn recognized the language as Cambodian, but he wasn't close enough to catch what they said.

The guard then saluted, and the three men turned around and headed back down the road. When they were out of sight, the guard relaxed a little but remained standing outside the shack.

Three minutes passed. Wilburn bent over and whispered, "Take him."

This time, the silenced XM-21 sniper rifle spat. Three hundred meters away, the Khmer guard slumped to the ground, a 7.62mm bullet in his head. The faint clatter of the AK-47 falling from his lifeless hands was the only sound.

Like a shadow, Wilburn climbed quickly up the muddy bank and dashed across the road. Chief saw him check the guard's body and then duck into the bamboo shack. He came out a moment later and looked down the road. It was clear. He motioned for the Indian to join him.

Chief turned around and repeated the motion to the men behind him before he ran across the road and took a firing position in the shadow of the shack covering the approaches.

One by one, the raiders silently climbed the bank and fanned out in the brush on both sides of the dirt road leading back to the temple. Lieutenant Vance ran up and crouched down beside Wilburn. The sergeant pointed down the trail and stuck up two fingers. He wanted to take another man down the road with him and scout out the defenses. The lieutenant nodded his approval.

Wilburn ran over to where the other Green Beret crouched and waved him to follow. Macmillan got to his feet and started up the trail.

The rest of the men settled back to wait for their return. Vance was nervous. He didn't like having Wilburn gone. His plan seemed like a good idea back up on the mountain, but now he wasn't so sure. They had really hung their asses out in the wind. They didn't have half enough information about the base they were hitting and there were too many things that could go wrong. He shivered as the night breeze cooled his wet uniform.

Vance wasn't the only one who was a little nervous about what was going to happen next. Treat Brody had an unusual sense of foreboding. He had been in far worse situations than this a dozen times and he usually kept a cool head. But for some reason, this was just a little too spooky for him. Maybe it was the eerie effect of the moonlight shining through the trees and turning the jungle into a mottle of silvery gray and dead black. Maybe it was just knowing that they were probably biting off more than they could chew.

Whatever it was, Brody kept glancing over his shoulder as if he were expecting something to come up from behind and bite at any moment. He clenched his hand around the pistol grip of his M-16 a little tighter and unconsciously rested his thumb on the selector switch at the side of the receiver.

One twitch of his thumb, and the weapon was on rock and roll.

Colonel Duc took his time about inspecting the guard posts. He was in no hurry to have to go back inside the temple and watch the two Russian officers rutting like animals. For once he was pleased with what he had seen of the guards. Except for the soldier at the boat landing, who had been inside his guard shack instead of standing outside, everything was in good order. When he got back to the command post, he complimented the young guard officer.

"The men looked very good tonight, Comrade Lieutenant. Everyone, that is, except for the guard at the boat landing. See that he is properly punished in the morning."

Duc left the command post and wandered over to the two big Mi-8 helicopters parked under the camouflage netting. The dappled moonlight filtering through the net made them look like monsters from a bad dream, demons crouching.

He thought of what the Russian colonel had said about flying his gunship in coordination with other helicopters as a fire team. He knew that Yakanov was tactically correct, but he still preferred to work alone as he had done all along.

The gunship team concept that the Yankees used was a good one, but it was for other pilots to use, not him. It lacked emotional satisfaction. He wanted to hunt the enemy down by himself and he was not willing to share his kills with anyone. Even if it meant that there would be fewer dead Yankees, there was more pleasure in it for him. He saw their blood flow by his own hands, and his alone.

He walked over to the edge of the cleared chopper pad and looked out into the moonlit jungle. In the cool of the night, the place didn't stink like it did in the heat of the day. He missed the mountain breezes of his father's summer home and would be glad to leave this jungle hellhole. He hoped that Yankanov's new base was somewhere not as hot and stifling.

He was turning to go back when he heard a faint clinking of metal in the trees to his left. He froze in place and listened. There it was again.

There were no guard posts in that area. Someone was out there but it was not one of his men.

He ducked behind the helicopters and crouched low in the shadow of his own gunship. Reaching down to his belt, he

179

drew a Chinese-made Tokarov pistol. He slowly pulled back the slide to chamber a round and peered around the side of the chopper's fuselage, listening intently.

CHAPTER 24

Kangor Wat, Cambodia

"We found where they're keeping the chopper," Sergeant Wilburn whispered to Lieutenant Vance when he reported back from his reconnaissance of the temple area. "But we've got us a little bit of a problem. There's two of 'em there now."

"Two helicopters?"

"Yes, sir. They're parked in a cleared area to the left of the temple as you go in, and they're going to be a real bitch to get at."

Vance was afraid of that. "Okay, what's the layout?"

Wilburn drew his Randall knife from a sheath that was taped upside down on his assault harness. Kneeling beside the lieutenant, he drew a rough diagram in the dirt on the moonlit road.

"This road here leads into the temple. It's about a klick and a half further down. To the left of the big temple is a cluster of small bamboo buildings. One of them is that mess hall you showed me on the aerial photo, and I think that the other one is a barracks. There's a fuel dump right next to the temple and what I think is the ammo storage area.

181

"Now here's where we're going to have the problem. The choppers are parked right next to the side of the temple, boxed in by the barracks and the supply dump. The only way we can get a clear shot at them is to go straight down the road. And we don't stand a chance in hell of doing it that way."

"Where are their defensive positions?"

"They're pretty well set up for a bunch of gooks hiding in the jungle. We spotted two machine-gun bunkers right in front of the temple covering the road with interlocking fields of fire. Their outer perimeter is in the jungle about three hundred meters away from the temple. And their positions are well concealed. We almost ran into one of them on our way in.

"If we still had the RPGs with us, we could go down the road, take out the bunkers, and then have a straight shot in to blast the choppers. But we're not going to be able to do that with thumper grenades. They don't have the range. It looks like we have to sneak in through the jungle, bypass their positions, get right in close to the choppers, and take them out with hand grenades. Getting out, however, is going to be a real bitch."

"Do you think we can do it?"

Wilburn hesitated for a moment. "To be honest with you, sir, we might as well just shoot ourselves right now and get it over with. We can probably get in, but I don't think we'll ever get out. As soon as we hit the choppers, all hell's going to break loose. That barracks probably holds twenty or thirty men, and I have no idea how many are inside the temple. Any way you slice it, we'll be right in the middle of more gooks than I think we can handle."

"Ell tee," Brody cut in. "I think I've got a plan."

"What that?" Vance was willing to listen to him tonight, because he was all out of ideas.

"I know that you don't want to split us up, but I agree with the sarge. If we try to go in the way we planned, we're going to get all sorts of fucked up. We need a diversion, something to draw the gooks away from the choppers."

"That might not be a bad idea," Wilburn agreed. "What'd you have in mind?"

"Well, Sarge, why don't me, you, and maybe a couple more of the guys sneak around through the woods and try to come in from the side. There's a better chance of four or five of us making it in undetected than if we all try to go together."

"That's a good point," Vance had to admit.

"Then, Ell tee, you can take the rest of them and make a probing attack down the road. That'll draw most of the gooks over to your area and give us a chance to sneak in close and blow up the choppers. We can *di-di* out the back, and you guys can pull back by the river. We can all meet back at the mountain when it's over."

Vance looked over at Wilburn. "What do you think, Sergeant?"

"Well," he rubbed the back of his neck. "It's still dicey, but it'll probably work better than if we all try to infiltrate in one group."

Vance glanced down at his watch. "It's almost twenty-two hundred hours. How long do you think it'll take you to get into place?"

Wilburn thought for a moment. "Why don't you give us an hour. Plan to start your attack at twenty-three hundred. We'll wait until we hear you firing before we make our move for the choppers. If you can keep 'em busy for ten or fifteen minutes, we should be able to get in and get the job done."

"Okay, Brody," the lieutenant turned to him. "Who do you want to take with you?"

"How 'bout Two-Step and Jungle Jim, sir. JJ's got one of the radios and a seventy-nine. That'll give you Corky on the M-Sixty and Two-Step can trade his thumper for someone's sixteen so you'll have a seventy-nine with you, too."

"Is that going to give you enough firepower?"

"Don't forget me, Brody," Wilburn said. "I've got my over-and-under, so we'll have two grenade launchers with us."

"That sounds okay," the officer said. "Get your people ready."

"Yeah," Wilburn said, getting to his feet and sheathing his knife. "We'd better get moving, Brody. We're going to need all the time we can get to move into position."

Colonel Duc waited in the darkness by the side of the helicopter for several minutes, his heart pounding. He heard nothing more from the shadowy jungle.

He was almost ready to dismiss the clanking noise as having been made by monkeys. Suddenly he remembered what Colonel Yakanov had told him about the Yankees frantically trying to locate his gunship base.

He had not given much credence to Yakanov's statement at the time, but he quickly convinced himself that the Russian was right. The noises he had heard in the jungle were Yankees coming to kill him.

The thought that Americans would dare to violate the sanctuary of neutral Cambodia made him furious, but that they were coming after him had the colonel almost foaming at the mouth. They would live only long enough to regret it. He vowed to destroy every last one of them. As Duc hurried back to his command post, he thanked the goddess of good fortune who had led him outside the temple this evening.

He wasn't going to let the Russians know what he had heard, however. Colonel Yakanov would never believe him and would only laugh. Even though the Russian was the one who had warned him, he would think Duc was panicking.

There was no doubt in the North Vietnamese's mind that Yankees were out there. He could feel them hiding in the jungle, just as he had always been able to tell when the students at the university were laughing behind his back.

He broke into a run.

The Cambodian officer of the guard was startled when Duc came bursting into the command post.

"Yankees," the colonel panted. "There are Yankees in the jungle around us."

184

The lieutenant reached for the handle of a hand-cranked alert siren.

"No!" Duc snarled, slapping his hand away. "Pass the word quietly. I do not want them to know that we are ready for them."

"Yes, Comrade Colonel."

The officer called for his runners and told them to pass the word to all the guard posts. The lieutenant was careful to keep the expression on his face completely neutral, but he was thinking that the mad-dog colonel had finally gone completely out of his paranoid mind.

Well aware that he was under Duc's critical eye, the lieutenant knew he had to keep busy. He picked up the field phone and rang through to all the machine-gun posts, telling them to keep an extra-sharp eye out for intruders.

Finally, he tried to ring through to the guard house on the river bank. The phone rang and rang, but no one answered it. Maybe the guard was outside taking a piss. He would try again in a couple of minutes.

"Everyone has been notified of the alert, Colonel," he said, being careful to speak with respect. "What are your orders now?"

"We wait," Duc answered, peering into the jungle beyond the temple grounds. "They are out there, I can smell them. But we will wait for them to come to us." He laughed. "Yes, they will come to us."

Back in the temple, the Russian's party was winding down. The colonel's whore lay on her back, snoring. The vodka he had poured down her throat had finally knocked her out, but not before she had serviced the bearlike Russian several times. The young Cambodian girl sat with her head in her hands, sobbing quietly. She was also trying not to move, hoping that the pain in her lower belly would go away.

She had known that there would be pain when she finally lost her virginity, all the village women had spoken of that, but the experience had been far more painful than she thought

185

it would be. The Russian's male member was the biggest thing she had ever seen between a man's legs. She wondered if all Western men were equipped that way. If they were, she felt very sorry for their women.

"Well, Zerinski," the colonel said in Russian. "What do you think of our 'comrade,' Colonel Duc."

"That slant-eyed little bastard really is a mad dog. Did you see how he was looking at me when I was trying to get that girl warmed up a little?"

Yakanov laughed. "You probably took his pet piece of ass. Well, she'll be of no use to any of these scrawny little bastards now that you have broken her in. You might as well take her back with us. She ought to be good for a couple more weeks."

"That's not a bad idea, comrade."

"How soon do you think we can get out of this pest hole tomorrow?" Yakanov asked.

"At least by noon. From what I understand, the machine is not too badly damaged. At least we can get it up in the air and fly it back to the new base where our own mechanics can go over it thoroughly."

"What are you going to do about Duc?" the younger officer asked.

Yakanov grinned. "Well, I am afraid that the colonel is going to find himself meeting the fate of all mad dogs. He is just too dangerous to be allowed to run free. He stole that helicopter from me once and he is likely to do it again. So, I am afraid that I have no choice. He must be eliminated."

"It is fortunate that my agent was in place in Pol Pot's headquarters when he showed up with it."

"Yes, it was. If he had not been there, we would have never known where he went. Your KGB people should work on getting even more agents into operation."

"I know, Comrade Colonel, but it is very difficult to find Vietnamese that we can trust. Even the ones who call themselves Communists are not trustworthy. All these slant-eyed bastards are the same. They steal from their mothers' graves."

"I know. It's no wonder that the Americans in Saigon cannot keep a secret. Everytime they tell the Vietnamese about one of their operations, they run to sell the information to the highest bidder."

"I know that I will be very glad to get back to working in Europe. At least the agents that I buy there stay bought. These treacherous bastards have no loyalties at all."

"But for now, Comrade Captain, we need them to keep the Chinese worried."

"Another bunch of treacherous slant-eyed bastards. It is fortunate for us that the Vietnamese and Chinese have been enemies for hundreds of years."

"It does keep them busy with each other most of the time and gives us a place to test our weaponry. You have to admit that the Americans have brought quite a few ingenious weapons systems over here, and it's nice to have a chance to see how they work."

"We need a war ourselves, Colonel, somewhere like this where we can update our weapons and tactics."

"I know. It has been too long since the glorious Red Army has had the opportunity for a 'live-fire exercise.' That is why we are here."

"But this is a pest hole, Comrade, and this is not even a decent war."

"I know, I know. But this is the only place we have now. And it could be worse. There are more miserable places in the world. You should be stationed in the Middle East for a while. And while we are here, we can amuse ourselves by enjoying the good things that this part of Asia has to offer. In the Arabic countries, all the women reek of sheep fat."

"Speaking of that, Colonel, would you like to sample this whore?" Zerinski looked toward the young Cambodian girl.

"No, thank you. I have had about all the excitement that this old body can handle for one evening. But don't let me stop you. Go right ahead."

"Thank you, I think I will." Zerinski turned to the girl and motioned for her to come.

CHAPTER 25

Kangor Wat, Cambodia

Macmillan led Lieutenant Vance's assault group through the thick brush at the side of the road. Vance followed only a few meters behind, trying not to lose him in the deep shadows. From what Wilburn had said about his recon of the temple, the enemy machine-gun bunkers were just around the bend in the dirt road. The officer went to ground when he saw Macmillan stop and crouch in the shadows.

The officer remembered his military-history classes back at West Point. The instructor, an infantry lieutenant-colonel who was a veteran of both World War II and Korea, was fond of reminding his students that a plan of battle, no matter how well thought out, rarely survives the initial contact with the enemy. Vance hoped that this would be an exception to that rule of warfare.

He turned around and motioned for the men behind him to fan out on their side of the road. The Indian sniper slipped beside him and checked out the area to their front with his sniper scope. He tapped the officer on the leg and pointed to a shadowy area off to his right front.

Vance peered out across the moonlit road into the darkness, but he couldn't make out a thing. He turned back to the sniper and shrugged his shoulders. Chief handed him the rifle and motioned for him to look through the Starlite scope. Vance put the weapon up to his shoulder and brought the sight reticle to his eye.

Sighting along the barrel, the sniper gently nudged it in the right direction.

There it was! Through the ghostly green glow of the Starlite, Vance made out a roughly rectangular shape that was darker than the surrounding area. It was a bunker. He pulled his head back from the scope and located it with his naked eye.

Wilburn had said that there were two of them. Where was the other one?

Chief located it, too, and this time, Vance found it without the scope. He nodded, turned, and motioned behind him. Corky slipped beside him with his M-60 machine gun, and Farmer followed close behind with Two-Step's M-79 grenade launcher.

Vance pointed out the positions to the two grunts. Corky quietly flipped the bipod legs down and put his gun into place. Laying behind it, he zeroed in on the left bunker while Farmer lined up to fire at the one on the right. Chief focused his scope rifle on the dark aperture of one of the bunkers and waited for the lieutenant's signal.

Vance tapped him on the leg. He fired.

The soft, coughing sound of the silenced rifle was the signal for everyone else to open up on the two bunkers. In an instant, the silent, moonlit jungle was lit with machine-gun and M-16 tracer fire and the explosions of the 40-mike-mike grenades.

Corky and Chief took out the crew of the machine gun in the left-hand bunker. But Farmer's grenades fell short of their target.

The Khmer RPD machine gun in the remaining bunker opened up on them with its characteristic high-pitched chatter, delivering a withering hail of return fire. The green 7.62mm tracers were right on target.

Vance took a round high in the chest. He gave a small cry and fell over on his side.

Chief slung his silenced rifle over his shoulder and crawled over to the fallen lieutenant. In the light of the tracer fire, his Starlite scope was useless, the sensitive optics burned out by the visual light. Grabbing Vance under the arms, the sniper dragged him into the brush and laid him behind a tree trunk.

The Indian quickly checked him over. The officer was still breathing. He moaned softly when Chief pulled his fatigue jacket away from the wound. Chief put his ear next to the entry hole and listened. He could not hear air leaking from his lungs. At least he didn't have a punctured lung. He slid his hand under the wounded man, but couldn't find where the bullet had exited. That was bad. The bullet was still lodged in his body. He needed to be dusted off ASAP.

Chief quickly took the field dressing from the first-aid pouch on Vance's field belt. Ripping it out of its plastic cover, he put the plastic over the entry wound to keep air from leaking into his chest cavity. Then he tied the bandage over it. He laid the lieutenant down on the ground and tried to make him comfortable.

There was nothing else he could do.

Back in front of the bunkers, the remaining men found themselves in deep trouble. One of the Khmers had brought up an RPG-7 rocket launcher. The night was lit by the bright flash of the back blast as it launched an antitank rocket at their positions.

''RPG!'' someone screamed. The grunts buried their faces in the dirt and waited for the explosion.

The rocket overshot their position and impacted harmlessly in the jungle. But with the RPG in action, it was only a matter of time before the gooks found the correct range and dropped a round right in the middle of them.

It was time to get out of there—fast.

Macmillan ripped off a long burst from his CAR-15 submachine gun, dropped the empty magazine on the ground, slammed a fresh one into place, and pulled back on the charging handle.

"Pull back!" he yelled over the roar of the firing.

Chief reached down, slung Vance over his shoulder, and headed back for the road. He slung his sniper rifle across his back and pulled out his GI-issue .45-caliber pistol. With the heavy night scope and silencer mounted on the rifle, it was too awkward to aim and fire with one hand. The pistol was all he had to fight with now.

Corky covered Bunny and the sniper's withdrawal, his pig rapping out long bursts in the direction of the rocket launcher. As soon as they faded into the jungle, he slung the ammo belt for his sixty over his shoulder and grabbed the carrying handle on top of the smoking barrel.

Tucking the butt stock under his right arm, he fired a short burst and backed into the brush.

The flash of an exploding grenade illuminated Farmer, who was still kneeling in the open at the side of the road, still trying to put a thumper round into the last bunker.

"Move your ass, Farmer!" the machine gunner yelled at him. "Get going!"

Farmer fired off the last grenade in his bandolier and beat feet. Running down the road, he saw Macmillan covering their withdrawal and slid in beside him to lend a hand.

"Keep going!" the Green Beret yelled, triggering off another quick burst from his CAR-15. "I'll meet you at the river."

Farmer fumbled at the last thumper ammunition bandolier around his neck, pulled a 40-mike-mike round out of its plastic carrier, and slammed it into the breech of his seventy-nine. Snapping it shut with a flick of his wrist, he threw the thumper up to his shoulder and fired one last shot back down the road.

"Catch you later, Sarge," he shouted. He spun around and ran for the boat landing.

In the jungle on the other side of the temple complex, Brody, Wilburn, JJ, and Two-Step were also fighting for their lives.

It had taken them far longer than they had planned to make

their way through the jungle to the outer ring of the Khmer defenses. They had not yet gotten into position to make their run for the choppers when Vance opened up on the bunkers.

Thanks to Colonel Duc's raging paranoia, the entire perimeter was on full alert. When the firing started, every one of the Khmer troopers opened up into the jungle, shooting at shadows.

Wilburn was slightly ahead of the other three men when the shit hit the fan. At the first burst of AK fire, he dropped to the ground, pinned down in a blazing crossfire between two Khmer positions.

"Brody!" the Green Beret shouted over the roar of AKs blasting away on full automatic. "Pull back! Get you people out of here!"

Jungle Jim snapped his thumper to his shoulder and fired it like a rifle, aiming at the muzzle flashes in the jungle ahead of Wilburn.

The bright explosion shreaded the camouflage in front of the Khmer position. Someone screamed as the deadly 40mm grenade frag found a target.

Breaking the launcher open, JJ stuffed another one of the fat cartridges into the breech, snapped it shut, and fired again.

Brody threw himself behind a nearby tree when the initial burst of fire broke out. Laying the barrel of his sixteen around the side of the trunk, he put down a steady stream of covering 5.56mm fire while Two-Step sprinted up to rescue the trapped Wilburn.

Bright balls of orange flame leaped from the muzzle of the Indian's sawed-off shotgun as it roared again and again.

Another one of JJ's little thumper grenades flew into a bunker aperature and detonated the ammunition stored inside. The night was lit by the blinding flash.

For a stunned moment, the Khmers' fire stopped.

"Wilburn! Get out of there!" Two-Step yelled up to the trapped man. Pumping the shotgun's slide as fast as he could, he fired off the remaining rounds in his magazine. It sounded like the sawed-off riot gun was on full automatic fire.

Under the covering hail of Two-Step's steel ball bearings,

Wilburn jumped to his feet and dashed back into the jungle. Once he reached cover, he whirled around, fired off the thumper round in the launcher barrel of his over-and-under, flicked the rifle over to rock and roll, and laid down on the trigger.

Now it was the Indian's turn to make it back.

Two-Step rolled onto his side. Digging shotgun shells out of his belt pouch, he stuffed them into the empty magazine of his riot gun. He jacked back on the slide to load one into the chamber.

"Cover me!" he yelled as he got to his feet. He fired off three rounds as fast as he could pump the slid, spun around, and raced for safety.

Under the withering hail of full automatic fire from Brody and Wilburn's sixteens, he made it into the dense jungle.

"Get the fuck outta here!" he yelled as he passed the big tree Brody was crouched behind.

"You got that shit right!"

Covering each other as they retreated in bounds, the four grunts faded back into the darkness. Behind them, the Khmers continued to tear up the jungle, frantically firing at shadows.

Duc had trained them well.

"Don't let them get away!" Duc screamed into the field phone in his command post. "Go after them, you fools! Go after them!"

Reports had just come in to the command post that the Yankees were breaking off contact and running into the jungle. The North Vietnamese officer was so enraged that his face was flushed and his eyes bugged out. The Yankees were getting away. He threw the field phone down.

The young Cambodian lieutenant was doing his best to keep track of the progress of the battle, but he was not having an easy time of it. On top of trying to sort out the conflicting battle reports from the outposts and bunkers, he had to keep out of the way of the pistol Duc was waving around in his hand.

The colonel suddenly turned to one of the runners in the command post and screamed. "Get my gunship ready for take off. Now!"

"In the dark, sir?"

Duc slashed the barrel of his Tokarov across the man's head. "I said get my machine ready," he screamed like a woman. Droplets of spit hit the man in the face. "Right now!"

The man ran to get the colonel's crew chief.

Duc snatched a map off the table and dashed for the door. He stopped suddenly and spun around. "If they get away," he snarled at the guard officer, "you die!"

The Cambodian lieutenant shuddered and reached for the field phone again. He prayed to the good Buddha that the intruders were captured. If they were not, he would have to give serious thought to deserting.

Colonel Yakanov and Captain Zerinski stood outside the main entrance to the temple and watched the fireworks in the jungle.

"It looks like the Americans finally found him," the colonel observed.

As soon as the shooting started, the two men had armed themselves with the Stechkin machine pistols they carried in holsters on their broad leather field belts, and came out to see what was happening. Their 9mm weapons had a selective fire capability and a twenty-round magazine, making them perfect for close-in work when a submachine gun was too much to carry.

The Russian flyers kept well back in the shadows cast by the crumbling portico of the temple. They wanted to stay out of the field of fire. With the confusion of a nighttime shootout, there was too great a chance that the Cambodians would mistake them for the attacking Americans.

"Well, do you think that Duc will stay on his side of the border now?" Zerinski asked Yakanov.

"I doubt it," the colonel answered. "That is the greatest weakness about a man like him. He always lets his emotions rule common sense. He hates the Yankees so much that if they don't kill him this time, he will go after them at the first chance he has. I am afraid that I am going to have to eliminate him as soon as we get back. This commando raid is one thing, but I don't want the American air force running bombing missions against our airfields.

"If he annoys them any more, I am afraid that they just might decide to take out all the helicopter landing fields in North Vietnam to make sure that they get him. The Americans are like that. They tend to overreact when they have had enough. And I, for one, simply cannot allow that to happen. I cannot risk the lives of our gunship test team just because of a crazy man like Duc."

The Russian flyers heard the distinctive sound of the electric starter motors winding up the turbines on one of the Mi-8 helicopters. The high-pitched whine was followed closely by the wop-wopping of the big, five-bladed rotor as it came up to speed.

"That fool!" Yakanov nearly screamed. "He's going to try to go after them in the dark!"

CHAPTER 26

Kangor Wat, Cambodia

At the boat landing, the men tensely waited in a small perimeter at the river's edge. Everyone had pulled back safely except for the Special Forces sergeant, Macmillan.

Chief and Farmer had already put the wounded Lieutenant Vance on Bunny's air mattress, and they were ready to go. As soon as the Green Beret joined up with them, they would take to the water and try to make their escape.

While they waited, Bunny frantically tried to reach Sergeant Wilburn on the radio. "Bravo One, Bravo One, this is Bravo Two, over.

"Bravo One, Bravo One, this is Bravo Two, Bravo Two, come in please.

"Fuck!" The radio operator hung the handset back on his assault harness. "I can't get anybody," he told the Indian sniper.

Chief nodded silently and took off across the clearing to where Corky was covering the road with his machine gun. He crouched beside the gunner.

"Look, man," the Indian said. "We can't get through to Wilburn. I think we'd better get our collective asses out of here while we still can. Those gooks are going to be all over us like stink on shit before too long.''

''Okay,'' Corky looked up at the sniper. ''You guys go on ahead. Take the ell tee and *di-di* on outta here. I'll stay here just a little bit longer in case Macmillan shows up.''

''Are you sure?''

''Yes! Just get the fuck outta here, man. I'll catch up with you guys later.''

The Indian got to his feet. ''Take care, man. I'll see you back at the mountain.''

''Right.'' Corky didn't even look up from his gun.

''Okay, let's go!'' Chief said when he returned to the men clustered on the shadowed river bank.

''Where's Corky?'' Farmer was worried.

''Back down the road. He's says he's going to hang back 'till Macmillan shows.''

Farmer looked down their river escape route. He knew what he had to do now and got to his feet. ''You guys go on ahead. I think I'll go back up and give Corky a hand with that.''

Chief shook his head. The two grunts were buddies so he knew what was going through Farmer's mind. ''Okay, man. We'll keep an eye out for you up on the mountain.''

''Catch you later.''

As Farmer headed back to Corky's position, the remaining men slipped down into the water and started up the river against the current. It was slower going that way, but they had no choice and moved as fast as they could through the warm, dark water.

Bunny didn't even think about being afraid this time. He was much more concerned about getting out of there in one piece. Little things like phobias didn't mean much to him at that moment.

''Corky!'' Back down the road Farmer called out softly.

''Over here,'' the gunner whispered from deep shadows at the side of the trail.

Farmer slid in beside him. ''What the fuck you doing here,

man?'' the Chicano asked. "I told that sniper to get you people the fuck outta here."

"I didn't want you to get lonely." The darkness hid the grin on Farmer's face.

"You're one crazy motherfucker, amigo." Corky shook his head, but he was glad of the company.

"What do you think happened to him?"

"Who?"

"Macmillan."

"Fucked if I know, man. If he don't show up here pretty soon, though, it's going to be Alpha Mike Foxtrot time, 'adios, Motherfucker.' We're going to have to unass this place before we're hip deep in gooks."

"What do you think went wrong?"

"Christ, man, I don't know, but they were sure the fuck waiting for us."

"How could they have known we were coming?"

"Beats the shit outta me."

Just then a figure stumbled out of the shadows. He collapsed in the middle of the moonlit road bed and lay motionless.

"It's Mac!"

They got to their feet and ran for the fallen man. In the silvery moonlight, the wet blood soaking the front of his camouflaged tiger suit looked shiny black.

Corky knelt by his side. Handing his gun to Farmer, he picked the wounded man up in his arms and carried him into the brush.

Sergeant Macmillan's eyes fluttered open, and he saw the two grunts kneeling beside him. "I thought that I told you fuckheads to get out of here," he wheezed. "Oh, Jesus." He closed his eyes for a moment.

"We had to wait for you, Sarge," Farmer replied. "You're coming with us."

"I can't make it." The Green Beret coughed and spat up blood. "Got hit in the guts. I can feel it bleeding bad inside."

"We'll get you outta here, Sarge."

'No!" The wounded man painfully raised himself to a sitting position. "Give me your grenades and get the fuck outta here. The gooks are right behind me."

Corky pulled the hand frags off his belt and handed them to Macmillan without a word. He had seen enough men die to know that there was absolutely nothing they could do for him.

"Let's go, Farmer," he said softly.

Farmer hesitated. "Sarge. . ."

"*Di-di*, goddamnit!"

The two grunts turned and ran down the road for the river bank. When they slipped into the warm water and started upstream after the others, behind them they heard the dull crump of grenade explosions and the screams of wounded men.

At the landing strip in front of the temple, Duc twisted the throttle to the powerful twin turbines of his Mi-8 gunship and pulled pitch. The big Russian helicopter rose to a hover a few feet off the ground. The nose dipped when Duc nudged forward the cyclic and took off down the narrow runway. The helicopter cleared the trees and Duc circled the temple to gain altitude. He called back on the radio to his command post to get their latest information about the intruders.

When the Cambodian lieutenant reported Macmillan's rear-guard action along the road to the boat landing, Duc banked the chopper and headed toward the river. The Yankees must have gone that way.

Brody, Two-Step, JJ, and Wilburn were headed through the jungle for the river themselves when Duc's gunship passed a few hundred feet over their heads.

The men instinctively threw themselves flat as it flew over them with a whining roar. Brody glanced up. Its shape blocked the moonlight that filtered through the trees. He shivered. He remembered his nightmare of the evening before, the dream of being chased by a big, shadowy thing in the dark sky that he could never quite see. Now he knew what the monster in the nightmare had been. It was the Russian gunship.

A chill ran through him. Did that mean he was going to die? He shook off the thought.

There was no chance that the pilot of the chopper could see them under the trees. Brody had flown the doorguns on several Huey Night Hawk missions out of An Khe, and he knew that it was almost impossible to spot targets on the ground at night. Even if the enemy gunship had searchlights mounted on her belly like the Night Hawks did, if the men kept to the shadows, the pilot would never see them. They would be safe as long as they were careful and kept to the trees.

When the sound of the beating rotors faded into the distance, he got back to his feet and forced the chopper from his mind. There were other more pressing matters concerning him. The other men stood up and they moved out.

From the drag position at the rear of their little column, Brody concentrated on following Two-Step through the brush and keeping an eye on their back trail. The chopper was probably coordinating with the ground-search patrols. He couldn't relax until they were back on the mountain.

Wilburn had taken point and had his compass out, guiding them straight back to the mountain. Their plan to go down the river was out now. There was too great a chance of the enemy chopper spotting them. He was a little worried about the men in Vance's assault group, and wondered why they had not called in to make a report. They should have once the firing had started, and there was no further need for radio silence.

The whole mission had been one big foul-up from start to finish, but it was no one's fault. They had just had a long string of bad luck, starting when Ringer's Mike Force ran into NVA Regulars.

Some missions were like that. No matter how well planned, if the gods of war were against it, it was all over.

At the head of the column, Wilburn was beginning to wonder if any of them were going to make it out alive. He had to get everybody back to their mountain camp and see if he and the lieutenant could salvage anything from the mess.

Colonel Duc savagely flung his gunship around in the moonlit sky, searching for the damned Yankees.

He had flown the length of the road from the temple to the river and had found nothing. Even across the river, the road leading up into the hills had been clear for several kilometers.

They could not have just disappeared into a hole in the ground. There had not been enough time for them to escape. They had to be hiding somewhere fairly close to Kangor Wat. He was determined that he would find and punish them for daring to attack him.

He heard his call sign in his helmet headphones and reached for the radio. "Tiger, Tiger, come in, this is Kangor Base."

"Kangor Base, this is Tiger." Duc recognized the voice of the Khmer lieutenant on the radio.

"This is Kangor Base. One of the search parties has found the guard at the boat landing. He is dead. His body was thrown inside his shack. Also, there are signs that the Yankees have gone into the river there. But there is no indication that they climbed out anywhere on the other side. Over."

"This is Tiger. Keep searching the river banks on both sides. Out."

Duc was jubilant. They were using the river as an escape route. Now he had them.

The North Vietnamese colonel quickly flew back to the boat landing and brought his gunship low over the river. He observed that at a certain height, the moonlight reflected off the water and he could clearly see the surface. He rolled back on the throttle to cut his airspeed even more, coming almost to a hover. Then he started his search.

A few hundred meters upstream, he thought he saw something moving in the deep shadows of the tangled brush along the banks. Lining up on the break in the trees, he triggered off a single 57mm high-explosive rocket from the pods mounted on his weapons pylons. The flash of the explosion lit up both banks of the river. He thought that he saw more movement and fired another rocket.

This time he saw something moving on the opposite bank. He circled around and he gave the shadows a quick burst from his 23mm canons.

A thousand meters further upstream, the grunts were moving as fast as they could against the current. Bunny was still on the radio trying to reach Wilburn. The RTO had no way of knowing that the antenna base on Wilburn's PRC-77 had stopped a piece of frag in the jungle and was not receiving his transmissions.

Wilburn didn't know about the radio malfunction, either, because he could still hear the hiss of the squelch when he put the handset to his ear. He tried calling the other team, but with the antenna damaged, his radio would not transmit.

To their rear, the men moving up the river heard the explosions of Duc's rockets coming closer and closer to them.

"We've go to get our asses out of here." Farmer was tense. He felt trapped. "That chopper's going to be right on top of us any second now."

"You got that shit right," Corky said. He didn't like being in the river, either. "If he catches us here, there's no place to run. We'd better take our chances in the woods."

Though the machine gunner didn't like the feeling of being trapped in the river, he was still reluctant to leave it. He knew how to get back to the mountain as long as they went back the same way they had come in, but he wasn't too sure that they could find their way back through dense jungle. Also, it was easier to take the wounded lieutenant down the river. In the jungle, they would have to carry him somehow, and that would be a real bitch.

They didn't really have any choice, however. The enemy gunship was coming closer and closer, and it was the woods or nothing. Corky found a break in the thick brush along the bank and climbed out to take a look.

It was clear. He turned back and motioned for the others to follow.

The men in the water pushed the air mattress onto the bank with Vance still on it. They didn't have time to cut poles and make a litter, so Corky let the air out of the mattress and cut slits in the side of the tough fabric for handles.

All four of them grabbed onto the makeshift litter, lifted Vance, and headed out through the dense foliage. They had to get as far away from the river as they could before the gunship showed up.

Chief took point. He was pretty good with a compass and he could also scope out the terrain with the Starlite on his sniper rifle.

After they had gone several hundred meters into the jungle, the sniper halted them for a short break so he could get his bearings. Taking out his map, he plotted their course and ran a compass azimuth to the mountain. Carrying the lieutenant and fighting the jungle, it was going to take them twice as long to get back, but it couldn't be helped.

He got to his feet and set off along the azimuth. They couldn't let themselves be found in the jungle when the sun came up, and dawn was just a few short hours away.

CHAPTER 27

Inside Cambodia

It was early morning, and the thick ground mist still covered the jungle below the raiders' mountain campsite. After marching all night with their wounded officer, Corky's group had finally reached the camp. Treat Brody and Jack Wilburn were anxiously waiting for them when they staggered up the last few meters of the hill.

"What the fuck took you guys so long?" Brody asked the gunner. Corky turned and pointed back down the hill to the men struggling with Vance's litter.

"Oh, shit." Brody was stunned. "Is he dead?"

"No," Corky shook his head. "I don't think he's hit that bad, but we've got to get him outta here as soon as we can."

"Let me talk to Wilburn."

Brody found the Special Forces NCO examining his radio, the one that had not worked the night before. He found the damage made by the bullet. "Now what the fuck are we going to do?" Brody asked him.

Now that Vance was down, the command of the group had fallen on Wilburn's shoulders.

Wilburn looked around at the handful of exhausted men

clustered in the small clearing on the mountainside. Some of them were trying to choke down cold C-rations, but most of them were simply trying to get a little rest after the all-night march. They were also trying hard not think about their situation.

The sergeant turned back to Brody. "Well, for starters, I think that I'd better call in and let them know that we stepped on our foreskins."

He wiped a hand across his forehead, smearing the camouflage paint. "Then I'll see if I can get you guys and your ell tee extracted."

"What do you mean, you guys? Aren't you going to come with us."

Wilburn looked grim, and his blue eyes were hard. "No, Brody, I'm not. I came here to kill that goddamned chopper. And it ain't dead yet, so Ole Panama Jack ain't going nowhere."

Brody glanced over to where Two-Step and Gardner were tending Lieutenant Vance. The wounded officer kept slipping in and out of consciousness. There was little they could do for him except to make him comfortable. If he was going to survive, he needed to have a Dustoff soon.

"How would you like some help with that little project?" Brody asked, patting the butt stock of his sixteen.

"Why do you want to get involved?"

"Well," the grunt looked Wilburn straight in the eye. "Let's just say that I want to. Me and my guys will be more than glad to stick around for a while and give you a hand with that little chore."

"I appreciate that, man." The Green Beret sounded sincere. "I really do. It's a little more than I can handle by myself, but I owe that sorry motherfucker in that gunship. And," his voice coarsened, "now that Mac is dead, I owe him another one."

"Don't forget, Wilburn," Brody said softly. "We owe him one, too."

"Yeah, I guess you do. How is your lieutenant doing anyway?"

"I think he's going to make it, if we can get him out of here. He's not hit that bad, but he's in shock. This is the first time he's ever been wounded and he doesn't know how to handle it."

"He's not a bad ell tee for a leg," Wilburn laughed.

"I've seen worse."

"That's a fact."

Wilburn got to his feet and reached inside his jacket for the SOI, the radio codebook that hung on a nylon cord around his neck. "Well, I'd better get on that Prick-Seventy-seven and see what they can do back there about getting us a Dustoff flight."

"Roger that."

"Lightning Six, Lightning Six, this is Hook Talon Bravo, Hook Talon Bravo, over."

"You wanted to see me, Colonel?" Rat Gaines stood in the door to Colonel Jordan's office at Battalion Headquarters.

"Yeah, Gaines. Come on in and have a seat."

Jordan lit a smoke and snapped the lid of his engraved zippo shut. "We just got a call from your boys over in Cambodia. It looks like Vance really got his ass in a crack this time."

"Oh, shit. What happened?"

"We're still not too sure about the details. All we know is that they got into a big pissing contest when they tried to get in close enough to hit the chopper. For some reason, the Khmer Rouge had been alerted and were waiting for them. Vance got himself wounded, and one of the other men on the team was KIA."

"Who?" Rat sat up straight in his chair.

"One of the Green Berets."

Gaines was relieved that it wasn't another one of his men, but he hoped to God that it wasn't Panama Jack. "Did they take out that gunship, sir?"

"No, they didn't. And they report that there's two of them parked there now."

"Shit! Now what do we do?"

"We don't." Jordan's voice was cold.

"I don't understand, sir." Gaines was confused. "What do you mean?"

The colonel looked disgusted. "I mean that word came down from USARV that we are to do nothing at this point. If your people make it back across the fence, that's fine. But if they don't, that's just tough shit."

Jordan savagely butted his smoke and reached for another one. "Sometimes this fucking war is enough to gag a maggot off a gut wagon."

Something was wrong, dead wrong. "What happened, Colonel?" Gaines asked softly.

"It looks like one of our ARVN allies in Saigon leaked the mission to the Cambodes, and Sihanouk is screaming his fat head off about intervention again. He's got Congress spooked, and they're putting pressure on the White House. Johnson called Westmoreland and told him to cancel the operation."

"But, Colonel, we've got recon teams working across the fence in Cambodia all the time. I don't see what the difference is."

"I know that, and you know that, but Congress doesn't. Also, this mission isn't just a recon. It's a strike mission."

"So?" Rat's voice was cold. "They told you just to write those men off. Is that it, sir?"

Jordan locked eyes with his company commander. "That's about it, Rat."

"Goddammit, sir, they're never going to make it all the way back to the border on foot, you know that. That whole area is swarming with Khmer Rouge and NVA units, and they'll be alerted for them. Look what happened to Ringer's Mike Force on their way in. This sucks, Colonel. It sucks heavily!"

"I know it does. And that's why I wanted to talk to you."

The battalion commander leaned forward across his desk, a wolfish expression on his face, the same expression he had worn in the days of his first tour as an ARVN Ranger advisor in the Delta when he had been known as Mack the Knife.

"There's not a hell of a lot that I can do about it, Rat. Officially, that is. But," he grinned, "how'd you like to put your commission on the line again?"

Gaines pulled one of his thin cigars from the breast pocket of his fatigue jacket and lit it up. He blew a perfect smoke ring into the already smoky air in the colonel's office.

"Sounds fine to me, Colonel. I found the fucking thing in a box of Wheaties anyway."

Jordan laughed. "I thought you'd feel that way. Okay, here's what I've got in mind. . . . "

Rat's Jeep raised a trail of dust as he raced down to the Python Flight operations shack. He skidded the vehicle to a halt in the graveled parking lot in front of the colorful sign reading 'Home of Python Flight. You Call — We Maul'.

"Anybody seen Warlokk?" he called out, running into the pilot's ready room.

One of the pool players looked up from his shot. "Last I saw him, sir, he was down in the maintenance bay checking out his replacement bird."

"How 'bout hauling ass over there and telling him that I need to see him 'rat now.' "

"Roger that."

The pilot parked his pool cue up against the table and headed out the door at a dead run. Everyone in Echo Company had learned that when their company commander said that he wanted something done "rat now," he meant exactly now, not even a split second later.

Gaines went on into his office and picked up the phone.

"Sergeant," he addressed the battalion ammunition NCO on the other end of the line, "this is Captain Gaines. I need to have a half-dozen LAWs down on the alert pad in thirty minutes or so. . . . No, I don't have a fucking requisition. If you have any questions about it, Sergeant, why don't you just call Colonel Jordan and ask him if he wants me to have them.

Do you need his extension number? . . . Good, I didn't think so. Half an hour and they'd better fucking be there."

He put the phone back down in its cradle. "Fucking REMFs," he muttered.

"You wanted to see me, sir?" Lance Warlokk stood at the door.

"Yeah, Lance! Come on in and grab a chair."

"What's up?" The thin, scar-faced warrant officer dropped into the folding metal chair across from Rat's desk.

"First, how's the head?"

"It was just a bump, sir. Not a concussion. It's as good as ever. The flight surgeon has already cleared me for duty."

"Good. How'd you like to take a little solo flight?"

The veteran pilot grinned. "Sure! Why not?"

"Don't you even want to know where you're going?"

"Fuck it, it don't mean nothin'!"

Rat laughed. "Good."

Joe Schmuchatelli poked his head around the door to the office. "What's going on, Captain? They're preflighting our bird."

"Come on in, Alphabet. I was just getting ready to send someone after you."

The co-pilot-gunner noticed the map of Cambodia on the wall. "Oh, oh. What's up now?"

Rat leaned back in his chair and took a deep drag on his cigar. "S.O.S., same old shit. I'm going into Cambodia again against orders."

He blew the smoke out. "But this time, Joe, I can't take you with me."

"What do you mean, I ain't going?" Alphabet flared up. "What is this shit, Rat?" The co-pilot-gunner was pissed. He had flown into Cambodia in Rat's left-hand seat the last time the captain had jumped the fence to pull some of his people out, and he sure didn't want to be left out this time.

"Joe," Gaines patiently tried to explain. "It's a totally different deal this time. There's a whole lot more at stake here, and if we get caught this time, it's really going to be serious. USARV's gotten into the act on this one and they're working on orders directly from the White House.''

"So? Big fucking deal." Alphabet wasn't impressed with high-level politics at all. "I don't give a shit. I didn't vote for that son of a bitch."

"Joe, look. Jordan's going to turn a blind eye on this one. In fact, he's helping us. But if we're caught with our pants around our ankles, it's kiss-your-ass-good-bye time. We'll all go to jail, Jordan included. I'm going to try to make a small Mike Force team in to reinforce that mission and take out a couple of casualties. All I can risk on this mission are two ships and two pilots. We're going to fly in as low and as fast as we can to avoid the radar, and get in and out without being detected by either side.''

"But, Captain—''

"Joe, wait! Listen to me for a minute. You're going to get your chance, believe me, but right now I need you to do something else.''

"Bold Lightning, Bold Lightning, this is Python Lead on your push. Over." From the rear cockpit of *Sudden Discomfort,* high in the sky west of Kontum, Rat Gaines called ahead to Ringer's Mike Force camp.

"Python Lead,'' came the voice in his helmet head-phones, "this is Bold Lightning, send your traffic over.''

"This is Python. Is Lightning Six anywhere around there today? Over.''

"This is Lightning, that's affirm. Want me to get him on the horn? Over.''

"This is Lead. That's a negative. Just tell him that I am inbound to his location. Echo Tango Alpha six mikes, over.''

"Python, this is Bold Lightning. Roger, wilco. Anything further, over?''

"This is Python Lead, negative. Out.''

Lightning Larry Ringer was waiting on the chopper pad when Rat flared out to a landing. The Green Beret officer ran up to the Cobra before the rotors had even had a chance to stop turning.

"What's going on, Rat?" he shouted.

"Larry, old buddy!" Gaines stepped out of the cockpit and took his helmet and gloves off. "I've got a proposition for you. How'd you like to take another little trip?"

"Cambodia, right? I monitored the transmission."

"That's affirm." Rat fished in his pocket for a cigar and lit up.

Ringer shook his head. "Here we go again. This calls for a drink."

"You got that shit right!"

Inside the team house, Ringer, Sergeant Thompson, and Gaines sat at the wooden table by the radio room, intently studying a map of the mountainous terrain around Kangor Wat.

Ringer took a short shot from the beer in his hand and looked up from the table. "If you can provide an insertion, it's a go. If Fifth Group happens to ask, I can always tell them a bunch of my Strikers up and went home on me. And," he looked over at his team sergeant. "If CCN calls, Thompson can always tell them that I'm drunk and shacked up somewhere in Kontum."

"Are you going, too?"

"Sure, why not." Ringer had a big, boyish grin on his face. "If they catch me, what are they going to do? Send me to Vietnam?"

Rat laughed. "Well, my man Warlokk will be here in about a half hour or so with a slick, so get your people rounded up, and we'll move out as soon as he touches down."

"Roger that." Ringer stood up. "Lon," he called out to his interpreter. "Get your skinny ass in here."

CHAPTER 28

Inside Cambodia

"Oh, fuck." Wilburn slammed the radio handset down and looked out over the forested valley below the mountain without really seeing it. He was trying to assimilate what he had just heard on the radio. He didn't believe it, but he knew that it was true. He didn't understand why shit like that always happened to him. He was a good troop, he always paid his bar tab on time, and he didn't cheat the whores too much, so why him?

"What's wrong?" Brody asked, catching the expression on his face.

"We got a problem here, son, a real problem," the Green Beret answered wearily. "Saigon has called the mission off."

"What do you mean!"

"They wrote us off with a big *xin loi,* 'sorry 'bout that.' As of right now, we don't exist. There won't be any extraction, Dustoff, or resupply."

"What! They can't do that!"

"Welcome to the Nam, old buddy. They just did, the motherfuckers."

"But why?" Brody's voice rose.

"Beats the fuck outta me, man. Probably somebody playing fucking politics again." Wilburn was disgusted. He was a professional soldier and long as he had been in the Nam, he had never gotten used to the political games played back in Saigon. "This happens every fucking time I get mixed up in a Cambodian operation."

He rubbed the not quite completely healed wound in his leg. The piece of cannon frag from Duc's gunship attack on his team had nicked the thigh bone and it still ached like a son of a bitch.

"Since they won't extract us, with the ell tee wounded, we're going to have to give up on my idea of taking out that gunship and concentrate on just getting our asses out of here alive."

"They can't even give us a Dustoff?"

"Nope."

"That sucks."

"You got that shit right, my man."

Wilburn got to his feet. "Well, we'd better let the rest of the guys know what's going down and see about rigging a litter for Vance."

The men took the news about as well as could be expected. No one could understand what had happened or why they had been abandoned. Not even Lieutenant Vance could give them a rational explanation for what had gone wrong. Politics weren't taught at West Point.

"They can't just leave us here. I've got to talk to them," the officer pleaded with Wilburn. "Try to make them understand."

"Sir, they understand," the Green Beret said patiently, trying to quiet the wounded man. "I talked to your battalion commander himself. He said that the orders came down from higher and that there's nothing he can do about it. The mission's been scrubbed, and that's that. We're all on our own. So, if you'll just take it easy, sir, I'll get us ready to go."

Vance lay back. He was scared. He knew that his wound wasn't serious if he could get to a hospital. But this was condemning them all to die. The men could never make it all the way back carrying him. Before he slipped into unconsciousness, Vance vowed that he would make them leave him behind. At least that way they would have a chance.

Two-Step took the news stoically and set about readying himself for what he believed was going to be his last mission. First, he carefully cleaned his shotgun, reloaded it, and then honed the blade of his K-Bar knife to a razor-sharp edge. Then he combed out his long black hair and tied his light blue infantry neck scarf around his head for a sweatband. He regretted that he had never learned a warrior's death song from his grandfather. If he knew one, this would be the time to sing it.

He dug into his ruck and got out his camouflage paint sticks and his stainless-steel shaving mirror. Looking in the mirror, he painted broad stripes on his cheeks like the ones worn by his Plains Indian ancestors. He might die in the jungles of Cambodia, but at least he would die looking like a Comanche warrior.

"I've never seen a redskin in green and black war paint before," Chief said. The Indian sniper had walked up while Two-Step was putting the finishing touches on his war paint. "Ain't that supposed to be in red and yellow?"

"I think the ancestors will forgive me," Two-Step replied seriously. "They'll get the idea that I'm on the warpath."

"That's no shit."

"You want some?" Two-Step asked, offering the paint to his Indian brother.

"We reservation redskins usually don't go in much for war paint like you wild Indians do. But thank you, I think I will!"

The sniper squatted down beside Two-Step. Taking the mirror and the camouflage stick, he started applying the paint to his face.

"You know," he said as he worked, "my grandfather went on the warpath once down in California over cattle stealing. That's how he got sent to the reservation in Oregon. The army caught him and his buddies. And I guess if it's good enough for that old Indian, it's good enough for me."

When he was done, Chief had painted half of his face

214

black from hair line to neck. The other half was painted light green. "There. Now I'm ready to take me some scalps."

Two-Step laughed.

Farmer sat on a boulder with Gardner, overlooking the valley. The two grunts were cleaning their weapons while they kept an eye on the approaches to the mountain. "What do you think's going to happen, JJ?" Farmer asked.

Gardner shrugged and snapped the breech of his thumper closed. "I don't know. I guess we'll just have to try to fight our way back."

"Like we did the last time, right?"

"Yeah, just like the last time."

Back when the two grunts had both been cherries, FNGs, their first mission had taken them into Cambodia to rescue their platoon sergeant, Leo Zack. The Black Buddha had been wounded in a firefight and captured by the NVA. They tracked him all the way into Cambodia and, with a little help from Rat Gaines's gunship, rescued him from a North Vietnamese prison camp. After a desperate all-night march, they got back into South Vietnam and fought off the pursuing NVA troops until the Air Cav swooped down to rescue them all.

This time, though, Gardner knew that there would be no last-minute rescue. They were completely on their own and at least three days' march from the border.

"We made it last time okay, didn't we, JJ?"

Gardner looked at the slightly built young soldier. For once Farmer's face wasn't wearing its usual farm-boy grin. He was scared shitless, and it showed. Not for the first time, Gardner felt protective of Farmer. Farmer looked like he should be somebody's kid brother, and it was easy to want to protect him.

"Yeah, man," JJ said, keeping fear from his voice. "We sure as hell did and we'll make it okay this time, too."

Farmer grinned, his mind relieved. If big Jim Gardner said that it was going to work out okay, it would. JJ was hardly ever wrong about anything.

Brody and Wilburn were off to one side, away from the other men, going over their maps, trying to figure out the fastest way to get out of Cambodia. There were three main routes that they could take back, but each one had a distinct disadvantage involved.

Had they been fresh and not encumbered with the wounded officer, they could just split for the fence, running day and night straight up one side of the hills and down the other until they reached it.

But carrying a litter, that just wasn't possible. They were going to have to try to pick a route that kept to the valleys as much as possible, something that wouldn't bust their asses going up and downhill. It was going to take them at least three days to get back, and even that would be pushing it to the max.

"Sergeant Wilburn," Bunny called out from his radio watch. "There's somebody named Lightning who wants you on the horn."

Wilburn and Brody both ran for the radio.

"Hook Talon Bravo," came the familiar voice from the Prick-77 handset. "This is Lightning Six on your push, over."

"Lightning," Wilburn nearly shouted, hitting the push to talk switch on the side of the handset. "This is Talon Bravo. Go ahead."

"This is Bold Lightning Six. Be advised that I have been informed of your circumstances. Python Lead is at my location right now, and we are waiting for your return just like the time I waited for you to get back from your visit to Vung Tau last year. We'll be waiting for you and will have anything that you need. How copy? Over."

"This is Talon Bravo. Roger, good copy. Over."

"This is Lightning Six. Roger out."

"What the fuck was that all about?" Brody asked. "What does Vung Tau have to do with us being stuck out here in the middle of fucking nowhere?"

Wilburn looked at him with a big grin on his face, the first smile that anyone had seen all morning. "Lightning Larry just told me that he's on his way here with your captain."

"You're shitting me!"

216

"Nope," Wilburn continued. Smiling, he explained. "Last year I took an in-country R and R to Vung Tau for three days and I kinda got hung up in a whorehouse with a girl and a string of pearls. I was supposed to meet Ringer in Saigon, and when I didn't show up, he flew down and snatched my young ass right out of the saddle to go back to Saigon with him."

"Well fuck me dead."

"That's the best way to go that I can think of," Wilburn laughed.

The good news brightened everyone's day, including Lieutenant Vance's, when Wilburn woke him to give him the information.

"Did he say when he'd get here?" the wounded officer asked.

"No, sir, he didn't. But I imagine that he'll get here as soon as he can. He knows that you need a medevac and that we're low on ammo."

Vance lay back down. It was beginning to look like he might make it after all. He closed his eyes and went back to sleep.

It was a tense wait until the men heard the wop-wopping sound of a helicopter drawing closer.

"Hook Talon Bravo, Hook Talon Bravo, this is Python Lead. Over."

"Python, this is Talon Bravo," Wilburn answered. "We hear you, over."

"This is Python Lead. Roger. Talk us into your location. Do not pop smoke, I say again, do not pop smoke. Over."

"This is Talon Bravo. Wilco. We are on the south face of the mountain about halfway up the slope. There is a small clearing. You'll be able to see us. Over."

"This is Python, roger. We'll be there in zero two. Out."

As the grunts eagerly searched the sky, the olive-green-and-tan Cobra with the shark's mouth painted on her nose came into sight and passed right in front of them, circling the mountain. The pilot waved from the cockpit as he flew by.

Cheers broke out, and the grunts waved back at their company commander. Rat Gaines had come to their rescue again.

Flying in low over the valley, a second chopper approached, a slick this time. As the gunship circled the mountain, the Huey came straight on in, flared out, and touched down at the center of their clearing in a swirl of dust.

No sooner had the skids touched dirt than Captain Ringer leaped out of the chopper, followed by four of his tiger-suited Mike Force. One of the Nungs had his arms full of M-72 light antitank weapons and the others quickly pulled ammo crates, ration boxes, and water cans out of the cargo compartment.

Ringer ran over to where Wilburn was standing, away from the worst of the rotor blast. "PJ, you okay?"

"Yes, sir, I'm fine, but Mac's dead."

"Yeah, I know. He was a good man. You still want to nail that gunship?"

"You're fucking A, sir."

"Glad to hear that. That's what I'm here for. Let's do it."

The Green Beret officer turned to Brody. "Sarge, how 'bout your people? Do they want to go along with us?"

"We're in," Brody answered grimly, knowing that he had just committed his men to a long walk home. If they got home at all.

"Okay. Are any more of your people wounded?"

"No, sir, just the ell tee."

"Good. Get your lieutenant loaded on board so Python can get out of here and we can get to work."

The grunts quickly loaded Lieutenant Vance into the back of the slick and strapped him down for the ride back to An Khe.

As soon as they were clear, Warlokk carefully pulled pitch, bringing the Huey up to a hover. He had landed the slick with its nose pointing into the mountain, so he had to get the machine turned around before he could take off.

Coming to a hover, he slowly swung the tail boom around and inched forward until he cleared the trees around the landing zone, with the nose of the ship hanging straight out over

218

the edge of the mountain. Just the weight of the chopper resting on the rear of the skids kept her from toppling over.

Winding the turbine up to an ear-shattering scream, Warlokk dropped the slick over the side of the mountain. The chopper fell like a brick, her rotors desperately trying to find enough bite in the hot, high-altitude air. By skillful use of his cyclic and rotor-pitch collective, Warlokk translated the speed of his fall into forward movement that generated lift.

Within seconds, he was going fast enough to pull up and away from the forested valley before he crashed.

"Man, that fucker can really fly that thing," Ringer said in awe, watching the desperate maneuver.

"You got that shit right, sir."

"Lightning Six." The call came from Gaines's Cobra. "This is Python Lead, over."

Ringer took the handset from Bunny. "This is Lightning. We are a go, over."

"This is Python. Good luck, out."

From the mountainside camp, the men watched the slick disappear over the jungle with the Cobra flying high cover. They were on their own again.

"Okay, people." Ringer looked around at the men. "Let's get the map out and see how we're going to get this half-assed operation back on the road."

CHAPTER 29

Over the Cambodian border

Despite the caution that Rat and Warlokk had taken to stay low to the ground, the Khmer Rouge radar screens at the Kangor Wat airstrip still picked up the blips of the two choppers when they left the mountain campsite.

The two Russian gunships were already in the air, searching for the American raiding party, and Colonel Duc was immediately informed of the sighting. Since Colonel Yakanov's ship was the closest to the two intruders, the Russian pilot was vectored in to make the interception.

"Rat," Warlokk's voice came over his headphones. "I've spotted a bogie at two o'clock high, about three miles out and closing fast, over."

"Roger. I've got him, too. Split for the border, Lance. I'll try to keep him off your tail, over."

"Roger that, Lead. Good Luck."

Rat twisted his throttle all the way up against the stop and pulled in maximum pitch. He laid the Cobra over on her side in a banked turn and headed for the enemy gunship.

Rat grinned as the Russian machine grew larger in his gun sight. This time he was going to get that bastard. This was not going to be like his last chopper dogfight. This time he had something decent to fight with. His 20mm cannon wouldn't range out quite as far as the Russian 23mm guns did. And instead of two cannons, he only had one. But his H.E. shells packed almost the same punch as the shells fired by the HIP's bigger guns. And this time he wouldn't have to get right up on him to score a hit.

It was going to be just like one of those classic World War II fighter dogfights he had so avidly read about when he was a boy—two pilots in their machines facing each other in a cloudless sky. For a moment, Gaines imagined that he was sitting in the cockpit of a P-51 Mustang high over Nazi Germany, trying to keep Messerschmitt Bf-109s off the B-17 bombers he was escorting.

The Russian chopper had spotted *Sudden Discomfort* and turned away from Lance's fleeing slick. As the two gunships got closer, Rat saw that this machine did not have a red tail boom like the gunship he had tangled with before. It had to be that second HIP gunship that the guys on the ground had reported based at Kangor Wat. He wondered who was flying it—the same pilot or someone else? He was closing into firing range when he heard a heavily accented voice in his headphones.

"Pilot of the American Cobra, this is the Red Falcon. Do you hear me? Over."

"Red Falcon, this is Python Lead, the Cobra pilot. I hear you loud and clear. Do you have a message for me? Over."

"Cobra, this is the Red Falcon. I am Colonel Yuri Yakanov, of the Soviet air force. Who am I speaking to, please?"

"This is Captain Rat Gaines, United States Army Aviation. You're a little far from Moscow, aren't you, Colonel? What are you doing here? Over."

"Ah, Captain Gaines. I came all this way just to see you and your interesting machine. I want to see how it will stand up against my Mil gunship. Also, I want to know your name so I can record it in my logbook when I shoot you down."

"If you think that you're going to shoot me down, Ivan," Rat snapped back, "I hope you brought your fucking lunch."

"Please? I do not understand your meaning."

"I say again," Rat spoke a little slower, trying to suppress his Georgia accent. "I hope that you brought a lunch with you, Colonel, because shooting me down is going to be an all-day job."

"Now I understand," the Russian replied. "You make a joke. That is very good. I will have to remember it. The last time I shot down an American pilot, he did not have time to make any jokes."

"Well, Ivan, I'm not just any American pilot. I'm the best snake driver there is."

"Oh, Captain, I certainly hope so. There is no joy in killing a man who does not know his trade."

"Colonel, what do you say we quit bullshitting each other and get on with it?"

"I am ready, too. I propose that we both make right-hand turns and when we come around again, we will start."

"That sounds just fine with me, Ivan. Let's do it. Out."

As Rat started his turn in the sky, he sorely missed having Alphabet in the front seat to help him keep a close watch on the guy. The Russian was obviously not just some gook in a gunship. He sounded like he was a real pro. And if there was any truth in what he said about the last American he shot down, he was a blooded MiG fighter pilot.

Gaines wasn't a professional fighter pilot, but this time, at least, he had a better idea of what the HIP could do and what its weaknesses were. He was going to keep out of the way of its higher speed and make better use of the Cobra's greater maneuverability. For one thing, he was going to make sure that the Russian didn't get a height advantage on him. That had almost been fatal the last time.

He locked the nose turret in the dead-ahead position and checked the arming switches to his 20mm cannon pod. Pulling out of his turn, Rat lined up on the enemy ship. Their closing speed was almost three hundred and fifty miles per hour. By jet-fighter combat standards, this was not fast at all. Phantoms and MiGs closed at well over fifteen hundred miles an hour. Nevertheless it was two or three times as fast as anything that a helicopter pilot usually had to deal with.

The Russian pilot started firing at the maximum range of his guns. Rat saw the fire wink from the nose of the ship. He threw his Cobra into a skidding right-hand turn. He whipped the tail back around to line up the nose of his ship and triggered off a short burst from the 20-mike-mike cannon in return.

The Russian gunship banked off to its right to avoid the fire. Gaines threw his machine onto her side in a hard-banked left turn. Halfway through, he slammed the cyclic over to the other side, rolling the Cobra over onto her right. A sharp kick down on the right pedal brought her tail around. He was in a firing position behind and off to the side of the Russian machine.

Yakanov saw Rat's maneuver and knew that he had to shake the Cobra off his tail. Twisting the throttles to his twin 1,500 SHP turbines past their stops into overrev, he pulled in maximum pitch and put the nose into a deep dive. The heavy HIP pulled away from the smaller Cobra like a falling rock.

"Jesus Christ," Rat said to himself in total disbelief. "Look at that son of a bitch go!"

He glanced down at his own airspeed indicator and saw that it was reading almost a hundred fifty miles an hour. There was no way he could catch up with the fleeing enemy machine. "He must be doing a hundred and seventy five!"

Rat followed Yakanov into a dive as the Russian put his ship down on the treetops. The green and gray stripes of the HIP's camouflage paint blended in with the jungle foliage, making it difficult for Rat to to spot him until he saw the sun glint off the HIP's spinning rotors.

Suddenly the enemy gunship pulled into a sharp, skidding right-hand turn. Using the brutal torque of the five massive rotor blades to spin him around, Yakanov completed a hundred-and-eight-degree turn faster than any chopper Rat had ever seen.

This time, the Russian bore straight in, firing as he came.

It was Rat's turn to give way. He broke to the right, but this time the Russian pilot followed, turning with him as he continued firing. Big, glowing orange balls of 23mm tracer rounds flashed past Gaines's canopy.

Rat's instinct was to dive away from the HIP, but he knew that that would be a fatal mistake. He had seen that the heavier Russian gunship could easily outrun him in a dive. His only hope now was in his Cobra's greater maneuverability. And maybe a little diversion.

He whipped the chin turret over to the side and pressed the trigger to the minigun. With a sound of heavy canvas ripping, the mini-Gatling gun spat out four hundred rounds of 7.62mm tracer and ball ammunition at the Russian gunship.

That startled Yakanov. He had obviously forgotten that the nose turret of a Cobra was flexible. He hauled his HIP sharply out of the line of fire. Finally, it was Rat's turn. Gaines kicked his tail around to face the Russian again and put the Cobra into a slight dive to build up speed.

As the two ships closed, Rat squeezed the trigger for the 20mm cannon pod. The muzzle blast of the heavy gun shook the Cobra's airframe.

South of the mountain, Colonel Nguyen Cao Duc, over-revved the turbines of his gunship to speed him to the aerial battle. He was incensed that the arrogant Russian was engaging the American Cobra—his Cobra! He knew that the Yankee gunship had to be the same one that he had encountered before, the one that had damaged his machine.

That was the first time that any American had ever inflicted damage on an aircraft that he was flying. Duc took it personally. He had been insulted. He owed the Yankee pilot and was going to make sure that he got his revenge by killing him personally.

Six thousand feet in the air, east of the mountain, between Kangor Wat and the South Vietnamese border, Duc came upon Rat and Yakanov's deadly aerial ballet.

He saw the slim, sharklike shape of the green-and-tan Cobra dive down upon the bigger gray-and-green-striped Mi-8. Flame winked from the cannon pod under the stub wing of the Cobra, and Yakanov's machine took hits in the center of its fuselage.

Yakanov hauled his HIP gunship around, turning into the Cobra's fire. The Russian pilot was a master of aerial combat and knew what he was doing. Now the Cobra was facing the two 23mm cannons in the HIP's nose. Flame blossomed from the front of the Mi-8 as Yakanov fired.

Duc threw his own machine up into a steep climb. He wanted the height advantage for his death strike.

He didn't think that either of the other pilots had seen him arrive since they were concentrating so thoroughly on killing each other. As soon as he had an opening, he was going to flash out of the sky like a striking hawk and kill the Yankee dog.

No one was going to shoot holes in Nguyen Cao Duc's aircraft and live to laugh about it. No one.

When Duc had gained two thousand feet on the dueling helicopters, he circled in the sky like a vulture waiting to swoop down and feed.

As he waited, the thought came to him that it would save him a lot of trouble if the Russian colonel were to fall victim to the Yankee's guns. Maybe he could insure that that took place, killing two birds with one arrow as the proverb had it.

Rat was concentrating on bringing his cannon to bear on the elusive HIP gunship. Though he had gotten some hits on him, the Russian pilot was proving to be a master at aerial combat. Right when Gaines thought he had cold meat on the table, Yakanov slipped away.

He banked the slim fuselage of his Cobra sharply onto her side and brought the nose around. There he had him again, this time in a deflection shot.

An aerial deflection shot was the hardest one in the world to make. Gaines had read about deflection shooting in his books on World War II dogfighting and he didn't even have a compensating gun sight to help him compute the firing angle. But it was the only shot he had, so he took it.

Nudging the cyclic to give him a little more lead, he squeezed the trigger to the 20 mike-mike.

Again the cannon roared, shaking the airframe. The muzzle blast on the portside stub wing acted as a brake, pulling the Cobra slightly out of line to the left. Rat saw his shells fall short behind the enemy gunship. He kicked her over to the right to compensate and fired again.

Again he saw strikes on the rear of the HIP gunship. He bore in closer, triggering the cannon in short bursts.

In the HIP, Yakanov was frantically trying to shake the American off his tail. It was time to cut and run—if he could. The American was true to his word. He was good. The thought flashed through the mind of the Russian that maybe he was getting older than he liked to admit. His reflexes were not what they once had been.

It had been a long time since the Russian had cut his teeth flying MiG-15s in one of the volunteer squadrons operating out of Red China during the Korean War. Taking on American B-29 bombers and their F-86 Sabre Jet escorts, he had reached ace status very quickly back then, but he had been much younger.

With Captain Gaines hot on his tail, Yakanov was beginning to believe that he had better leave the aerial combat to someone a little younger. He had one last trick to try first, though, before he gave up.

He hauled back on his cyclic, kicked down on the left pedal, and feathered the rotor blades to minimum pitch all at the same time.

The heavy Russian machine put her nose up and skidded sideways, losing speed as fast as if he had opened a dive brake.

The maneuver caught Rat completely by surprise. His speeding Cobra flew right past the HIP.

Yakanov pulled his pitch back in and dropped the nose of his ship. The Cobra was right in his gun sight.

The Russian pilot was just pressing the cannon trigger

when he saw a flash of light in the sky above him and glanced up.

It was Duc's gunship and it was diving right at him! The muzzles of the two 23mm cannon flashed as Duc opened up on him!

Instinctively, Yakanov tried to evade the attacking chopper, throwing his machine to the side. The big helicopter was not as maneuverable as his old MiG fighter. He felt the impact and heard the explosions as the cannon rounds hit his ship. Warning lights flashed on his instrument panel and the RPM warning buzzer screamed in his ears. He was hit bad and going down.

He feathered the rotor blades, trying to go into autorotation, but he was too close to the ground. He braced himself for a crash landing in the treetops when another burst of Duc's cannon fire hit the cockpit. The plexiglass canopy in front of the Russian shattered and blew away. The exploding shells tore into his body.

Colonel Yuri Yakanov, ace Russian flyer, was dead before his gunship hit the ground.

Rat had thrown his Cobra all over the sky when he overshot the HIP. Hunched down behind his seat armor, he frantically tried to get out of the way of the cannon fire that he knew was coming. Then he glanced up and saw the second Russian gunship, the one with the red tail boom, drop down out of the sky on top of him. He tried to bank out of the way, but it was too late. The other chopper had started firing.

Gaines could hardly believe it when he saw the 23mm tracers pass behind the Cobra. The HIP couldn't have missed, not at that range. He shot a look behind him and saw the Russian's machine take the hits instead.

Rat didn't know what was going on and didn't have time to worry about it. He had been cold meat a moment ago, and now the Russian was going down in flames. A small red light on the instrument panel caught his eye and he glanced down. It was the underwing armament panel. He was out of 20mm ammunition.

It was time for him to get out. He would figure out what

happened when he got back to An Khe. Gaines hauled his bird around and, putting the nose down, punched the overrev button. He ran for the border at max RPMs.

CHAPTER 30

Kangor Wat, Cambodia

Colonel Nguyen Cao Duc smiled behind his face shield as he circled around the thick column of greasy black smoke that marked the site of Colonel Yakanov's destroyed helicopter.

The Yankee machine had gotten away, but now that he was not going to have to move his base of operations as the Russian had wanted him to do, Duc was content to let the Yankee escape. He would have other occasions to seek out and destroy the American pilot, even if he had to fly into South Vietnam and strike at the the Yankee Air Cavalry base at An Khe. At the moment, it was more important that he dealt with Yakanov's subordinate, the KGB officer who was masquerading as a flyer.

As he made one last circuit of Yakanov's funeral pyre, Duc decided that Zerinski simply would have to disappear. If anyone at Pol Pot's Khmer Rouge headquarters inquired about him, he would say that the Russian captain had been in the gunship with the colonel when the Cobra shot them down. It was a simple enough story. No one would doubt him. And no one at his base would dare say otherwise.

Duc felt a fierce sense of satisfaction about the Russian's death. He had tried to take Duc away from his mission of killing as many Yankee imperialists as he could. Yakanov had proven himself to be just one more filthy, barbaric Westerner who did not understand the meaning of vengeance.

Banking his red-tailed gunship around to the west, Duc headed back to his airstrip at the temple. He wanted to take care of Captain Zerinski before he went looking for the Yankee raiders. They could wait awhile until he had secured his rear area. There was no telling what the KGB man might do when he learned of Colonel Yakanov's demise.

KGB Captain Gregor Zerinski had, in fact, already learned of his comrade's fate. He had been monitoring the radio in the command post when Duc called back to say that the American Cobra had shot the Russian down. Something in the tone of the North Vietnamese's voice made him suspicious, particularly when Duc said that he was coming back to the base instead of taking off after the Cobra.

Zerinski had a nasty feeling that there was considerably more to Yakanov's death than falling victim to the American's guns. Yakanov was too good a pilot and too experienced to have that happen so easily.

Looking around at the expressionless dark eyes of the Khmer Rouge in the command bunker, the Russian realized that he was out on a limb. He was the only white man in a jungle camp miles from anywhere, and he was completely at the mercy of a madman. The fact that he was a fellow Communist wasn't going to count for much if the treacherous Colonel Duc decided that he wanted him out of the way. Zerinski quickly decided that he would take his chances in the jungle rather than waiting for the Vietnamese colonel to dispose of him.

At least in the woods, he knew what he was dealing with. Like all the Russian advisors sent to North Vietnam, he had been through a tough jungle-warfare and survival school run by the Cubans. He could handle himself in the countryside.

The Russian nonchalantly walked back to the room in the temple where he and Yakanov had spent the night. Out of

230

sight of prying eyes, he quickly gathered up the rations they had brought from their helicopter the day before, all the extra ammunition magazines for his Stechkin APS machine pistol, and his flying jacket.

Going back to the main hall of the cavernous stone structure, he went to the guard's quarters off the main entrance. There were a few more things that he was going to need on his jungle expedition—a pack, a canteen, a rifle, and a machete.

Holding his Stechkin at the ready, the KGB officer ducked his head around the corner of the doorway. The barracks area was almost empty. Most of the Khmer guards were out beating the brush to pick up the trail of the Americans. Only two men were in their bunks. Considering Duc's fanaticism, they would have to be on the sick list with something serious to have been exempted from duty today.

Sick or not, Zerinski didn't want any witnesses to his supply run. Duc would figure out where he had gone, and he wanted as much of a head start as possible.

He silently edged his way around the door into the dimly lit room. The Cambodian closest to him was awake in his bunk, reading a comic book. Sticking the machine pistol in the front of his belt, the Russian drew a slim-handled dagger from the inside of his boot top and crept up behind the guard.

Clamping a hand over the Cambodian's mouth, he pulled the man's head back hard. The dagger slashed across his throat. The slightly built Asian struggled briefly, but the only sound was the bubbling of blood from his severed windpipe. He was dead within seconds. Zerinski laid him back down on his canvas cot.

The second man was sleeping off a fever. He died the same way.

Zerinski quickly grabbed an AK-47 assault rifle, a Chi-Com-style magazine carrier full of loaded magazines, a rucksack packed with supplies, and a broad-bladed jungle knife. Slinging the ruck over his shoulder, he slipped out by one of the side entrances and hid in the shadows of the outer gallery for a moment until he could get the field gear arranged to his liking.

He surveyed the area outside the temple. No one was in the area. He dashed across the open ground and took cover behind the latrine at the edge of the jungle where he waited for a moment. No one seemed to have noticed him. Slipping into the underbrush, he headed for the jungle perimeter to the north. With everyone out looking for the Americans, he thought he'd be able to get through Duc's defenses with little trouble.

The KGB officer ran an agent network in southern Laos, and he had several good contacts who could funnel him back into North Vietnam. He figured that, with luck, he could make it back to Hanoi in just a few weeks.

Even though his Cobra was quite a bit faster than the Huey slick that Warlokk had been flying, Rat had been delayed long enough by his dogfight that he didn't get back to An Khe until after Lance had touched down on the Dustoff pad and off-loaded Lieutenant Vance.

Rat taxied over to the edge of the Python pad and shut his bird down. He climbed out of the cockpit and told the crew chief to refuel and service the machine. Then he ran over to his Jeep and fired it up. It was a short trip to the receiving entrance of the 45th Mobile Surgical Hospital.

Grabbing the first nurse he saw in the hall, he asked, "A chopper brought a wounded officer in here a little while ago. Do you know where they took him?"

She looked down at her clipboard. "Lieutenant Vance? I think he's still in OR Three. Down the hall and third door on the right."

"Thanks."

Rat peeked through the window in the door to the operating room and saw a team of doctors working on their patient. He backed away and took a seat on the bench in the hall. He had to find out how Vance was doing before he reported back to Colonel Jordan. He was still waiting when

First Lieutenant Lisa Maddox came down the hall and spotted him.

"Rat!" the nurse called out. "What are you doing here?"

"Oh, Lisa!" He got to his feet. "I'm just waiting to see how Vance makes out."

"Jake? Is he in there?"

"Yeah. He got popped last night."

"I didn't hear anything about it." Lisa knew all the men in the Blues, including their lieutenant. "Is he hurt badly?"

"No, I don't think so, but it took a long time to get him here, so there may be complications."

"What happened?"

Gaines looked away for a moment. "You really don't want to know, Lisa."

She saw the look on his face and decided that she really did need to know. Something was bothering Rat Gaines, something important, and she wanted to help him if there was any way that she could.

"Is there anything I can do, Rat? Anything at all?"

He hesitated. He was tempted, but he just didn't have the time. He had to be ready to fly back into Cambodia on a moment's notice. It was great temptation to take the rest of the afternoon off and tell her his troubles over a couple of drinks. But not this time.

"No, Lisa. Thank you anyway. I've just got to sit this one out."

"Rat Gaines, something funny's going on again, isn't it? I can tell. What are you up to this time?"

Rat grinned. That's what he got for spending so much time with the blond nurse and letting her get to know him as well as she did. He felt like an errant husband who had been caught with his hand in somebody else's honey pot.

"Look, Lisa, I'll tell you about it later, I promise. Right now, I just need to find out how Vance is doing so I can get back to Colonel Jordan and let him know."

Lisa decided to believe him and didn't ask any more questions. "I'll go in and see." she offered.

When the blond nurse came out of the OR a few minutes

233

later, she was smiling. "He's going to be okay. He's got an infection in the wound, but the lung wasn't hit, and there's no major damage. He'll be back on duty in two to three weeks."

"Great." Rat grabbed his black Stetson and started for the door.

"Rat!" she called out after him. "You want to have dinner tonight?"

He turned around. "I'd love to, Lisa, but . . ."

Before he could finish his sentence, he saw her face fall and he mentally kicked himself. It had been a long time since he had seen her. In fact, he had been so busy with the Cambodian mission that he hadn't even known that she was back in An Khe.

They hadn't spent any time alone together since the night that they had almost made love. It had been interrupted by an emergency night extraction that he'd been called out on. The day after that, she'd been sent away on a TDY, temporary duty assignment, to fill in at another hospital for someone who was on an emergency leave. In fact, they had not had a chance to even talk about that evening yet.

"On second thought, Lisa, that's a great idea. But if you don't mind, we'll have to eat in the club. I'm on call tonight and may have to move out smartly."

"Seven o'clock?"

"Sure, that's fine," he answered. "And if I'm not there on time, wait for me. I may be hung up for a few minutes."

"Good-bye," she called. Gaines exited the door at a run.

". . . So that's about it, sir." Gaines finished his report to the battalion commander. "Ringer's operating on one of his bootleg frequencies so we can keep in touch with him without anyone else listening in. I've got one of my people monitoring the radio, and Warlokk and I are ready to pull an extract as soon as they call for it."

Colonel Jordan studied the map, his burning cigarette forgotten in the overflowing ashtray. "Do you know when he plans to hit the base again?"

"No, sir. He said that he wanted a chance to take a look at the situation on the ground and then decide what they could do about it. The only problem is that since I ran into the enemy gunships, they know that we flew in there for something. And that something had to be to resupply or reinforce the assault team. They're likely to be looking for Ringer right now."

"At least with the wounded taken out, if he decides that they can't hit it, they have a decent chance of evading."

"I don't know about that, Colonel. I'm afraid that whole area is just a little too hot right now for a walk in the sun."

"Yeah, you're probably right." Jordan butted his smoke and lit another one. "I was hoping that we could keep your exposure over there to a minimum, but if he calls for an extraction, you're going to have to go in and get them out."

"Yes, sir. The shit's really going to hit the fan if Saigon finds out about this."

"For both of our sakes, let's hope to hell that they don't."

"I guess that's about it, sir. Oh, and one other thing. I'm going to put my XO, Mike Alexander, in charge of the Blues for now and I'm thinking of making that a permanent assignment. I think it's time that they had some new blood running that show."

"You're probably right about that. How long has Vance been down there?"

"It's been over a year, sir."

"Yeah, it's time that someone else had a shot at it, and I think Alexander will be good there."

"He's got a lot of fire and he's been begging me to get him out in the field."

"We'll see how long that lasts."

Both men chuckled when they remembered how gung ho they had both been as young officers. Every infantry lieutenant worth his pay wanted to lead a platoon rather than get stuck behind a desk, but sometimes the realities of ground combat—particularly in Vietnam, where the terrain and climate were harder to deal with than the enemy—changed the minds of many a would-be combat leader. Somehow, though, Mike Alexander had struck Gaines as being a real good candidate for the grueling life of a grunt officer.

"Well, sir, I'd better get back down to my orderly room and make sure that they're keeping everything under control."

"Right. Keep me informed."

"Yes, sir. If you need me, I'll either be there or down at my operations room."

Jordan watched the stocky southerner walk out the door. He was beginning to develop a real appreciation for the man's abilities as a commander. If he didn't get the ax over this little operation, Jordan saw a great career ahead for Rat Gaines.

The colonel butted his smoke. He wished that he could get a little more involved with the mission but he had the rest of his battalion to look after. Not for the first time he wished that he was still a major back in the Delta.

Life had been a lot simpler when he had been Mack the Knife instead of Crazy Bull Six.

CHAPTER 31

Camp Radcliff, An Khe

First Lieutenant Mike Alexander was ready and waiting for his CO when Rat Gaines got back to the Echo Company orderly room.

"I've got the Blues ready to go whenever you want them, sir."

"Good, come into my office for a moment."

In the plywood cubicle that Rat jokingly referred to as his office, he plopped down in his chair. "Have a seat, Mike."

The executive officer was in his full war gear, everything but camouflage face paint and his weapon. He clanked when he sat down.

"It looks like you just nominated yourself to be the new Aero Rifle Platoon leader," Rat commented.

Alexander had a hard time keeping a big grin off his face. He didn't want to be seen as taking advantage of Vance's injury, but war was war, and he was sick and tired of commanding a desk.

"Well, sir, I knew that Lieutenant Vance had been wounded, and since I am the ranking lieutenant . . ."

Gaines chuckled. Alexander was the only other lieutenant in the company.

". . . I just figured that since you were busy flying helicopters, it was up to me to keep things going until Vance gets better."

"And maybe get yourself a little CIB time on the books?"

"There is always that, sir." This time Alexander couldn't help it. He grinned from ear to ear.

"Well, I can't argue with that one. Now, go get Sergeant Zack in here and I'll brief you two on what's going on."

"Roger that, sir."

Gaines looked after Alexander's vanishing figure as he dashed out the door. At least the young officer had some fire in him. Vance had been running the Blues for over a year so it was time someone else got a chance at some command time down there. As soon as Vance got out of the hospital, Rat decided to put him behind the XO's desk for a while.

An hour later, when Alexander and Zack walked into the Blues' tent, word had already gotten out about their new platoon leader. Someone called out in a stage whisper, "Oh boy! Here comes our cherry ell tee."

"Just what we fucking need," someone else added. "A fucking butter bar."

"Oh no, he ain't no butterbar. This FNG is a first louie."

"There ain't no fucking rank among lieutenants, asshole. They're all cherries."

"At ease!" Zack called out, cutting them short.

The grunts fell silent. They knew better to mouth off when the Black Buddha had told them to shut up. If they weren't careful, the ex-boxer would drag their smart young asses out behind the shower tent and teach them manners.

"Obviously you men have heard that I'm going to be your new platoon leader," Alexander began. "And just as obviously, this is my first combat assignment in Vietnam. However," he paused. "This is not the first infantry platoon that

238

I have ever run. But I am sure that none of you are very interested in my two-oh-one file."

Somebody laughed.

"Instead, I want to tell you a little about my background. Number one, my old man was a career NCO, a first sergeant in an airborne battalion. I was raised on army posts all over the world and I have seen or heard all of the shit that any soldier has ever dreamed up. Now there are many ways to run a military unit, but there is only one way that really works. You men do your jobs, I'll do mine, and we'll all be better off for it."

Someone giggled. "You tell 'em, coach."

The lieutenant chose to ignore it for the moment.

"Now for a start, I want every one of you people out in the company street in five minutes for an inspection. Full combat equipment and ready to move out."

The troops sat with their mouths hanging open. No one moved.

"Get it!" Alexander barked.

The Blues jumped.

Out in the street in front of the tent, Alexander smoked a cigarette and talked quietly to Zack as he waited for the five minutes to pass.

The time came. No one came out of the tent.

"You want me to go in and get them, sir?"

"No, Sergeant, not yet." Alexander waited patiently.

At about the six-minute mark, the grunts started drag-assing out the door. They stood around in front of the tent, smoking and joking. After a couple of minutes of that, Alexander turned to Zack. "Platoon Sergeant, fall the platoon in."

"Yes, sir."

"Platoon, fall in!"

This time the men lined up more or less in two rows. There was a lot of grab-assing, shoving, pushing each other around, and talking in ranks. Finally they quieted down.

Alexander marched up in front of Zack. The sergeant called the platoon to attention.

He rendered a crisp salute. "Aero Rifle Platoon ready for inspection, sir."

Alexander returned his salute. "At ease!"

The grunts relaxed.

"First squad leader, front and center." Alexander called out.

A man at the end of the first rank pointed to himself and squeaked, "Me, sir?"

"Are you the squad leader?"

"I guess so, sir."

"Then I mean you!"

The soldier stepped out and stood in front of the officer. Alexander didn't say a word. He just looked at him. The trooper squirmed under his steady gaze and came to a more formal position of attention as the officer's eyes traveled up and down his body.

"What's your name and rank, soldier?"

"Uh, Williams, sir. Sergeant E-Five Matt Williams."

"Is your squad ready to move out, Sergeant Williams?"

"I guess so, sir."

"You guess so?"

"Ah, yes, sir."

"Let's see. Follow me."

Alexander stepped smartly in front of the first man in the front rank. The man had a quizzical look on his face. "Sergeant Williams," Alexander snapped out. "Call your Squad to attention."

"Sorry, sir. First squad A-ten-hut!"

The man in front of Alexander came to his own personal version of attention. "Your name and rank, soldier."

"Genelli, sir. Spec Four."

Alexander's cold blue eyes ran up and down the man, taking in everything from his scuffed jungle boots to his battered brush hat. Around his neck was a big brass peace symbol on a chain.

"Are you wearing your dog tags?" he demanded.

"Ah, no, sir. I lost 'em and I ain't got new ones yet."

"How is Graves Registration going to know who you are when you get wasted on a hot LZ?"

"I don't know, sir," the young soldier gulped.

"Don't you want your mama to know her boy got killed defending his country? Maybe you'd like Suzie Sweet Shorts back home to be notified of your untimely demise, too?"

"Uh, yes, sir."

Alexander thrust his face closer to the man and yelled at the top of his lungs. "Then, troop! As soon as this inspection is over, you march your ass over to the orderly room and you tell the company clerk that you need a new set of dog tags! Is that clear?"

"Yes, sir!"

Alexander stepped over to the next man in line. The soldier came to a real position of attention. Snapping his M-16 up to port arms, he barked out his name. Alexander took the rifle from his hands and gave it a quick inspection. It was spotless.

He couldn't say the same about the soldier himself, but his uniform and equipment were serviceable, and he looked like he was ready to go to war.

"Good work, soldier."

"Thank you, sir."

The officer made a mental note to talk to Zack about making him the new first squad leader.

The next man's uniform was almost in shreds. His boots had holes in the leather, and he was wearing a baseball cap instead of a brush hat. Alexander turned to the squad leader. "Can you tell me why this man is in an unserviceable uniform?"

"We have a real hard time getting new clothes from supply, sir."

"And why is that?"

"Damned if I know, sir."

"Sergeant Zack," Alexander turned to the platoon sergeant. "Have you been having problems with S-Four?"

"Yes, sir, we have. As you are aware, we only have an E-Five running the company supply room, and they've been

241

giving him the runaround over there at the Battalion Four shop.''

"See me after the inspection."

"Right, sir," Zack grinned. Maybe this new ell tee could get a few things taken care of.

The rest of the inspection went very much the same way. Some of the men were in ragged, unserviceable uniforms, some didn't have the proper field gear. Too many of them simply didn't give a shit. That was going to change real fast.

When the inspection was over, Alexander had the men file back into their tent and take seats on their bunks. He wanted to have a little chat with them.

"I know that most of you think that an inspection is a pretty chickenshit thing to do in Vietnam," he started out. "But I don't rightly give a flying fuck what you people think."

No one said a word. They weren't used to their platoon leader talking to them that way.

"You men are supposed to be the hotshot Aero Rifle Platoon of the Seventh Cav. You get to ride around in helicopters instead of humping the brush for weeks on end. You get to wear a little blue neck scarf and play king stud down in Sin City. The whores might think that you're heroes, but I'm not impressed. Not a bit. As far as I'm concerned, most of you people aren't worth what little the army is paying you."

That got an angry growl from most of the grunts, but the lieutenant ignored it.

"First off, just so there is no misunderstanding, I'm not trying to make parade-ground soldiers out of you or to get you looking as pretty as MPs. I don't really give a shit how you look just as long as your weapons and equipment are clean and serviceable, and that you have your basic load ready to move out at a moment's notice. As far as I'm concerned, anything else is pure bullshit."

He looked around the tent, locking eyes with every man, one at a time.

"But, as I've seen here today, too many of you aren't ready for combat and that shit don't cut it in my book. The sole reason for your existence is to be able to go anywhere and do anything on a moment's notice. And anything that prevents you from doing that pisses me off. I don't care if it's your attitude or your equipment. If you can't do your job, I'm going to be deep in your shit.

"You two squad leaders, you have fifteen minutes to get your men ready, completely ready for combat. Anyone not ready in that time will find himself a little lighter on the sleeves and humping the brush down in a rifle company faster than it takes to say it."

"Yes, sir!" they both answered.

"Also, you squad leaders will give me a list of all your men's unserviceable clothing and equipment in ten minutes. Move out!"

The troops scattered.

The fat sergeant first class behind the desk in the Battalion S-4 shop looked up when Alexander walked in. "Can I help you, sir?"

Alexander didn't say a word. He just looked around the big supply room, taking in all of the neatly stacked boxes and shelves full of clothing and equipment. It was a beautifully arranged supply room, just beautiful. He shook his head slowly.

"Sir?" the sergeant repeated.

"Is the S-Four in?"

"No sir. He's at a supply conference down at the Fifty-fourth General Support Group in Nha Trang. I'm in charge here today."

"Well, Sergeant Warner," Alexander read the name tag on the man's brand-new jungle fatigue jacket. "I'm here to pick up a few things for my unit." He dug a list out of his pocket.

"Ah, Lieutenant . . ."

"Alexander. First Lieutenant Michael P. Alexander, Echo Company executive officer and platoon leader of the Aero

Rifle Platoon." He smiled. "I'm sure that you'll need my name for your records."

"Do you have valid requisitions, sir?"

"I'll tell you what I have, Sergeant." Alexander's eyes locked on him. "I have men in my unit who are getting ready to go out in the field in rags and unserviceable boots."

"Uh, yes, sir. But you have to have requisitions. I can't issue you anything without valid requisitions"

"Can you write, Sergeant?"

"Why, yes, sir, of course."

"Good. You just sit your fat ass over there behind that desk and start writing requisitions. As soon as you get one done, I'll sign it and then you can file it away or whatever you do with it."

"But, sir," the sergeant squeaked, "you can't do it that way."

Alexander stuck his face right up against the sergeant's nose. "Are you telling me what I can't do, Sergeant?" he said sweetly.

"But, sir, there are procedures and—"

"I'm sure that there are, Sergeant, and that's what the army pays you for. Following procedures. Now, you sit down and start earning your pay while I find some uniforms and boots for my men."

"But sir . . . ."

"Would you like it any better if I got the battalion commander on the horn and had him talk to you about procedures?"

"No, sir."

"Then get your ass to work, Sergeant."

"Yes, sir!"

Half an hour later, when everything was said and done, Alexander walked out of the supply building with his arms full of new uniforms, TA-50 equipment, and boots. Everything he had on the list. Inside the S-4 shop, Sergeant Warner was seriously considering finding a new job.

CHAPTER 32

Kangor Wat, Cambodia

"What do you mean that you cannot find him!" Duc screamed at the Khmer sergeant standing in front of him. The North Vietnamese officer had completely lost control. "You incompetent fool! He has to be around here somewhere. He cannot just disappear."

"Comrade Colonel." The unfortunate sergeant hurriedly tried to talk his way out of certain execution. "We have looked everywhere, and the Russian has not been found. We discovered two of the men in the temple guard barracks with their throats cut. We think that the Russian did it."

That made Duc pause in his tirade and think for a moment. What had made the KGB man want to try to escape? Had he somehow learned what had happened to his colonel? It appeared that Captain Zerinski had more brains than Duc had credited him with.

The North Vietnamese colonel suddenly realized that it had become just as important that he find the KGB officer as the Yankee commandos. If the Russian got back to the Khmer Rouge headquarters alive, he could very well cause trouble.

"Tell your men to search the jungle and look for the Russian's trail. He has not had enough time to get very far yet. They are to capture him immediately and bring him back to me. Now!''

"At once, Comrade Colonel.'' The sergeant saluted and left the command post as fast as he could. He would search the jungle as he had been ordered, but it was a useless exercise. Dozens of his troops had been tramping around in the jungle outside the temple since early morning, looking for the Americans. It would be impossible now to tell one man's set of tracks from another.

The Cambodian NCO started seriously thinking of deserting. Maybe he could hide out with his wife's family. They lived in a remote hilltop village and no one would ever find him there. He really did not want to have to tell the crazy North Vietnamese colonel a second time that he could not find the Russian long-nose.

Duc turned to one of his command-post runners. "Go get the girl who was with the Russian last night,'' he ordered. "The young one. Bring her here to me immediately.''

"Yes, Comrade Colonel.'' The runner saluted and ran out the door.

Perhaps the girl knew something about Zerinski's plans. The colonel doubted it. The Russian was much too smart to talk to a whore. But it would not hurt to interrogate her on the off chance that she had overheard something.

He went to the big map on the wall and studied it again. He was still puzzled by the sudden appearance of the Yankee helicopters.

According to his radar operators, there had only been two machines, and one of them had been the Cobra that had engaged the Russian colonel. He had not spotted the other machine, but the radar people said it looked like a Bell Huey on their screens, not one of the larger American helicopters like the Chinook. Why had they flown across the border, and what did that mean?

From the reports of the attack on his base last night, Duc concluded that there had to have been at least thirty men in the raiding party. Since the Huey could only carry ten men, he felt certain that the Yankees had not escaped as he had initially feared.

If anything, the lone Huey had probably brought the Yankees a resupply, probably of ammunition. They would have needed more after the firefights last night. If that was the case, it meant they were still out there, waiting for nightfall, and that they planned to attack his base again. If they were waiting, where were they?

It had to be far enough away to not be easily found by his search parties, but close enough to strike, probably within two hours' march of the temple, or not more than fifteen kilometers away. Other than the jungle, the only terrain feature within that radius was the volcanic mountain to the northeast. He wished that he had taken a look at it on his way back in.

He suddenly remembered that it was in the vicinity of the mountain where the radar operators said they first saw the blips of the Yankee machines. The mountain was their base camp—they were hiding there now, he was certain of it.

"Colonel, I have the girl."

Duc turned and looked at her. She was still beautiful, but as far as he was concerned, she was soiled. She kept her eyes downcast as was proper for a peasant in the presence of a government official. It was not going to save her.

"Look at me, girl!" he commanded.

The girl raised her eyes to meet his. He could not read anything in her face except fear. He decided that he would definitely have to interrogate her to learn what she knew.

"Throw her in the tiger cage for now. I will deal with her later."

"Yes, Comrade Colonel." The guard saluted and took the girl away.

Duc went back to studying his map. First, he wanted to check the mountain.

The North Vietnamese pilot went to the door and yelled for his crew chief to ready his machine. He turned to the duty sergeant and barked, "Have the the guard officer report to me."

On the side of the mountain, Ringer, Wilburn, and Brody were making plans for another attack on the Russian gunship. Now that they had rocket launchers again, they could go back to their original plan of attack and take it out from a distance.

The 66mm LAWs didn't have the range of the RPGs that Ringer had originally brought with him, but since they were all that they could get on short notice, they would have to do—if they would fire.

There had been lots of problems with the damp climate of Vietnam corroding the delicate, electric firing systems of the M-72 LAW. But the ones that Warlokk had brought them all had fairly new dates on their packing materials.

"This time we'll wait till three in the morning," Ringer said. "The slopes will have been up all night waiting for us, and that's going to have slowed them down quite a bit."

Brody nodded his agreement. That was when the Viet Cong and North Vietnamese always liked to hit American bases, between two and four in the morning when the guards were the least alert. They would use their own tactics on them for a change.

"I think we can infiltrate their perimeter again," Ringer continued. "Since we didn't break through last night, they'll probably be expecting us to try it from another side this time, maybe from the north or the east. So we won't disappoint them. We'll hit them there with a diversionary attack while the rocket team sneaks in from the west side again."

"Who are you going to send in with the rockets?" Wilburn asked.

"You. And ask for volunteers to go with you, two men. I'll take the rest of them and the Nungs to run the diversion for you."

"Sounds good to me."

Just then, one of the men on guard shouted. "Chopper's coming!"

The three men jumped up and ran over to see. Python

hadn't called to say that he was coming back, so it had to be the enemy machine.

Down in the valley, they saw the big HIP gunship settle down in a clearing two klicks away. The pilot kept the rotors turning. Small figures of khaki-clad troops poured out of the rear doors of the Russian machine and ran into the surrounding jungle.

"Looks like the party's over," Brody said grimly. "Those motherfuckers are running an Eagle Flight against us."

"Now you're going to find out what it's like to be on the other end of an air assault for a change," Ringer commented.

"No, thanks, sir. I'd rather sit this one out if you don't mind."

"I really don't think we're going to have a hell of a lot of choice in the matter. I think they've figured it out that we're hiding up here."

"We can always try to get the fuck out, sir." Brody said hopefully.

"You probably got that shit right, Brody," Ringer answered, taking one last look at the HIP. "Okay, boys, let's get a move on!"

The grunts looked over their shoulders at the Russian chopper and quickly got their gear together. None of them liked being on the other side of an air-mobile operation at all. Before they were ready to move out, the gunship made two more landings on the other side of the mountain to drop off more troops.

They were surrounded.

"You said there was a back door to this place?" Ringer asked Wilburn, looking at his map.

"Yes, sir, there is. Follow me."

With Wilburn and one of the Nungs taking point, the small group headed down the brushy slope of the volcanic mountain as fast as they could. Their only chance of survival was to reach the cover of the jungle as quickly as they could and make a run for the Vietnamese border. There weren't enough of them to fight it out with the Khmer units closing in on them. It was going to be hard enough just to get away. The game had gotten completely out of hand.

"We found their camp, Colonel," the Khmer sergeant in charge of one of the ground parties radioed to Duc. The pilot was circling in the air above the mountain. "But they have gone."

"Where did they go?" the pilot radioed back.

"It looks like they are heading east back toward Vietnam, sir. We are tracking them now."

"Keep on them, you fool. You will regret it if they get away!"

"Yes, Comrade Colonel."

Duc put his helicopter into a hard bank and headed back to base. He wanted to have more troops on hand in case the unit chasing the Yankees ran into a fight. The HIP could lift twenty-four fully equipped troops in addition to its full weapons load, so he could carry more than enough reinforcements if they were needed.

The troops were waiting for him when he touched down in front of the stone temple.

"Hurry up!" he screamed, waving them to the rear doors of his machine. "The Yankees are getting away!"

Before the Khmer soldiers had even gotten the rear doors closed and locked, Duc wound up the turbines and started the heavily laden helicopter down the narrow runway. With the load he was carrying, he waited until the last possible moment before pulling pitch and rising into the air. With the men in the back, he had two full platoons that he could commit to the chase.

The Yankees would never get away now.

Wilburn was up on point with Chief and his sniper rifle in the drag position when he ran into the first of Duc's search teams. He went to ground behind a banana tree and waved Chief forward.

250

The Indian's camouflage uniform and war paint made him almost invisible as he crept up through the foliage to Wilburn's side. He brought the XM-21 up to his shoulder and scoped out the area in front of him with the day scope mounted on the weapon.

He quickly spotted the two khaki-uniformed Khmer soldiers hiding under the trees ahead of them. He nodded up at Wilburn and held up two fingers. Wilburn pointed off to their right and made walking motions with the first two fingers of his right hand.

Chief nodded again. Wilburn wanted him to find a clear path to get around them. He scanned the jungle in that area, but found no more enemy. He nodded affirmatively.

Wilburn took off in that direction leaving Chief to keep the two Khmer covered with the silenced rifle. The sniper waited until the next man in the formation, one of Ringer's Nungs, reached his position. He pointed out the Khmers to the mercenary and put a finger to his lips to signal silence. The Nung made a slashing motion across his neck and grinned a gold-toothed smile.

Chief shook his head violently to indicate no. The Nung shrugged. He seemed genuinely disappointed that he was not going to be allowed to cut their throats but he followed the track Wilburn had taken into the jungle anyway.

It was the first time that Chief had ever been around any of the Special Forces' famous and feared Nung CIDG troops, and he was impressed. The small men moved like tigers through the jungle and they always seemed to have a secret smile on their faces.

When Ringer finally got up to his position, Chief pointed out the two Khmers to him. The Special Forces officer frowned and briefly consulted his map. The enemy soldiers were right on their main escape route and were going to have to be bypassed. This detour was going to cost them time, but it couldn't be helped. They could not risk a firefight. Shots would tell the other search parties which way they had gone.

Ringer motioned Chief to go back up to the drag position and then followed him with the rest of the men.

251

CHAPTER 33

Camp Radcliff, An Khe

When he gave his report to Colonel Jordan, Rat Gaines had purposefully not said anything about his dogfight with Colonel Yakanov. He wasn't really sure why he held it back, but he did.

Part of the problem was that there were too many questions about the battle that were eating at him. He didn't have answers yet and he wanted to figure it out before he said much about it.

First and foremost in his mind was the second HIP that had gunned the Russian down. That was the one thing that made no sense to Gaines at all. The only thing he knew for sure was that it had not been an accident. There was no way that the other pilot could have confused his Huey Cobra with Yakanov's Mi-8 HIP. The HIP was more than twice the size of his own chopper. There had to be some other reason for the Russian's treacherous death at the guns of one of his own aircraft.

Gaines wasn't concerned about Yakanov's death. He knew full well that if the Russian had not been killed, he would have certainly gunned Gaines out of the sky.

Rat would have liked to have known more about the Russian flyer. For instance, he wondered what the man was doing flying a gunship out of a remote airbase run by a North Vietnamese officer. It was another part of the equation that just didn't make any sense.

It was well known that the Russian air force had observers and technical advisors stationed in North Vietnam. They always sent a large advisory mission to client states who were at war with the Western world. They also sent fighter pilots. He had even read recently of aerial encounters over North Vietnam. American fighter pilots had seen Westerners flying MiGs marked with the North Vietnamese Air Force yellow star. And there was no question that they were Russians.

The Russians had gotten into the game every chance that came their way in the years since World War II. Fighting in someone else's war was the only way Russian pilots got real combat flying experience. Endless training was no substitute for the real thing.

Starting with the Russian volunteer squadrons flying MiG-15s out of Red China during the Korean War, Ivan had flown and fought against American, British, and French pilots everywhere from Cuba to Egypt. There was even a persistent rumor that the MiGs that had shot down UN General Secretary Dag Hammerskjold over the Congo had been piloted by Russians acting on KGB orders.

Finding Yakanov getting combat time over North Vietnam was understandable, but Gaines would have expected the Russian to pilot a MiG-21 jet fighter out of one of the airfields defending Hanoi. He didn't understand what an experienced Russian fighter was doing flying a helicopter gunship out of a base deep in the jungles of Cambodia.

Gaines would probably never know what had really happened up there, much less why. But if the other HIP gunship had not gotten involved, he certainly would have been shot down.

He shook himself and vowed that as soon as more Cobras came on the line, he was going to find another pilot and brush up on his air-to-air-combat maneuvering. He realized that he probably would never again have to use them in an actual dogfight, particularly if Ringer and his boys blew up that other HIP gunship. But Rat Gaines wanted the security of knowing that if he ever did get into a dogfight again, he was ready for it.

His crew chief stuck his head around the corner of his office door.

"Captain Gaines? Your bird's all ready to go again, sir. She's been refueled and rearmed."

"Thanks, Chief."

The crew chief turned to go. "Oh, by the way, sir. Did you know that you had a large-caliber hole in your tail boom as well as a nick in the trailing edge of one of your rotors?"

Rat blanched. "Uh, I ran into a little ground fire on my last mission."

"Well, we took care of it and she's as good as new again."

"Thanks a lot, Chief."

"No sweat, sir."

Gaines stared out the window at the helicopters on the flight line. Sometimes fate took a strange turn. It could just as easily have been large-caliber holes in his body.

"Captain Gaines," someone shouted from the radio room. "Captain Gaines, there's some guy named Lightning on the horn for you."

Rat jumped up, ran for the radio, and snatched the microphone out of the operator's hand.

"Lightning Six, this is Python, over."

"Python, this is Lightning. We've got us a little problem here. . . ."

In terse sentences, Ringer told Gaines that they were on the run again and were going to split for the border. He also told him that the second Russian gunship was running airmobile operations against them.

"This is Python, roger, copy. Look, Lightning, I'll try to put something together ASAP and get right back to you on it. Over."

"This is Lightning. I'll be waiting. Out."

"Shit!" Rat slammed the radio microphone back down.

254

He desperately tried to think of what he could do to help them.

He grabbed his hat and raced for his Jeep. He had an idea that might work, but he needed to talk to Colonel Jordan about it first. It was a little complicated and a lot illegal. Gaines wanted to have his battalion commander's help in planning it, as well as his blessing. Rat knew full well that if he got caught, he would take the fall, not the colonel. But he still wanted Jordan's okay before he took off.

Gaines slammed his Jeep into reverse and sprayed gravel as he sped out of the parking lot, headed for Battalion Headquarters. Lieutenant Muller jumped to attention, obviously startled when Gaines suddenly stormed into the commander's outer office.

"I'm working as hard as I can on getting your supply sergeant, sir," the lieutenant said hurriedly, trying to save himself from another ass-chewing.

Rat had almost forgotten his earlier conversation with the adjutant. He had to stop for a moment to think of what he was talking about now. "That's fine. Is the old man in?"

"No, sir, he's over at Brigade right now." Muller stood at attention as if he were still in officer candidate school at Fort Benning, and Gaines were a tac officer.

"At ease, Lieutenant." Gaines shook his head wearily. If Muller would only learn how to relax, people wouldn't get on his case all the time. "When's the colonel due back?"

"He didn't say, sir."

"Oh shit!" Gaines thought for a moment. "Give me a call the moment that he gets in. I have to talk to him ASAP."

"Yes, sir."

Back in his Jeep, Gaines headed over to the flight line. He needed to talk to Alphabet, Warlokk, and Cliff Gabriel. He hated to ask them to put their lives on the line again, but it had to be done if anything was to be salvaged out of the Cambodian mission.

* * *

Twenty minutes later at the alert pad, the men of Gaines's Aero Rifle Platoon sat on their rucks waiting for their lift.

Standing by himself off to one side, Lieutenant Mike Alexander waited anxiously for the choppers. This was his first air assault, and he was a little apprehensive but he hid it behind the big grin plastered across his face.

It was natural to have apprehensions, but he was also having the time of his life. He was finally going to make an Eagle Flight with his new command, the Blues. It was what Alexander had joined the army for—the chance to lead men into battle. Playing war games in the frozen winter woods of Germany, crashing around in M-113 armored personnel carriers; it had been a lot of fun, but only a war game. Today, he was going to the real thing.

Like all young officers going out on their first combat operation, Alexander prayed he wouldn't do something stupid. There would be no umpires with white bands around their hats to tell him that he had just done something wrong. From now on, a mistake meant the death of his own troops.

A slight change in the wind brought the smell of burning kerosene from the exhaust of a helicopter. It was exciting. He imagined that as the smell of horse shit had been in the nineteenth century to the men of the old horse cavalry, the odor of burning kerosene was a hallmark of the new helicopter cavalry, the First Air Cav. After all, he was in one of the most famous cavalry units of all time, the 1st Battalion of the 7th Cavalry, once the outfit of General George Armstrong Custer.

Alexander had read of the exploits of the 7th Cav in the days of the Indian wars, and the battle of the Little Big Horn. It had been a little like the situation they faced in Vietnam, an outnumbered cavalry unit fighting off a screaming horde of people defending their own familiar ground. He was confident that this time, however, he would not face another Little Big Horn, not when helicopters could rush reinforcements to a battle in minutes while others provided aerial rocket artillery fire for the men on the ground. Not for the first time, Alexander had a sense of participating in history, of taking part in something very important.

Platoon Sergeant Leo Zack stood behind his new platoon leader, his shaved head gleaming in the sun. He, too, was a little apprehensive about their mission, but not for the same reasons.

He didn't like even the thought of going back into Cambodia again, after what had happened to him the last time he had been there. Cambodia was bad news for sure, but he owed it to Brody and his men to pull them out, just like they had pulled him out of a North Vietnamese prison camp across the fence.

The Black Buddha shook himself and tried not to think about NVA Major Tran, who had held him captive for four hellish days. It had been the first time in his life that he had been absolutely certain that he was going to die. And at the same time, the experience had been so bad he had actually welcomed it.

He fervently hoped that he would get a chance to meet Major Tran again someday on the Vietnamese side of the fence. There were a few things that he wanted to settle with him in a one-on-one situation.

Two Huey slicks finally made their appearance. They taxied over to the alert pad and settled onto the perforated steel-planked runway in front of the waiting grunts.

"Let's go, boys and girls, saddle up!" Zack yelled.

Alexander felt his pulse quicken. Spurts of adrenaline shot through his body. He grabbed his gear.

The other men ducked under the spinning rotors, raced to scramble on board the two machines, and took their accustomed seats on the floor plates, facing out the open doors. Two men in each chopper went into the door gunners' pockets on each side and took their places behind the empty M-60 doorguns.

Alexander waited till the rush was over and climbed aboard the lead ship with his platoon sergeant. Zack waved him to a place on one of the canvas-covered troop seats against the back bulkhead and handed him a flight helmet. He secured his seat belt, plugged the helmet cord into the chopper's intercom, and called up to the pilot. "We're ready to go back here."

"Roger that," Warlokk clicked in on the intercom circuit. "Wait one."

Warlokk and Gabe were flying the two slicks without co-pilots. Gaines was trying to keep the number of people who were in on the escapade down to a bare minimum. That's why the grunts were manning their own doorguns.

"Python Lead, this is Python Three One," Warlokk radioed to Gaines, who was already airborne and circling overhead in *Sudden Discomfort*. "We are ready for takeoff. Over."

"Python Three One, this is Lead. Roger, pull pitch now."

As if they were tied together with a rope, the two Hueys rose off the pad in a hover and started down the runway, one right after the other. Both pilots knew that Rat Gaines liked his people to look good when they took off from the Golf Course. He couldn't stand sloppy flying and he was right up there watching them, so they wanted to do it right.

As soon as the choppers picked up enough speed, the pilots increased pitch on the rotor blades, and they rose into the air. They still kept in perfect formation as they turned and headed out over the perimeter wire and bunker positions around the sprawling First Air Cav base camp.

Rat Gaines was right ahead of them in his shark-mouthed Cobra gunship. The two slicks quickly formed up behind his machine as he banked west toward the Cambodian border.

Python Flight was going to war.

CHAPTER 34

The Cambodian border

Rat Gaines's Cobra gunship swooped low over the small clearing several klicks on the wrong side of the Cambodian border. In the front gunner's cockpit, Alphabet swung the chopper's nose turret from side to side like a bloodhound, seeking out anyone who might be lurking in the tree line surrounding the clearing. Rat circled the LZ twice to make sure it was safe before he climbed back up into the sky.

"Python Three One, this is Lead," he radioed to Warlokk, who was leading the flight of the two slicks full of Alexander's Blues. "The Lima Zulu is green. I say again green. Over."

"This is Three One. Roger green, rolling in now."

As Rat flew top cover, the two slicks flared out over the tall elephant grass, the blast of their rotors flattening it in big rings around the choppers. Before the skids had even touched down, the grunts on board jumped to the ground and ran for the tree line.

The instant that the last infantryman was completely clear of the rotors, the two Hueys lifted out and headed back across the border. They barely skimmed the treetops on their way out, keeping as low as they had on their flight in.

"Blue Six, this is Python Lead. Send status, over."

"Python Lead, this is Blue Six," Lieutenant Alexander answered Gaines's call. "We are on the ground and moving out now. Over."

"Blue Six, this is Lead. Roger, good luck, out."

The Cobra made one last pass over the landing zone before it headed out in the same direction that the two slicks had taken.

The three helicopters had made their approach to the small LZ a couple of miles inside the Cambode border at treetop level. They had come in low not so much to deceive the enemy radar, but to hide from their own radar sets covering the border. The irony of the situation was not lost on the pilots.

Since Saigon had abandoned the original mission, under no circumstances could Rat let anyone find out that he had a rescue mission of his own under way. If somehow the rescue was discovered, however, his cover story was the picture of simplicity. No one would really believe it, but it was realistic enough that it would save face if they were found out. It might even save Rat's career.

Late yesterday, he had entered a compass malfunction on his Dash-13, the daily maintenance log for his Cobra. No one had had a chance to see that the compass fault was corrected before he took off on what was supposed to be a routine ground recon mission.

The dense, mountainous, jungle terrain in Cambodia and South Vietnam was the same along the border. There was no way a man could know where he was if his compass was off. Even the commander on the ground wouldn't know that he had been dropped off at the wrong location, unless he had a great deal of experience operating in that area.

It was a thin cover story but it was the best that Gaines and Colonel Jordan had been able to come up with on short notice. If they were found out, the story was bolstered by the fact that Lieutenant Alexander was on his first mission in the jungle and could not be expected to know any better, either.

After all, everyone knew that the most dangerous thing on a battlefield was a lieutenant with a map.

In a hurried conference behind the closed door of the colonel's office, both Gaines and Jordan had explained to Alexander that he was putting his ass in the fire alongside theirs if he volunteered to go on their clandestine operation.

"I don't want you to feel pressured to do this in any way," Colonel Jordan explained, offering him an easy way to back out. "If you'd rather not get involved with this, I give you my word that I won't hold it against you. Sergeant Zack can take the Blues out on his own."

"No, sir." Alexander was adamant. "I wouldn't miss this for anything. After all," he grinned broadly. "I can always plead ignorance. Any court-martial board would believe that."

Gaines and Jordan laughed.

"You're right, but let's hope that it doesn't come to that." Jordan quickly got serious again.

Now that he was on the ground, Alexander was excited. This was just the sort of thing that he had always dreamed of doing, leading a commando operation deep into enemy territory. This was one hell of a mission for his first time out.

"Sergeant Zack," the officer called the platoon sergeant over to him. "Are the men ready to move out?"

"Yes, sir."

"Well let's get at it then."

"Right, sir."

Zack formed the men into a patrol formation. Taking point himself, they moved out as fast as they could, heading due west. The way the captain had it figured, they would be able to join up with Brody's people right about nightfall.

Gaines's gunship and the two slicks were going to stay on the ground at a small Special Forces camp just a few klicks inside South Vietnam. There Gaines would monitor the situation using Ringer's bootleg radio frequency. If something went tits up again, and the Blues needed to be pulled out fast, Gaines would scramble the slicks and escort them back to pick them up. If all went as planned, everyone would just walk out and no one on the outside would be the wiser.

If everything went as planned.

Considering the way that the whole thing had gone from the start, however, Gaines was positive that something would go wrong again. Had Gaines been a praying man, he would have asked for a little divine help with this one. But he knew that God had forsaken Vietnam a long time ago. No help would be forthcoming from that quarter.

Colonel Jordan sat in the radio room of his TOC, chain-smoking his Marlboro cigarettes. He had one of his big radios tuned to the frequency that Ringer and Gaines were using for their clandestine operation.

The air in the operations bunker was tense. Far more people than Jordan felt comfortable with knew what was going on, but it couldn't be helped. There was no way an operation this size could have stayed secret for very long. Now everyone was waiting just as anxiously as he was.

Even so, Jordan's secret was safe. Nearly every man in Camp Radcliff had heard about Saigon's instructions not to help the men across the border. Their buddies were cut off over there, and it could just as easily have been one of them who had been abandoned. No one was going to do anything that could possibly keep their friends from getting back home safely. That included shooting their mouths off.

Also, the Air Cav rumor network in Camp Radcliff had kicked into full operation. It was impossible to hide the fact that Lieutenant Vance was laying wounded in the hospital and that he was the only man who had returned from the operation. If Vance had been brought out, what had happened to all the other men who had been with him?

In fact, the rumors were reaching out well beyond the perimeter of the Air Cav base camp. Mike Force commander Larry Ringer and two men from Recon Team Sleeper were also not accounted for. When Special Forces Command and Control North in Kontum tried to get ahold of Ringer, they finally figured out what was going on. The man trying to cover for Lightning's absence back at the Mike Force camp had finally admitted that his captain had gone back across the border to finish up the job he had started.

The brass understood that at CCN. Larry Ringer had a reputation. He hated doing a half-assed job. But the problem still remained. Saigon had shut down the mission and Ringer was over there without official sanction. The Green Berets, however, were not about to leave one of their own hanging in the wind, and certainly not because a bunch of politicians in Washington had gotten spooked over Prince Sihanouk's ranting and raving.

The Green Berets started reaching into their bag of clandestine operational resources and pulled out a few little items. They also started calling in all their markers to people who owed them favors. The commander at CCN vowed that he was going to take a strip off Ringer's ass as soon as he got him back. But to do that, he had to get him back first. Life around their AO would be entirely too dull without Lightning Larry around to liven things up.

In the 45th Mobile Surgical Hospital, Jake Vance woke to find that he had a visitor, his father, Lieutenant General Joseph R. Vance III.

Since Vance's father was a general, the army had notified him as soon as it learned that his son had been wounded. General Vance had been on an inspection tour of army bases on the west coast and it had been no problem for him to fly down to Travis Air Force Base outside of Fairfield, California and hop a ride on the first C-141 Starlifter headed for Vietnam.

After a long trans-Pacific flight, the fast, four-engined jet transport had touched down at the big airfield at Da Nang. A friend of the general's at the marine base there met him at the ramp and whisked him away on a helicopter to Camp Radcliff and the First Air Cav's 45th Mobile Surgical hospital.

There were times when being a general officer could really pay off.

The general walked into Vance's room. "How're you doing son?"

Jake had never seen his father looking that bad. His eyes were red, he desperately needed a shave, and his normally crisp khaki uniform looked like he had slept in it for a week.

"Fine, sir, just fine," Jake answered, sitting up in the narrow hospital bed. He wanted to reassure his father. He was surprised to hear such concern. He was not used to hearing his father speak that way, and it made him very uncomfortable.

"The doctor says that you're going to be okay, son. That you'll be ready to return to your unit in just a few weeks."

"Yes, sir."

"What's this I hear about your having been hit on a mission in Cambodia? What in the world were you doing over there, Jacob?"

"Well, sir, it's a long story."

The general pulled up a chair and sat next to the bed. "Why don't you tell me then. I've got all day and I think that I have a high enough clearance to hear just about anything that you say."

The younger Vance laughed.

"Well, sir, it all started when our Charlie Company got hit by a Russian gunship a few weeks ago."

"Russian?"

"Yes, sir. It was confirmed. Anyway . . ."

Vance told his father the story of the mission into Cambodia, being wounded in their abortive raid on the gunship base, and of Captain Gaines and Lance Warlokk flying in to pull him out.

"Where are the rest of your men?"

"They're still over there, Dad. They stayed on to try to finish the mission."

"Even after everything was called off?"

"Yes, sir. They had to stay anyway, so I guess they figured

that they might as well finish the job they had been sent to do.''

''What do you mean that they had to stay anyway?'' The general's voice was hard. ''Wasn't a recovery operation set up for them?''

''No, sir.'' Jake's voice was bitter. ''They were expected to walk out.''

''You're shitting me!'' the general exploded. ''What goddamned idiot issued those orders?''

Jake was shocked. Rarely had he ever heard his father use profanity.

''I don't really know, sir. I guess some idiot in Saigon. The sergeant said he was told it came down from the top.''

The general's eyes flashed. ''I'll see about that.'' He snapped his folded overseas cap against the palm of his hand like it was a swagger stick.

''I'll be back in just a little bit, son. I've got to pay a courtesy call on your division commander. Maybe he can shed some light on this for me.''

''Yes, sir.''

Jake Vance lay back in his bed, relieved. Now something would be done about the people he had had to leave behind.

He didn't know what, but he was confident that his father could arrange something. The three silver stars his father wore on his collar pulled a hell of a lot more weight than a silver lieutenant's bar. His father had always been very good at getting things done his way.

That was how Jake Vance had gotten into the army in the first place. His father had insisted that his only son follow his own career and go to West Point. Jake had wanted to study engineering, but his father had wanted another generation of Vances to follow the colors.

When he first came to Vietnam, Jake had had a difficult time trying to tell his father how the war was being conducted. The general had not wanted to believe some of what Jake had written to him about. Now, for the first time, Vance felt that his father believed him. And for the first time, he felt that his father was proud of him.

CHAPTER 35

Inside Cambodia

Colonel Duc had been smart. The North Vietnamese pilot had landed his Khmer ground troops in a large circle surrounding the small group of fleeing Americans. He had effectively blocked all the roads and trails leading away from the mountain. He had them trapped and he knew it.

Captain Ringer and his small group were in a real bind and it had gotten progressively worse as the day wore on. Every time they tried to break out of the tightening ring, they ran into more small parties of Khmer Rouge troops. It was becoming almost impossible to get around them.

"Okay, people, this is getting serious now." Ringer turned to Brody and Wilburn when they finally stopped for a rest break. Looking at Wilburn he asked, "PJ, why ain't this shit ever easy?"

"You got me, sir."

"Jesus!" He wiped the sweat from the back of his neck. "Anyway, we've been lucky so far, but we've got to do something about this ASAP before they squeeze the circle shut and zero all of us.

"We're beating ourselves to death running around here the

way we are, trying to dodge every gook we run into. So here's what we're going to do." Ringer laid his map out on the ground. "I'm going to take Wilburn, the sniper, and two of my Nungs and try to carve our way out of here. Brody, I want you and your people to act as our rear guard."

"No sweat, sir."

"We'll be out in front of you a couple thousand meters or so, and we'll keep in touch on the horn. I'm going to head west." His finger tapped a location on the map. "And if I can't find an exit, I'm going to make me one out of dead slopes. You stay back, out of sight, watch our tail, and wait for my call. If we get into a firefight, don't come to reinforce us. You just sit tight right where you are unless I call for you, understand? I don't need any John Waynes today."

"Yes, sir!" Brody laughed quietly. He fully understood their situation and knew that the Green Beret captain was right.

"Let's give the folks a few more minutes and we'll take off."

"Right, sir." Brody stood up. "I'll go talk to my people."

"Brody?"

"Sir?"

"I've been meaning to ask. How'd you ever get mixed up in this anyway?"

"Just lucky, I guess, sir."

Ringer laughed.

"That's what I thought."

Colonel Duc orbited high in the sky, waiting for more reports from his ground troops. So far, the search teams had found very little. The colonel was becoming angrier by the minute.

"Mongoose, this is Tiger," he called impatiently to the Cambodian sublieutenant in charge of the ground operation. "Come in."

"Tiger, this is Mongoose. Over."

"This is Tiger. It has been over an hour since you reported. Have you found anything yet? Over."

"This is Mongoose. No, Comrade Colonel. Not yet. Each time we pick up their trail, it fades out and we cannot follow it. Over."

"This is Tiger. You had better find something very soon. Out."

Duc glanced down at his instrument panel. He only had enough fuel on board for another twenty minutes of flight time. He decided to go back to Kangor Wat and refuel. That way, when they found the Americans, he would be able to stay right on top of the Yankee dogs until he had blasted them out of existence.

"Mongoose, this is Tiger. I am returning to base to refuel. I will be back in twenty minutes. Over."

"This is Mongoose, acknowledged. Out."

Duc banked his Mi-8 gunship sharply away to the south and headed back to Kangor Wat.

On the ground, Brody and his men heard the helicopter's rotors fade into the distance. They had gone to ground a few minutes before, ducking back into the thick undergrowth when the big green-and-gray-striped Russian chopper passed over their heads and started circling. At first, Brody was certain that they had been spotted.

He got to his feet and made the move-out signal. Up at point, the young Nung, one of two that Ringer had left behind, took up the trail again. Two-Step followed behind the Chinese mercenary in the slack position.

The Indian had always thought that he was good in the woods, but he realized that he could learn a lot from the Nung. The slender Oriental moved through the jungle like he had been born in it, leaving almost no tracks behind him. The black, tan, and two-tone green stripes of his tiger suit blended perfectly with the leaves and branches as he snaked his way through.

Suddenly, the Nung froze and carefully lowered himself to the ground. He slowly turned around to look back at Two-Step and pointed a finger at his own eye. He had spotted something. The Nung raised three fingers. There were three of them. Two-Step cautiously crawled up beside him to take a look himself.

Slowly he parted the leaves in front of him and saw two olive-uniformed Khmer troops standing in the middle of the trail examining something on the ground. A third man looked into the jungle around them, his AK ready.

One soldier wore red collar tabs, and had to be their leader. He stood up and looked down the trail that Ringer's party had taken. Obviously, he had found tracks. The Khmer said something to the man standing guard.

The Nung put his head close to Two-Step. "We must stop them, kill them now," he whispered. "They find *Dai Uy* Ringer's trail."

The Indian nodded and loosened the K-Bar knife in his boot sheath.

"I go to right, you go to left." The Nung flashed a quick grin and slithered off into the jungle.

Two-Step slung his shotgun across his back, barrel down and followed the Nung's instructions. This was going to be a little closer than he really liked. There were three of the Khmers and only two of them. And they had to have a perfectly silent kill.

A single gunshot would bring the rest of the searchers right down on top of them.

Broken Arrow crept within a few meters of the Cambodians and was just off of the trail in the brush when he heard a moaning sound from the other side of the trail. The Khmers heard it, too. Their AKs snapped up.

The moaning sound came again.

Two of the Khmers carefully parted the brush with the muzzles of their assault rifles and discovered the Nung laying there. Peering through the leaves, Two-Step could see that his face and neck were covered with blood.

The enemy dragged the mercenary's limp body onto the trail and rolled him onto his back. One of them kicked him in the ribs. The Nung moaned again, his eyes closed to mere slits.

The three soldiers relaxed, their AKs held down at their sides. This one was of no danger to them. He looked to be almost dead.

The Nung muttered something. The Khmer who had kicked him leaned over, trying to hear what it was.

The Nung's hand shot out, grabbed the Khmer by the throat, and jerked him down to meet the knife blade that he brought up from his side.

The other two Cambodians were stunned, they froze for a fatal instant.

From flat on the ground, the Nung twisted around and delivered a kick to the closest Khmer's crotch. The man screamed and fell to his knees. The Nung delivered another smashing blow to the man's throat, crushing it.

Two-Step had leapt from the brush when the Nung grabbed the first Khmer.

The third enemy soldier was just raising his rifle when the Indian's arm wrapped around his head and jerked it to one side with a snap. The razor-sharp blade of his K-Bar slashed the Khmer's throat, cutting all the way through to his spinal column.

It was over in seconds.

The second man was struggling to breathe through a crushed windpipe, his eyes bugging out of their sockets. The Nung calmly slit his throat, wiped the blade of his fighting knife on the man's jacket, and smiled up at Two-Step.

"Good, no?"

"Yeah, that was great."

The Indian sat down to catch his breath. That was the damnedest thing he had ever witnessed.

He had never seen a kick delivered from a prone position like that. He had picked up a few moves from the Oriental martial arts since he had first come to Nam, but that move had been unbelievable.

"We go now," the mercenary said. "Maybe somebody hear man scream."

"Yes, we'd better move out."

270

Two-Step went back down the trail and motioned the rest of the men forward.

Brody looked at his Comanche buddy with disbelief when he saw the knife wounds in the three bodies. He knew that Two-Step was good with a knife, but he hadn't known he was that good.

"The Nung got two of 'em," the Indian explained, reading the expression on Brody's face.

"Jesus."

"Here, help me get 'em off the trail."

The dead Khmers were quickly dragged off and dumped out of sight behind the brush at the side of the trail. Dirt was sprinkled over the wet blood and the grunts brushed away the signs of the fight before they took off. A good tracker would be able to tell that there had been a fight there, but it was the best they could do in a hurry.

The Nung went back up on the point again and they moved out fast.

Ahead, Ringer and Wilburn stopped again. Another small group of Khmers were ahead of them, blocking the trail.

"We're going to have to take to the woods," Wilburn whispered in the captain's ear. The enemy boldly walked up the trail.

"Yeah, I think you're right. These bastards are all over the place."

"I'll go on back and bring Brody's people forward." Wilburn dropped back down.

"Right," Ringer replied. "I'll stay here and keep an eye on these assholes."

With the Khmers on their trail, they were going to have to strike out through dense jungle. It was getting dark fast and the Special Forces officer didn't want to move through the jungle at night. For one thing, it was noisy. Far more importantly, there was too great of a chance of stumbling into someone in the dark.

So far, they had made pretty good time. He really hated

to stop, but they were going to have to find a place to lay up until the next day, someplace high enough so they could stay out of the way and watch all the approaches. At first light in the morning, they would try to break out again. Right now, all they could do was hide.

Coming in from the east, Alexander also saw that it was getting dark. He was worried because they had not covered as much ground as they should have.

They had stopped cold for over an hour while Sergeant Zack took two of the men and made a recon of a major trail they had crossed, a trail that showed signs of recent heavy traffic. They brought back an empty tin of canned herring packed in Red China and an empty pack of North Vietnamese cigarettes. An NVA regular unit had stopped for a meal in the last couple of hours. The inside of the can was still wet with fish oil.

Since the enemy's tracks ran in the same direction they were going, Alexander had been forced to take another route, and it had cost them valuable time. Now that it was getting dark, he went back to where Sergeant Zack was walking beside the radio man.

"Do you think we should stop?" he asked the veteran sergeant.

"Yes, sir, I think we should. If the NVA are in this area, there's too great a chance of us running into them in the dark. We'd better hole up and just wait it out. We won't be any help to the others if we get into a firefight at night. Also, Captain Gaines won't be able to fly in and bail us out, either."

Alexander was anxious. He wanted to keep going, but he knew that the veteran sergeant was right. With just the two squads, he didn't have enough men to get into a pissing contest with a passing NVA unit.

"Okay, Sergeant, as soon as you can find a good spot, we'll stop and wait till morning."

"Yes, sir."

272

"Oh, one more thing," Alexander grinned. "Can you help me find where in the hell we are on this map, so I can call it in to Captain Gaines. You know how bad we lieutenants are with maps."

Zack smiled. "Be glad to help, sir."

CHAPTER 36

Camp Radcliff, An Khe

Early that evening, a meeting was held behind closed doors in Colonel Jordan's office. Rat Gaines, Captain Mike Torrence of Charlie Company, and General Vance were already there. They were waiting for the representative from Special Forces Command and Control North.

So as not to be conspicuous, General Vance had changed into an unmarked set of jungle fatigues with no name tape. It wouldn't do to have someone asking what a three-star general was doing wandering around the First of the 7th Cav Headquarters.

"Good evening, gentlemen."

A tall Special Forces major wearing starched ARVN camouflage fatigues walked in the door. The man was thin with close-cropped blond, almost white, hair and faded blue eyes.

"I'm Major Snow from CCN," he said with a faint European accent. "I understand that you're trying to retrieve a package from Indian country. I think that I can help you."

The Green Beret officer, once a refugee from the Hungarian Revolution, handled Roadrunner and Project Delta support operations for CCN. He was known as the master of under-the-table deals. If it would result in a dead communist, he'd do it no matter who liked it or who had said that he couldn't.

Snow's only reason to be in Vietnam was to kill Asian communists until he could return to his homeland and kill the Russian and Hungarian kind back there. His hatred for the followers of Marx and Lenin ran deep. During the street-fighting in the revolution in Budapest, a 122mm cannon shell from a Russian JS III tank had taken out a flat in an apartment building. Snow's wife and baby daughter had been in the flat.

When the Hungarian revolution failed, he escaped to Austria and made his way to the United States where he enlisted in the army. Snow was the *nom de guerre* he had taken because his Hungarian name was too hard to pronounce. The men he worked with all called him the Ice Man. And with good reason. When he planned an operation, he was as cold and hard as ice.

The introductions were made quickly, and the group got to work. From the briefcase he carried, Major Snow pulled out a large topographical map, a series of aerial photographs, and a long, typed list.

"Before we get started, gentlemen, there's one thing I want to settle first." Snow locked eyes with General Vance. "I understand, sir, that you are here in a completely unofficial capacity."

"Yes I am, Major, that's correct. I'm visiting my son in the hospital."

"Well, sir, we are planning to engage in an unauthorized operation that, if discovered, will have all of us in jail at the very least. It's not going to look too good if it's discovered that you had anything to do with it. Are you sure that you want to get involved?"

Vance met the major's stare squarely. His voice was cold and steady. "Yes, I do."

"Okay, that takes care of that." Snow relaxed a little. "Here's what I've put together."

He pointed to an area on the map. "Captain Ringer is

275

here tonight. He will stay there until first light, if he can. If he is hit and has to withdraw and evade, he will try to head west.

"Now," Snow looked up at Jordan. "Lieutenant Alexander and the Aero Rifle Platoon are lagered here for the night." He pointed to another location to the east of Ringer. "I figure that it will be another two or three hours in the morning before he can link up with Ringer.

"Now here's the bad news. Our radio interception is reporting increased NVA movement in this area. The Vietnamese are concerned about all the Khmer Rouge activity along the Ho Chi Minh Trail. As you know, they are very protective of their traditional supply routes. They are moving units into this area as well. If the interceptions are correct, and they usually are, Alexander is going to run into heavy NVA activity when he attempts to make his link-up. Ringer is going to run into them as soon as he crosses over this ridgeline and tries to run for it."

"Then they're trapped." General Vance sounded angry.

"Well, not really, General. That depends on how much of a diversion we can create to draw them away from that area."

"Something like an air assault?" Jordan asked.

"That would probably do it, but there is no way that we could keep an air-mobile operation secret. My understanding is that the Air Cav is under specific orders not to cross the border under any circumstances whatsoever."

"That's correct," General Vance leaned forward. "I talked to the division commander earlier today. He doesn't like it any more than we do, but his hands are tied."

"Well," the Hungarian leaned back in his chair. "How about if I bring in my own private Air Cav? And, Colonel, you provide the troops."

"What are you talking about?"

"I can have four lift ships and two gunships anywhere you want at first light tomorrow."

"Where are you getting them?" The general was incredulous.

"Well, sir, let's just say that the choppers carry no markings, not even tail numbers, and the pilots all wear Hawaiian shirts and shoulder holsters."

The general looked puzzled, but Rat grinned broadly. "Air America, sir," he clarified. "The CIA's private air force."

"How are you getting those kind of assets?"

"Trade secrets, sir," the major smiled thinly. "They owe me a few. The biggest problem that I see now is that Russian Mi-8 helicopter flying out of Kangor Wat. It's the only wild joker in this whole thing. If that pilot happens to get wind of what we're doing, the gunship's got enough firepower to knock this whole operation out of the air as well as take out all the men on the ground."

"You just leave that bastard to me," Gaines said quietly. "I'll see that he doesn't interfere with our party."

Snow looked at him.

"Don't worry, Ice Man," Rat said. "That fucker's cold meat."

After all the details had been hammered out, Gaines drove as fast as he could over to the officers' club for his dinner date with Lisa. He had already called to warn her that he would be late and he knew that she was not going to be very happy with him.

As he walked in the door, he saw that he need not have worried. He located her by heading to the largest group of guys standing around and found her right in the middle.

"Go away, Rat!" someone called out as he walked up.

"Thanks, guys, for keeping my date from getting lonesome while I was defending my country."

"Gaines, you wienie."

Rat bowed. "Lisa? Shall we have dinner?"

The nurse looked at him. Seeing that he wasn't drunk, she stood up. "Okay, let's go."

At the table, the waitress quickly took their orders. Rat ordered coffee with his meal.

As soon as the waitress was gone, Lisa leaned over the table. "You mind telling me what's going on?"

The pilot looked at her blandly. "What do you mean?"

"Goddamnit, Rat, I'm not blind. You don't drink coffee this late at night. Plus that little song and dance you gave me at the hospital this morning about Vance. Look, Rat, I'm not trying to get national secrets out of you or anything, I'm just worried. I don't know what's going on and I'm scared."

He reached across the table and took her hand. "Lisa, I know you are and I wish that I could tell you more about it. But believe me, this time I can't. This one's just too serious."

The nurse didn't say a word. She just kept looking at him, the concern plainly evident on her face.

He squeezed her hand, trying to make her understand. "I'll tell you all about it as soon as it's all over. I promise."

"Okay, Rat." She leaned back in her chair.

Gaines relaxed a little and made small talk until their food came. He dove into his hamburger and fries and didn't even make his usual derogatory comment about the origin of the mayonnaise.

Lisa ate her club sandwich in silence. There was so much she wanted to talk to him about, but she could tell that it was not the right time. His mind was not on her at all. It was too bad. She believed he would like to hear some of what she wanted to say.

"Rat?"

"Uh, yes." He snapped his mind back to the club.

"Why don't you take me back to my quarters?"

"Sure thing."

He rose and picked up his hat before leading her out of the club. He didn't even respond to the comments of his buddies when he passed their tables.

He had little to say on the short Jeep ride to the hospital. He pulled up in the graveled parking lot in front of the nurses' quarters.

" 'Night, Lisa. I'll call you tomorrow evening."

"Sure, Rat. Good night." The nurse's voice was cold and harsh.

278

On the drive back to his operations building, Gaines wondered what in the world she was pissed off about. He decided to worry about it the next day.

Just as night fell in the jungle, the Americans reached the top of a small, sparsely covered ridge. "What do you think?" Ringer quietly asked Wilburn.

The sergeant looked around, at the already pitch-black jungle. "It'll do. We've got good coverage of the approaches."

"That's what I thought. We'll use a patrol star tonight."

"Right, sir."

As each one of the men reached the top, Wilburn had them pull into a tight defensive perimeter. Instead of digging in like the grunts were used to doing, Wilburn put them in a patrol star formation. The men lay down on their bellies, facing out with their feet touching in the center. They would lie unmoving in that position all night, awake or asleep. Even if they had to urinate, they were to roll onto their side, do it and lay back down. No one was to move until the morning.

If anyone heard anything or saw movement, he was to tap the boot of the man next to him and point it out with hand signals. The man would pass it down the line to the next man in the circle. No one would say a word until first light the next morning.

Since there were so few of them, defensive positions would have been useless. Their only chance was to lie low, completely silent, and hope that the Khmers would miss them in the dark.

They put their claymores out in the trees around them, but they were not trip-wired. They were rigged for command detonation, not early warning, and they would only be used as a last resort if the men were discovered and forced to pull out. Their weapons were ready in their hands and their hand grenades within easy reach, but they didn't want to fight. Their survival depended on not being discovered.

Once they were in position, a few of the men tried to eat.

Most of them were too exhausted to even open a C-ration can. The Nungs had their cold rice and pork-fat balls in their packs and they offered to share them with Brody's men. They had few takers.

Ringer told the men that he wanted half of them to try to sleep, but everyone was too wired to relax. They were all awake and alert. Even Farmer, who usually could sleep anywhere at anytime, didn't drop off. The dark jungle below their ridge scared him.

Later that night, Brody was startled awake with a hand over his mouth. In the silvery moonlight, he saw Two-Step beside him. The Indian put a finger to his lips to indicate silence. He had been dreaming again and had made noises.

It had been his old nightmare, and he didn't want to return to it. He brought his arm up close to his face and looked at his watch. The luminous dial read 2:35 in the morning. In the silvery light, the jungle below them looked like the landscape in his dream. He shivered and tried to stay awake.

Colonel Nguyen Cao Duc was disgusted. The Cambodian girl knew nothing. The Russian KGB officer had not divulged anything to the slut. She had said that she knew nothing from the beginning, even before he had started working on her. But he had not believed her. He questioned her long enough now, however, that he realized she was telling the truth. She could not have remembered a lie through his interrogation.

He went over to the dresser against the wall and splashed water from the pitcher on his hands and forearms. Bloody, red water collected in the wash basin.

On his bed, the young Cambodian girl tried not to whimper as she sucked air through bruised lips. She had long since stopped struggling against the bonds that tied her hands and feet to the corners of the bed. Now she was only waiting for the Vietnamese to finally kill her, praying that he would kill her so that the horrible night would finally end.

While Duc was disgusted that he had not learned anything

280

from her, he was also very pleased at the way the interrogation had gone. She had been a good subject to work on.

He looked at her naked, battered body. It had been a long time since he had enjoyed an interrogation quite as much as this. The girl felt his eyes on her and she whimpered like a wounded animal.

CHAPTER 37

Kangor Wat, Cambodia

Colonel Duc woke feeling refreshed and confident. He knew that he would catch up with the Yankees today and deliver the punishment they deserved. He dressed in a clean flight suit and walked briskly to his command post.

"Where are the messages?" he barked at the duty sergeant.

"Here, Comrade Colonel." The NCO instantly handed him a clipboard.

Duc quickly flipped through the copies of last night's radio reports. The search parties had still not found any signs of the Yankees. Evidently, the lieutenant in charge was completely incompetent. It was time that he got back in the air himself to coordinate the search.

"Have my helicopter readied for takeoff. Also, I want another ten men ready to go up with me."

"Right away, Colonel."

The HIP gunship had been rearmed and refueled during the night, and a preflight inspection had been completed by the time he walked over to it. The ten Khmer soldiers clambered into the troop compartment in back as he strapped himself into the cockpit.

In two minutes, the powerful twin turbines were whining, and the massive five-bladed rotor was a blurred, spinning disk. Duc taxied out to the end of the runway and twisted the throttles all the way open. Like a huge bird of prey, the green-and-gray-striped Mi-8 rose into the air and headed to the north.

As good as his word, Major Snow's private air force showed up right on schedule. At first light, Rat Gaines's Python Flight had air-lifted Colonel Jordan and one platoon of Charlie Company to a small LZ close to the Cambodian border. After the insertion, most of the Python choppers took off and flew back to An Khe. Only Rat's gunship and Warlokk's slick, which was doubling as Jordan's C and C bird, remained on the ground.

The grunts had just secured the perimeter of the LZ when six choppers came roaring in low out of the north, two C model gunships and four slicks. Four of them were painted dull black, but the last two were polished aluminum. Not a single marking was to be seen on any of them, not American stars, not tail numbers, not even warning stripes.

"Python, Python," a slightly accented voice came over the radio. "This is Frosty, over."

"This is Python, you're right on time. The LZ is secure, over."

"This is Frosty, roger."

The six machines flared out and landed in trail. Major Snow and his own radio operator jumped from the back of the lead gunship and ran over to Gaines and Jordan, who had set up a field CP at the edge of the clearing.

"Good morning, Colonel, Rat. Are your people ready to go, sir?"

Captain Mike Torrence, the CO of Charlie Company who was supplying the grunts for the morning's diversion, stepped up. "We're ready, Major, and I'll be going along to do the C and C myself."

"Good, that'll make things a little easier."

Torrence turned to the lieutenant at his side. "Get 'em moving, Blake."

"Roger, roger, sir." He turned to his men. "Let's get it, boys and girls."

Three of the platoon's four squads ran for the waiting birds and scrambled on board. The last squad remained behind to provide security for the LZ.

When the troops were on board, Snow gave the pilot in the lead ship a thumbs-up. The pilot was wearing a Hawaiian shirt over his nomex flying suit and a straw cowboy hat instead of a flight helmet. He nodded affirmatively to Snow and spoke into his microphone. One by one, the choppers lifted off, circled high in the sky, and headed west for Cambodia.

The Air America machines flew high enough so that the radar sets on both sides of the border would pick them up. This was not a mistake. Since all of the Air Cav's helicopters were accounted for, the army's command would not know who was violating the orders not to go into Cambodia. To the enemy radars, however, the six choppers would appear as an air assault and the alarm would go out.

"Okay," Snow said, looking around the clearing. "That's on the way. Now let's see about the rest of this operation."

Gaines took the radio handset from the RTO. "Blue Six, Blue Six," he called. "This is Python, over."

"Python, this is Blue Six," Alexander's voice came over the handset. "Send your traffic, over."

"Blue Six, this is Python. Be advised that we have reports of increased enemy movement in your area, located between you and the Lightning element. Use extreme caution. We are trying to draw them away from you at this time. Over."

"This is Blue Six. Roger, copy. We have already seen signs of them. I anticipate an Echo Tango Alpha of three hours. Over."

"This is Python, roger. Be careful and keep in touch. Out."

"Lightning, Lightning, this is Python, Python, over."

"Python, this is Lightning," Ringer answered. "I hear you weak, but steady. We are under way now. There is no sign of that gunship yet, and we are not being pursued at this time. Over."

"This is Python, roger. Be advised that Blue 2 is working his way in to meet you and we are trying to pull the November Victor Alpha away to the north. Over."

"This is Lightning, roger, I monitored your call to the 2 element. I will be in contact with him for the marry up. Over."

"This is Python. Out."

Gaines gave the radio handset back to the RTO.

"Well, that's about it. Now we wait."

Snow glanced at his watch and bent over the large acetate-covered map spread out on the ground. "Charlie Company should be making the first of their landings right about now."

Colonel Duc had just finished talking to the lieutenant on the ground when he received a call from his base telling him that they had intercepted a North Vietnamese Army radio broadcast reporting American air assaults in the jungle to the north.

Duc quickly checked the location on his map. It was too far to the north to be an attempt to rescue the Yankees he was chasing. They could not have possibly marched that far overnight.

It was tempting, but Duc decided to stick to the area he had chosen to search.

Just then, the lieutenant on the ground called him again. "Tiger, this is Mongoose. We have found signs of them. They ran into one of our outposts yesterday and killed the men, but they left a trail. We are following it now."

"Mongoose, this is Tiger, give me the location quickly!"

Duc copied the grid coordinates on his map. "This is Tiger, I am on my way there now. Keep on them!"

He banked his ship over and headed in that direction. The location he had been given indicated that the Americans were still trying to make it to the border, just as he had expected them to do. He didn't know what was going on up north, but he was certain that it had nothing to do with his prey.

He was circling a ridgeline to the east of the kill site when the lieutenant called him again.

"Tiger, Tiger, this is Mongoose." The young Cambodian officer could not contain his excitement. "We have found where they spent the night. There are signs of at least a dozen of them and they are moving to the east. We are in pursuit."

"This is Tiger, acknowledged. Have ten of your men find a clearing where I can land so I can pick them up and transport them on ahead."

"This is Mongoose. Right away."

Major Snow put down the radio handset and looked up from his map. "I think it's working. CCN says that they're picking up radio traffic directing the NVA units into the area where your people are making their air assaults."

Jordan checked the map coordinates. " 'Bout time we pulled them out then, don't you think?"

"Yes, sir. I'll give Frosty a call."

So far their plan was working. Charlie Company's phony air assaults had worked to draw the NVA troops north. With the two Air America gunships prepping the LZs for them, Torrence's grunts had flown in, shot up the empty countryside, and gotten back on the slicks. They had hit enough LZs and had expended enough ammunition that the NVA thought they were being hit by a full-sized invasion. Instead of moving south to investigate what the Khmers were doing, the Vietnamese were hurrying back to cover their supply lines to the north.

With the North Vietnamese regulars out of the way, all Ringer and Alexander had to worry about were the Khmers. And so far, Ringer had been able to keep one step ahead of them.

* * *

The Americans were all together in a group again, heading down a ridgeline to the east as fast as they could go. Chief was on point with Wilburn and one of the Nungs, using his scoped rifle to check out the valleys below.

"Oh oh," he said. "We got company."

"Where?" Wilburn asked.

"Over there to our right, six hundred meters or so. They're moving parallel to us, about a dozen of them."

"Fuck! Better hold it up here while I tell the captain."

"Roger."

Ringer came up and Chief pointed out the Khmers to him. The captain pulled his map out and studied it for a minute.

"PJ, there may be another route a klick or so to the north." His finger traced a curved line. "Let's pull back from here and try to get around them that way. Tell Brody to hold the rear again. We'll go ahead and check it out."

"Yes, sir."

At the base of the ridgeline, Brody quickly placed his people into an X-shaped ambush covering Ringer's rear. With that formation, no matter which direction the Khmers tried to come, they could bring fire on them.

A tense fifteen minutes later, Brody received a radio call. "Two, this is Lightning. It's clear. Move out. Try to stay five hundred meters behind us, over."

"This is Two, wilco, out."

Brody gave the handset back to Bunny and stood up. "Okay, let's go. Two-Step, you take point, I'll do slack. Corky, take drag."

They had only gone four or five hundred meters when Brody heard Corky's M-60 open up behind them.

"Bunny, stay here and call it in!" Brody shouted as he ran back to the drag.

Bunny keyed the mike. "Lightning, Lightning, this is Blue Two Tango, over."

"Lightning, send it," came the curt reply.

"This is Two Tango, we are in contact with an unknown-sized enemy force at our rear, over."

"Do you need help? Over."

"Not at this time, over."

"Keep me informed. Lightning out."

Bunny crouched down at the side of the trial, his M-16 ready, and nervously scanned the jungle around him.

"I'm a goddamned FO, not a fucking grunt, I'm not supposed to be out here all by myself." he muttered.

For the hundredth time on this mission, Bunny wished that there was some artillery close enough for him to call on. Even one tube of 105mm would get them out of this fucking mess. He vowed that he was never going outside of the artillery fan ever again. A guy could get killed without artillery support.

When Brody reached the contact, Corky had rolled behind a tree and was hosing down the trail. Two dead gooks were laying out in the open where the M-60 had cut them down. From the intensity of the enemy fire, however, he knew that there was still a squad or so of them out there. At least they didn't have a machine gun. All he could hear were the AK-47s, which was bad enough.

He turned sharply and waved Two-Step around to their left flank. The firing wasn't so heavy there.

On the other side of the trail, Gardner and Farmer were working together as a team. Every time Gardner stood to fire his seventy-nine, Farmer jumped up beside him and ripped off a magazine of 5.56mm on full auto to keep the Khmers heads down. So far, it was working real well.

Farmer poked his head up to take a look and a burst of AK tracer cut through the air in front of him. On second thought, maybe it wasn't working as well as they had thought. JJ whirled and fired a thumper round at the source of the tracer. It stopped.

On the flank, Two-Step cautiously crawled forward until the bark of the AKs sounded like they were right in front of him. He looked around the tree trunk and saw six Khmers in a group five meters in front of him. He ducked back behind the tree, pulled a hand frag from his side pocket, and checked the load in his sawed off.

He pulled the pin on the grenade, let the spoon fly off,

counted two and lobbed it fifteen feet to the Khmer position. With the short count on the fuse, the grenade exploded in the air over their heads.

Before the frag had even stopped flying, the Indian stepped out into the open, his deadly pump gun held down at his hip.

Working the slide as fast as he could, he emptied the magazine. The stainless steel-balls tore through the vegetation into the surviving Khmers. The few who had escaped the blast of the grenade were blown off their feet.

Two-Step ducked back behind the tree and quickly reloaded. Jamming the last shell up into the sawed-off's magazine, he charged the enemy position.

They were all dead.

Dropping down among the bodies in their fighting hole, he scanned the jungle, looking for more gooks on his side of the trail.

It was clean.

When Brody heard the roar of Two-Step's shotgun, He yelled at Corky and charged. Cordova held the trigger down on his sixty, smoking the barrel as he sprayed fire into his side of the trail.

Gardner sent two grenades after Corky's tracer rounds.

"Cease fire!" Brody yelled. "Cease fire!"

It was suddenly quiet.

The Indian stepped out of the brush and joined Brody. The two grunts quickly checked all the bodies. "You see a radio?" Brody asked.

"Nope."

Brody turned and saw his RTO standing over one of the dead Khmers. "Bunny, call Lightning. Tell him that they definitely were Khmers but that we didn't find a radio on any of the bodies."

Bunny passed the message to Lightning who ordered them to move out again.

Two-Step was loading shotgun shells in the magazine under the barrel of his sawed-off when he cocked his head to the side.

"Quiet!" he hissed. "Listen!"

CHAPTER 38

Inside Cambodia

The grunts froze. In the distance, they heard the faint, whining sounds of a chopper approaching. It did not sound like a Huey. The sound drew closer.

"Hit it!" Brody shouted.

They all headed up the trail after Ringer, running as fast as they could to get back into cover. Through the breaks in the trees, they saw the dark shape of the Russian gunship flash over their heads. It passed the site of their contact and banked around.

Brody's heart froze. they had not dragged the bodies off of the trail. The pilot was sure to see them.

The gunship circled like a vulture. Suddenly, it banked away, flew higher into the air, and turned back. By twos and fours, rockets lanced out of its side pods and exploded in the jungle. The cannon muzzles under the nose spat flame as the 23mm H.E. rounds shredded the trees.

Brody didn't have to say a word. Everyone was running as fast as they could. Behind them, the chopper stopped firing, and they heard it settle to the ground.

There would be another tracking team on their ass in just a few moments.

They ran even harder.

Running alongside his squad leader, Bunny handed him the radio handset. It was Lightning.

Brody held his hand up. They stopped and took cover beside the trail. "The captain says we gotta hold it up here for a minute," Brody said softly.

The panting grunts quickly spread out and dropped down into brush. Right ahead of them was a small clearing with a trail leading in the right direction. Ringer's people were checking it now to see if it was clear.

Gardner and Two-Step hurriedly rigged their last claymore with a trip wire fifty meters back the way they had come. It was all they had left to slow the gooks down. If the trail leading from the other side of the clearing was safe, they wouldn't have to stay and fight it out. But with fresh tracking teams all around them, Ringer couldn't tell if the trail was still open until his Nungs had reconned it.

Once they were in position, the men checked their remaining ammunition and waited, hoping that they had gotten away from their pursuers. Two-Step kept looking over his shoulder for the signal that the way was clear. Even with all the extra shotgun shells he had loaded for this mission, he was running low and didn't want to get into another heavy firefight in the thick jungle. Their only chance was to fade back into the brush and go as fast as they could.

Corky laid out a hundred-round ammo belt for his sixty. He only had about six hundred rounds left. It was enough if they didn't get into a major pissing contest. If they did, he was in a world of hurt. On full rock and roll, his M-60 burned up over five hundred and fifty rounds a minute.

The rest of the men were in better shape than the machine gunner. They had sufficient ammunition for several more short skirmishes, but no one had enough left to get into a major firefight.

After a tense fifteen-minute wait, Wilburn stuck his head out of the foliage on the other side of the grassy clearing. He gave them the all-clear and the arm-pumping signal to hurry up.

"Treat!" the Indian hissed. "Let's go."

They could hear faint shouts from the pursuing Khmers behind them. They had no time to waste.

The men got up from their hiding places and started across the tall grass into the clearing when they heard the dreaded sound of the HIP's twin turbines. It was coming on fast.

"Brody! That fucker's found us again," Farmer wailed. He had been chased enough by helicopters for one day.

"Hit it!" Brody hissed.

The grunts dove into the thick brush for cover. The last of Ringer's people disappeared into the brush on the other side of the small clearing. But the gunship pilot had seen them and dove down.

Brody hugged the damp ground and waited for the roar of the HIP's cannons and rockets to start up again. There was nothing they could do to stop the Russian gunship.

"Python, Python," Bunny radioed to Gaines. "This is Blue Two Tango, Blue Two Tango, over."

"This is Python, send your traffic, over."

"This is Two Tango, that gunship's here again, sir." Bunny's voice broke, he was panicked.

"This is Python, roger. Echo Tango Alpha your location twelve, I say again twelve mikes, over."

"This is Two Tango. Roger copy twelve minutes. Can you hurry, sir?"

"This is Python, just take it easy, son." Under pressure Rat's Georgia accent became even more pronounced. "I'll be there as fast as I can. Out."

"He said twelve minutes," Bunny shouted over to Brody.

Brody grimaced. It might as well be twelve days. They would all be dead long before the captain could get there.

Suddenly, Brody remembered the Huey that the gooks had taken out with an RPG one time, right outside the wire at Firebase Belinda. He didn't have an RPG with him, but they still had their LAWs.

"Somebody gimme a LAW," he shouted. He was sick of

292

being chased through the woods like a slope with the Air Cav after him. He had had enough.

Farmer dug into the top of his ruck for the LAW he was carrying and handed it to his squad leader. Brody snatched the antitank weapon out of his hand and frantically pulled the lock pin from the end of the launcher. He jerked the carrying strap off, letting it drop to the ground, then unlatched and extended the fiberglass launching tube to its full length with a smooth pull. This caused the front and rear sights to slide out of their housings and pop up.

The rocket launcher was ready to fire.

He put the tube up on his right shoulder and peered through the sights. Though the antitank weapon's sights had been designed to hit moving vehicles, they were not graduated to track something moving as fast as a helicopter. He was going to have to apply Kentucky windage to the max here.

He lined up on the nose of the diving HIP and moved the weapon ahead of the sight picture.

Squeezing the firing switch on the top of the launcher, the rocket ignited with a whoosh and flew up into the air, trailing white smoke.

As Brody watched, the rocket shot directly behind the gunship, missing it completely. He had not given the chopper enough lead.

"Fuck!"

He scrambled to ready the launcher again as the HIP swept down onto Ringer's position, its rocketpods and nose cannons blazing. Over the roar of the exploding rockets and the bark of the 23mm cannons, Brody heard the screams of wounded men on the other side of the clearing. He had to kill that gunship before it killed all of them.

As Duc hauled his machine around into a hard bank to line up for his next run, Brody ran out into the small clearing with another LAW.

Fighting his way through the tall elephant grass, he tried to get right in the diving HIP's flight path to get ahead-on shot. He was concentrating so hard on the Russian chopper, he didn't notice that the sharp blades of the tough elephant grass were cutting his unprotected arms to bloody shreds.

In the air, Duc watched Brody run into the open. He saw that the Yankee had some kind of weapon with him, a short rocket launcher. He nudged the cyclic over to the side to line up on the man and triggered off one of his 57mm rockets before zooming past him to hammer the American position in the opposite tree line again.

Brody saw the rocket leap out of the pod on the right side pylon and come straight at him, trailing dirty white smoke.

He threw himself off to the side, landing on the hard ground with a bone-jarring thud.

The rocket exploded with a deafening roar. The deadly sharp fragments of its warhead sliced through the tough grass like hot knives.

Brody shook himself. With his ears still ringing from the blast, he staggered back to his feet. He raised the launcher again and aimed it at the chopper as it flashed past overhead.

He pressed down hard on the firing switch. Nothing happened.

"Motherfuck this thing!" he screamed as he tried to close the launcher and reopen it to recock the firing mechanism. The Russian helicopter was just banking away from its gun run on Ringer's position when Brody tried to fire the LAW again. Once more, nothing happened. The delicate electrical firing mechanism had been damaged when he threw himself to the ground to escape the HIP's rocket.

With a scream of rage, he hurled the dud rocket launcher away from him. He dashed back for the edge of the clearing.

"I need another one!" he yelled.

Gardner had already opened his LAW and readied it for firing. He handed it to Brody and ran into the clearing with him.

JJ raised his thumper to fire on the chopper, too. He had no idea if the little M-79 grenade would even reach it. He knew that the 40mm round traveled so slowly that one could actually see it fly through the air, but he figured that if he waited until it was almost on top of them, he might have a chance of hitting it. He flipped the sights on the front of the barrel back down. He didn't need them. This was going to be purely eyeball shooting.

"Come on down, you sorry gook motherfucker," Brody said softly. "Get your ass back down here so I can kill you fucking dead."

Brody was so wired with adrenaline that his muscles quivered. He had to relax his grip on the firing handle to keep from launching the rocket too soon. He had lost his brush hat, and the breeze blew his sweat-soaked blond hair into his eyes, stinging them. He hardly noticed it.

This was the last time that he would run from this helicopter. He had run from it in his dreams and he had run through the jungle to get away from it, but he would run no more. He would live or die right where he was.

The green-and-gray-striped machine made a slow turn in the sky and started back down. In the cockpit, Duc saw that the Yankee with the rocket launcher was back. He had someone with him this time. Duc laughed at their stupidity. His finger tightened around the trigger to the two 23mm cannons in the belly of his ship.

The North Vietnamese pilot started firing when he was a thousand meters away, well beyond the range of the shoulder-fired rocket. He saw the H.E. cannon rounds impact all around the two men, but they seemed to be protected, as if they were standing behind an invisible shield.

He fired another short burst, but they were still standing. He released the trigger and rolled back on his throttle as he bore down upon them. He decided to get close enough to them that he could not possibly miss.

Gardner grunted with pain. He had picked up a piece of cannon shell shrapnel in his side and it burned like fire. He didn't even bother to see how badly he had been hit. In just a few seconds, he would be dead anyway. If by some odd chance he lived through this, he would have time to look at it. Right now, he had to concentrate on tracking the rapidly closing Russian gunship.

Brody stood silently beside him, the LAW launcher on his

295

shoulder. He tracked the Russian helicopter through the sights and waited. This was his last round and it had to be good. If he missed this time, or if the LAW misfired again, they were all dead.

As the enemy gunship bore down on top of them, Gardner wondered why it wasn't firing at them. He thumbed the breech safety off and lined the M-79's barrel up with the diving chopper.

For some reason, at the last moment before he fired he wondered who was fucking his wife back home.

Brody took a deep breath and held it. Slowly, he tightened his fingers around the rubber firing handle on the top of the LAW. Right as he felt the rocket's motor kick in, he saw the cannon muzzles under the nose of the Russian ship blossom with flame and heard Jungle Jim's thumper fire.

The explosion of a cannon shell knocked Brody off his feet, but the little rocket he had fired was right on target.

Duc saw the rocket, too. Instinctively, he ducked. His hand nudged the cyclic control ever so slightly causing the antitank rocket to miss the cockpit. Instead, it went over his head, exploding behind him in the engine compartment.

That did not save Colonel Duc.

One of the massive turbines screamed as it ran out of control. It overheated in an instant and burst into flames.

The slight movement of the chopper that had made the LAW rocket miss the cockpit allowed Gardner's slow-moving thumper grenade to impact against the internal fuel tanks buried in the top of the helicopter above the troop-carrying compartment.

Hundreds of sharp pieces of frag from the antipersonnel round tore scores of holes in the thin-walled fuel cell. JP-4 jet fuel sprayed out, filling the interior of the HIP. The vapors were ignited by the burning, runaway turbine. Duc had just enough time to look behind him and scream before he was engulfed in flames when the fuel exploded.

Brody and Gardner both heard his screams over the high-pitched whine of the turbine and the roar of the explosion.

The blazing wreckage of the Russian helicopter plunged into the jungle. It exploded again on impact.

Brody stood there for a moment, the now empty LAW launcher hanging in his hand, and watched the chopper burn. The remaining 57mm rockets in the pods started cooking off in the flames, adding to the destruction. The burning 23mm cannon ammunition sounded like very loud firecrackers at a Chinese New Year celebration.

A thick column of dirty black smoke rose into the clear blue sky.

Finally, Brody dropped the empty launcher and turned to Gardner. The big man was on his knees in the tall grass, his hand pressed tightly against his side. Blood seeped through his fingers.

"JJ!" Brody yelled. "You're hurt!"

Gardner toppled over onto the ground.

CHAPTER 39

Inside Cambodia

Far to the north of the Americans, Gregor Zerinski stopped for a short break. Taking one of the Khmer canteens from the side of his belt, he unscrewed it and brought it to his lips. The water inside was so foul that he almost spat it out. It was stale and reeked of sweat. He forced himself to swallow it anyway and shuddered as it went down.

Wiping his mouth on the back of his hand, the Russian looked at the jungle around him and back down the faint trail he had been following. He had been on the run now for well over two hours, and there was still no sign of pursuit that he could detect. He felt that he could afford to stop and rest for a while.

He was surprised that Duc was letting him get away so easily. When he had first heard Duc's chopper in the distance, a little over an hour ago, he was certain that the North Vietnamese was flying out to drop men into blocking positions along the routes back to the north, the routes that he would most likely be taking.

He ran even faster for as long as he could, but nothing developed. He wondered why Duc had not tried to stop him.

The North Vietnamese had to have known that the KGB agent went north and, to make speed he had to keep to the roads and trails. According to the map, just a handful of men could have blocked the trails leading to the north.

The North Vietnamese had to know that if Zerinski got away, it would be the end of Duc's renegade operation. Zerinski would report his location, and the Russians would have no compunction against bombing the ancient Khmer temple flat. They didn't care that Kangor Wat was a thousand years old and they cared even less about what Prince Sihanouk thought or said. They would simply bomb the place into rubble and then blame it on the Americans.

Zerinski stopped on a ridgeline. He made his way over to the edge and looked down in the valley below him. He searched the sky for Duc's helicopter, but didn't see it. He spotted a big column of greasy black smoke rising up into the sky over to the east.

He wondered what it was, but quickly put it from his mind. All he could worry about now was making his long walk through the jungle to Laos. When he was safely in the hands of his man in the Pathet Lao, he would worry about Colonel Duc.

He went back to his pack and rummaged through it until he found the Russian canned rations he had stashed away. Opening a tin, he wolfed the sausages down and followed them with more of the rancid water. As soon as he came to a stream, he would rinse and refill the canteens. Right now he had to get going again.

Shouldering his stolen Khmer pack, the tall, blond Russian officer started back down the trail. He wanted to keep moving as long as he had the daylight. He still had a four-day journey ahead of him.

Two-Step, Corky, Farmer, and Bunny raced into the clearing. Brody was kneeling at Gardner's side, ripping his fatigue jacket away from the wound.

"How bad is it?" Two-Step was the first one to reach them.

"I don't know," Brody replied. "It don't look good. He's bleeding real bad."

He ripped a field dressing out of its cover and slapped it over the wound, tying the strings around Gardner's waist. A jagged piece of steel had sliced into his side, breaking a rib and exposing another one. Brody had no idea of the extent of internal injuries.

Brody looked around the clearing. "We've got to get him under cover. Let's carry him over to Wilburn and have him call to see if Captain Gaines can take him out in his Cobra."

"He'd fucking better," the Indian said flatly. "JJ won't last long if we have to move him very far."

Farmer knelt down beside Gardner. Tears filled his eyes, but he didn't even notice them. He looked over at Brody. "He'll make it, won't he, Sarge?"

"I don't know, kid." Brody sounded tired. "I don't know. Here, help me move him under cover."

Farmer took his legs while Brody picked the big man up by the shoulders, and they carried him the rest of the way across the clearing.

"I called a dustoff request in to your captain," Wilburn said as Brody laid Gardner under a tree. "He's on his way to pick him up and he says that he'll have a medic waiting at the border by the time he gets him back there."

"I don't know if he'll make it that long. He's losing a lot of blood."

"I've got a bag of blood expander in my ruck. I'll get it."

"Great."

It might keep Gardner alive until he could reach the Dust-off chopper. Blood expander, known to the medical world as Ringer's Lactate—no relation to the famous Green Beret—was a saline and electrolyte solution. It couldn't carry oxygen the way whole blood would, but it could be carried in a medic's pack and it didn't need to be refrigerated. Blood expander would keep a wounded man alive by keeping his blood pressure high enough to prevent cardiovascular collapse from stopping his heart. Many a man in Vietnam owed his life to blood expander, and many infantry units carried the small plastic bags in their rucks as a matter of course.

Like all of the Green Berets, Wilburn had been trained as a field medic back at the JFK Special Warfare Center at Fort Bragg, North Carolina. He quickly got the drip tube loose and inserted the needle into a vein inside Gardner's arm.

"Here," he handed Farmer the clear plastic bag of the colorless, lifesaving fluid. "Hold this."

"Sure." Farmer's voice was shaky, but his hand was steady.

Farmer knelt at Gardner's side, holding the bag high enough to allow gravity to feed the blood expander into him. JJ couldn't be dying, not Jungle Jim. Gardner was the one back in the barracks who always looked out after Farmer and tried to keep him out of trouble. JJ was the big brother that Farmer had never had. Gardner even laughed at his dumb jokes and listened to his stories of life on the potato farm back in Idaho. Farmer didn't know what he'd do without Gardner around. The other guys were okay, but he didn't feel as close to them as he did to JJ.

Corky came over and laid his hand on Farmer's shoulder. "He'll be okay, amigo. The captain will get him out of here in time."

Farmer looked up at him, grateful for the reassurance. The tough Chicano had been in-country as long as anyone he knew, and he had to know about these things.

"Thanks, Cork."

"No sweat, man. He'll make it."

Captain Ringer came up to him. "Gaines is inbound right now," he said. "His ETA is two minutes."

"Thank you, sir."

"You want to go back with him, son?"

"Oh no, sir, I couldn't do that. The guys need me here."

"Let me talk to Brody."

"No, sir, please. I can't run out on them."

"Someone has to hold the blood-expander bag," Ringer explained.

"Okay then, I'll go." Farmer was relieved to have a reason to stay with his friend.

"Okay, let's carry him out into the open so Rat can pick him up."

With Farmer holding the IV bag high over his head, Brody and Two-Step carried Gardner back into the open clearing. Wilburn followed them with the Prick-77 radio.

"Lightning, this is Python Lead," Gaines radioed. "I am approaching your reported location. Can you hear me yet, over."

"Python, this is Lightning. That is a negative, over."

"This is Python, roger."

The men in the clearing waited tensely, their ears straining for the sound of the rotors. With the Khmers all around them, they couldn't pop smoke for Gaines. He was going to have to find their small clearing on his own.

"Lightning, this is Lead. I can't see you down low. I'm going to have to go higher and see if I can spot you. Over."

"Lightning, roger."

Now things got even more tense. Rat had been keeping close to the ground to stay out of radar range. Up higher everyone could see him, both the gooks and the Americans. But one of his men was down and Gaines wasn't going to let him die if he could help it.

He hauled back on his cyclic stick and watched the numbers on his altimeter unwind. He leveled out at three thousand feet above the jungle. Now he could see.

On the ground, Brody spotted him, a black speck in the sky headed away from them and far to the north.

"Gimme the radio," he barked.

Wilburn handed him the handset.

"Python, Python, this is Blue Two. You are north of us about two klicks out and headed in the opposite direction. Make a one-eighty and bear to your portside. Over."

"Two, this is Python. Roger."

The men watched breathlessly as Rat banked his ship around and headed back in their direction.

"Python, this is Two. Bear left, I say again bear left. Over."

"Python, roger."

Brody ripped off his fatigue jacket. Running into the middle of the clearing, he waved it over his head like a flag.

"Blue Two, this is Python. I have you spotted. Be there in a flash. Out."

"Two, roger. Out."

With a whine of his turbine, Rat flared out in a hot landing right in front of the men. He kicked the rudder pedals, snapping the tail of the Cobra around and grounded the bird.

Brody and Two-Step picked Gardner up. With Farmer running alongside him, holding the bag of blood expander, they ran through the rotor blast. Gaines climbed down out of his cockpit and held the side of the gunner's canopy open. Farmer crawled in the small compartment. Still holding the bag of blood expander, he settled down into the gunner's seat.

Brody and Two-Step lifted the unconscious man up over the edge of the fuselage and laid him on top of Farmer. The small grunt was buried under the weight of his friend's limp body, but he didn't mind. Brody quickly buckled the seat belt around both men.

Rat lost no time getting back into the air. He flicked the switch of the governer to the off position and, with his turbine on overrev, he streaked for the border and the waiting Dustoff. The turbine would be trash by the time he got it back, but he didn't care. Uncle Sam would buy him a new one.

Colonel Duc's death plunge did not make the Khmer troops give up their search for the Americans. If anything, it spurred them on to even greater efforts.

For some totally unknown reason, the mad-dog North Vietnamese colonel had been a favorite of their leader Pol Pot. When Pot learned of Duc's death, they knew that they had better have something to show for it, like the bodies of the Americans. Duc was a madman, but he was completely sane compared to the Khmer Rouge leader. The things that

303

Pol Pot did to people could not even be talked about, much less contemplated. They had to find the Americans now or they would all die.

The second that Rat's gunship was clear, Ringer turned to Wilburn and Brody. "We'd better get this thing on the road again. They know we're here now."

"Roger that, sir. I'll get Dan and move out."

Brody's reduced squad, Corky and Two-Step, took the rear guard again as they headed east. Bunny and his radio went with Ringer.

"Blue Six, Blue Six," the Special Forces officer called. "This is Lightning, Lightning, come in."

"Lightning, this is Blue Six. Over."

"This is Lightning, send your coordinates, over."

"This is Six, we are at nine-three-eight two-seven-four. Over."

Ringer quickly checked his map. They were only two klicks away, an hour in this terrain.

"Blue Six, this is Lightning. Head two hundred and sixty-eight degrees, I say again two-six-eight degrees. You should reach us in less than an hour. Over."

"This is Six. Roger, copy two-six-eight. Over."

"Lightning out."

Ringer had just handed the microphone back to Bunny when firing burst out behind them. "Move it!" he shouted.

They might not make that last hour.

CHAPTER 40

On the border

First Lieutenant Nurse Lisa Maddox stood impatiently beside the Dustoff chopper that had landed in the small clearing. In the tree line was a small group of men at some kind of command post, and a Huey C-model gunship circled protectively overhead. Other than that, the place was empty. She scanned the skies looking for the helicopter that, she had been told, was bringing out a critically wounded man.

Back at Camp Radcliffe, she had been given some bullshit story about why the medevac chopper couldn't fly directly to the casualty. Instead, they had been vectored to fly into the small clearing, way out in the middle of nowhere.

How she was supposed to do her job properly when this was going on, she didn't know. Trying to save a man's life meant every last second counted. She couldn't understand what she was doing sitting on the ground at a time like this. It had not even occurred to her that the wounded man might not be in South Vietnam. She just assumed that this was another military fuck-up of some kind, and she was disgusted.

She heard beating rotors and the whine of an overrevved

turbine in the distance. An olive-green-and-tan Cobra gunship was coming in low and fast. It drew closer, and she saw the shark's mouth painted on the nose. It was Rat Gaines's bird, *Sudden Discomfort*. As the speeding Cobra came closer, she saw someone in the front seat of his gunship. Actually, it looked like two people!

She shouted to the pilots of the Dustoff, and they cranked the turbine of their Huey for a fast start. The two medics jumped down from the ship bringing a litter and blood-plasma bags.

The Cobra made a hot landing almost at her feet, its spinning rotor disk almost touching that of the Dustoff. Rat opened his canopy and jumped out. "Over here!" he shouted, running to open the front canopy.

The wounded man was lying in the gunner's seat and Farmer was with him, holding the bag of blood expander.

The medics ran up, and Rat handed the patient down to them. Gently they moved him onto the litter. Farmer climbed out of the cockpit and followed them as they ran for the medevac ship.

Rat didn't even seem to notice Lisa as he scrambled to get back into the cockpit of his bird. She took a closer look at the patient and recognized him. He was the one they called Jungle Jim, one of the new guys on the Blues.

That meant that Rat's people were in contact somewhere. But why had he flown this man out instead of letting the Dustoff come to him? If the Cobra could get in, so could the medevac.

Gaines's ship leapt into the air and streaked away to the west. Then it hit her, Gaines was flying to Cambodia. He had some kind of a Sneaky Pete operation going on again. No wonder he didn't want to talk to her at dinner last night. Now she understood.

The nurse jumped into the back of the Dustoff and the pilot pulled pitch. The medics had already plugged plasma into his vein. Carefully she took off the field dressing to examine his wound. It was nasty enough with the broken rib exposed, but she couldn't tell how badly he was cut up inside.

She radioed ahead to the hospital to have the OR ready for an abdominal wound with possible perforations of the bowel. An Khe assured her that everything would be ready and requested the patient's blood type. She gently pulled the dogtag chain from around Gardner's neck and read O positive, calling that information in as well.

Their ETA was nineteen minutes.

She glanced over at the other soldier. Farmer had not said a word so far, just watching everything she had done with wide, frightened eyes. He looked like a high-school kid with his red hair and big blue eyes, hardly old enough to have been a grunt.

"Are you hurt, too, soldier?" she asked.

"No, ma'am," Farmer answered. "I'm fine. How's JJ?" he asked, his eyes pleading for reassurance.

"He'll be okay," she said. "The hospital's waiting for him, and we'll have him in the OR in just a few more minutes."

The relief was plain on his face.

"You're in Echo Company, aren't you?" she asked.

"Yes, ma'am," he answered.

She wondered what kind of mess Rat had gotten himself into this time.

Just before he had landed, Rat monitored Ringer's transmission. Alexander and the Blues had not linked up with them yet. Ringer and his men were in deep *kim chee*.

As soon as he had cleared the trees around the LZ, Gaines reached down and flicked on his arming switches. He still had a full ordnance load on board and he could slow them down for quite a while. Maybe he could even hold them off long enough to allow Snow to get his Air America people in there.

"Blue Six, this is Python, over."

"This is Blue Six, go ahead."

"This is Python, Lightning ran into trouble. Can you move any faster? Over."

"This is Six. Roger, we copied Lightning's last transmission and we're moving as fast as we can. Echo Tango Alpha his location one five. Over."

"This is Python Roger. Contact him to coordinate the link-up. Over."

"Six, wilco. Out."

Rat switched radio frequencies and called back Major Snow at the jump CP. "Frosty, This is Python, over."

"This is Frosty, go."

"This is Python, I am en route to Lightning's location to cover him. Blue Six element is also in en route as fast as he can go. Estimated link-up in one five. Can your cowboy element provide on-site support? Over."

"This is Frosty. I will have to check on ordnance and fuel remaining. They're due back this location in one zero, over."

"This is Python, roger, copy. I think I'm going to need the help. Over."

"Frosty, roger, out."

Back at the CP in the clearing, Major Snow turned to Colonel Jordan. "I don't know if my people are going to be able to assist without refueling and rearming."

Jordan looked grim. "I think that Rat has some people standing by. Let me try to raise them. I'm not too sure how much longer our cover is going to last here anyway, so we might as well go ahead. I'll have them come with the lift element that's taking Torrence's people back, so at least they'll be covered this far."

The battalion commander reached for the radio. "Crazy Bull, Crazy Bull, this is Crazy Bull Six, over."

"Bull Six this is Crazy Bull Three, over." Jordan's operations officer answered so fast that he must have been sitting right on top of the radio back in the battalion TOC.

"Three, this is Six, we are ready for extraction. Also, send the Python element that is waiting on pad alert. Over."

"This is Bull Three, roger. out."

Jordan looked back down at the map. "When they show, I'll divert them to go after Gaines while the rest are pulling Charlie Company out."

"It'll be tight."

"Roger that, but there's still a chance that we'll be able to keep it covered."

Back at the 7th Cav alert pad, Lance Warlokk and Alphabet were strapped into Lance's C-model Huey gunship. Cliff Gabriel sat alone in his slick, *Pegasus,* right alongside them. Both of the pilots were waiting for a call that their commander needed them. When the operations officer in the TOC called, Warlokk was pulling the starting trigger in the throttle before he even rogered the message.

In the co-pilot-gunner's seat. Alphabet ran through a quick checklist, and as soon as the rotors were up to speed, Warlokk called over to Gabe.

"Gunslinger, this is Lawless, you ready?"

A curt "roger" was his only reply.

Warlokk reached up and switched the radio over. "Gold Course control, this is Python Three One, request takeoff clearance, over."

"Python Three One, this is Control, wait for the rest of your lift, over."

Warlokk didn't even bother to answer the tower. He threw a thumbs-up to Gabe and both machines started their taxi out to the runway.

"Python Three One, you are not cleared for takeoff. Do you roger, over?"

"Control, this is Python," Warlokk replied, twisting the throttle all the way against the stop and pulling pitch. His gunbird's tail lifted, and they started down the runway. "Say again please, you are coming in weak and broken. Over."

"Three one, Three One," the radio operator in the control tower screamed, almost in hysterics. "You are not cleared for take off!"

"Roger, tower," Warlokk's calm voice came in clearly over the radio in the control tower. "Understand cleared for take off. Rolling now."

By this time the two Hueys were fifty feet off the ground, their turbines whining as the rotor blades clawed the air.

"That guy must be new around here," Warlokk grinned over to Alphabet. "I guess he doesn't know that I'm always cleared for takeoff."

Side by side, the two choppers cleared the perimeter of Camp Radcliff and headed west.

Lieutenant Mike Alexander was racing down the trail. In the distance, he heard the sounds of heavy firing. Lightning was in contact.

"Sargeant Zack," he called out.

"I hear it," the black NCO panted. He was getting a little too old to be running around in the jungle like a crazy man. "They're less than a klick ahead."

Alexander dropped back to let the RTO catch up. With the heavy Prick-25 radio on his back, he was having a hard time keeping up with his lieutenant. The platoon leader snatched the handset from him. "Lightning, Lightning, this is Blue Six, over."

"Lightning, go." Alexander heard gunfire over the radio. His heart beat faster. He was headed into his first firefight.

"This is Six, we are less than a klick from you approaching from due east. Be on the lookout for us, over."

"Lightning, roger. There are bad guys between you and me, too. Be careful, but get your ass here as soon as you can. Over."

"This is Six, roger, copy, we're coming as fast as we can. Out."

Alexander put on a burst of speed and ran up to the point. "Lightning says there's gooks between us," he panted.

"Yes, sir," the running grunt panted, equally breathless.

A burst of AK fire sent both of them flat on their faces and scrambling for cover. From his prone position, Alexander ripped off a burst from his sixteen. Behind him he heard Zack yelling at the men, getting them out on the flanks.

Another burst of AK fire went past his head, and he started

crawling backward. The point man had found cover and was returning fire.

Alexander rolled to his left behind a thick clump of bushes. Bullets kicked up dirt where he had been lying. He couldn't see the enemy positions and so far all he had heard were the AKs, no machine guns.

He heard the characteristic thump of an M-79 behind him. The 40mm grenade exploded in the trees in front of him, but it didn't make the enemy slack off at all. If anything, the firing intensified.

There were shouts in front of him. He knew that the Khmers were bringing up more people. He had to get the situation under control pretty fast or he would be the one pinned down and Ringer would have to come and bail him out.

He pulled a hand grenade from the ammo pouch on his field belt. Holding it in his left hand, he pulled the pin. Getting to his knees, he ripped off a full magazine from his M-16 in his right hand, spraying the bullets from side to side. When the rifle bolt locked to the rear on an empty magazine, he lobbed the grenade with his left hand.

This grenade had the desired effect; he heard a scream, and the enemy fire slackened for a moment.

The platoon leader dropped the empty magazine out of the bottom of his rifle and slapped a new one into place. Pulling back the charging handle, he peered through the bushes. Spotting a muzzle flash, he opened up on it, burning through half a magazine.

No more AK fire came from that position. It looked like they were getting it under control after all.

He was taking another frag from his pouch when he heard shouts and heavy firing to his right front. Zack had gotten his men around them and was hitting them on the flank.

He got to his knees and lobbed the grenade. This time, it seemed to have no effect. He yelled over to the point man. The grunt turned his head.

"Let's take 'em!"

The man looked at Alexander like he had lost his mind. He slowly shook his head.

Alexander slapped a fresh magazine into his weapon and got to his feet. Running in a crouch, he dashed up to the next available cover, a tree trunk, firing as he ran.

No shots were fired back at him.

He ducked his head around the tree and fired off a short burst.

"Cease fire!" someone shouted from in front of him. "Cease fire, goddamnit."

Sergeant Zack stepped out into the open, his shaven head glistening with sweat. "We got 'em, sir. There was only four of 'em."

"Only four?" Alexander was surprised. He was sure that they were facing at least a full squad.

"Yes, sir, and you got two of them."

Alexander grinned. His first firefight and he had killed two men.

"Okay, Sergeant," he said, "let's get 'em moving. The captain's waiting for us."

"Yes, sir."

The Blues quickly formed up and moved out.

CHAPTER 41

Inside Cambodia

This time Brody's people had the point with Ringer. Wilburn, Chief, and the two Nungs held the rear. Their plan, if it could be called a plan, was to find a good defensive location and hold up until either Alexander and the Blues linked up with them or Rat got back with his gunship.

Either way it wasn't going to be easy.

"Left front, two hundred meters," Wilburn whispered in Chief's ear. The rear guard had dropped well back, and they were trying to slow things up a little. They found a little rise in the ground overlooking the main trail and pulled into an ambush position. With the two Chinese mercenaries out on the flanks, Wilburn was spotting targets for the Indian sniper.

"Got him." Chief slowly focused the day scope on his rifle, ranging in on the target, a Khmer point man. The sight reticle on the day scope had two stadia marks on the vertical cross hair. When the top mark was lined up with the top of a man's head and the bottom with his feet, the target was dead meat.

He took a deep breath, held it, and slowly squeezed the

trigger. The silenced rifle spat. With a strangled cry, the Khmer went down on his knees and pitched onto his face.

"Fuck!" Chief had missed his aim point and had hit him in the upper chest. He was still dead, but he had cried out.

AKs opened up into the jungle in front of them, firing blind.

Chief ducked back down under cover and waited for Wilburn to find another target. So far, the gooks didn't know where they were. Not only did the silencer quiet the heavy-caliber sniper rifle, it also acted as a flash hider, making it very difficult to spot the muzzle flash.

"Twelve o'clock, two of 'em down low at the base of a tree. Hundred and fifty meters."

"Got it."

Chief fired at the man on the left, shifted his aim, and fired again. The second man screamed in pain. He had only been wounded. He rolled back behind the tree and started calling out in Cambodian.

"Trung si." Dan, the younger Nung, called over to Wilburn. "He tell others where we are. We go now."

"Yeah, let's get it."

The four men crawled backward until they were clear and faded back into the brush. Running down the trail, they looked for another good ambush point.

"Lightning Five, this is Six over." It was Ringer calling.

Wilburn had one of the radios on his back. He took the handset from his assault harness. "Five, go ahead."

"This is Six, we've found a good position. Keep coming on down the trail till you hit a small clearing. We'll be off to your left front with the clearing at our backs. I think we can hold them here. Over."

"Five, roger, copy."

The men ran harder, keeping an eye over their shoulders. Dan, the Nung, dropped back to cover the rear.

"You go, *Trung si,* I stop them."

Dan slipped into the brush along the side of the trail. The colors of his camouflage uniform blended in perfectly with

314

the vegetation. He readied a grenade and checked the magazine in his M-16.

Three Khmers came pounding down the trail. Dan waited until they were right on top of him. Springing out into the open, he opened up on full automatic, hosing them down with a full magazine of 5.56mm. He waited a second and threw the grenade as hard as he could farther back down the trail.

The explosion was followed by cries of pain.

Dan dashed on up the trail after Wilburn, changing the magazine in his rifle as he ran.

Wilburn rounded a shallow bend in the trail and saw Ringer's position a hundred meters ahead. Chief and the other Nung had already reached cover. He heard a long burst of AK fire from behind him. He spun around. Dan had been hit.

The Chinese gave a sharp cry and pitched forward.

Wilburn ran back, but the mercenary was dead. An AK round had caught him in the head. Wilburn reached down, grabbed Dan's harness with one hand, and started dragging the body to cover.

Wilburn was a brother to the Nungs and had been adopted into one of their families. It was not as important to a Nung that he was killed in combat as it was that he be buried in his family's cemetery. The Green Beret could not leave his brother's body behind to lie in foreign soil, his spirit wandering restlessly.

Brody's people saw what he was doing and started firing to cover him. Wilburn was only twenty feet from safety when a round took his leg out from under him. He fell hard, dropping Dan's body. He glanced down and saw the round, oozing hole in his pant leg. It was the same one that had been hit on his last trip into Cambodia.

Brody jumped up from behind a log and dashed out to help him to his feet. The two men ran the last few steps back to cover behind the fallen log.

"You okay?" Brody panted.

"Fucking leg!" Wilburn spat, reaching for his field dressing. "Why can't they hit my other fucking leg for a change?"

Taking the knife from his harness, he ripped the pants leg open. The round had made a neat round hole through the muscle on the outside of his thigh. It was clean and was not bleeding badly. He put the dressing over it, tied the strings around the torn pants, and rolled over into a firing position. There was still work to be done.

The Khmers had spotted them and were spreading out in an assault line. They could hear the gook sergeants shouting at their men. The AK fire was heavy, but the Americans were not firing back unless they had a good target. They were too low on ammunition to waste a single shot. Even Corky was being real careful with his sixty, trying to snap out only short bursts instead of suppressive fire.

Only Chief had plenty of ammunition left and he was using it up. The bad thing about the silencer on the XM-21 sniper rifle was that it did not hold up well under sustained fire. Gas pressure built up in it, and it blew out. When Chief felt the silencer give way, and his next shot sounded clearly, he reached up to the right side of the rifle's breech and switched the selector over to fully automatic.

Now he had a scoped, 7.62mm automatic rifle. He started snapping out three-round bursts, but it wasn't helping much. The enemy fire wasn't slacking off one bit. There were just too goddamned many gooks and too few of them.

"Lightning, Blue Six, over."

"Lightning!" Ringer shouted over the roar of the small-arms fire. "Send it!"

"This is Six. I am only a hundred meters behind you. Watch for me."

"Blues coming in!" Ringer yelled to alert everyone.

The first men to break into the perimeter were Alexander and Leo Zack. The sergeant took a quick look at the situation. "First squad to the right, Third to the left," he shouted. "Move it!"

The two squads scrambled to spread out on either side of Ringer's small group. They dove for cover and got to work.

Zack found a place behind Brody's log. " 'Bout fucking time,'' the grunt told him.

Zack handed him a bandolier of loaded M-16 magazines.''Shut up and get busy,'' he snapped back.

Zack was in no mood to deal with Brody's smart talk. This little war wasn't over yet, not by a long shot. If they didn't regain fire superiority real soon, they were going to be overrun.

''Get those thumpers going!'' the sergeant shouted.

Corky caught movement to their front and snapped out a burst at his target, but his smoking gun clicked silent after only a few rounds. ''Ammo!'' he yelled out. ''Need ammo!''

The gunner from the first squad, rolled up a two-hundred-round belt and threw it over to him.

''Thanks, amigo.''

Corky flipped up the feed tray and laid the linked belt in place. Snapping the cover back down, he hauled back on the charging handle and got back to work. His first burst took out the target.

With twice the number of guns on line now, the grunts started getting serious. The two thumpers made quite a bit of difference, too. The deadly little grenades dropped down on top of the hidden Khmers as fast as the gunners could pump them out.

''Keep firing!'' Zack yelled. He raised his head up to see how they were doing and a string of green tracer fire almost took it off. The gooks had finally gotten a machine gun into action, an RPD.

The Russian RPD machine gun fired a lighter cartride than did the American M-60. In the jungle, the shorter range didn't matter. And the RPD fired two hundred rounds a minute faster. It was nothing to mess with.

The RPD opened up in full song. The bullets chewed in to the Americans' position, sending all of them diving for cover. The Blues' three M-60 gunners tried to take the deadly Russian gun out, but the Khmer gunner had them zeroed in. Every time the grunts stuck their heads up, the RPD fire sent them back down again.

Third Squad's sixty took a hit, sending splinters of metal back into the face of the gunner and wrecking the gun.

They had to do something fast!

Chief edged the barrel of his sniper rifle around the side of a tree and focused in on the Khmer machine-gun nest. They had built a hasty bunker of fallen logs, and it was going to be a difficult shot. A burst of fire into the tree made him duck back down. That gook gunner was good. The Indian sniper shifted his position and tried again.

This time he got a shot at what he thought was the machine gun's spotter, a man crouching beside the gun. It was a snap shot and he missed. The fire was just too heavy to take the time to aim and squeeze the trigger properly.

Under the covering fire of their RPD, the Khmers crept up closer. Two-Step checked the load in his pump gun. They were almost close enough for him to use the short-range weapon. But when they got that close, it would be all over.

"Lightning, Lightning, this is Python Lead." Rat's voice was loud over the radio. "I am inbound to your location. Echo Tango Alpha one mike. Over."

"This is Lightning," Ringer shouted back. "Roger. Blue Six has linked up, but we're under heavy fire from a machine-gun bunker. We're at the edge of a clearing and the target is to the west of us. Popping smoke now, over."

"Somebody throw a smoke!" he yelled.

Bunny ripped a smoke grenade off his assault harness and lobbed it out in front of them.

"This is Python, I have strawberry over."

"Lightning, roger, a red. A hundred meters west of that. Go get 'em Rat!"

"Roger. Rolling in now."

Rat brought his ship around in a hard bank over the small clearing. Since he was flying without a gunner, he could only fire the weapons when they were pointed dead ahead. He aimed his ship at the jungle beyond the red smoke and cut loose with everything he had.

318

The rockets from the Cobra gunship slammed into the Khmers' positions. The explosions threw bloody body parts up into the trees. He pulled up and hauled *Sudden Discomfort* around to make another pass, this time parallel to the Americans' front.

In the Khmers' machine-gun bunker, a jagged shard of hot steel sliced into the gunner at the Cambodian lieutenant's side. Blood and tissue spattered him and the man screamed as he died. They almost had the Yankees, but they couldn't stand up against the shark-like gunship. The Khmer lieutenant couldn't let the Yankees get away. He knew that if he returned empty handed, he would be executed, along with all of his men.

He pulled the RPD machine gun out from under the gunner's body and checked to see that the magazine drum was full. He raced out into the open carrying the gun. Propping the barrel up on a low-hanging limb, he waited until Gaines swept down closer. He centered the diving Cobra in his sights, remembering to give the speeding machine plenty of lead as he squeezed the trigger.

"Yankee you die!" he screamed.

CHAPTER 42

Inside Cambodia

The stream of bright green 7.62mm tracer from the RPD machine gun flashed past Rat's canopy.

''What the fuck!'' he shouted as he stomped down on the rudder pedal, wrenching his ship out of the line of fire. He felt the Cobra take hits on the armor plating around the cockpit. The overworked turbine screamed as he frantically pulled maximum pitch and overreved. He had to get out of there.

More tracer rounds flashed past. The Cobra shuddered as she took more hits. Gaines felt a vibration in the cyclic. The rotors were damaged.

He was frantically jinking the ship from side to side when, from the corner of his eye, he saw a Huey Hog dive past him, her rotors a blur. Rockets lanced from the pods on her side pylons and the thumper in her nose turret belched flame into the jungle.

It was Warlokk!

In the left-hand seat of Warlokk's gunship, Alphabet played his firing controls like a master, saturating the area that the tracers were coming from.

The Khmer officer with the RPD shifted his fire to the new

threat. Alphabet saw him lean out from behind his tree with the machine gun. Acting on reflex, he triggered off a salvo of 2.75s. One of the speeding rockets caught the gook right in the chest.

When the flash of the explosion settled, there was no more gook with a machine gun and no more tree, either.

"Lead," Warlokk radioed. "This is Lawless. You okay?"

"This is Lead. Yeah, I've got a little rotor damage, but she's flyable. Thanks a lot, guys."

"Lead," Warlokk's gunner clicked in. "This is Alphabet. That's what you get for not taking me with you, over."

Gaines laughed. "Lead, roger. I'll take that under advisement. Take over for me until Cowboy and Gabe get here. Over."

"Lead," Gabe's voice broke in over the radio. "This is Gunslinger, I'm one minute out, and Cowboy is right behind me. Over."

"This is Lead, roger, wait one till Lawless can clear the Lima Zulu. Over."

"Gunslinger, roger, copy."

Warlokk and Alphabet flew low over the treetops, but no one shot at them. The Khmers were disappearing into the jungle as fast as they could go. With their officer gone, there was no reason for them to stick around and get killed by the dark Yankee death birds. Enough of them had been killed already today.

"Gunslinger, this is Lawless. The LZ is green, I say again green, over."

"Gunslinger, roger. Coming down now."

With Warlokk flying cover, Gabe flared his ship out to a landing.

In the tree line, Ringer shouted to Brody. "Get it, Sarge. Get the rest of your people out and take Wilburn with you. We'll cover for you."

Brody hesitated, looking at the captain.

"Go!" Lightning shouted again. "We'll wait for Cowboy."

Two-Step and Brody got on each side of Wilburn, and

throwing his arms over their shoulders, they helped him into the open and the waiting slick. Corky and Bunny ran behind them, covering them as they loaded the wounded man into the back of the bird.

Corky crouched down low by the side of the ship and waved Bunny on in. Throwing his sixty up into the troop compartment, the gunner pulled himself inside and yelled, "Hit it, Gabe!"

The pilot pulled pitch and *Pegasus* leapt into the sky.

"Everybody okay?" Gabe yelled back.

On his way back to the doorgun position, Brody grabbed up the spare flight helmet and keyed the intercom. "We've got to cover Ringer and the ell tee!"

"Roger."

Gabe banked his chopper over so Brody could fire his doorgun as Warlokk swept down lower to search for anyone who wanted to make an issue of their extraction. They found no takers for their action, though.

"Lightning, this is Cowboy, we have you in sight. Coming down now. Over."

As Brody watched, two of the all-silver, Air America slicks flared out for a landing. He saw Ringer and the Nung drag the body of the other Nung out with them. Alexander and the two squads of the Blues followed.

As soon as they had all cleared the tree line Brody opened with the door gun, sending suppressive fire over their heads back into the jungle. He didn't have a target, but he wanted to discourage any gooks who had not gotten the word yet.

The two men threw the body into the rear compartment of the lead slick and clambered on board after it. The grunts followed quickly, climbing into both choppers. When the last man, Leo Zack, was on board, Cowboy Flight pulled pitch.

As soon as the slicks had clawed their way back into the sky, they were joined by Warlokk's gunship flying off to the side and Rat's Cobra doing top cover.

Brody keyed his mike. "Gabe, we've got a wounded man back here, we need to call ahead on him."

"Roger." Gabe switched over to the dustoff frequency and

322

told An Khe that he was inbound with one Whisky India Alpha.

"They want to know his condition," the pilot called back.

"Routine," Brody answered, meaning that the wound was not life threatening.

Gabe radioed that information as well.

"They're waiting for him."

"Lead, this is Gunslinger," Gabe called Gaines. "I'm going to make a run for the Dustoff pad. See you back at camp."

"This is Lead, roger copy."

Gabe pulled away from the formation and cranked up maximum RPMs.

Wilburn sat on the canvas troop seats against the rear bulkhead while Brody carefully checked the field bandage on his leg.

"Goddamnit, Brody," the Green Beret protested. "It's not that big a deal, I've gotten hurt a lot worse opening a fucking beer can. Just let me off at Ringer's compound and I'll have our medic take a look at it later."

"Forget it, Sarge, you're coming with us. You got hit working with the Cav, and the Cav is fucking well going to take care of you. Also, we've got the best-looking nurses in-country. I'll have to introduce you to Lisa, Lieutenant Lisa Maddox. She's got to be the prettiest woman in the entire United States Army."

"I don't fuck officers," Wilburn snarled.

Brody laughed. "Wait till you see this one. She might just change your mind."

The medics were waiting with a stretcher twenty minutes later when Gabe greased *Pegasus* in for a landing on the Dustoff pad outside the 45th Surge. Despite Wilburn's heated protests that he could walk on his own, the medics made him lie on the litter and they hurried him inside the hospital.

Brody cleared his doorgun and put the link belt back into the ammo can before he climbed down onto the skid. "Thanks for the ride, Gabe," he said to the pilot. "We're going to get off here and go check in on Gardner."

323

Gabe stuck his head out of the pilot's window. "Next time you need me to come and pull your ass out, Brody, how 'bout finding a nice quiet place somewhere in Vietnam, for Christ's sakes. That Cambodia shit sucks."

Brody laughed. "You got that shit right."

The grunts all unloaded their weapons and slung them over their shoulders before following Brody in the back door of the hospital.

Brody went right up to the nurses' station. "I'm looking for one of my men, ma'am, Jim Gardner, Echo Company, First of the Seventh? He came in here earlier this morning."

The nurse, a rather plain-looking second lieutenant wrinkled her nose. She didn't comment on the fact that Brody badly needed a bath as she checked the patient list on her clipboard.

"Gardner, James J. Right? Well, he's out of surgery, but he can't have any visitors yet."

"How is he, ma'am?"

"He was hurt pretty badly, but the surgery went well. He'll be back to duty in three weeks or so."

Brody was relieved. He liked having the big man in his squad. "When can we see him?"

"Probably tomorrow morning."

"Thank you, ma'am. Thank you very much."

Brody turned back to his men and grinned. "Well, guys what do you say to a hot shower and a couple of cool ones?"

"You got that shit right, amigo," Corky replied.

"That's a big rodg," Bunny added.

Just then Farmer came down the hall and saw them walking out. "Hey, guys," he shouted as he ran after them. "Wait up! JJ's going to be okay."

"Yeah, we heard," Brody answered. "Why don't you come on back with us. We're going to get cleaned up and have a beer. We'll see him in the morning."

"Sure," Farmer said when he caught up with them. "But, can we stop off at the mess hall first, Sarge? I'm starved."

"Farmer," Corky slowly shook his head. "You are the hungriest motherfucker I have ever seen."

Farmer just grinned.

General Vance was waiting at the pad when Colonel Jordan stepped out of the chopper. He landed twenty minutes after all the rest of his people because he had a side trip to let Major Snow off at Ringer's Mike Force compound. This time the General was wearing his proper uniform, so Jordan rendered him a salute.

"Colonel," Vance said extending his hand, "I just wanted to let you know that all of the cats stayed in the bag. No one knows a thing."

"The radar didn't report anything, sir?"

The general grinned. "Oh, they saw you all right, but the reports of the sightings are going to get mislaid somehow."

Jordan didn't believe what he was hearing. "You didn't have anything to do with that, did you, General?"

"Well, Colonel, as you well know, when you've been in the army as long as I have, you get to meet a lot of people. It just so happens that the officer responsible for the radars used to work for me a long time ago. He's a good man and he understood the situation completely."

Jordan was relieved. "Thank you, General. My men and I appreciate that a great deal."

"It was nothing. I should thank you and your Captain Gaines for taking care of my son."

"We tried, sir."

The general glanced down at his watch. "Well, I have to be getting down to Saigon. Westmoreland is holding a plane for me. Take care, Colonel, and if there's anything I can do for you, don't hesitate to let me know."

"Don't worry, sir," Jordan said, saluting again. "Believe me, I will."

His driver roared up in his Jeep. "Ready to go, sir?"

Jordan threw his flight helmet into the back and swung into the passenger seat. "Roger that. Take me back to the TOC."

CHAPTER 43

Camp Radcliff, An Khe

Two weeks had passed since the Cambodian mission, and things were just starting to get back to normal around Echo Company. Not much had been going on. The men of the Blues were lounging around in their tent in the afternoon when their platoon sergeant, Leo Zack, stuck his shaved head in the door.

"A-ten-hut," he called out.

The grunts slowly got to their feet, wondering what was going on. The Black Buddha never played this kind of state-side bullshit on them.

A pale Lieutenant Jake Vance walked in the door, followed by their new platoon leader, Lieutenant Alexander.

"As you were," Alexander called out.

Everybody relaxed and sat back down on their bunks.

Vance looked around the room at the men he had led for so many months. They had had some real good times together and some real bad. He was not the kind of officer who made friends with his men, but he knew that in a strange way, he would really miss some of them. He wouldn't miss the responsibility of commanding them, however. Although he had tried as hard as he could, he had never liked it.

"I just wanted a chance to say good-bye to you men." He looked around the tent. He had never been any good at public speaking or making inspiring talks to the troops.

"Good-bye lieutenant," someone sang from the back of the tent.

Vance felt his face start to get red, but he laughed instead of getting pissed off. He had finally learned how to take a joke.

"But even though I'm leaving, I've still got time to give you your monthly troop lecture on Jeep safety."

Now everyone groaned.

Vance smiled. "Well, maybe I'll pass on that one this time. Lieutenant Alexander will be handling that little duty from now on. I just wanted a chance to tell you that I have really enjoyed being your platoon leader, and that you're the best bunch of men that an officer could ever want to lead."

Someone laughed out loud.

"Most of you, that is."

More laughter.

Vance was a little surprised at how at ease he suddenly felt. Now that the life-and-death responsibilities of being their platoon leader were off his shoulders, he found that it was easier for him to relax around the men.

"Also, I am sure that you'll all be pleased to learn that my orders for promotion to captain have just come down. Now you won't be able to make any more jokes about dumb-shit ell tees."

Cheers broke out this time. Honest cheers.

"Way to go, Ell Tee," someone yelled. "Now you're a real officer."

Vance grinned. "Now when I find one of you clowns out of line, I can really get on your case. Lastly, because I'm sure that you are all very anxious to get back to spit-shining your boots, I've got a new assignment. I'm going down to Saigon and I'll be working in Operations."

His voice got serious. "Hopefully, the next time that

someone behind a desk in Saigon tries to leave you guys holding the bag, I'll be able to tell them what it's like up here in grunt country.''

"You tell 'em, Ell Tee!''

Just then, Treat Brody came racing into the tent. "Hey,'' he yelled out, waving a letter in his hand. "Guess what! The Snake's coming back. He's due in here next week.''

Cheers broke out.

Vance groaned and turned to his replacement. "Now I'm really glad that I'm turning this mob over to you, Mike. One year with Snakeman Fletcher is more than any sane person should have to put up with.''

"What do you mean?'' Alexander looked puzzled. "Who's the Snakeman?''

Cheers and laughter broke out in the tent.

Vance grinned broadly. "You'll find out, Ell Tee. Believe me. You'll find out.''

GLOSSARY

ALPHA The military phonetic for *A*

AA Antiaircraft weapons

AC Aircraft commander, the pilot

Acting jack Acting NCO

Affirm Short for affirmative, yes

AFVN Armed Forces Vietnam Network

Agency, the The CIA

AIT Advanced individual training

AJ Acting jack

AK-47 The Russian 7.62mm Kalashnikov assault rifle

AO Area of operation

Ao dai Traditional Vietnamese female dress

APH-5 Helicopter crewman's flight helmet

APO Army post office

ARA Aerial rocket artillery, armed helicopters

Arc light B-52 bomb strike

ARCOM Army Commendation Medal

ARP Aero Rifle Platoon, the Blue Team

Article 15 Disciplinary action

ARVN Army of the Republic of Vietnam, also a South Vietnamese soldier

ASAP As soon as possible

Ash and trash Clerks, jerks, and other REMFs

A-Team The basic Special Forces unit, ten men

AWOL Absent without leave

BRAVO The military phonetic for *B*

B-40 Chinese version of the RPG antitank weapon

Bac si Vietnamese for "doctor"

Bad Paper Dishonorable discharge

Ba-muoi-ba Beer "33," the local brew

Banana clip A thirty-round magazine for the M-1 carbine

Bao Chi Vietnamese for "press" or "news media"

Basic Boot camp

BCT Basic Combat Training, boot camp

BDA Bomb damage assessment

Be Nice Universal expression of the war

Biet (Bic) Vietnamese for "Do you understand?"

Bird An aircraft, usually a helicopter

Bloods Black soldiers

Blooper The M-79 40mm grenade launcher

Blues, the An aero rifle platoon

Body count Number of enemy killed

Bookoo Vietnamese slang for "many," from French *beaucoup*

Bought the farm Killed

Brown bar A second lieutenant

Brass Monkey Interagency radio call for help

Brew Usually beer, sometimes coffee

Bring smoke To cause trouble for someone, to shoot

Broken down Disassembled or nonfunctional

Bubble top The bell OH-13 observation helicopter

Buddha Zone Heaven

Bush The jungle

'Bush Short for ambush

Butter bar A second lieutenant

CHARLIE The military phonetic for *C*

C-4 Plastic explosive

C-rats C rations

CA A combat assault by helicopter

Cam ong Vietnamese for "thank you"

C&C Command and control helicopter

Chao (Chow) Vietnamese greeting

Charlie Short for Victor Charlie, the enemy

Charlie tango Control tower

Cherry A new man in your unit

Cherry boy A virgin

Chickenplate Helicopter crewman's armored vest

Chi-Com Chinese Communist

Chieu hoi A program where VC/NVA could surrender and become scouts for the Army

Choi oi Vietnamese exclamation

CIB The Combat Infantryman's Badge

CID Criminal Investigation Unit

Clip Ammo magazine

CMOH Congressional Medal of Honor

CO Commanding officer

Cobra The AH-1 attack helicopter

Cockbang Bangkok, Thailand

Conex A metal shipping container

Coz Short for Cosmoline, a preservative

CP Command post

CSM Command sergeant major

Cunt Cap The narrow green cap worn with the class A uniform

DELTA The military phonetic for *D*

Dash 13 The helicopter maintenance report

Dau Vietnamese for "pain"

Deadlined Down for repairs

Dep Vietnamese for "beautiful"

DEROS Date of estimated return from overseas service

Deuce and a half Military two-and-a-half-ton truck

DFC Distinguished Flying Cross

DI Drill instructor

Di di Vietnamese for "Go!"

Di di mau Vietnamese for "Go fast!"

Dink Short for *dinky-dau*, derogatory slang term for Vietnamese

Dinky-dau Vietnamese for "crazy!"

Disneyland East The Pentagon

Disneyland Far East The MACV or USARV headquarters

DMZ Demilitarized zone separating North and South Vietnam

Dog tags Stainless steel tags listing a man's name, serial number, blood type and religious preference

Donut Dolly A Red Cross girl

Doom-pussy Danang officers' open mess

Door gunner A soldier who mans a door gun

Drag The last man in a patrol

Dung lai Vietnamese for "Halt!"

Dustoff A medevac helicopter

ECHO The military phonetic for *E*. Also, radio code for east

Eagle flight A heliborne assault

Early out An unscheduled ETS

Eighty-one The M-29 81mm mortar

Eleven bravo An infantryman's MOS

EM Enlisted man

ER Emergency room (hospital)

ETA Estimated time of arrival

ETS Estimated time of separation from service

Extract To pull out by helicopter

FOXTROT The military phonetic for *F*

FAC Forward air controller

Fart sack sleeping bag

Field phone   Hand-generated portable phone used in bunkers

Fifty   The U.S. .50 caliber M-2 heavy machine gun

Fifty-one   The Chi-Com 12.7mm heavy machine gun

Fini   Vietnamese for "ended" or "stopped"

First Louie   First lieutenant

First Shirt   An Army first sergeant

First Team   Motto of the First Air Cavalry Division

Flak jacket   Infantry body armor

FNG   Fucking new guy

FOB   Fly over border mission

Forty-five   The U.S. .45 caliber M-1911 automatic pistol

Fox 4   The F-4 Phantom II jet fighter

Foxtrot mike delta   Fuck me dead

Foxtrot tosser   A flamethrower

Frag   A fragmentation grenade

FTA   Fuck the army

GOLF   The military phonetic for *G*

Gaggle   A loose formation of choppers

Get some   To fight, kill someone

GI   Government issue, an American soldier

Gook   A Vietnamese

Grease gun   The U.S. .45 caliber M-3 Submachine Gun

Green Berets   The U.S. Army's Special Forces

Green Machine   The Army

Grunt   An infantryman

Gunship   Army attack helicopter armed with machine guns and rockets

HOTEL   The military phonetic for *H*

Ham and motherfuckers   The C ration meal of ham and lima beans

Hard core   NVA or VC regulars

Heavy gun team   Three gunships working together

Hercky Bird   The Air Force C-130 Hercules Transport plane

Ho Chi Minh Trail The NVA supply line
Hog The M-60 machine gun
Horn A radio or telephone
Hot LZ A landing zone under hostile fire
House Cat An REMF
Huey The Bell UH-1 helicopter, the troop-carrying workhorse of the war.

INDIA The military phonetic for *I*
IC Installation commander
IG Inspector general
IHTFP I hate this fucking place
In-country Within Vietnam
Insert Movement into an area by helicopter
Intel Military Intelligence
IP Initial point. The place that a gunship starts its gun run
IR Infrared

JULIET The military phonetic for *J*
Jackoff flare A hand-held flare
JAG Judge advocate general
Jeep In Nam, the Ford M-151 quarter-ton truck
Jelly Donut A fat Red Cross girl
Jesus Nut The nut that holds the rotor assembly of a chopper together
Jet Ranger The Bell OH-58 helicopter
Jody A girlfriend back in the States
Jolly Green Giant The HH-3E Chinook heavy-lift helicopter
Jungle fatigues Lightweight tropical uniform

KILO The military phonetic for *K*
K-fifty The NVA 7.62mm type 50 submachine gun
Khakis The tropical class A uniform
KIA Killed in action
Kimchi Korean pickled vegetables

Klick   A kilometer
KP   Kitchen Police, mess-hall duty

LIMA   The military phonetic for *L*
Lager   A camp or to make camp
Lai dai ˉVietnamese for "come here"
LAW   Light antitank weapon. The M-72 66mm rocket launcher
Lay dead   To fuck off
Lay dog   Lie low in jungle during recon patrol
LBJ   The military jail at Long Binh Junction
Leg   A nonairborne infantryman
Lifeline   The strap securing a doorgunner on a chopper
Lifer   A career soldier
Links   The metal clips holding machine gun ammo belts together
LLDB   *Luc Luong Dac Biet*, the ARVN Special Forces
Loach   The small Hughes OH-6 observation helicopter
Long Nose   Vietnamese slang for "American"
Long Tom   The M-107 175mm long-range artillery gun
LP   Listening post
LRRP   Long-range recon patrol
LSA   Lubrication, small-arms gun oil
Lurp   Freeze-dried rations carried on LRRPs
LZ   Landing zone

MIKE   The military phonetic for *M*
M-14   The U.S. 7.62mm rifle
M-16   The U.S. 5.56mm Colt-Armalite rifle
M-26   Fragmentation grenade
M-60   The U.S. 7.62mm infantry machine gun
M-79   The U.S. 40mm grenade launcher
MACV   Military Assistance Command Vietnam
Ma Deuce   The M-2 .50 caliber heavy machine gun
Magazine   Metal container that feeds bullets into weapons; holds twenty or thirty rounds per unit
Mag pouch   A magazine carrier worn on the field belt

Mama San An older Vietnamese woman
MAST Mobile Army Surgical Team
Mech Mechanized infantry
Medevac Medical Evacuation chopper
Mess hall GI dining facility
MF Motherfucker
MG Machine gun
MI Military intelligence units
MIA Missing in action
Mike Radio code for minute
Mike Force Green Beret mobile strike force
Mike-mike Millimeters
Mike papa Military police
Minigun A 7.62mm Gatling gun
Mister Zippo A flamethrower operator
Monkey House Vietnamese slang for "jail"
Monster Twelve to twenty-one claymore antipersonnel
   mines jury-rigged to detonate simultaneously
Montagnard Hill tribesmen of the Central Highlands
Mop Vietnamese for "fat"
Motengator Motherfucker
MPC Military payment certificate, issued to GIs in RVN
   in lieu of greenbacks
Muster A quick assemblage of soldiers with little or no
   warning
My Vietnamese for "American"

NOVEMBER The military phonetic for *N*. Also, radio
   code for north
NCO Noncommissioned officer
Negative Radio talk for "no"
Net A radio network
Newbie A new GI in-country
Next A GI so short that he is the next to go home
Niner The military pronunciation of the number 9
Ninety The M-67 90mm recoilless rifle
Number One Very good, the best

Number ten Bad

Number ten thousand Very bad, the worst

Nuoc nam A Vietnamese fish sauce

NVA The North Vietnamese Army, also a North Vietnamese soldier

OSCAR The military phonetic for *O*

OCS Officer candidate school

OCS Manual A comic book

OD Olive drab

Old Man, the A commander

One five one The M-151 jeep

One oh five The 105mm howitzer

One twenty-two The Russian 122mm ground-launched rocket

OR Hospital operating room

Out-country Out of Vietnam

PAPA The military phonetic for *P*

P Piaster, Vietnamese currency

P-38 C ration can opener

PA Public address system

Papa San An older Vietnamese man

Papa sierra Platoon sergeant

PAVN Peoples Army of Vietnam, the NVA

PCS Permanent change of station, a transfer

Peter pilot Copilot

PF Popular Forces, Vietnamese militia

PFC Private first class

Piece Any weapon

Pig The M-60 machine gun

Pink Team Observation helicopters teamed up with gunships

Phantom The McDonnell F-4 jet fighter

Phu Vietnamese noodle soup

Point The most dangerous position on patrol. The point

man walks ahead and to the side of the others, acting as a lookout

POL Petroleum, oil, lubricants

Police To clean up

POL point A GI gas station

Pony soldiers The First Air Cav troopers

Pop smoke To set off a smoke grenade

Prang To crash a chopper, or land roughly

Prep Artillery preparation of an LZ

PRG Provisional Revolutionary Government (the Communists)

Prick-25 The AN/PRC-25 tactical radio

Profile A medical exemption from duty

Project Phoenix CIA assassination operations

PSP Perforated steel planking used to make runways

Psy-Ops Psychological Operations

PT Physical training

Puff the Magic Dragon The heavily armed AC-47 fire support aircraft

Purple Heart, the A medal awarded for wounds received in combat

Puzzle Palace Any headquarters

PX Post exchange

PZ Pickup zone

QUEBEC The military phonetic for *Q*

QC *Quan Cahn*, Vietnamese Military Police

Quad fifty Four .50 caliber MG's mounted together

ROMEO The military phonetic for *R*

RA Regular army, a lifer

Railroad Tracks The twin-silver-bar captain's rank insignia

R&R Rest and relaxation

Ranger Specially trained infantry troops

Rat fuck A completely confused situation

Recondo Recon commando

Red Leg An artilleryman
Red Team Armed helicopters
Regular A well-equipped enemy soldier
REMF Rear echelon motherfucker
Re-up Reenlistment
RIF Recon in force
Rikky-tik Quickly or fast
Ring knocker A West Point officer
Road runner Green Beret recon teams
Rock and roll Automatic weapons fire
Roger Radio talk for "yes" or "I understand"
ROK The Republic of Korea or a Korean soldier
Rotor The propellor blades of a helicopter
Round An item of ammunition
Round Eye Vietnamese slang for "Caucasian"
RPD The Russian 7.62mm light machine gun
RPG The Russian 77mm rocket-propelled grenade anti-tank weapon
RTO Radio telephone operator
Ruck Racksack
RVN The Republic of Vietnam, South Vietnam

SIERRA The military phonetic for *S*. Also, radio code for south
Saddle up To move out
Saigon commando A REMF
SAM Surface-to-air missile
Same-same Vietnamese slang for "the same as"
Sapper An NVA demolition/explosives expert
SAR Downed chopper rescue mission
Sau Vietnamese slang for "a lie"
Say again Radio code to repeat the last message
Scramble An alert reaction to call for help, CA, or rescue operation
Scrip *See* MPC
SEALS Navy commandos
7.62 The 7.62 ammunition for the M-14 and the M-60

SF   Special Forces
Shithook   The CH-47 Chinook helicopter
Short   Being almost finished with your tour in Nam
Short timer   Someone who is short
Shotgun   An armed escort
Sierra Echo   Southeast (northwest is November Whiskey, etc)
Sin City   Bars and whorehouses
Single-digit midget   A short timer with less then ten days
   left to go in The Nam
Sitrep   Situation report
Six   Radio code for a commander
Sixteen   The M-16 rifle
Skate   To fuck off
SKS   The Russian 7.62mm carbine
Slack   The man behind the point
Slick   A Huey
Slicksleeves   A private E-1
Slope   A Vietnamese
Slug   A bullet
Smoke   Colored smoke signal grenades
SNAFU   Situation normal, all fucked up
Snake   The AH-1 Cobra attack chopper
SOL   Shit Outta Luck
SOP   Standard operating procedure
Sorry 'bout that   Universal saying used in Nam
Special Forces   The Army's elite counterguerrilla unit
Spiderhole   A one-man foxhole
Spooky   The AC-67 fire-support aircraft
Stand down   A vacation
Starlite   A sniper scope
Steel pot   The GI steel helmet
Striker   A member of a SF strike force
Sub-gunny   Substitute doorgunner
Sweat hog   A fat REMF

TANGO   The military phonetic for *T*
TA-50   A GI's issue field gear

TAC Air   Tactical Air Support

TDY   Temporary duty assignment

Terr   Terrorist

Tet   The Vietnamese New Year

"33"   Local Vietnamese beer

Thumper   The M-79 40mm grenade launcher

Tiger suit   A camouflage uniform

Ti ti   Vietnamese slang for "little"

TOC   Tactical Operations Center

TOP   An Army first sergeant

Tour 365   The year-long tour of duty a GI spends in RVN

Tower rat   Tower guard

Tracer   Ammunition containing a chemical that burns in flight to mark its path

Track   Any tracked vehicle

Triage   The process in which medics determine which wounded they can best help, and which will die

Trip flare   A ground illumination flare

Trooper   Soldier

Tube steak   Hot dogs

Tunnel rat   A soldier who goes into NVA tunnels

Turtle   Your replacement

201 File   One's personnel records

Two-point-five   Gunship rockets

Type 56   Chi-Com version of the AK-47

Type 68   Chi-Com version of the SKS

UNIFORM   The military phonetic for *U*

UCMJ   The Uniform Code of Military Justice

Unass   To get up and move

Uncle   Short for Uncle Sam

USARV   United States Army Vietnam

Utilities   Marine fatigues

VICTOR   The military phonetic for *V*

VC   The Viet Cong

Victor Charlie   Viet Cong

Viet Cong   South Vietnamese Communists

Ville   Short for village

VNAF   The South Vietnamese Air Force

VNP   Vietnamese National Police

Void Vicious   Final approach to a hot LZ, or the jungle when hostile

Vulcan   A 20mm Gatling-gun cannon

WHISKEY   The military phonetic for *W*. Also, radio code for west.

Wake-up   The last day one expects to be in-country

Warrant officer   Pilots

Waste   To kill

Wax   To kill

Web belt   Utility belt GIs use to carry gear, sidearms, etc.

Web gear   A GI's field equipment

Whiskey papa   White phosphorus weapons

White mice   Vietnamese National Police

White team   Observation helicopters

WIA   Wounded in action

Wilco   Radio code for "will comply"

Willie Peter   White phosphorus

Wire, the   Defensive barbed wire

World, the   The United States

X-RAY   The military phonetic for *Z*

Xin loi   Vietnamese for "sorry 'bout that"

XM-21   Gunship weapon package

XO   Executive officer

YANKEE   The military phonetic for *Y*

Yarde   Short for Montagnard

ZULU   The military phonetic for *Z*

Zap   To kill

Zilch   Less than nothing

Zip   A derogatory term for a Vietnamese national
Zippo   A flamethrower
Zoomie   An Air Force pilot

ABOUT THE AUTHOR

THE AUTHOR served two tours of duty in Vietnam as an infantry company commander. His combat awards and decorations include the Combat Infantrymen's Badge, three Bronze Star Medals, the Air Medal, the Army Commendation Medal, and the Vietnamese Cross of Gallantry. He has written many magazine articles about the war. He and his wife make their home in Portland, Oregon.

At Song Re Valley, First Air Cav tangle with a deadly Russian sniper who is shooting Hueys out of the sky. When an air strike napalms the jungle to flush out the long-range killer, Sergeant Brody and his men are caught with a wall of flames on one side and VC hordes on the other. The Blues take out the Russian rifleman once and for all in a bloody . . .

CHOPPER 1 #12: SNIPER KILL